ROWENA CORY DANIELLS

EXILE

BOOK TWO OF THE
OUTCAST CHRONICLES

SOLARIS

First published 2012 by Solaris
an imprint of Rebellion Publishing Ltd,
Riverside House, Osney Mead,
Oxford, OX2 0ES, UK

www.solarisbooks.com

ISBN: 978 1 78108 013 9

10 9 8 7 6 5 4 3 2 1

A CIP catalogue record for this book is available from the
British Library.

Designed & typeset by Rebellion Publishing

Printed in the US

Also by Rowena Cory Daniells

When King Charald presented me with his unwanted, half-blood son to rear, I knew nothing could prevent me from turning the boy into a weapon, least of all sentiment.

Taken from High Priest Oskane's Private Journal

Chalcedonia and the Five Kingdoms

Prologue

ASHER LOVED HER, but she was not his to love. They were both half-bloods. It was Hueryx, the T'En scholar, who had claimed her, and Hueryx was the father of her unborn child.

But that didn't stop Asher loving her and, when she walked into the brotherhood scriptorium in tears, he put his brush down. 'Sasoria, what's wrong?'

'It's not fair,' she whispered, fierce mulberry eyes ablaze. One hand settled protectively on her swollen belly. When her pregnancy went past seven small moons, they knew the infant would be T'En and she would have to give him up. 'I don't see why I should hand my child over to a sisterhood to raise.'

'The covenant–'

'Is wrong. Wrong and cruel!'

Asher didn't know what to say; as much as he sympathised with her, he understood why the sisterhoods had forced the covenant on the brotherhoods.

Four hundred years ago one of the brotherhood leaders had attacked another all-father, kidnapping and killing his brotherhood's T'En sons. There were reprisals, and more precious T'En boys had died. Before it could spiral out of control and a whole generation could be wiped out, the sisterhoods had intervened. Imoshen the Covenant-maker had rescued the T'En boys and made the brotherhood leaders swear a gift-enforced oath to hand over all T'En children.

'The sisterhood will return him when he's seventeen,' Asher said. 'By then, he'll be old enough to survive the rivalry in the brotherhood ranks.'

'By then, he'll be grown up. He won't acknowledge me.'

By then, the boy would have his gift and he'd be a danger to Malaunje until he learnt to control it. 'Be thankful you have Vella.'

'Little Aravelle.' Sasoria smiled at the thought of her one-year-old Malaunje daughter. 'But when she grows up, she'll be forced to give up her T'En babies, too. It's wrong, Asher, and it's tearing me apart.'

A sob shook her. He opened his arms and she went to him.

The scriptorium door swung open.

'Asher, I need–' Scholar Hueryx swept in. He saw Sasoria and beckoned her.

Asher watched, helpless, as Sasoria went to the full-blood scholar. Hueryx kissed her tears away. Asher could feel the lure of Hueryx's power as he tried to entice Sasoria to drop her defences. Once imprinted with his gift, she would be his devotee, bound to him for life.

So far, she had resisted, but one of these days her defences would fail and Asher would lose any hope of winning her back.

'I have amazing news,' Hueryx said. 'All-father Rohaayel broke the covenant. He kept his T'En daughter hidden from the sisterhoods for seventeen years–'

'No! He dared to keep a T'En girl?' Sasoria was shocked and delighted. Healthy T'En infants were rare, and girls were even rarer. 'What does it mean? Can we...' Her hand settled on her belly.

'I don't know,' Hueryx admitted, forehead crinkling. 'But the power of the sisterhoods is being tested, and I've been called to the brotherhood's inner circle.' He gestured to Asher. 'Find me the covenant book. I'll need the exact wording of the original gift-enforced oath.'

Scholar Hueryx was the brotherhood's historian. As his assistant, Asher transcribed and illustrated the beautiful books. He knew exactly where to find the tome.

When Hueryx left, Sasoria brought little Aravelle into the scriptorium. The toddler played on the floor, while Asher worked and Sasoria ground pigment to mix coloured inks.

It was dusk before Hueryx returned. By then, Sasoria slept on the daybed in front of the fire, with Aravelle in her arms. On seeing them, Hueryx smiled, signalled for silence and waved Asher over. As the scholar led him to the far side of the chamber, Asher could feel Hueryx's power. It called to him, and he resented it fiercely.

'I need you to do something for me,' Hueryx whispered. His wine-dark eyes glittered with excitement. 'There's going to be trouble tomorrow–'

'A brotherhood uprising?'

Hueryx nodded. 'The all-fathers have finally united. Tomorrow, when the all-mothers are about to execute Rohaayel, our most powerful gift-warriors will ambush them. With the all-mothers dead, the gift oath will be severed.'

'And you'll save Rohaayel.'

'What? No, he has to die. He knows nothing of this. He's a means to an end. Once the all-mothers are dead, we'll confront their seconds and force them to dismantle the covenant.'

'And if they don't?'

'We'll kill them all. Many of us will die, but after the most powerful females are dead and we prevent the young ones from learning how to use their gifts, as Rohaayel did with his daughter, the brotherhoods will have the upper hand.'

'You're afraid there will be reprisals.'

'Yes. But hopefully, once the T'En females learn the all-fathers have united, they'll dismantle the covenant. This is inner circle business, Asher. I only tell you, because you must promise to protect Sasoria if I die.'

'Of course.' He looked down to hide the hope in his eyes, but he suspected Hueryx knew.

The next morning, they stood on the balcony to watch the all-father and his seconds leave the palace. The three brotherhood leaders wore their torcs of office on their broad shoulders. Their silver hair was bound in elaborate plaits. With their long-knives on belts slung low on their hips and their chests bare to reveal their duelling scars, they looked beautiful and dangerous.

Hueryx hugged Sasoria. 'This is a historic day. We'll be able to say we were there when the brotherhoods reclaimed the right to raise their own sons.'

On the street below, the all-father and his two seconds met up with other brotherhood leaders. There was no laughter, no boasting or jesting. They greeted each other with a single nod then strode off, determined to confront the sisterhoods.

'I don't understand,' Sasoria said. 'If Rohaayel raised his daughter, why did Imoshen turn him in to the sisterhoods?'

Hueryx shrugged.

Asher frowned. Downstairs the Malaunje whispered that Rohaayel had tried to get a powerful sacrare grandson from Imoshen. Rohaayel had planned to take the boy and kill Imoshen, but she'd found out and run to the sisterhoods seeking sanctuary. As for the sacrare boy, some said he'd been stillborn, others said he'd died when Imoshen made her way across Chalcedonia in the middle of winter. Asher didn't know what to believe.

Sasoria rubbed her lower back.

'You're tired. You should rest.' Hueryx picked up the toddler who had been playing at his feet and handed her to Asher. The scholar kissed Sasoria's cheek and his voice grew thick with emotion. 'Know that I love you.'

She laughed, unaware that this could be goodbye and kissed him fondly. 'You'll come as soon as it's official?'

Hueryx nodded.

Asher led her to the scholar's private chamber.

'Thank you,' she said. 'You don't have to stay.'

But they both knew he would. He'd been her lover before Hueryx took a fancy to her, and he was going to outwait the T'En scholar.

'I'll watch over Vella while you rest.' As he kissed Sasoria's cheek, he sensed Hueryx's gift residue on her skin.

She squeezed his hand. 'I used to wish this baby had been born a half-blood like us, but now...'

Now she had hope.

Sasoria slept and soon the toddler curled up next to her. Meanwhile, Asher tried to imagine their brotherhood with T'En children running around. There would be lots of little boys. It was rare for a T'En man to produce a full-blood daughter, but it did happen.

He must have nodded off, but he woke the instant Hueryx returned. The scholar drew him into the hall and, gauging from his expression, the news was bad. 'What happened?'

'The sisterhood leaders told Imoshen she had to execute Rohaayel. The brotherhoods sent their best gift-warriors to kill her, but she...' Hueryx shook his head, stunned. 'An untrained seventeen year-old girl killed ten T'En gift-warriors. She made the brotherhood leaders back down, and they hate her for it.' He glanced to the closed door where Sasoria slept. 'This is going to break her heart.'

Asher realised the shock would weaken Sasoria's defences, making it easy for Hueryx to imprint his gift on her. 'I'll tell her.'

'No. I'm the one who gave her hope. I'll tell her.'

For the rest of the afternoon Asher tried to concentrate on illustrating the beautiful histories, but all the while his stomach churned. It didn't help that outside their palace walls the all-fathers battled over Rohaayel's brotherhood. There was fighting in the streets, and he could smell burning. When he went to the window, he saw Rohaayel's palace was alight. Such a waste.

A door opened behind him. 'Asher?'

'Sasoria.' He turned. She'd been crying. He held out his arms and she ran to him. To his relief, he sensed very little of Hueryx's gift residue on her.

Her hug was fierce and brief. 'We have to run away.'

He wanted nothing more but... 'The kingdom is full of True-men.'

'Mieren,' she corrected him with a fond smile. 'You hide it so well, I forget you were raised by Mieren parents. They must have loved you very much to keep you.'

'They paid for it.' He'd been thirteen when the fisher-folk murdered his parents in their beds and set fire to their cottage. He'd escaped and made his way to the Wyrd city.

'My poor Asher,' she whispered. 'But it will be different for us. Have you heard of the village of free Malaunje?'

He shook his head.

'They say it's high in the mountains. We must go tonight, while the brotherhoods are in upheaval. I'll pack. You find out where the village is.'

But no one knew. Most said it was a myth. This didn't deter Asher. Sasoria was his. He'd been raised in a tiny fishing village to the south. There were hundreds of islands off the coast of Chalcedonia, islands where Hueryx's brotherhood and the True-men would never find them. He'd make a life for them there, a good life.

So he loaded Sasoria and little Aravelle into the rowboat. As Asher took the oars, he realised he would be glad to leave the island city. He was born a free Malaunje, and that was how he wanted to live.

It was season cusp so both moons were full but, with Rohaayel's palace blazing and the fighting in the streets, no one noticed them row across the lake. They headed south west for the coast and freedom.

PART ONE

Chapter One

'SORNE'S VISIONS NEVER failed to come true. You told me we'd be victorious!' Spittle flew from the king's lips. 'You told me the Wyrds would crumble. You said you'd seen me leading my war barons down the causeway and into the Wyrd's city.'

'And so you shall.' Zabier's mouth was almost too dry to speak. His heart raced and he felt sick with terror. He'd never seen the king this bad before. Charald had been so intent on orchestrating the attack, he hadn't slept for three days.

'How? How are we going to take the city now? The Wyrds fought off my barons, closed the causeway gate and murdered every man trapped inside. I've promised my people a kingdom free of Wyrds. I've promised the barons the spoils of the city. But what do I have instead? I have a nest of Wyrds wanting to talk terms. *Terms!*'

'In my vision, you take the city,' Zabier assured him. It had seemed a safe bet. Charald had conquered every mainland kingdom around the Secluded Sea. But the king was nearly sixty and most True-men were lucky to live to fifty.

As Zabier watched the king pace, he seriously considered slipping pains-ease into his wine to calm him.

Words poured from the king. He'd been fighting to retain the throne since the age of fifteen, and he had the details of every battle in his mind. He spoke of men long dead, barons who had failed him, barons who had proved loyal; he spoke of his cousin who had seized the crown when his back was turned and how his son, Prince Cedon, had died.

That was the night Zabier had been named the Father's-voice, messenger of the god. It was more than a decade ago, but Zabier would never forget. The failed offering, the deaths of Prince Cedon and of Zabier's brother, Izteben...

'Three queens I've had, and what have they given me?' As the king gestured, Zabier noticed his hand trembling. 'Seven stillborn children, a prince who never lived to grow up and now a crippled prince. What good is a son with a club foot?'

'Why does the Warrior god test me like this?' Charald demanded. 'I've done everything He asked of me. I conquered the kingdoms of the Secluded Sea in His name and set up temples to the seven gods of Chalcedonia. Why, the last two offerings were full-blood Wyrds, silverheads. Sorne never made that kind of sacrifice, yet his visions always came true. Oskane... Where is Oskane?' The king frowned, looking around as if the old priest might be sitting in a corner.

Zabier licked dry lips and ventured, 'High Priest Oskane died the same night—'

'Of course. That was the night my treacherous cousin seized the throne. Now my cousin's daughter has produced a healthy True-man son, when all I have is a useless cripple. The barons have heard. They eye my throne and...' Charald ran on about the ambitious barons.

If they knew their king's mind was failing, they would turn on him. Until recently, Zabier had dreamed of seducing Queen Jaraile, planting his own child on the throne and assisting her to rule until his son was of age. But a closer acquaintance with the barons had convinced him it was safer to have less ambitious goals. After all, as high priest of the greatest church, he was the most powerful man in Chalcedonia after the king.

If only his visions would come true.

'Three years ago, before he died, Sorne promised me a healthy son,' Charald said. 'Then again, two nights ago, when the Warrior returned him from the dead, he said he'd had a vision of my son ruling Chalcedonia.'

Zabier looked down to hide his contempt. Religion was the king's one blind spot, and Sorne knew it. He'd used the king's faith to 'return from the dead' and reclaim his trust. Charald turned to Zabier. 'I haven't seen Sorne since the night of the sacrifice. Where is the Warrior's-voice?'

Sorne. Always Sorne. Zabier managed to summon a smile. 'He was exhausted after his vision. I'll see if he is well enough to come to you, sire.'

IMOSHEN KNELT TO inspect the tiles. They'd been mopping the blood, sweeping up broken glass and loading enemy bodies onto carts since midnight. As far as she knew, the warriors down in the brotherhood quarter were still hunting down invaders.

She came to her feet and dusted off her hands. 'Not a speck of blood. Excellent.'

A dozen fresh-faced Malaunje lads and lasses watched her intently. Her gift surged and she knew they needed reassurance. She was a raedan, able to read people's emotions. It was a good gift for the all-mother of a great sisterhood. 'When the palace is ready we'll hold a cleansing ceremony.'

This cheered them, but nothing would remove the knowledge that Charald's army had made it past the brotherhood palaces at the low end of the island, through the free quarter and right up into the sisterhood quarter.

'How can they do it, all-mother?' one earnest youth asked, angry tears glittering in his mulberry eyes. 'How can they kill defenceless children?'

'They're Mieren, born without the gifts or the Malaunje affinity for them. They aren't as aware of each other as we are. They can't share what they feel as we do. This makes it easier for them to be cruel.'

Leaving the weapons practice courtyard, Imoshen went to the solarium to see to the wounded. There were so many injured they lay in the hallway, and the herbalists had enlisted several assistants. Moving from bed to bed, Imoshen said a few words to each of the wounded until she came to the person she needed to see.

She might be the sisterhood's all-mother but she was also Iraayel's choice-mother. It didn't matter to her that he wasn't a child of her flesh. She'd loved him from the day he was born, and last night he'd led the lads against king Charald's men. T'En boys aged thirteen to sixteen might be as tall as full grown Mieren, but they didn't have the muscle. Iraayel had ordered the lads to build a barricade at the top of the stairs. If he hadn't been there, the Mieren might have made it as far as the nursery. Imoshen shuddered to think of her baby daughter in the hands of King Charald's men and her gift surged.

All around her, voices grew louder and people sat up as they responded to the overflow of her power; she restrained her gift and approached Iraayel, only to find Saffazi with her choice-son. Half a year older than Iraayel, Saffazi was usually the one getting him into trouble. Now she sat holding his hand, her expression intense. Last night, the two sixteen-year-olds had killed in defence of the sisterhood.

Seeing Imoshen, Iraayel sat up. 'Tell them, I'm all right. I don't need to be here taking up a bed. Tell them.'

Imoshen smiled. 'Last time I saw you, you were uninjured, the attack was over and I sent you to make sure the palace was free of invaders. What happened? Did you corner one of the Mieren?'

'No... I learnt to make sure dead men are dead before I load them onto the cart.'

Iraayel and Saffazi exchanged a look, then laughed.

But Imoshen couldn't. The thought of what might have happened terrified her.

'Silly boy,' she said somewhat thickly and hugged him tight.

As she pulled back, he caught her arm. 'Saf stayed with me all night. We were afraid the shades of those we'd killed would come after us, seeking vengeance.'

'That was brave of you.' Imoshen wasn't surprised. She'd always known the girl had steel in her. Leaning over, she kissed Saffazi's cheek and let her power rise to offer gift-infused thanks.

'But you didn't need to worry.' She was surprised they knew of the danger, as neither of them had begun their initiate training. 'I asked the oldest and most powerful of my inner circle to protect us from the shades of dead Mieren. Besides, when people die a violent death, they're confused and easy prey for the beasts of the higher plane.'

She smiled at their relieved expressions. 'I must go. It's nearly time for the all-council.'

Leaving the solarium, she headed for her chamber. No sleep last night, on her feet all day; why didn't she feel tired?

'There you are.'

As Gift-tutor Vittoryxe fell in step with her, Imoshen repressed a sigh. She knew the gift-tutor meant well, but Vittoryxe was inclined to lecture.

'You're headed for the all-council?'

'Soon.' Imoshen wasn't looking forward to it. The leaders of the brotherhoods and sisterhoods would elect a causare to talk terms with the Mieren king.

'You'll be elected causare,' Vittoryxe said, as if she believed Imoshen wanted this and envied her. 'As the next causare, it will be up to you to save us from King Charald the Oath-breaker. Only you have the raedan gift, only you can read him and use this insight against him.' Vittoryxe took Imoshen's arm, her gift rising with her intensity. 'You must remind King Charald that it was *his* ancestor who signed the accord that gave us this island. Back then, it was fit for nothing but goats. Without land to farm, we had only knowledge to trade.'

They came to a point where the hallway divided. Vittoryxe turned to her. 'Now we have a network of estates across Chalcedonia and trading partners throughout the known world. We bring wealth to Chalcedonia, and the Mieren benefit from having us here. We've done nothing to provoke them. Why did King Charald attack us?'

Back when Imoshen had helped heal Sorne, she'd seen the king through his eyes. After eight years serving Charald as he conquered the kingdoms of the Secluded Sea, Sorne knew the man who wore the crown. Imoshen had read him. He was a true servant of the Warrior god – he fed on war. 'King Charald hates us and loves war.'

'He's always hated us. And no one loves war, war is terrible,' Vittoryxe said.

'Gift-tutor?' A servant waited to speak with her.

'This will be about the gift training chamber. The Mieren desecrated it. You go. I'll be joining the inner circle soon.'

They parted. It was true Imoshen was a raedan, but that only allowed her to read people. She couldn't sway their minds. She'd told Vittoryxe why the king attacked them, and the gift-tutor hadn't believed her. What was she going to do?

Deep in thought, she passed a corridor. Something moved in the corner of her vision and, with a harsh cry, a man hurtled out of the shadows towards her. She caught a flash of metal as his blade came down. Her gift rose. Imoshen side-stepped the blow and reached for him. All she needed was bare flesh under her hand and she could tear his life force from his body, sending it to the higher plane, where it would be devoured by predators.

But her hand met cloth.

Her gift surged in frustration. The man made a disgusted sound in his throat as if he sensed it, before shoving her against the wall and drawing his arm back for a strike.

She focused her gift and reached for his face, but he jerked away from her touch.

This gave her the chance to duck under his arm. Picking up her long pleated trousers, she ran flat out down the passage, heading for the all-mother's chamber. She made it as far as the corner before he tackled her around the waist. As they hit the ground, her chin struck the marble and her teeth sank into her lower lip. Desperate, she tried to twist under him, reaching for his face. He reared back and raised his weapon to strike.

Hands caught his knife arm. Arodyti pulled him off Imoshen, lifting him to his feet. The sisterhood's hand-of-force gave a grunt of pain as he elbowed her in the stomach. Arodyti's shield-sister caught his other arm and, between them, they slammed him up against the wall, pinning him. His blade clattered away, spinning on the marble.

Sounds echoed strangely in Imoshen's ears. She heard frightened, angry voices as her inner circle of high-ranking sisters ran out into the hall.

Feeling light-headed with relief, Imoshen pulled herself to her feet. Her gift urgently needed to be used; shivers ran through her.

Egrayne reached them. The sisterhood's voice-of-reason had been a gift-warrior; she grabbed the man's knife, stepping in to hold it to his throat.

Something warm ran down Imoshen's chin. When she wiped her mouth, her hand came away glistening with blood.

'Read him,' Egrayne ordered. 'Find out why they attacked us.'

'He's probably just a man-at-arms, with no idea what's going on,' Imoshen said.

'Read him,' Arodyti urged. 'We have to know what we're up against.'

He didn't speak their language, but he must have felt Imoshen's gift gathering, because he grimaced in disgust. She read fear, mixed with contempt. But if she wanted to know his motivations she had to dig deeper, she needed touch.

As she lifted her hand to his face, he jerked his head aside. The knife dug into his throat and he winced.

Imoshen placed her palm on his cheek and probed. 'He has natural defences.'

'He would,' Arodyti muttered.

'Break them,' Egrayne snapped.

Imoshen glanced to her in surprise. 'If I do that I could shatter his mind.'

'He was going to kill you.'

Yes, and she'd been ready to wrench his life force from his body and send it to the higher plane. But that was in self-defence. 'You're asking me to shatter his walls and immerse myself in his mind.'

His filthy, angry Mieren mind. She couldn't do that without being affected by him. His breath came in short gasps and she could smell fear on his skin. He revolted her, but she also pitied him.

'He waited behind after the others left. He let Malaunje go past because he wanted to kill a full-blood,' Arodyti said. 'He knew you were important by the richness of your clothes. He chose to kill you because we need you. Now we need you to find out what he knows.'

They were right. Imoshen let her gift build with every breath, and rise up against his defences.

In her mind's eye, he stood on a rock and the tide was coming in. She was the tide. She came at him in ever rising waves until he lost his footing and fell into the sea.

She had him.

Terror. Disbelief. This could not happen to him.

But it had, and now she could sift through his thoughts. This went beyond her raedan gift; it was the destructive dismantling of a man's mind.

She picked through his memories, working backwards: the attack on her; waiting for a suitable victim; the actual attack on the city and running up the road to the palaces; waiting for the order to attack; marching to get here; saying goodbye; boasting to friends.

Ah, here it was – the call to bear arms.

A man stood on a mounting block outside a smithy, exhorting the locals to come and kill Wyrds. He spoke of the brown fields of True-men and the green fields of the Wyrds. He claimed the Wyrds had stolen the water and weren't suffering from the drought. He claimed the Wyrds had denied the Seven, and the gods had sent the drought as punishment.

Kill the Wyrds; end the drought.

Kill the Wyrds; strip the city.

Kill the Wyrds; return home a rich man.

Kill the Wyrds...

Kill them because they were different, with their gifts and their strange eyes and their six fingers. They frightened him.

There, that was the core reason. Kill what he feared.

How could she reason with this?

Imoshen felt tainted by his hatred. Her legs crumpled under her. Barely able to think, she felt Egrayne catch her and slide an arm under her shoulder.

'What happened?' Frayvia asked. The Malaunje woman took her other arm and helped her along.

Egrayne explained about the attack, as they entered the inner circle meeting chamber and lowered her into a chair.

'You're her devotee, help her,' Egrayne urged.

Imoshen felt Frayvia's hand on her forehead. She refused to activate their link and inflict the Mieren miasma of hatred on her devotee.

'Should we send for All-mother Reoden?' Frayvia asked. 'Or is it a gift injury?'

Imoshen struggled to speak. She didn't want them to call on Reoden. With so many injured, the healer would already be exhausted.

'Give her air.'

'Give her some water.'

'She's covered in blood.'

Her inner circle hovered and fussed.

'I'm fine,' Imoshen said. She wasn't fine. She despaired.

'What did you learn from him?' Egrayne asked.

'Yes. Why did King Charald attack us?'

They asked as if there was a logical reason and, once they knew what it was, they could fix the problem. Imoshen gathered her thoughts. 'He was just a man-at-arms and didn't know King Charald's reasons, only the reasons he was given.' She explained about the drought and the belief he would reap gold. 'But mostly, he came to kill Wyrds because we're different. He fears what's different and seeks to destroy what he fears.'

The sisters fell silent.

As Imoshen look up at them, she felt the dried blood on her neck. 'I need to bathe and dress, or I'll be late for the all-council.'

She came to her feet, moving with care. Frayvia helped her through to the bathing chamber, stripped her, sponged the blood from her body, clucked over her and helped her dress. Hot tears scalded Imoshen's cheeks. The thought of what they faced seemed insurmountable.

But, when she returned a little later, dressed in pleated trousers, vest and formal knee-length robe, with her hair properly arranged, she was clear-eyed and cool-headed. Vittoryxe had joined her inner circle and they had recovered their spirits.

Listening to them speak, it was clear they believed Imoshen would be elected causare and she would use her gift and come up with a way to convince the king to honour the accord. After all, it was his ancestor who gave them this island. He must respect the agreement.

Imoshen wondered why they did not feel despair. But they had not felt the fear and hatred she'd felt in the Mieren's mind. If all of King Charald's war barons and their men were like her attacker...

She turned to Egrayne. 'Perhaps one of the all-fathers would be a better causare.'

The voice-of-reason grabbed her arm and drew her away.

'What happened when Rohaayel was executed?' Egrayne asked. 'What happened to his brotherhood?'

People rarely spoke of Imoshen's father and the memory made her flinch. 'After he died, the other all-fathers fought over his brotherhood. That night, his palace burned and there was blood in the streets.'

'Exactly. That is how the all-fathers resolve disputes.'

'She's right,' Gift-tutor Vittoryxe said. 'The male gift influences the way they think, making their impatient and prone to violence. It's even worse when they get together. Their gifts feed each other. They can't afford to look weak, or an ambitious male will try to take their brotherhood, so they don't back down. Is this the kind of causare you want to deal with King Charald?'

No, it isn't, but...

'Honestly.' Vittoryxe lifted her hands in frustration. 'Do you know how lucky you are? You don't deserve your raedan gift, Imoshen. You have no ambition. The causare who saves us from King Charald the Oath-breaker will go down in history!'

At that moment, Arodyti returned. She had changed into her ceremonial armour; she strode towards them, radiating determination. 'I'm ready. Let's go.'

Chapter Two

THE RUINED PALACE was littered with the dead.

Tobazim tried not to see the details, but he had to look for enemy bodies. He stepped over the corpses of Malaunje children, the elderly and warriors who had died defending them. It hit him hard; he'd sought sanctuary in the city after the king's barons had attacked his home. They'd struck the winery without warning and killed indiscriminately. Almost everyone he knew and loved had died that night.

'Come here,' Learon called from the boat-house.

Tobazim found him standing near the gate to the lake. His choice-brother was big, even for the T'En, and it was thanks to him that Tobazim, Athlyn and about a dozen Malaunje had escaped the winery.

Learon crouched, gesturing to the metal grille that protected the boat-house from the lake. 'That's how they got into the palace. They broke the gate.'

Tobazim prodded the bent bars, feeling his gift rise. He could sense the forces required to twist the metal. 'The noise of last night's revelry hid their entry.'

'And we were right next door. We were the first to hear the screams.' Learon came to his feet, brushing off his hands. He looked disgusted. 'It wouldn't have been this bad if our brotherhood had let us go to their aid right away.'

'Lower your voice. Only we know our all-father held his warriors back.'

'What kind of all-father lets another brotherhood suffer?'

A vindictive one. 'Kyredeon misjudged,' said Tobazim out loud. 'He thought Chariode's brotherhood would be weakened, not destroyed. He had some sort of vendetta against Chariode.'

'And that makes it acceptable?'

'Of course not, but we're not in a position to criticise our all-father. Come, there's no more Mieren bodies down here.' He went down the passage and out into the courtyard. His choice-brother caught up and walked beside him. 'Now that we've gotten rid of their dead, we can deal with our own. We've lost so many, I wouldn't be surprised if we have to dig more crypts.'

Learon swayed and began to pitch forward. Tobazim reached out to save him. The instant he touched Learon's bare skin, he knew what was wrong, but he could not save himself as he, too, was swept to the higher plane.

A dozen vengeful shades surrounded them. They had to be the spirits of the Mieren he and Learon had killed when they helped close the causeway gate.

How had the shades found them? The all-father's inner circle should have protected the brotherhood's warriors. Considering the number of dead, though, it wasn't surprising some had slipped past and sought out their killers.

On the higher plane, his choice-brother's true nature was revealed. Learon would die to protect those he loved. Inspired by his purity of purpose, Tobazim drew on his gift to form an axe and prepared to defend Learon's back. Unlike his choice-brother, he was not a gift-warrior, but he had the training to protect himself on the higher plane.

As Learon forced the empyrean plane to take shape around them, it became the winery courtyard, reminding Tobazim how they'd stood under the lantern-lit tree the night the barons attacked.

Without an innate gift and training, the Mieren could not hold their true form on the higher plane. Each shade had reverted to the man's inner essence, and they appeared as all manner of beasts.

The shades rushed them. Tobazim swung his axe with a precision. Each time he cut a shade, the creature dissolved, unable to hold its essence together. The hungry higher plane did the rest, absorbing the shades' energy.

A foul squat creature with broad shoulders and slavering teeth came in low and tried to tear out Tobazim's groin. He sidestepped, smashing its brains out. While he was distracted, something raked his side, clawing him and raising red-hot trails of fire.

From the corner of his eye, he caught a glimpse of Learon hacking at something twice his size: a conglomeration of shades that had banded together with one goal in mind, to avenge their deaths.

A clawed paw swung towards Tobazim's head. He ducked, then drove the end of the axe up and under his attacker's jaw. The shade fell back. The impact of its fall shattered it, and another of the creatures along with it.

Fear kept Tobazim moving. With every wound they leaked power. If he and Learon received too many injuries, they would not be able to hold themselves together. They would be absorbed, leaving their bodies nothing but husks on the earthly plane.

Claws and teeth sought to break his skin. Each time he shattered a head or broke a spine, the shade collapsed and was absorbed.

Something the size of a small pony leapt in from the side, knocking him off his feet. The axe flew from his hands, and he felt the greedy earth soak up the power he'd used to form the weapon, leaving him diminished. Vicious jaws opened and lunged for him. Weakened by the loss, Tobazim fought to keep the creature's massive maw from closing on his head.

Learon caught the creature around the neck and hauled it away. Tobazim sprang to his feet, formed a hunting knife, and gutted it.

The creature dissolved, and Tobazim realised it had been the last of the shades. Learon's body leaked bright power in several places. His choice-brother gestured to Tobazim's chest and he looked down to see a wound. They should heal these injuries on the empyrean plane, or else they would carry them across to their physical bodies, but he was exhausted... staggering, dry-mouthed, mind-numbingly exhausted.

The lanterns faded as if someone had dimmed them. Learon was weakening. Shadows crept in from the corners of the courtyard. Tobazim saw empyrean predators slink out of the shadows, attracted by the power they'd shed. If only they had a barred cage to protect them, they'd have time to repair their bodies.

Even as he thought this, long roots unfurled from the tree's branches, sinking into the ground to form vertical bars; reminding Tobazim of the winery's giant fig with its buttress roots. It occurred to him that they needed crossbars like the grille of the boat-house gate, and horizontal tendrils grew from the bars.

Forming a blade had taken concentration and effort, a skill learnt only after days of practice. Forming this grille came instinctively to him, drawing on his ability to build. Now they were protected within a cage. As the predators paced around them, he felt their furious intent and poured more of himself into maintaining the cage.

Learon ran his hands over his own body. A construct, a projection of his self-image, it obeyed his commands and healed.

Something threw itself against the bars, making Tobazim stagger. Learon caught him.

Tobazim felt the heat of Learon's hand on his chest, as his choice-brother sealed his wound. They had to go back, but so much of Tobazim's concentration was needed to maintain the cage, he could not make the transition.

He tried to push Learon away, gesturing for him to go.

His choice-brother held on to him. Tobazim felt the cage give way, felt the beasts rush them as Learon dragged them both back to the earthly plane.

Back in the real world, he lay panting like a fish out of water. When he could focus, he realised he was on his side in the courtyard of the ruined palace.

Learon crouched over him. Tears of relief filled his eyes. 'I thought I'd lost you.'

'I'm all right.' Tobazim pushed himself up, his arms shaking. It was hard to talk, and his muscles ached as if he'd been at weapons training all day. 'I wouldn't have made it back without–'

'I couldn't have held them off without you.' Learon came to his feet and offered his hand. Tobazim accepted it, and his choice-brother hauled him upright. They staggered like a couple of drunks, laughing.

Tobazim sobered. 'We should get back.'

They left the ruined palace by the front gate and went down the street to their brotherhood palace next door. As Tobazim stepped into a courtyard, he smelled oregano chicken cooking and his stomach rumbled. 'Hungry?'

Learon grinned. 'Starving.'

Tobazim headed through the entrance courtyard. The palace was a rabbit warren of buildings, added by a succession of all-fathers, all eager to make their mark. Every day, Tobazim had to fight his gift's instinct to tear down and rebuild.

He heard Learon give a grunt of surprise, followed by a loud thud, and spun around, drawing his long-knife. He half expected to find that one of the Mieren had sprung from the shadows and tackled his choice-brother, but it was their brotherhood's own hand-of-force, shoving Learon up against a wall.

Oriemn had his hand on Learon's throat. 'Last night you deliberately disobeyed me. I told you to wait for my signal.'

Learon could not speak to defend himself.

'We didn't take up arms until the brotherhood gate was opened,' Tobazim defended his choice-brother. 'Then we went to help close the causeway gate.'

'Where did you get to before that?'

'We went to help the women and children escape from the rooftop garden next door.'

The hand-of-force let Learon feel the force of his gift before he stepped back. Learon sagged against the wall, rubbing his throat.

'Then it's thanks to you two we have to feed and house over two dozen of Chariode's Malaunje women and children.'

'Hand-of-force Oriemn?' A lad came running, his bright copper hair glinting in the sunshine. 'The all-father wants you.'

'This isn't finished,' the hand-of-force told them, then strode off.

'Oriemn can't punish us for saving lives,' Learon muttered.

'No, but he can make life hard for us.'

'Why? Saving those Malaunje should add to our brotherhood's stature. Kyredeon should be grateful.'

'He should, but...' Life in the Celestial City was not what they'd been led to expect. They'd done their initiate training under scholars who'd upheld the values of the High Golden Age – brotherhood, honour and duty. Here...

Tobazim's stomach rumbled. They'd expended a great deal of energy on the higher plane. 'We need to eat.'

They were returning to their chamber when pretty Paravia stopped them. Today, her long copper hair was bound in a single no-nonsense plait.

Learon lifted the braid and leaned down to kiss the back of her neck, but she danced out of reach. 'I've been asked to sing at the farewelling ceremony in front of the whole brotherhood to honour our dead. I'm so nervous.'

'You'll be wonderful,' Learon told her.

'You can't sing a note. What would you know?' But she smiled. 'I must go. I'm helping settle the Malaunje from Chariode's brotherhood. The things they saw...' Tears glittered in her wine-dark eyes. She kissed

Learon's cheek, then Tobazim's. 'You did a wonderful thing, saving them.'

Then she slipped away.

Tobazim flushed as he rubbed his cheek. He felt a failure. He wished he could have done more.

Learon slung an arm around his shoulder. 'Come on.'

'Wait.' Seventeen-year-old Athlyn had found them. Also from the winery, he was the only other T'En survivor. 'I've been looking all over for you. If we hurry, you'll see them.'

'See who?'

But he was already leading them upstairs, through the brotherhood's many wounded, who had spilled out of the infirmary. Athlyn led them out onto a second-floor balcony overlooking the street.

'What are we looking at?' Learon asked.

'There.' Athlyn pointed, as All-father Kyredeon and his voice-of-reason and hand-of-force left the palace through the gate below. They wore their brotherhood torcs and formal robes.

Athlyn nudged Tobazim. 'And there goes All-father Hueryx and his two seconds.'

'What's going on?' Tobazim whispered. 'Where are all the brotherhood leaders going?'

Ceyne, the sawbones, joined them on the balcony. He looked pale and tired. 'The sisterhoods have called an all-council to elect a causare. Someone must negotiate with King Charald.' He stretched and rubbed his neck. 'The brotherhoods are furious. The sisterhoods have nominated All-mother Imoshen for causare.'

Tobazim frowned. 'The one who executed Rohaayel and the gift-warriors?'

Ceyne nodded. 'The all-fathers have never forgiven her.'

Learon whistled. They watched two more all-fathers go by with their seconds.

'Wait a moment,' Tobazim said. 'There are nine brotherhoods but only six sisterhoods. The all-fathers can outvote...'

Ceyne was shaking his head. 'Two all-fathers have nominated themselves for causare, Hueryx and Paragian. Unless one of them steps down, they'll split the brotherhood vote and Imoshen will win.'

'Then one of them will have to back down.'

Ceyne laughed bitterly. 'Have you ever known a brotherhood leader to back down?'

Chapter Three

SORNE WOKE WITH a dry mouth and a full bladder. His head felt fuzzy, as if he'd been drinking all night, but he never took more than one glass of wine; a half-blood could not afford to let down his guard among True-men. He sat up gingerly, trying to recall last night without success. When he tried to force the memory, it felt like prodding a bruise.

Meanwhile, King Charald's angry voice carried clearly through the tent walls.

Sorne rolled to his feet, looking for a chamber pot. He was a little unsteady, but he found the pot and undid the drawstring of the too-short breeches.

Why was he wearing borrowed clothes? How had he ended up here? And where was he?

Diffused light dappled the tent walls. He could smell camp fires, hear King Charald in a rage, men shouting as they organised other men and pipers playing... it all added up to an army camp.

But where was the camp?

Sorne laced up, poured water into a bowl and washed his hands. He went to wash his face, but caught Charald saying something about the Wyrd city.

And it came back to him. Finding the standing stones; the lightning storm and the True-men about to conduct the full-blood sacrifice, who turned out to be...

Graelen.

Sorne's knees gave way as he sank to the ground with a groan. He hadn't been able to save Graelen. In the end, the adept had sacrificed himself to save Sorne. And Graelen had died believing Sorne would warn the city. He'd meant to; he'd planned to go straight to Imoshen.

Stunned, Sorne came to his feet and took a mouthful of watered wine.

Had King Charald's army reached the city yet? Did he still have time to warn them? Sorne looked around for some boots. He'd have to steal a horse and find...

Find Valendia. How could he have forgotten his sister?

He'd been trying to find Valendia when all this madness started. He had a flash of True-men mobs wandering the port and the bodies of Wyrds swinging from shop signs.

He'd searched the crypts under the church, but he couldn't find Valendia. She'd been hidden by–

His brother walked in, dressed in a long brocade robe over a white under-robe and flat cap. That explained where he was; this tent was richly appointed as befitted the high priest, voice of the Father, greatest of the seven gods of Chalcedonia.

'I see you're awake.' Zabier's eyes glittered strangely. 'Good. We're running out of time. The Wyrds want to talk terms.'

'Zabier... What have you done with Valendia? Did you send her to the retreat?'

Zabier laughed. 'Why would I do anything so obvious? She's safe as long as you cooperate.'

Sorne's heart sank. 'Brother–'

'I'm not your brother and she's not your sister. You're just a brat our mother wet-nursed,' Zabier corrected, then gave him a thoughtful look. 'You're still addled. I should never have given you that second dose.'

So he'd been drugged. That explained his thick head. 'What did you give me?'

'Pains-ease.'

'But that's only good for minor hurts.'

'Shows how much you know. In the pure form it brings visions.'

'Do those visions come true?'

Zabier gave him a sour look. He retreated three steps and called through the tent flap. 'Holy warriors, come here.'

Two burly priests entered the tent.

'Clean him up. Dress him in the robes of the Warrior's-voice–'

'We only have the spare robes for the Father's-voice,' one of them said. 'No one told us we'd need–'

'I don't care, as long as he looks the part of a religious visionary. Hurry up. The king is waiting.'

Before last night, Sorne would never have believed Zabier could turn on him. They hadn't always seen eye to eye, but they were brothers, or at least choice-brothers. Now there was a restless energy about Zabier that he did not like.

Shocked and heart-sore, Sorne did not resist as the burly male priests stripped him, rubbed his body with sacred oils and dressed him in a robe that only came to his calves. He tried to make sense of everything, but his brain was still sluggish.

After a while, something came back to him. 'Last night you said–'

'That was two nights ago. Last night Charald attacked the Wyrd city. Haven't you listened to a thing I've said? The king has to meet the Wyrds to talk terms.'

'The city walls held?'

'We breached the walls. The barons' men rampaged through the streets and palaces, but the Wyrds rallied. They shut the gates. They've been throwing bodies onto the causeway all day. We've been carting them off to the pits.' Zabier gestured for the two burly priests to leave. 'The war barons are furious, the king is livid and' – he glanced over his shoulder to make sure they were alone – 'I look like an idiot. I told them I'd had a vision of them marching across the causeway, triumphant. It seemed a safe guess, considering Charald's past successes and your vision of half-bloods being loaded into carts by True-men.

You...' Zabier shook his head. 'The king still believes in your visions.'

'Because there's only a couple that haven't come true, yet.'

'So you say.' Zabier came closer still, lowering his voice. 'Charald swallowed your story about the Warrior god sending you back from the dead. That's why the king wants you with him when he confronts the Wyrds.'

Sorne looked up, horrified. He'd failed to warn the city. When Imoshen learned he was one of the king's party, she'd think he'd betrayed her.

'What?' A nasty smile split Zabier's face. 'Afraid of full-bloods?'

Sorne didn't answer.

'The king and his war barons were afraid, but I've convinced them malachite protects them from the silverheads' gifts.'

Sorne looked up. 'Why would you tell them that?'

'As long as they believe it helps, it does. Resisting the Wyrds' gifts requires faith. I know more about silverhead power than any other True-man. More even than Oskane did. I've had fifty priests researching them. So don't try to trick me. I know you didn't sacrifice that full-blood. I know that when he took his body to the higher plane, he killed himself. What I don't know is why.' He eyed Sorne thoughtfully.

Sorne had no intention of telling him.

Zabier went on. 'I know you are vulnerable to the full-bloods' power because of your tainted blood. I know I am safer than you, as long as I don't let them touch me, or come in contact with their blood. All these years the Wyrds have kept True-men at bay with the threat of their gifts, and it was mostly bluff. They're really only powerful on the higher plane. And while they gift-work, their bodies are vulnerable here. Few silverheads have gifts that can be applied on the earthly plane. Now that we've called their bluff and their city is besieged, they want to talk terms.'

Sorne nodded, trying to keep up. Neither Zabier nor the king knew that his allegiance lay with the Wyrds. He was in the perfect position to spy for Imoshen. 'The Wyrds have no king. Who is negotiating terms?'

'Their leaders have some sort of temporary king they call a causare. All you have to do is keep back, stay quiet and follow my lead.'

They both glanced to the tent entrance, as King Charald called them. Sorne went to rise, but Zabier stopped him.

'Don't think I won't hurt Valendia. She betrayed me. All these years I've kept her safe from True-men and Wyrds, pure and untainted, and then I find her in the arms of that... that filthy Wyrd.' Zabier shuddered.

Sorne had no trouble believing Zabier would hurt their sister. What amazed him was that Zabier had kept her safe until now, while sacrificingWyrds.

Zabier went to a chest and selected a pile of malachite pendants. 'Come on.'

Outside, servants lit lanterns. Charald strode about in full armour like a man of twenty. Clearly in a good mood, he jested with his war barons as the men arrived with the royal banner. Everyone wanted to be one of the party for this historic moment. The barons had never liked Sorne, and it was only his ability to communicate with the Warrior that made him useful to the king. He'd been 'dead' for several years now and he didn't know what alliances the barons had formed, so he hung back to observe.

Someone caught Sorne's arm in a firm grip. 'There you are!'

'Nitzane?' Sorne drew him around the corner of the tent.

Nitzane grinned. 'I knew you were on a secret mission for the king. Didn't I say so, when I ran into you in Navarone?'

That was when Sorne had overheard Nitzane fail to convince his brother, the king of Navarone, to help him unseat King Charald. Nitzane believed Charald was behind the accident that killed his wife.

Now that Nitzane got a good look at Sorne, his eyes widened. 'Last time I saw you, the left side of your face was a mess of burn scars. Now it's smooth as the rest of your face. When they said you'd come back from the dead, I wondered how you managed to convince them, but I see you've been up to your old tricks.'

'I made a bargain with the Warrior.' Sorne didn't like lying to Nitzane, who was one of the few True-men he considered a friend. 'I gather you weren't at the sacrifice two nights ago?'

'Just got here. Arrived home to find a couple of barons had attacked the Wyrd winery next to one of my estates. Killed everyone and burned the building to the ground.'

This was news to Sorne, but he wasn't surprised. Charald would have wanted to test Zabier's advice.

Today, he'd heard the king raving; Charald did not trust Nitzane. 'You need to watch your back, the king–'

'I have Ballendin with me. And I have more men-at-arms than any other baron.'

'All the more reason to be on your guard. Find out which barons you can trust–'

'Why? Is the king going to assassinate me?' Nitzane leant close. 'Marantza's death was no accident.'

'She was attacked?'

'No, the bridge collapsed.'

'And you had someone inspect it for sabotage?'

'What? No, I–' Nitzane hesitated. 'Marantza was the king's heir. Our son is next in line to the throne after Charald's son. The king had her killed.'

'You could be right. But you've no proof.' Sorne shrugged. 'Come on.'

He glanced around the corner of the tent. Luckily their departure hadn't been noted. Zabier was distributing malachite pendants and giving the Father's blessing.

Sorne looked east, across the lake to the Wyrd city. Its white walls, towers, domes and minarets glowed in the light of the setting sun, reflecting in the lake's still waters.

From this distance the city looked pristine. You could not tell that a battle had just taken place here.

The T'Enatuath were his people. Sorne had been raised to hate them and groomed to destroy them. It had taken him this long to undo Oskane's lies.

He hadn't been able to save the city from the first onslaught, but perhaps he could save his people from King Charald.

'WE'RE LATE.' EGRAYNE was not happy, but when they entered the empowerment dome, they found that everyone else was late, too.

Good, Imoshen needed time to face her ghosts. To the others this was the dome where Egrayne helped young T'En uncover their gifts, but to Imoshen it would always be the place where she had been forced to execute her father.

She'd done what she had to, to keep her choice-son and devotee safe, but it had killed something in her and it had been many years before that part of her recovered.

As for the all-fathers, they had never forgiven her for killing one of them and the gift-warriors who tried to ambush her. She didn't see how they would ever accept her as causare.

'Good news,' Egrayne said, taking the seat beside her.

Imoshen blinked.

'Two all-fathers have nominated themselves for causare. The brotherhood vote will be split.' Egrayne grinned. 'With the six all-mother votes, you'll be elected.'

Imoshen's heart sank. 'In recorded history there's only been one causare, and she only held the position long enough to negotiate the accord with King Charald the Peace-maker. I'm a bit confused as to what exactly a causare does. If I'm elected, I'll be authorised to work out terms with King Charald?'

'No. The all-council will tell you what the terms should be. You take those terms to the king. If he refuses and the brotherhoods think you've failed, they can say they have no confidence in you as causare and nominate someone else. Then we vote again.'

Imoshen frowned. 'But the brotherhood and sisterhood leaders have to obey the causare.'

'Not if they don't agree. The causare represents us, she doesn't rule us. We're not Mieren, to blindly follow a king.'

'You mean I'd have all the responsibility and none of the power?'

She nodded.

'Why would anyone want to be causare?'

'Because someone has to do it. You're the best person for the job. You're a raedan and the brotherhoods fear you.' She leant closer, lowering her voice. 'Power is held by the powerful.'

Imoshen looked down. She wasn't as powerful as the all-mothers believed. She'd killed the brotherhood gift-warriors, but it had been a matter of guile and trickery, not power.

If it came down to a confrontation between herself and one or more of the all-fathers, then her people were lost. The brotherhoods would rise against the sisterhoods and the division would destroy the T'Enatuath. They needed to be united against King Charald. Which brought her back to this all-council.

'So, in the role of causare I wield as much power as I can get away with, without driving the brotherhoods to unite against me?' she asked Egrayne.

Her hand of force nodded. 'You're a raedan, you'll know how far to push them. And they'll know...' She glanced to the far side of the dome. 'And here they come.'

Egrayne led Imoshen down to the stage directly under the dome. As the powerful T'En males poured in and took their places on the tiered seats opposite them, Imoshen glanced over her shoulder to the sisterhood leaders.

They were decked in silks and brocades, with jewelled pins in their long silver hair. They wore their torcs of office on their shoulders and formal robes, but they looked strained and tired. If they were anything like her, they'd been awake since yesterday morning, had spent the night fighting and the day cleaning up after the attack.

All-mother Reoden looked particularly exhausted. Being a healer meant she had the added responsibility of deciding who was most in need of her gift. Imoshen felt for her.

The healer came down to the last row of seats and took Imoshen's chin in her hand to study her swollen lip. 'What happened to you?'

'The same as what happened to so many of us, but I was lucky. Arodyti came to my rescue.' She felt Reoden gather her gift and caught her wrist. 'No, you've exhausted yourself.'

'And you're about to meet King Charald. You can't go looking beaten.'

'She's right,' Egrayne said.

'But we haven't voted yet,' Imoshen protested.

They both ignored her.

She felt the caress of Reoden's gift as her lip was healed. Before Imoshen could thank her, one of the brotherhood leaders declared the all-council open. The three candidates were called forward and presented.

All-father Paragian; she remembered his warriors claiming all the other brotherhoods' banners one spring festival. How everyone had cheered. She'd heard his people were devoted to him.

All-father Hueryx, on the other hand, was shorter and slighter of build. He'd been a scholar. He had one of those clever, sharp faces and a mouth that was inclined to mock.

Their voices-of-reason stepped forward and delivered short speeches listing why their all-fathers should be voted causare. She thought they made good points. Then Egrayne put forward Imoshen's case – her gift would give her a unique insight into the Mieren king.

Not that this would do any good, if Sorne was right about the king.

Imoshen hated being the centre of attention. She looked straight ahead, concentrating on the patterns of light glimmering on the golden tiles scattered through the dome's mosaics.

Then they put it to the vote. Each brotherhood or sisterhood had one vote. Two of the leaders were missing as they'd been out on estates when the attack happened, but a high-ranking brother and sister would give their leaders' votes. It was done with a show of hands. The two brotherhoods went first: Hueryx four votes, Paragian five.

She had the six sisterhood votes.

Egrayne stepped forward. 'It's official. Imoshen will be causare of the T'Enatuath, until the emergency is over or until another causare is appointed.' She drew Imoshen forward to stand beside her. 'I give you T'Imoshen.'

There was no applause. Imoshen was not welcome.

'We need to work out the terms,' Egrayne whispered in her ear. 'Start the discussion.'

But the council had begun late and it was almost time to meet King Charald. 'I suggest we go down to the causeway gate now,' Imoshen said. 'Walk with me. We can discuss terms on the way.'

So they left the dome, going out onto the broad causeway road. The all-fathers and all-mothers crowded around her. Each had an opinion, each believed he or she was right and each set out to convince her and everyone else of this.

By the time they reached the gate, she'd heard enough.

'Light the lanterns,' Imoshen ordered. Dusk had turned to night. She faced the leaders of the T'Enatuath. Paragian's brotherhood had drawn gate duty tonight and his warriors looked down from the wall-walk above. 'This is what you want. The sisterhoods believe King Charald should honour the agreement made with his ancestor. They believe we have both T'En and Mieren law on our side.' The females nodded. 'The brotherhoods believe the king is without honour because he attacked unprovoked and without making a declaration of war. His attack failed. They believe we can fight off another attack.'

'We were unprepared, feasting,' young All-father Saskeyne said. 'Next time they wouldn't even get into the free quarter.'

'Do I have the right of it?' Imoshen asked and the brotherhood leaders agreed she did.

Frustration made her gift rise. Sisterhood and brotherhood alike, they believed they were negotiating terms. She believed Charald was expecting their surrender. Help was not going to come. Their city was alone, surrounded by their ancestral enemy. If she went out there to talk terms and came back with an offer of surrender, the brotherhoods would revolt and confront King Charald, precipitating the destruction of their people. Maybe they were happy to die a glorious death, but she had children to think of.

'I see...' And they had to see, too. 'I want All-fathers Paragian and Hueryx to come with me to witness this.'

They were surprised and pleased. Egrayne was not.

'You must not show weakness,' Egrayne whispered, as the warrior escort lined up.

'I have my reasons.'

Chapter Four

THEY MADE SORNE wear a hood, and it infuriated him. At least today they had a good reason. The True-men didn't want the Wyrds knowing they had a half-blood in their ranks. They were afraid the malachite pendant he wore would not be strong enough to protect him from the full-bloods. They didn't know that Oskane's daily scourgings had been good for one thing. They'd armoured him; he'd even been able to bear the pain of an empyrean stomach wound for four years, until the T'En had healed him.

As the short winter day ended, King Charald, his priests and twelve barons stepped onto the causeway. It was wide enough for two carts to pass. The king's party advanced in a pool of golden lantern light.

The causeway stretched to the white stone walls of the city, which seemed to have retained some of the daylight so that they shone with a soft radiance. From this angle, the city appeared tall and narrow, stretching up to the sisterhood palaces on the peak. Lamps glowed in many windows and on the streets. He heard the barons mutter at this profligate waste of oil.

By the time they reached the halfway point, no Wyrds had come through the city gate.

'Where are they?' Charald complained. 'The evening star has risen. Are they going to insult me by not appearing?'

Sorne recognised the signs. The king was working himself into a lather.

'The gate is opening, sire.' Zabier stood at Charald's side.

Sorne was behind them in the next rank, standing with the barons. Behind them, the king's banner swayed, suspended between two poles. From each corner hung several long, silver trophy braids, collected from dead Wyrds on the battlefield three hundred years ago. During the Secluded Sea campaign, those silver braids had impressed their enemies.

It had taken Charald eight years to conquer the kingdoms of the Secluded Sea, and Sorne had worked himself into a position of trust. Each time the king conquered a city, town, or port, he would meet with the defeated officials. Towards the end, many had capitulated without a fight. It was better to pay a ransom and survive than to have their city sacked.

From what Sorne had overheard today, he gathered Charald had promised his people a kingdom free of Wyrds and his barons the spoils of the city. This did not leave much room for negotiation.

'No more foreigners suckling at the Wyrds' tit,' one of the barons muttered, gesturing to the foreign quarter.

Set out from the wall, and to the left of the causeway, was a cluster of two- and three-storey buildings. They had been built on stilts over the lake by merchant princes from distant kingdoms. Right now the foreign quarter looked empty and Sorne suspected Charald's men had sacked it.

'Here they come,' someone said.

A glow filled the tunnel under the causeway gate, and a shiver of fear passed through the gathering.

'Let's see how arrogant they are, now that we've called their bluff,' Charald said and the barons muttered approvingly.

The True-men's bravado amused Sorne. It was the first time he'd seen Charald's party afraid of the inhabitants of a besieged city. When the Wyrds stepped out onto the causeway, their lanterns cast light up the wall to the defenders on the walkway above them. Sorne caught the glint of armour, pale faces and helmets.

The first three T'En who approached wore shimmering silk breeches, sandals and knee-length robes of rich brocade. On their shoulders they wore wide, jewel-encrusted torcs, revealing their ranks and affiliations. Their long silver hair was dressed in elaborate styles, held in place with jewelled pins. The men's chests were bare, displaying old duelling scars. The woman...

Was Imoshen.

He'd had no idea she ranked so high amongst her people.

As the warrior escort took up position, Sorne saw them look to the banner's trophy braids and their mouths grow tight with anger. The two males remained one step behind Imoshen, who came to a stop when there was still a body length between her and the king.

'A woman?' one of the barons muttered. 'Their causare is a woman? I thought it was an elected position, not inherited.'

'One of the males will be the causare,' Charald said softly over his shoulder. 'They've put a beautiful woman out front to distract us.'

Zabier said nothing. Sorne glanced to the back of his head. If Zabier knew as much as he claimed, he'd know the T'En women's gifts were more powerful than the men's.

'I am Causare T'Imoshen, of the T'Enatuath,' she introduced herself, speaking Chalcedonian with a slight accent.

'High King Charald, conqueror of the five kingdoms of the Secluded Sea, ruler of Chalcedonia,' Zabier introduced the king.

Charald rested his hand on his sword hilt and waited, drawing out the T'En's discomfort. Whoever spoke first revealed weakness.

Imoshen took a step forward. 'King–'

'That's near enough.' Zabier held up his hand before she could come close enough to touch the king.

'King Charald,' Imoshen began again, 'your ancestor signed an agreement, giving our people this island. Why have you broken the accord?'

'The accord is nothing but scribbles on parchment.'

Both the males behind her stiffened, and Sorne guessed their gifts would be rising. He was glad he was too far away to sense their power; he did not want his gift addiction to surface again. While Oskane's scourgings had given him the strength to fight it, repeated exposure to power had made his hair go white by the time he was twenty-five, and the craving for power had slipped under his guard. The pain of the empyrean wound had completed his downfall. He was as addicted as any devotee, just not to one specific T'En. As long as he avoided their power, he could keep the craving under control.

'Do you want to renegotiate the accord?' Imoshen asked, as if Charald was a reasonable person. Didn't she remember Sorne's insight into the king?

'What I want is a Chalcedonia free of Wyrds. I want all your kind to pack what you can carry and leave this city, leave this kingdom.'

Behind her, the two males went utterly still, and exchanged quick looks. The warrior escort looked stunned. Only Imoshen was not surprised.

'This is our home,' she said. 'We have enough food for years and plenty of fresh water. We can shut the gates and go about our lives, while you sit out here in the winter snows, and the dust and flies, while your men die of the flux and their fields lie fallow, while their women sleep alone and their children forget them–'

One of the barons cursed, but Charald laughed.

'Shut the gate. See if I care. While you sit on your arses behind your walls, my barons will be riding for your estates. They'll pull down the gates, march in, put everyone to the sword and burn their bodies.'

'Barbarian,' the taller of the two males gasped.

'There's no negotiating with him,' the other agreed. They both spoke T'En, unaware that Sorne understood.

King Charald glanced over his shoulder to the barons as if to say, *See, one of them is the true causare.*

'We have wealth,' Imoshen said. 'We can pay a tithe to the crown for the use of this island.'

'Pay him?' the tall one muttered in T'En, clearly not impressed. 'Why should we pay for what we already own?'

Hadn't anyone ever told him you only own what you can stop others from taking? Charald had proven that repeatedly.

'Why should I accept scraps when I can have it all?' As Charald addressed the tall male behind Imoshen, she tilted her head to study the king and his barons. Sorne felt the brush of her gift on his senses, subtle and alluring. Female gift power rolled over him, over all the barons. Several of the men fidgeted, responding to the sensation. But none objected, and Sorne suspected they were too focused on the interplay between their king and the T'En male to notice it.

'We broke through once. We can do it again,' Charald said. He gestured to the big T'En man. 'Next time, speak for yourself, causare. Next time, come prepared to surrender.'

'We have not used our gifts on True-men,' the smaller, sharp-eyed man said in Chalcedonian. 'Do you really want to push us? You can't resist our gifts.'

Charald gave a bark of laughter. 'Your gifts? I piss on your gifts. You know why?' He beckoned Sorne to step forward. 'Because I have this priest, returned from the dead not two days ago.' And he thrust Sorne's hood back to reveal his face with the missing eye.

All of the Wyrds gasped.

'Warrior's-voice,' the sharp-eyed male muttered in Chalcedonian.

'I see you've heard of my half-blood,' Charald gloated. 'Have you heard what he can do? He's the one who discovered how to contact the gods. The Warrior has been blessing him with visions since he was seventeen. Through this half-blood the Warrior guided me, as I conquered the kingdoms of the Secluded Sea. He guided me here tonight.'

As Charald paused for effect, Zabier glanced to Sorne and the king. He looked as if he wanted to protest, but managed to hold his tongue.

Sorne also wanted to protest, but couldn't. If he was to be any use as Imoshen's spy, he had to let the T'En believe the worst of him. He had promised to let her know if Charald was going to attack. Now, after Charald's boasts, she would assume he'd lied to her.

Sorne did not try to catch her eye, not with Zabier watching him.

'Can you guess how he gets these visions?' Charald was enjoying himself. Sorne knew what was coming and he could not stop it. 'He sacrifices his own kind. Just two days ago, he sent a silverhead into the Warrior god's arms and was rewarded with a vision.'

The T'En stared at him in horror. All Sorne could do was look, stone-faced, straight ahead.

Without a word, Imoshen turned on her heel and walked away. The two men followed her, then the warriors, and lastly the servants with the lanterns.

Charald laughed, calling after them, 'That's right, go home and load your wagons, sew your jewels into the hems of your winter coats. Prepare for exile, Wyrds. You have until dusk tomorrow to agree to my terms, then I send my barons to raze your estates!'

As the causeway gate closed, the king rubbed his hands together and turned to his barons. 'That's put the wind up them. It'll go back and forth for a bit, but they'll be opening the gates and bending over before midwinter.'

He strode down the causeway, with the barons falling into step around him. 'Time to celebrate. Break open the wine.'

Sorne held back while the True-men jostled for position next to the king.

'You...' Zabier was beside him; fury twisted his features. 'You get all the glory. I'm the one who came up with how to avoid the Wyrds' gifts. I'm the one who made the half-blood sacrifices. All you ever sacrificed was gift-infused relics. You sicken me!'

Somehow, Sorne managed to restrain himself and leave.

'Yes, walk off. It's all you ever do. You left me to protect Ma and Valendia from King Matxin. You left again when Ma was dying. She called for you, right at the end, but you weren't there!'

Sorne ground his teeth. Back then, he'd been a fool, chasing glory and the respect of True-men. All it had gotten him was the empyrean wound and betrayal. It had taken him years to find out who he really was. Now he would not fail Valendia, and he would not fail his people.

As soon as they stepped through the causeway gate, Imoshen felt her legs go weak. Had Sorne betrayed them? She found it hard to believe, but if he hadn't, he was playing a deep and dangerous game.

The sisterhood leaders drew her to one side, but she was still aware of Hueryx and Paragian being swamped by brotherhood leaders demanding answers.

'King Charald is a barbarian,' Paragian said. 'He has a pet half-blood who sacrifices T'En to True-man gods!'

'Sacrifices T'En?' Egrayne repeated horrified. She looked to Imoshen for confirmation.

'...the king boasts he's come back from the dead.' Hueryx said, to his fellows. 'That he sacrificed one of us just two days ago.'

This incensed the men. Between their rising gifts and their furious exclamations, it was hard to think. This was what she'd feared; what would get them all killed.

Imoshen pushed through the sisters to climb a mounting block below a street lamp. She beckoned Arodyti. 'Give me your long-knife.'

The sisterhood's hand-of-force obliged. Imoshen struck the metal post. The high, clear note cut through the brotherhoods' deep voices and they all turned to her. 'The king is using the Warrior's-voice and talk of sacrifices to unnerve us.'

'Did your gift tell you this?' All-father Kyredeon demanded.

'I read a great deal of anger in the Mieren, cloaking their fear. In King Charald I read triumph and determination.'

'Yes, but what does the king want?' All-father Egrutz asked.

She read the brotherhood leaders. With their gifts on edge they were angry, eager for violence and ready to shout her down. They would take the hard facts better from one of their own, which was why she'd asked Hueryx and Paragian to go with her. 'What did King Charald want, All-father Hueryx?'

'He didn't want to negotiate, that was clear. He means to drive us out of the city, and out of Chalcedonia.'

'We can hold the city. We can double the guard on the wall!' a hand-of-force insisted and others agreed

Imoshen caught Paragian's eye. 'What will King Charald do if we hold out against his army?'

'He threatened to send his barons to break down our estate walls, kill every last T'En and Malaunje, and burn the buildings.'

Everyone protested.

'Hueryx,' Imoshen raised her voice. 'Does Charald strike you as the sort of man who would make good on his threat?'

The wiry all-father sent her a look that said he knew what she was doing, but answered anyway. 'The Mieren king will not hesitate.'

'And can our estates stand against the barons and their men?' Imoshen asked Paragian.

'They all have defences, but none could stand for long, not without hope of help coming.'

'We are dealing with a king who has conquered all the mainland kingdoms of the Secluded Sea,' Imoshen said. 'He has resources beyond anything we have–'

'What?' Saskeyne bristled. She read him. He'd come to the leadership of his brotherhood young and hadn't been seasoned by disappointment. 'Are you suggesting we walk out of here tonight? Because I'm not doing that. This is our home.'

Others agreed with him. A sea of angry faces shifted under the lamplight.

'You're the great raedan,' Kyredeon sneered. 'We were told you could read King Charald and find a way to negotiate with him.'

'I read him. He wants to be rid of us, and he believes we have our backs to the wall.' She looked around at the angry men, and the worried women. 'Are you willing to sacrifice everyone on the outlying estates, then sit here until we run out of food in two or three years' time?'

They muttered.

She waved an arm in the direction of the camped army. 'Charald can bring food in. He can rotate his army. The drought won't last. He can send his men home to harvest their crops and plant new crops, while we sit here and eat our stores. And when we've done that, we will be back where we are right now.' She waited a moment to let them take this in. 'Do you want to sacrifice everyone on our estates, to gain nothing?'

'We can assassinate him,' Saskeyne said. 'I could send one or two warriors to kill Charald and—'

'And then what? I read his war barons. They are greedy and ambitious. They'll fight over Charald's crown. One of them will win and then he'll reward his supporters by promising them the riches of the Celestial City, and we'll be back where we started. The Mieren will not negotiate.'

'But they fear our gifts,' All-father Dretsun said.

Imoshen sought Hueryx's eyes. 'What did Charald say about our gifts?'

'He said he pissed on our powers.'

This was greeted with stunned silence.

'Didn't you notice how his men were dressed?' Imoshen asked. 'When they attacked, much of their skin was covered. Somehow they've learned we need touch to use our gifts, that our powers have limitations. There are thousands of them and too few of us. Meanwhile, our people on the estates are vulnerable.'

'This lake stretches back towards the mountains, with many secluded inlets. King Charald can't patrol it all.' It was Saskeyne again. 'We can send out small groups of warriors. They can make their way through the countryside. They can warn the estates.'

'Warn them to do what?'

'Defend their walls.'

'Until all the warriors are dead, the walls fall and the defenceless are slaughtered?' Imoshen asked. 'Or are you suggesting these warriors can travel through hostile countryside escorting old folk, children and babies back here? When the Mieren track them down and surround them, no one will come to their aid. They will all die to the last child.'

Silence stretched.

'What do you suggest we do, Imoshen?' Egrayne asked.

It was the question she had been waiting for. 'We buy time by saying we'll accept exile.' There were protests at this, but she raised her voice and forged on. 'It'll save our estates, while we come up with a plan.'

'I say we send a dozen of our best warriors into the enemy's camp,' Saskeyne said. 'They infiltrate the barons' tents. They kill all the barons and the king.'

'Every king has an heir, every baron has a brother. Killing the king and his barons will make their heirs eager for vengeance. For every one you cut down, another will rise in his place, filled with righteous anger and ready to seek revenge. How will this lead to peace?'

Imoshen waited while they discussed alternatives. Her gift surged and she read them. The brotherhoods would fight to die a glorious death; the sisterhoods would fight to survive. Imoshen's gift told her the moment was right to call a vote.

'I say we buy time.' She raised her hand. One by one – some grudgingly, resentfully – the leaders of the T'Enatuath raised their hands.

'Our warriors will think us weak, if we accept exile,' Saskeyne protested.

'Our warriors will think us cunning, if we buy time,' Imoshen said. 'When the odds are against you, cunning is all you have.'

'So tomorrow we ask for time to prepare for exile,' Hueryx said, to her relief. 'How much time?'

'As much as we can get. Meanwhile, we send stealthy messengers to our estates, warning them to prepare for attack, or send their people here in secret. Saskeyne's right, the lake's shore is too big for King Charald to patrol. Tell your guards on the wall-walk to watch for refugees from our estates.'

'Meanwhile, we come up with a plan,' Paragian said and others agreed.

The brotherhood leaders hadn't accepted exile. They still thought they were negotiating to buy time to defeat King Charald. Imoshen glanced to Hueryx. He met her eyes, and smiled with dark humour.

'Yes, go back to your inner circles and ask for ideas,' Imoshen said. Maybe, just maybe, they would come up with something.

When she climbed down her knees shook so badly she had to lean against the mounting block. Returning the knife, she thanked Arodyti.

They'd bought some time and saved their people out on the estates. But they were still besieged, outnumbered and hated. And she had to persuade the brotherhoods exile was preferable to a glorious death.

Chapter Five

LAST TIME HE'D travelled with Charald's army, Sorne had worked himself into the position of the king's advisor. At twenty-five, he'd stood on the balcony of the conquered palace in Navarone and discussed how to recapture Chalcedonia. It had taken years to reach that point, and the barons had always resented Charald's half-blood priest. Now he was relegated to standing behind the king's chair again, like a servant.

Zabier had his place at the king's table, but he sat there sour-faced, nursing his wine and his grievances. Meanwhile, the barons and the king celebrated. They were so sure it would be a short, successful siege they were already dividing up the spoils of the city between them. From their point of view, it was much better to convince the Wyrds to walk away, leaving everything intact, than to sacrifice men to capture burnt-out palaces.

As the servants took the empty plates, Baron Eskarnor came to his feet, raising his glass. 'To King Charald, saviour of Chalcedonia!'

As the barons topped up their glasses to echo the toast, Sorne saw naked greed and ambition on their faces.

How could Imoshen save the city and their people? Originally, he'd meant to rescue Valendia and take her to Imoshen. But for now his sister was safer as Zabier's prisoner.

The king called for more wine and Zabier excused himself and beckoned Sorne, who followed him out. If only he could convince Zabier to trust him. They had more in common with each other than with any of these violent men.

When they entered the holy tent, Sorne looked for his travelling kit and realised he'd left it with his horse the night of the sacrifice. His mother's torc had been in that bag; a terrible sense of loss swamped him.

'I left my horse picketed over the hill from the standing stones,' Sorne said. 'You didn't happen to come across it, did you?'

'No.' Zabier gave him a suspicious look. 'Why? Did you have something valuable in your travelling kit?'

He was about to lie, when he realised Zabier could be motivated to help him. 'Do you remember the torc I used to wear for ceremonies?'

'The one that glowed when the walls between this plane and the higher plane were about to break?'

The torc was only thing Sorne had of his mother. Charald had ordered the young queen murdered so he could take another wife, one who would give him True-man sons. His mother had only been fifteen, which seemed impossibly young to him now that he'd just turned twenty-nine. He cleared his throat. 'I believe it glowed in the response to the gods.'

'The predators, you mean.'

Sorne blinked. Zabier had always been a believer.

'I'm not a fool. I know those things are beasts, not gods. We've already been through this, but I see the drug has left you with a patchy memory. You're going to perform the sacrifices for me then tell me your visions and I will tell King Charald. I've seen too many ceremonies go wrong to risk my life.'

'I'll need my mother's torc.'

'I'll ask if a horse was discovered that night, but I doubt if anyone will admit to finding it. The men-at-arms are little better than savages and the barons are just thieves in fine clothes.'

'You hid Valendia because you knew this war against the Wyrds was coming. You protected her.'

'Yes.' Zabier looked pleased.

Sorne picked his words carefully. 'What's going to happen to her after King Charald banishes all the Wyrds?'

'She'll be safe with me. She can have her music and a pet. What more does she want?' Zabier fought a yawn and failed, then gestured to the bunk. 'That's mine. You can sleep on the bedroll. Since my assistant isn't here, you'll perform his tasks. And remember, I'm a light sleeper.'

'I remember.' He found it hard to reconcile the boy he'd known with this man. 'You're high priest of Chalcedonia, advisor to the king. You've come a long way from the carpenter's cottage. What more do you want, Zabier?'

Thre was no answer. Zabier undressed and dropped the nightrobe over his shoulders, put out the lamp and lay down.

Sorne stretched out on the bedroll. He preferred it to True-man beds, which were never long enough.

'I want to be powerful enough so that I don't have to live in fear,' Zabier said softly. 'When you sailed off with King Charald I was thirteen. King Matxin named me Father's-voice and high priest, then forced me to perform sacrifices to frighten the barons. He gave me lists of names and told me to say the gods had revealed them as traitors. I had to obey him. Ma and Valendia's lives depended on it.'

'I'm sorry. I didn't know.' He didn't know how the man he'd met once and instantly trusted could have turned into the tyrant Zabier described. Yet other people described Matxin as a despot. 'I'm sorry, brother.'

Zabier shifted on his narrow bunk and Sorne thought he would protest. But he said nothing.

If Sorne could just win Zabier over, convince him that keeping Valendia locked up was no way for her to live and come up with a way to help Imoshen save the T'Enatuath...

His head ached and he gave it up for now.

*   *   *

IMOSHEN RETURNED TO the palace feeling exhausted. Everyone was subdued. Tired and heartsore, she suspected.

She was glad to retreat to her bedchamber. She moved quietly, so as not to wake Frayvia or the baby. Stripping off her finery, she dressed in a simple nightgown and slipped into the nursery.

Last night, she had shut this door on the sisterhood's T'En children, not knowing if the next person to open the door would be herself or an armed Mieren. Today she'd barely had time to see her infant daughter. Now all she wanted to do was hold her.

Imoshen found her devotee curled up with Umaleni. She stretched out beside her baby daughter; so small and vulnerable. A fierce love welled up in her. She would do anything to protect her child, her children, her people. But realistically, what could she do? Charald seemed set on a kingdom free of her kind.

Years ago, when she'd escaped the brotherhood and failed to save her infant son, she had travelled across Chalcedonia with Frayvia and Iraayel, who was only four at the time. She'd experienced first-hand the hatred of the Mieren. And today she had looked into the mind of the man who'd attacked her and found, behind all the logical arguments, a deep irrational fear of her race.

How could they fight this primitive fear?

A warm hand cupped her cheek.

She opened her eyes to find Frayvia watching her fondly. 'Your mind is racing. It makes my stomach churn. Sleep.'

'Sorry. Do you think Sorne would betray us?'

'Why? What's happened?'

Imoshen gestured to the window seat and they retreated there. As they settled under a blanket, she told Frayvia about the meeting with King Charald.

'Sacrificing T'En?' her devotee repeated. 'Poor Sorne.'

'You think he has no choice? King Charald is awfully proud of him.'

Frayvia exhaled slowly. 'I don't think he would willingly betray us. You read him when you healed him, surely you know?'

'Usually I read a momentary emotion, which only gives me a glimpse and I have to interpret it. With Sorne I read his core, and he is pure of heart. But what if he discovered something that made him hate us? A person of principle can do terrible things, if they believe what they do is justified. Remember how Kyredeon sent his warriors to murder Reoden's daughter? True-men are right to fear us. We are stronger than them and our gifts can shatter their minds.'

A wave of tiredness swept over Imoshen and Frayvia yawned. Imoshen realised she was unconsciously draining her devotee through their gift link. 'Enough talk for now.'

SORNE WAS NOT used to being confined. He'd spent all day in the tent with Zabier. Now he paced. Soon the Wyrds would meet with the king. He didn't understand why they'd made Imoshen their causare. Other than her gift, she had no qualifications. They were blinded by their reliance on the gifts to interpret the world. Surely one of the all-fathers would be better qualified? Then again, maybe not; the Wyrds lived segregated in the city or on their estates. Few went out into the larger world. Even those who sailed their trading vessels were limited in what they could observe. None of them knew True-men, or strategy, or King Charald like he did. He would have made a better causare.

The realisation stopped him in his tracks.

Since he was seventeen, he had been observing King Charald, the greatest living commander – perhaps the greatest ever, since no one else had succeeded in uniting the Secluded Sea under one leader before. He knew Charald was single minded and utterly ruthless.

The Wyrds were trapped in an ever-tightening noose, and it was up to Sorne to find a way out.

'I swear, if you don't stop pacing I'll...' Zabier rubbed his face and shoved his notes aside. 'What's the matter with you?'

'I need to walk.' He did his best thinking that way.

'Go. Then maybe I'll get some peace.' Zabier seemed edgy as he gestured to the chest. 'Wear the cape and hood.'

Zabier stood and went to the entrance, where an awning protected a table and chairs. When Sorne joined him, he found half a dozen of the new order of priests intent on dicing. They looked more like men-at-arms than priests.

'You didn't have these priests before,' Sorne said.

'My holy warriors? I wasn't sacrificing silverheads before.' Zabier raised his voice. 'Two of you are to escort the Warrior's-voice wherever he goes.'

'Don't trust me?'

'No, I don't. But then I don't trust the men-at-arms, either. Some of them might forget you are the Warrior's-voice and see only your tainted blood.'

Zabier had a point. Last time he had walked the army camp, King Charald had not been making war on Wyrds.

As Sorne set off with his escort of priests, he was reminded how Oskane used to call him and Izteben his holy warriors.

There had to be a weakness in King Charald's defences. Not physically, the king was far too experienced for that, but an army was made up of individuals, whose allegiance extended no farther than the next man in the chain of command.

While conquering the kingdoms of the Secluded Sea campaign, Sorne had seen Charald turn men against their kings and use them to his advantage.

Walking the camp revealed where each baron had pitched his tent, which told Sorne something of their allegiances. There were the five southerners who had risen to the position of baron while serving Charald in his Secluded Sea campaign. He had rewarded them with land and wealth upon returning to Chalcedonia. They were ruthless, ambitious men. Then there were the six original Chalcedonian barons who, when Charald's cousin had stolen the crown, had given their allegiance to King Matxin. When Charald returned, they had bent over backwards to prove their loyalty.

The southern barons had pitched their tents on the south side of King Charald's tent, while the Chalcedonian barons were camped to the north.

Clearly neither group trusted the other.

Baron Nitzane occupied an odd position, camped between both sets of barons. King Matxin had banished him and his brother because they were related to Charald through his marriage. They had gone straight to King Charald and served him loyally, so Nitzane and his brother had served with the southern barons. The king had rewarded the eldest brother with the kingdom of Navarone, which he ruled under High King Charald, while Nitzane now owned the estates that had once belonged to both his mother's father and his father, so he was also a Chalcedonian baron.

It struck Sorne that Charald was right to fear the young baron. If anyone could unite both the southern barons and the Chalcedonian barons against the king, it was Nitzane. This division of loyalties and mistrust could be turned to the Wyrds' advantage but, as yet, Sorne did not see how.

When he returned to the tent, Zabier appeared more relaxed. As they went outside to join the king, he noticed Zabier's eyes seemed glassy.

Sorne knew the signs. His brother was an addict.

From what Zabier had said, it had to be pains-ease. Sorne wanted to say something, but he had to be careful. He knew from personal experience that an addict could justify anything.

*   *   *

IMOSHEN DIDN'T LIKE Charald. There was something wrong with the king. And it wasn't just the way he kept addressing Hueryx and Paragian, even when she spoke directly to him.

'Winter is upon us. Soon the roads will be impassable,' Imoshen said. 'We need to send messages to our estates and they need to travel here or meet us at the port. Many of our ships are at sea. We need to recall them. It would make more sense to start the exile process in the spring, with the aim of leaving by midsummer–'

Charald gave a bark of laughter. 'I could order my barons to ride out and raze every one of your estates tomorrow. You leave in ten days.'

'If you razed all of our estates, there would be no reason for us to leave in ten days,' Imoshen said.

Charald had been watching her, and now his gaze slid past her shoulder to Paragian. She stole a look at Sorne. Was he serving the king?

'You can send your messengers now and leave on the first day of spring,' Charald told Paragian.

'The roads will still be deep in snow,' Imoshen said. 'If you want us to travel fast, then mid-spring would be best.'

'New small moon after spring cusp,' Charald said. 'That is my final offer.'

It was what Imoshen had hoped for. 'Very well, we'll hand the city over then.'

They had saved their estates and had until new small moon after spring cusp to come up with a plan. If it was possible. If it wasn't, it would give the brotherhoods time to adjust to the idea of exile.

SORNE FELL INTO step behind the barons as they left the causeway, crossed the town square and took the road past the shops and homes, up the northern hillside where the king had made camp.

When they reached the camp, they stopped in front of Charald's tent.

'So that's it,' Baron Aingeru said. 'We sit around now until the first new small moon of spring and wait for the Wyrds to leave?'

'Certainly not. Did you see the way they looked down their noses at us? Arrogant Wyrds,' Charald snapped. 'They need to know we're serious. This could be a ploy.' Charald gestured to the five southern barons. 'Eskarnor, Hanix, Aingeru, Odei and Fennek, take a war party, choose a Wyrd property near your estate and raze it. Bring back the silverheads' braids. When we add them to your banners, the Wyrds won't be so high and mighty.'

They all moved into Charald's tent to discuss which estates to attack. Sorne was surprised to hear Nitzane make recommendations. How could the baron talk of murdering Wyrds, yet treat him as a friend? Did Nitzane put him in a different category from other half-bloods?

Perhaps this was how Zabier could separate his love for Valendia from the act of sacrificing Wyrds.

By midday the following day, the barons had ridden off to attack the chosen estates. Imoshen and her people were in for a shock.

Chapter Six

EVERY DAY, IMOSHEN went to the rooftop garden to practice her exercises, striving to train her body and bring her mind, body and gift into alignment. She used to find the exercise patterns soothing, but today she looked out across the lake to a besieging army. Snow blanketed the hillside. She hoped they were freezing their balls off in those tents.

Twenty days under siege and life went on. In a way, it seemed her people had always lived under siege. They were wary of the Mieren, and they were wary of each other. When she'd come to the city at the age of seventeen, the divide between the T'En men and women had struck her as an undeclared civil war.

At least King Charald's attack had forced her people to put aside old grievances and unite against a common enemy, to some extent.

'No matter how hard you stare at them, they will not disappear,' her choice-son said.

'Iraayel.' She smiled, looking up. Just before the Mieren attack he'd turned sixteen. He was half a head taller than her and would not finish growing until he was around twenty-five. 'Your wound has healed well.'

'It was nothing. You know what I hate? The silences.'

'I don't understand.'

'The Mieren attack reminded me of the day Lyronyxe was murdered in front of Sardeon and I. That made me realise I haven't seen Sar in years. We used to be best friends, the three of us. So I went to All-mother Reoden's palace and asked to see him, but they turned me away. Why?'

Imoshen hesitated.

'When I thought back,' Iraayel continued, 'I realised it was like a door had closed in my mind that day and now it has re-opened. You never told me why the brotherhood warriors killed Lyronyxe.'

'You were only twelve. You poured yourself into your gift studies and began weapons training alongside the older lads. I waited, but you didn't ask.'

'I'm asking now.'

Imoshen could sense his gift rising and had to fight the instinct to take a step back.

Iraayel gestured to the brotherhood palaces. 'The all-fathers hate you because you killed one of their own. Yet now you're their causare.'

'Only because they divided their votes.'

'Lyronyxe was thirteen. What did she do to deserve their hatred? Why did All-father Kyredeon send his warriors to kill her?'

'He said he knew nothing about it and her death was an accident.'

'But you don't believe him.'

She didn't deny it. As Imoshen recalled Lyronyxe, the bright child she'd watched grow up, her throat tightened. 'She was a sacrare, born of two T'En parents. Reoden's gift is healing. We never knew who Lyronyxe's father was. Whatever his gift, it expressed itself in Lyronyxe this way: she would have been a gift-wright, like All-mother Ceriane.'

'Gift-wrights are good,' Iraayel insisted. 'They can heal a T'En when their gift corrupts.'

Imoshen chose her words carefully. 'A healer like Ree can use her gift to repair broken bones or knit torn flesh. If she can do that, she can take the living heart inside your body and squeeze it until it stops.'

He went pale. 'I never thought... but yes, that makes sense.' He frowned. 'You're saying a gift-wright–'

'A sacrare gift-wright,' she reminded him. 'Very powerful.'

'Could reach into a T'En's gift and turn it against them?'

Imoshen nodded.

'You think All-father Kyredeon had Lyronyxe killed so she would never grow up to threaten the brotherhoods. What kind of person does something like that?'

'A ruthless one.'

'But...' His voice shook and she could see he was close to tears. He turned and walked to the edge of the roof, where he gripped the stone balustrade.

She joined him, wanted to touch him, yet hesitated. Her gift surged, but she hadn't been able to read Iraayel since the day Lyronyxe was murdered.

He turned to face her. 'Why won't they let me see Sardeon?'

'He loved her. When she died, he went looking for her essence on the higher plane.' She saw Iraayel wince. 'Sardeon had no training. When I realised he had been sucked onto the empyrean plane, I went after him, found him and brought him back.' She took Iraayel's hand. 'At first Reoden said he was all right. But I haven't seen him since. All I know is that Gift-wright Ceriane has tried to help him.'

Iraayel swallowed. Tears clung to his lashes. 'All-mother Reoden is so kind. Yet she lost two children that day.'

Imoshen hugged him, and then pulled back to find Egrayne approaching.

The gift-empowerer looked grim.

'I'll go,' Iraayel said. He slipped away as Imoshen went to meet Egrayne.

'You spend too much time with him, Imoshen. It'll make it harder on you when he has to join his brotherhood.'

She didn't want to send Iraayel away, didn't see why she should, but she contained her rebelliousness and asked, 'Is there bad news?'

'Very bad,' Egrayne said as they left the roof top garden. 'Reoden's waiting downstairs with a Malaunje lad from one of her estates. He stole a Mieren boat and went to

All-father Tamaron's palace. They let him in, demanded answers, then sent him up here.' Egrayne led her along a corridor to an open door. 'They know. All the brotherhoods know.'

'Know what?' Imoshen asked.

'That King Charald hasn't kept his word,' Reoden said, when they reached her. She was pale and angry, her gift close to the surface. A lad of about fifteen stood at her side. 'Tell the causare what you told me.'

Imoshen's gift surged and she saw him as a bowstring pulled taut, ready to snap. 'Charald attacked his home.'

He nodded and gulped a breath. 'It was late, everyone had gone to bed. There was no warning. They must have poisoned the dogs. First we knew was the shouting, and Mieren running through the big house. I looked out the window and saw the barn on fire. The adults tried to stop them. I tried to get to my' – his mouth worked and he swallowed twice – '...my sisters, but I couldn't. The cook told all us kitchen hands to go out the back and run away. They were waiting for us. They came after us, hacked at us as we ran. They–'

'Enough.' Anger made Imoshen's gift rise.

'I ran away,' the lad whispered. 'I hid. I didn't go back. I–'

'Listen to me.' Imoshen took his hand in hers, letting her gift bring him comfort. 'You came here. You warned us. We needed to know. Thank you.'

And he dissolved into tears, as great wracking sobs shook his body. Reoden pulled him into her arms.

IMOSHEN AND EGRAYNE stepped out into the hall and looked at each other.

'The brotherhoods know,' Egrayne said. 'They're going to be furious. They'll want to retaliate.'

Imoshen's mind raced. 'Why did Charald do this, when we've already agreed to his demands?'

'I don't care why he did it. What do we do?'

'King Charald holds all the cards. Exile may be our—'

'Don't say that. Not even in jest.'

'I wasn't jesting. We need a way to influence him. But he knows not to let us touch him.'

'What if...' Egrayne's eyes widened. 'Have you heard the rumour about the playwright, Rutz? They say he can imbue words with power and sway people's minds. That's why he writes under a pen-name to hide his real identity. If the other all-fathers knew who he was, they'd execute him for fear of falling under his influence. Ask All-father Chariode...' She looked stricken. 'Rutz may have died the night of the attack.'

'That would be a useful gift right now,' Imoshen conceded. She happened to know for a fact that Rutz could not imbue his words with power, because Rutz was really Captain Ardonyx, the explorer. He was Imoshen's secret bond-partner and Umaleni's father. And even if he could imbue words with power, he was far to the south, on a voyage of discovery. But she did need to find out what had happened to Chariode's brotherhood. Iraayel was due to join it in less than a year's time.

'The lad has finally let me ease him into sleep,' Reoden said, as she reached them. 'I'm surprised he held out so long. He stole a horse and rode night and day to get here.'

'You need to call an all-council, Imoshen,' Egrayne urged. 'The all-fathers will want to hold Charald accountable.'

'Then I'd better call an all-council right away.' And divert the brotherhoods from doing something stupid.

By the time everyone reached the empowerment dome, they knew Charald had not kept his word and they were furious. After listening to the leaders of the T'Enatuath argue back and forth, Imoshen raised her hands for quiet. When this did not work, she went over to the singing bowl that was played during empowerment ceremonies, and tapped it. A single clear note rang out.

Silence fell under the dome.

'I'm guessing King Charald has broken his word to prove he has power over us,' Imoshen said. It was the only explanation that made sense.

'Do you expect us to sit here and let him decimate our estates?' Kyredeon demanded. 'You were elected to negotiate, not capitulate.'

'I have to have something to negotiate with. We need leverage on King Charald. Simply going in and killing him achieves nothing,' Imoshen said. There had been several offers from young T'En males willing to assassinate the king on a suicide mission.

'My inner circle and I have been trying to come up with ways to influence the king,' Imoshen said. 'We need T'En whose gifts do not require touch to work. In the past there were T'En who could take an intimate object belonging to another and use it to influence the owner's mind.' She'd been trying this, with limited success. 'There's a rumour that the playwright Rutz can imbue words with power. If this is true, now is the time for him – or someone like him – to come forward.'

No one spoke.

'What happened to the survivors of Chariode's brotherhood?' Imoshen asked. 'Were there enough of them to reform the brotherhood, or has it been absorbed by another...'

She ran down as the brotherhood leaders turned to All-father Kyredeon. Her heart sank. She did not want Iraayel serving him.

Kyredeon came to his feet. 'My warriors saved over two dozen women and children from Chariode's palace roof. Since the night of the attack, the survivors have taken shelter in my palace. We don't know if any of Chariode's brothers will survive out on his estates, so I'm making a formal claim to his brotherhood. Does anyone contest my right?'

No one did.

Kyredeon looked pleased. 'Then I'll ask around, see if the survivors know who Rutz is, or was. If he was here the night of the attack, I suspect he's dead.'

'Thank you, all-father.' The words stuck in Imoshen's throat. 'The rest of you, go back to your inner circles, see if anyone has a gift that doesn't require touch and can think of a way to apply it that gives us leverage with King Charald.'

ZABIER STOOD NEAR the king beside the brazier as they talked of camp business. The barons were complaining that there weren't enough camp followers to go around. Fights had broken out over women. Normally, he'd find this fascinating, but there was a restless beast inside him, pacing back and forth. If he slipped away and dosed himself with a few drops of pains-ease it would soothe the beast for now. But what he really needed was to immerse himself in the golden floating world of dreams.

All he had to do was swallow a decent dose when he went to bed. He knew his tolerance, knew just how much to take to put him into the blissful state. The things he saw...

No wonder he'd believed they were visions.

When King Matxin had declared him the high priest and Father's-voice, he'd needed visions. Assistant Utzen had claimed True-men saw visions when taking pure pains-ease, then supplied the drug. But Utzen had been King Matxin's spy and...

A moment of lucidity told Zabier his gradual addiction to pains-ease had been a deliberate ploy, engineered by King Matxin. It had been typical of Matxin to keep those he needed under his thumb.

Anger rolled through Zabier. What kind of man takes a thirteen-year-old boy, puts him in a position of power, then supplies him with a drug just to ensure his co-operation? Wasn't it enough that Zabier would have done anything to keep his mother and little sister safe?

Raised voices brought him back to this king's tent. The last of the southern barons had returned with a swag of trophy braids.

Arms loaded, Eskarnor strode through the gathering.

When Zabier had accompanied Eskarnor and Hanix to destroy the first Wyrd estate, the two barons hadn't bothered to hide their contempt for him. Now that Zabier sat beside the king and discussed tactics, they were more discreet. But he knew how they really felt, and resentment burned in him. Men of violence had no respect for men of learning.

As Eskarnor presented the trophy plaits to King Charald, Zabier glanced to Sorne. His irritating choice-brother did not react. Those braids had to be rich with gift residue, which Sorne should crave. Yet he appeared uninterested, standing in the background. His distance from the tent's brazier revealed how low he was in the pecking order.

Zabier listened in to what Eskarnor was telling the king. He didn't want the baron undermining his position.

'...snow made travel difficult,' Eskarnor said.

'Doesn't matter, you're the last to return. Time for the next step.' The king sprang to his feet, summoned his manservant to bring all the trophy plaits and went outside where he bellowed for the banner-men to bring the barons' banners and the pipers to bring their pipes.

As they trudged down through the snow, past the tents toward the houses of Lakeside, the sun came out from between the clouds, making the snow glisten. The silver trophy braids on the Chalcedonian barons' banners gleamed, but Zabier's eye was caught by a rich copper plait, woven into a silver one.

Valendia had hair like that down to her knees; rippling waves of copper that came alive in sunlight. He missed going to see her every evening, missed her happy chatter, the way she would pull out one of her musical instruments and play her latest piece for him.

It was not her fault that she had grown so beautiful that men craved her. Sorne was right; she had been completely innocent. That vile Wyrd had taken advantage of her, probably fed her a pack of lies to turn her against him. He should visit her and give her a chance to apologise.

Charald led everyone down through the houses and shops to the place where the causeway met the town's square.

Soon, under Charald's direction, the banner-men had created a display of bright banners with his in the front and the barons' arrayed in order of the sizes of their estates. Buckets had to be found and packed with snow to place the banner poles in, and the banners had to be arranged so that they could be clearly seen from the causeway. All this took time and the townsfolk came out to watch.

When Charald was satisfied, the banners blocked the entrance to the causeway. Naturally, all this activity had attracted interest and the top of the Wyrd city's wall was thick with spectators.

'We'll show them.' Charald rubbed his hands together and beckoned his manservant. 'You have the needles and thread?'

Zabier saw what he was up to. Unlike the original Chalcedonian barons' banners, none of the southern barons' banners were decorated with silver plaits. Now that they had the Wyrds' attention, the banner-men were going to add the trophy braids.

Charald signalled the pipers, who struck up a martial air, and made a ceremony of decking the four banners with long silver plaits. The banner-men had to climb onto chairs and sew or tie the trophies into place.

When the last banner-man climbed down, Charald stepped aside and had the pipers play once more, while the townsfolk cheered. In the fading light, Wyrds watched impotent from behind their city walls.

'That's done it,' Charald chuckled. 'They won't be so arrogant, next time we talk.'

Zabier was both impressed and horrified. Five estates burned and hundreds of people dead, because Charald didn't like the Wyrds' tone of voice.

Leaving the banner-men to watch over the banners, everyone filed through the streets, up to the camp where the barons joined the king for dinner.

TOBAZIM FELT HOT fury then cold disgust as he watched the Mieren attach the silver trophy braids to their banners. Charald had broken his word. All along the wall, warriors and scholars alike expressed their outrage.

'This is why, if there's a good chance we're going to die in battle, we cut off our hair,' Learon told young Athlyn. 'It was a lesson learnt in the war three hundred years ago.'

Athlyn had only just left his choice-mother's sisterhood to join the brotherhood when the winery was attacked. He was slight and pretty, and out of his depth in the city.

'Attacking estates, killing women and children... the Mieren king has no honour.' Athlyn's voice shook. 'Every time I look at those banners, I feel sick.'

Learon caught Tobazim's arm and drew him aside. 'When it gets dark enough, we should slip out, row across the lake and take the banners. Reclaim our people's braids.'

'I'll come,' Athlyn offered.

'It's the perfect way to win stature,' Learon told Tobazim. 'Kyredeon should have acknowledged our stature when we saved the Malaunje women and children. We're the reason he won Chariode's brotherhood, with all its estates and trading vessels. Yet he punished us.'

'We'd have to ask permission. Last time, we acted without permission he had us both dig crypts as punishment.'

'Did I hear you're going to take back the braids?' Haromyr asked. He was a young adept like them, eager for stature.

Within a few moments, they had a band of twelve, willing to go across the lake and strike a blow against the Mieren.

Learon led them along the palace wall-walk to where Hand-of-force Oriemn stood next to Kyredeon and the brotherhood's voice-of-reason.

In his enthusiasm, Learon barely waited for the voice-of-reason to acknowledge him. 'Hand-of-force, we want permission to take a dozen warriors across the lake to capture the Mieren banners and bring our people's braids home.'

Oriemn's eyes widened. He glanced to Kyredeon and the voice-of-reason, then back to Learon. 'You're too late. I'm already organising this. Go back to your chambers.'

Learon went to protest, but Tobazim elbowed him.

Oriemn had already turned away and the three brotherhood leaders were making plans to move quickly before another brotherhood came up with the same idea.

Tobazim and Learon made their obeisances then backed off. Learon managed to hold his tongue until they were alone, then turned to Tobazim. 'Did you see the look he sent Kyredeon? Oriemn stole our idea. Now he'll get all the stature.'

Tobazim caught his arm. 'Keep your voice down. We don't want to make an enemy of the brotherhood's hand-of-force.'

But he suspected they already had.

Chapter Seven

It seemed to Zabier that Charald was particularly loud that night: talking nonstop, telling stories of past battles. With all the barons present, the king could not afford a mental lapse. Zabier watched Charald closely. Although the king did forget a couple of names, he did not ask to speak to anyone who was dead.

As the barons said good night, Zabier breathed a sigh of relief. He found these evenings exhausting and was looking forward to his bed. But when he and Sorne returned to the holy tent, it was so cold Zabier had to build up the brazier. 'It's freezing. I don't know why Charald doesn't commandeer the finest house in Lakeside.'

'The king scorns creature comforts,' Sorne said, stripping down to his knitted underthings, then climbing into his bedroll. 'You have to remember he's been leading armies since he was fifteen. He had to be tougher than any of his generals.'

'I don't see why we have to suffer, just so he can make a point,' Zabier grumbled as he climbed into his bunk.

'It's only fear of King Charald that keeps the southern barons in line. They betrayed their own kings for gain. They'd betray Charald,' Sorne said.

Zabier resented Sorne's tone. He might have stayed behind when Charald sailed off to war, but he was no fool.

He was only just beginning to warm up when shouting drew them all out of their tents. Down below, beyond the rooftops of Lakeside town, flames illuminated the night.

'Someone's knocked over a candle,' Sorne said. House fires were common.

But a moment later, a man came with the news the banners were burning and everyone ran down through the camp, towards town.

As Zabier rounded a building, he spotted leaping flames on a tall structure. For a moment he could not make sense of it. Then he realised it was a straw man, propped at the entrance to the causeway. Hanging from the straw man's arms were the barons' banners, burning brightly.

It was hard to tell, but Zabier was pretty sure not a single trophy braid remained.

'COME QUICKLY, IMOSHEN.'

She followed Arodyti and Sarosune down the steps and out of the palace. 'What is it?'

'You saw the banners at the end of the causeway?'

'Everyone did.'

'You have to see this.'

At that moment, they stepped through the sisterhood gate. From up here she could see two sources of light. One was far away, outside the city at the end of the causeway. The other was inside the city, down near the causeway gate. Figures danced around the closer fire. Imoshen could hear shouts and laughter. Something about the tone made her shiver and her gift surge.

'Have you been down there?' she asked Arodyti.

'No, we saw it from the palace roof. The fire outside the city started first, then the one inside our gate.'

Straight down through the free quarter they went, heading for the causeway gate. As they drew closer, it became clear the brotherhoods had built a huge bonfire in front of the sisterhood boat-house, the very place where Reoden's daughter had been killed.

Figures danced around the leaping flames, drinking, laughing and chanting. Imoshen looked for blood and signs of rivalry between the brotherhoods, but tonight there was none. After twelve years in the city, she found it unnerving, the same way she'd found Kyredeon's bloodless claiming of Chariode's brotherhood unnerving.

Imoshen and her two companions were the only T'En women and, as they approached, the brotherhood warriors fell back. They stared, eyes feverish with excitement.

From a good three body lengths Imoshen began to sense the male gift, then she hit a wall of it, powerful, aggressive, violent and triumphant.

Arodyti swore and stopped dead. She glanced over her shoulder to Imoshen and Sarosune. 'Feel that? I've never come across anything like it.'

More and more of the brotherhood men turned towards them. This was what the sisterhood warriors must have come up against four hundred years ago, when they had rescued the boys from the brotherhoods. This primal, violent drive made her gift scream a warning. It surged and she read the tone of the crowd. These brotherhood men – Malaunje and T'En – were not entirely sane right now. One hint of weakness, and they would turn on the three sisters. 'We can't go back.'

Arodyti went first, then Imoshen, followed by Sarosune. The men parted for them as they made their way to the steps leading up to the gate wall-walk.

Imoshen felt light-headed, as if she was drunk. A quick glance to Arodyti and Sarosune revealed they were in the same heightened state, high on the men's gift power.

They stepped onto the wall-walk. It was wide enough for six men to walk abreast, and extended in a semi-circle around the low end of the island. So many tall, broad-shouldered men crowded the wall it was hard to see the lake's shore. The shouting and cheering almost deafened her, while the force of all those roused male gifts battered against her defences.

She made her way along until she recognised All-father Saskeyne's voice-of-reason; although, right now, he looked beyond reason.

Imoshen tapped him on the back.

He turned, saw her and shouted something. The all-father and hand-of-force pushed through the crowd to join him. Imoshen felt Arodyti bristle and Sarosune stepped closer.

'We've done it. We've shown those Mieren!' the all-father shouted.

Seeing she didn't understand, Saskeyne gripped her arm and pointed towards the shore. 'There!'

Imoshen made out a vaguely man-shaped object burning fiercely at the point where the causeway met the town.

'We showed them. Flaunt the trophies of our dead, will they? We took back the braids and we burned King Charald in effigy, burned him along with all his barons' banners!'

Imoshen stared at the burning man shape. 'How?'

'You told us to see what gift strength our brothers had. Turns out, we had four noets, very strong mind-manipulators. They captured the minds of the Mieren on watch. Any whose minds couldn't be enthralled, they shattered. We moved so fast, the Mieren didn't get a chance to sound the alarm.'

King Charald was going to be furious. This would confirm all the stories the Mieren told about her kind.

She was furious. How could she negotiate, if they deliberately taunted King Charald? But, at the same time, she realised the brotherhoods needed to retaliate. Seeing the trophy plaits of their dead had... 'What have you done with the plaits?'

'What?'

'Where are the trophy braids?'

'Safe.' He gave his voice-of-reason instructions.

Saskeyne's voice-of-reason led them up the causeway road to a two-wheeled hand-cart laden with plaits. There had to be sixty or seventy. Each of those T'En could have lived to be one hundred years old or more. When

Imoshen looked at the cart piled high, she saw six to seven thousand years of wasted life.

Snow started to fall, landing lightly on the braided hair. The plaits couldn't stay here.

'Bring the cart,' Imoshen told Saskeyne's voice-of-reason. 'And follow me.'

Imoshen went up the road, into the free quarter, then along one of the side streets to the dome of empowerment. Between them, they carried the long plaits inside and hung them over the rail that ran around the dome's central stage. The gift residue on each braid told Imoshen if its wearer had been killed recently, or if the hair had belonged to a long-dead T'En. It also told her whether each braid's owner had been male or female.

When they were done, Imoshen turned to the voice-of-reason. 'Tell the all-fathers to meet us here tomorrow at midday. Each brotherhood and sisterhood will claim their people's relics so they can lay them to rest in the crypts.'

And she would confront All-father Saskeyne.

HIS LEGS WEREN'T as long, but Zabier was right on the king's heels as he charged across the town square. They found the banner-men laid out neatly in a row, with their throats cut. Not one had put up a fight. A sign balanced against the entrance to the causeway read: *King Charald, King of Straw*.

'How could T'En warriors do this without anyone noticing?' Charald was livid. He threw the sign into the flames. 'Where were the townsfolk? The Wyrds had to set up the straw man, take the banners off the poles and hang them up. What were our sentries doing?'

No one could answer him.

The king returned to his tent, demanding explanations. Townsfolk were hauled before him. All of them had been inside their homes with their families; no one could tell him when it had happened, and no one had heard anything.

Charald's voice grew hoarse from shouting. His tremble, which he usually kept hidden, became more pronounced.

The king grilled the sentries, but they had been behind the houses at the camp perimeter, and they knew nothing. He sent them off to be whipped all the same.

Spittle flew from Charald's mouth as he ranted and raved. The tremble moved from both his hands to his head. Old grievances bubbled up, magnified tenfold. Even the dead were not excused, as he railed against anyone and everyone who had ever done him wrong.

No one dared to speak up. Anything they said would be twisted against them.

Usually, Zabier waited for the king's tirade to end while trying to alleviate the worst of his excesses. Tonight, there seemed to be no end in sight. Zabier was out of his depth and looked around for Sorne, but the half-blood was nowhere to be seen. He vaguely remembered him slipping away when they returned to the king's tent.

As soon as the king's attention was diverted, Zabier escaped. He found Sorne sitting in the holy tent by the light of a single candle.

Neither of them spoke for a moment.

Then Sorne looked up. 'He's getting worse.'

'Yes.'

'His temper feeds on itself. It's like he becomes drunk with it. You could try getting him to eat. Food will calm him.'

'I think he's beyond food.'

Sorne nodded. 'One of these days, he'll go too far and someone he's unjustly punished will slip a knife in his back. Or one of the barons will get tired of tip-toeing around him.'

Zabier thought it more likely the king's rage would completely unhinge his mind. When that happened, Eskarnor would make his move. Eskarnor had Hanix in his pocket. The two were from Dace and did not have a high opinion of Zabier, or the Chalcedonian church.

If the king was going to be replaced, his replacement needed to be one of the Chalcedonian barons, who knew the worth of the Seven and valued their high priest. But Zabier didn't want another king; he knew Charald's foibles and how to cope with them.

If he could just control his rages.

Zabier rubbed his face and sighed. 'The queen's father used to have a way with him. He'd sit sipping wine with the king and gradually talk him into a calmer frame of mind. Since he died unexpectedly, no one's–'

'Before I sailed, Baron Jantzen told me he was concerned by the king's rages. He said he was going to try the soothing powder from Khitan. Perhaps–'

'That's it!' Zabier opened his chest. 'I've never tried this before, but...'

Sorne came over.

Zabier held up a bottle of cloudy liquid. 'Pains-ease in its pure form.'

'Why do you have a whole jar of it when you're not a healer? Are you sick?'

Zabier waved him away, as he added some pains-ease to a carafe of wine. He hesitated over the amount to use.

'Charald never uses pains-ease,' Sorne said. 'He says a man should be able to bear pain. I've seen him jest while they sew him up.'

The king was a big man. Zabier decided to be sure and tipped in a further measure, then stirred it. He picked up the carafe.

'Do you want me to come with you?' Sorne offered.

And steal his thunder? Zabier shook his head. He wanted to be the one with the ability to calm the king.

Sorne returned to his bedroll and Zabier went to the next tent where the holy warriors slept. It smelled of sweaty men and ale. Several were awake, sitting in the dark.

'You and you, stay outside my tent until I return.'

When Zabier entered the royal tent with the carafe, he found the king's manservant placing bread and cheese on the table. They exchanged looks.

As Charald sent a messenger off to find someone he thought had insulted him, Zabier poured two glasses of wine. He'd been using pains-ease regularly for years now and had developed a tolerance for it. 'Have you eaten, sire?'

'I'm not hungry.'

'At least take some wine with me. Your throat must be parched.'

Charald came over, took the wine and tossed it back. As he replaced the wine goblet he noticed his hand trembling and clasped his sword hilt to hide it.

While waiting for the man to report to back, the king paced and complained to Zabier about past slights. Each time he went past, Zabier topped up his wine.

The king took his seat, still rambling.

Charald stabbed a piece of cheese and ate it quickly. Zabier cut bread and poured more wine. The king began to slur his words and the tremble became more pronounced. Zabier was amazed by his capacity to fight the drug.

Finally, sometime towards morning, Charald fell asleep with his head on the table. The manservant, who had been crouched in the corner dozing, looked up hopefully.

'My king?' Zabier whispered.

Charald snored and they both breathed a sigh of relief. Between them, they carried him to his bunk.

As Zabier came out of the tent, his eyes gritty with tiredness, he spotted the night-watch and beckoned. 'Go down to the causeway. Make sure there's no sign of that straw man. Not a single piece of ash.'

When Zabier returned to his tent, the two holy warriors were huddled in furs under the awning, which hung low with the weight of the snow. They returned to their tent and Zabier went to bed.

He'd just fallen asleep when Charald's manservant woke him.

'Come quickly. The king is deathly ill,' he whispered.

Zabier's mind was so fuzzy with exhaustion he had trouble making sense of what he said. 'Have... have you called the saw-bones?'

'No. He's asking for you and the Warrior's-voice.'

'Coming,' Sorne said. He was already on his feet. It was all very well for him. He hadn't been up all night.

Zabier forced himself out of bed. He wasn't going to let the half-blood insinuate himself into the king's good graces. Zabier gestured to the servant. 'Send for the saw-bones.'

'I don't think that's a good idea. The king's convinced Baron Nitzane's poisoned him,' the manservant said.

Sorne swore. 'You're right. If he accuses Nitzane in front of the saw-bones it will get out. Fear of Nitzane's popularity with the Chalcedonian barons is the only thing that's keeping Eskarnor in check. Go back to the king's side. We'll be right there.'

As soon as the manservant left, Sorne whispered. 'It's the pains-ease. I've seen this before. Some people have a bad reaction, and Charald's never had it. How much did you give him?'

'Not much,' Zabier lied.

'Looks like even a little was too much. Come on. We've got to keep him from accusing Nitzane. Believe me, you don't want Eskarnor crowning himself king of Chalcedonia. I've seen what that man is capable of.'

Zabier's fingers shook as he laced up his breeches. Sorne was already tying his bootstraps.

When they stepped out of their tent, the silvery light of a winter's dawn filled the sky to the east and their breath formed plumes of white mist. They heard grumbling and laughter where another tent had collapsed under the snow.

They found the king calm but violently ill. He'd already thrown up everything in his stomach and now he was dry retching. The spasms were so intense, Zabier's stomach heaved in sympathy.

The servant hovered, wringing his hands.

'Give us a moment with him,' Sorne said.

Zabier wondered what he hoped to achieve.

The spasm passed and the king lifted his head. He looked shocking, haggard and pale. He rubbed his face with a trembling hand. When his servant went to take the basin away, the king held onto it.

Charald beckoned and whispered. 'It was Nitzane. He means to have my throne for his son. He poisoned me.'

'Nitzane or Eskarnor,' Sorne said. 'One of the barons.'

'No, Eskarnor would meet me on the battlefield. Nitzane's not a leader of men. He'd use stealth and subterfuge.'

'What did you eat or drink, sire?' Sorne asked.

'Wine, cheese and bread.'

'The same wine, bread and cheese your high priest had?' Sorne gestured to Zabier. 'He's not ill. I think–'

The king lurched forward again. His manservant steadied the basin under his face. Charald heaved wretchedly, bringing up a little bile.

When it was over, the king gave a heartfelt groan, sinking back onto his bed. The servant took the basin, but stayed nearby in case. A shudder ran through the king and Zabier pulled up the covers.

'I've heard some of the men complaining of the heaves,' Sorne said. 'When you get this many men together, there's always illness. You'll be right by this time tomorrow.'

'I have to be.'

Sorne went to rise.

Charald caught his arm. 'I thought I was dying.'

Sorne covered the king's hand with his six-fingered hand. 'What, a mean old bastard like you?'

Zabier was shocked.

He was even more shocked when the king laughed. It was a weak laugh, but a laugh all the same.

A flash of pure hatred stabbed Zabier. He'd never made the king laugh. It was Sorne's fault he'd given the king pains-ease and now Sorne was covering for him, which infuriated him. If Sorne thought he was going to be grateful, he was very much mistaken.

As the manservant moved to get rid of the basin's contents, Sorne rose and stopped him. Zabier stayed by the king's bed, head bent in an attitude of prayer, straining to hear.

'No one is to come in here. No one is to know how ill the king has been. If anyone asks, tell them the king drank too much and is sleeping it off.'

The manservant nodded without looking to Zabier. Clearly, if Sorne stayed, before long everyone would be looking to the half-blood for orders instead of him. How did Sorne make them overlook his tainted blood?

After the manservant left, Sorne pulled up a stool at the end of the king's bed and spoke softly of events during the Secluded Sea campaign. He talked of men they both knew, battles and betrayal. He made Charald smile, chuckle even.

The king didn't throw up again, and, as Sorne diverted Charald with stories, Zabier realised Sorne loved the old man.

The fool.

THAT DAY, SORNE took his usual walk around the camp, followed by two of the holy warriors. Now that he'd spent more time in camp, he saw the allegiances more clearly. Eskarnor had emerged as the leader of the southern barons and Hanix was his right-hand man. Their tents were pitched side by side.

As Sorne walked through the Chalcedonian barons' tents, he spotted Baron Kerminzto watching him. Kerminzto was the queen's cousin. He could have presumed on this connection to win favours from the king, but he didn't. Sorne suspected he was a cautious, sensible man. Today, Kerminzto looked grim, but then so did everyone else.

When Sorne passed Nitzane's tents, he spotted the baron observing as Captain Ballendin conducted weapons practice and paused to watch.

'Charald's temper fits are getting worse,' Nitzane muttered by way of greeting. 'I swear I don't trust him.'

'He doesn't trust you,' Sorne whispered. 'He's convinced you poisoned him.'

'What? Rubbish. I can't help it if he drinks too much, or gets the camp trots.'

'Keep your voice down,' Sorne warned. 'Do nothing to give him reason to doubt your loyalty.'

'How can he blame me?' Nitzane objected.

'The same way you blamed him for the bridge collapse that killed Marantza. Coincidence and motive.'

Nitzane blinked. His eyes filled with tears. 'She didn't deserve it, Sorne.'

'I know, but that doesn't mean Charald was responsible.' And even if he was, Sorne needed Nitzane to support the king.

Chapter Eight

IT WAS A solemn occasion under the empowerment dome, as the all-mothers and all-fathers divided the braids between them. While it was possible to recognise another T'En by his or her gift, there was too little residue left on these plaits to identify anything but the genders.

Imoshen wanted to get through the formalities and make her point about the consequences of burning the banners, but there was still a pile of plaits dating from the war three hundred years ago. She watched with growing frustration and astonishment as the leaders of the T'Enatuath voted to build a memorial to those who had fallen in the previous war.

Then All-father Saskeyne's voice-of-reason sprang to his feet and claimed stature for their brotherhood. And, to Imoshen's amazement, the others acknowledged it. Her gift surged and she read them as a group; they were so intent on their own little world and so used to dismissing Mieren as beneath them that they did not grasp the larger implications.

She was causare, their nominated leader, but she led only by consensus. If she destroyed Saskeyne's stature, he would retaliate with aggression. If she tried to force her will on the brotherhoods, they would revolt.

She felt dark laughter well up inside her and wished Ardonyx was here. His biting satires had laid bare the flaws of their society, but most people had failed to see the underlying message. She sensed someone watching her and spotted Hueryx. There was a mocking light in his eyes.

Her gift surged and she understood his cynical comments sprang from frustration with their people.

She would not give in to bitterness.

When it seemed the leaders of the T'Enatuath would leave without addressing the real problem, Imoshen came to her feet.

'Before we go, there is one more thing. The Mieren king sent his barons to raze our estates even though we had agreed to give him what he wanted. He'll see the burning of his effigy and the banners as an insult. If he razed our estates without provocation, what will he do now?'

She waited for this to sink in, then gestured to Saskeyne. 'While this all-father's symbolic action has united us, we are still sitting in a besieged city and the people on our estates are vulnerable.'

'What are you saying, Imoshen?' Hueryx asked, giving her the opening she needed.

'I cannot do my job as causare if others take actions that undermine me. Before any of us take an action that is going to impact the rest, it needs to be brought to an all-council for approval.'

The brotherhood leaders did not like this. They argued it infringed on their authority. She said nothing, letting Hueryx put the case. Paragian was quick to grasp the implications and support him.

While the debate unfolded, Egrayne leant closer to her. 'Hueryx didn't address you as T'Imoshen. He should use the causare's title.'

Imoshen wanted to bury her head in despair or laugh. Her title was the least of her problems. 'If I can get the brotherhoods to agree to this, I'll count it a win.'

She watched the argument evolve and, when her gift told her the moment was right, came to her feet. 'I propose we bring actions that affect the T'Enatuath to an all-council for approval.' And she raised her hand.

Gift on edge, she memorised who raised their hand and in what order. All-fathers Kyredeon, Saskeyne and Dretsun were last to agree.

When the all-council was over, she walked back to the sisterhood quarter with the all-mothers and their seconds.

Outside the healer's palace, she caught Reoden's hand. 'Ree, my choice-son wanted to see Sardeon but he was turned away. Why?'

The healer drew her inside and took her up to her private chambers. As Reoden reached for the nursery door, Imoshen prepared herself for the worst. Like Iraaycl, Sardeon was sixteen. If he was still living in the nursery, he must need constant care.

The door swung open to reveal a pleasant room that opened onto a private rooftop garden. A child lay on his stomach in front of a fire reading a book. His feet swung in time to some internal music.

Imoshen looked up to the healer. 'Where's–'

'Sar?' Reoden called.

The child looked up. It *was* Sardeon. She had forgotten how beautiful he was.

'But...' He should have been sixteen, not twelve. Imoshen looked to Reoden in confusion.

'Go back to your reading,' Reoden told Sardeon. 'The gift-wright will be here soon.'

They stepped outside and shut the nursery door.

'He hasn't grown at all,' Imoshen whispered. 'What does Ceriane say?'

'She hasn't found anything like it in the records. We're hoping he'll grow out of it...' Reoden heard what she'd said and winced. 'We're hoping time will heal him.'

'Is he ready for me?' the gift-wright asked.

The healer nodded and the gift-wright left them.

'I'm sorry,' Imoshen whispered.

'I'm his choice-mother and a healer.' Reoden wrung her hands. 'I should be able to help him. I can't.'

'No one can help him, or me.' Scryer Lysitzi joined them. 'I'm crippled. My power is blocked. I should have known Kyredeon meant to kill...' Her voice faltered.

'You could have only known if I had asked you to scry looking for a threat to my daughter,' Reoden told her. Imoshen had the feeling it was an old argument. 'It's not your fault.'

Imoshen was shocked by the scryer's appearance. One side of her face was pulled out of alignment by a scar. 'At least let Ree heal your face.'

Instead of answering, the scryer gave a strange laugh and drifted out, muttering under her breath. Imoshen shivered.

'I have healed her face,' Reoden confessed. 'Every time I heal it the scar comes back.'

'It's tied to her gift?'

'It is now.' Tears slid down Reoden's cheeks.

'Oh, Ree.' Imoshen took her in her arms and kissed them away. They had been lovers and would be again, one day. 'Why didn't you tell me?'

'The shame–'

'The shame?' Imoshen could not believe her ears. 'If anyone should be shamed, it's Kyredeon's men, for killing an innocent child!'

As TOBAZIM FINISHED his exercises, he glanced over to Learon. Every evening his choice-brother came to him with complaints about the hand-of-force. Tonight it had been the way Oriemn belittled initiates when they made mistakes in training. He claimed it undermined their confidence. While Tobazim agreed, there was nothing they could do. He'd hoped the challenging exercise patterns would help Learon bring his mind, body and gift into balance.

But his choice-brother's expression was grim.

Learon picked up a cloth to rub his face. 'How can a young initiate learn when he's afraid of his teacher?' He tossed the cloth away. 'When we lived in the winery, I dreamed of coming to the city and winning stature. It all seemed so simple then. All we had to do was slip into a rival brotherhood palace and steal their banner to prove ourselves to the hand-of-force.'

'True.' Tobazim looked around for something to distract him, and noticed activity on the all-father's rooftop garden, across the other side of the courtyard from them. 'What's going on there?'

Under the brotherhood's banner, two Malaunje had constructed a tent with brocade trim and gauze curtains. Others arrived bringing a couch, two braziers, and a low table set with wines and delicacies.

'Looks like they're building a trysting bower,' Learon said.

'That's right, I heard Kyredeon had taken a new lover. Guess he's planning on moon bathing. It's supposed to enhance the gift when trysting. But,' Tobazim gestured to the sky, 'both moons are new and there's too much cloud.'

Learon didn't comment. The Malaunje finished constructing the bower then went downstairs.

'I bet Oriemn was furious when Saskeyne's warriors beat him to the trophy braids,' Tobazim said again.

'Serves him right. Stealing my idea.'

As they turned to head downstairs, Learon signalled for silence and pointed. A warrior crept across the rooftop garden. Another warrior followed him, keeping low, dashing from raised garden bed to bed.

'Are they ours?' Tobazim whispered.

'It'll be a rival brotherhood trying to steal our banner. Bet they're Saskeyne's adepts. Come on.'

'Wait, Lear.'

But he'd already taken off down the stairs.

Tobazim followed close on Learon's heels, so close that he sensed his choice-brother's eager gift. The palace was a warren of passages and courtyards. But Learon knew his way and did not hesitate. His long legs ate up the stairs, taking them three at a time, until he reached Kyredeon's private rooftop garden.

'Wait.' Tobazim caught up with him before he stepped outside. He could feel Learon's gift close to the surface. 'We should tell someone.'

'This is our chance to win stature. Turn the flat of your blade. Grab their arm-torcs, if you can.' If they took the other brotherhood's arm-torcs, the warriors would have to come back to retrieve them. Their humiliation would add to Tobazim and Learon's stature. Learon stepped out. 'Come on.'

Tobazim followed him.

A lantern burned in the bower, but the rest of the rooftop garden was dim. Empty raised garden beds dotted the area. At first glance, Tobazim could not spot the warriors.

Learon grabbed a rake and charged. 'Caught you!'

As the other brotherhood warrior sprang to his feet, Tobazim saw a flash of blade; that wasn't right. Although warriors could end up with broken bones, banner-stealing was not meant to cost lives.

The warrior deflected the rake with his first blade and lunged for Learon's throat with his second.

The attack was furious. Learon staggered backwards as he struggled to bring the rake around and into play.

Stunned, Tobazim was about to help him, when he caught movement in the side of his vision. He dodged instinctively. A blade whistled past his ear.

On the back foot, Tobazim edged away, fighting to control his gift. His attacker glanced behind Tobazim, who sensed another man's gift. Just in time, he threw himself sideways. Rolling across a garden bed, he came to his feet near Learon, grabbed a shovel and brought the end up.

Four warriors surrounded them. A patch of moonlight fell across their faces. Tobazim did not recognise them, and he thought he knew all of Saskeyne's young adepts by sight, if not by name. These were not hot-headed young brotherhood warriors out to strike a blow for stature.

'Who are they?' Tobazim whispered.

'I don't know,' Learon muttered. 'But they're not here to steal the banner.'

With that, Learon charged his two assailants, swinging the rake like a scythe; they scattered. He brought the blunt end up, driving it forward in the classic staff attack. It took one of the warriors in the chest, sending him sprawling.

He returned to protect Tobazim's back. Learon was a master-adept of both armed and unarmed combat; Tobazim was not.

Two more intruders darted out from the shadows, making six in total. Tobazim's gift leapt to his defence. He forced it down. As the intruders came closer, there was no yelling, no bravado, just deadly intent in their movements. They divided up, so that Tobazim and Learon each faced three attackers.

Tobazim did not like their chances.

'These are not them,' one of the intruders said.

'Too late. Kill them anyway. Then hide.' He sounded like someone who was used to giving orders and dealing in death.

Tobazim wanted to protest. They were all T'En. It did not feel right, fighting his own kind when thousands of Mieren besieged their city.

'Quickly,' the leader urged.

Tobazim flinched. He didn't want to die like this. He'd never had the chance to win stature with his gift, never trysted with a T'En woman, never known love...

Behind him, Learon grunted with effort as he diverted a strike.

The warrior on Tobazim's left darted in, trying to get around to his back. Tobazim remembered his old weapons-master telling him the weakest fighter always attacks from behind: deal with him quickly, then concentrate on the ones that come in from the front.

Tobazim swung the shovel at the knife-hand that arced towards him, smashing the man's hand and breaking bones. The blade went flying as the momentum of Tobazim's strike carried the intruder around, taking his second knife out of striking range.

Tobazim stepped in behind him. With his free hand, he caught the man's shoulder and pulled him backwards, slamming him on the ground.

The fallen man's companion stepped in front to protect him.

Tobazim cursed. What was he thinking? He should have brained the one he'd just taken down. This was not weapons practice.

He edged closer to Learon. They must not get separated. Meanwhile, he tried to keep his attackers moving so that one impeded the other.

The intruders' leader moved to one side to allow one of his companions to come at Tobazim, who shortened the arc of the shovel and drove it forward for the man's throat. It sank in, hitting something hard. The warrior went down. A horrible gargling sound came from his crushed throat as he struggled for breath.

Ignoring the downed man, Tobazim faced the leader.

The leader was a canny older warrior who circled him, then came in, moving so fast that Tobazim couldn't get the shovel around in time.

Darting back, he tripped over a body. As he went down, a long-knife passed within a finger's breadth of his throat. He just had time to realise he was a dead man when he hit the tiles and the wind was knocked out of him.

Beyond his attacker, Tobazim saw All-father Kyredeon, his hand-of-force and a Malaunje woman step out of the stairwell. Seeing the altercation, she darted back.

The attackers' leader turned towards the newcomers.

Hand-of-force Oriemn drew his long-knives, tossed one to Kyredeon and stepped between his all-father and the intruders. Three of the four remaining intruders went to deal with the new threat.

Learon had lost the rake somehow and was now facing a warrior with nothing but his fists.

Tobazim rolled to his knees. Noticing the gleam of a blade on the tiles, he grabbed the hilt and sprang to his feet to help Learon. He was in time to see his choice-brother break the intruder's neck and spring to help Kyredeon's hand-of-force, pulling one of the intruders off Oriemn's back.

All-father Kyredeon had snatched a blanket from the couch and wrapped it around his forearm, and was using it as a shield to deflect the blades, while striking with his own knife.

Tobazim darted in, looking for a target. He saw an intruder with a knife in one hand, hugging his broken hand to his chest, and knew it was the one he had failed to kill. This time, Tobazim came at him from behind, caught him around the throat and drove the knife between his ribs, straight into his heart.

It was up close and intimate; it was one of his own people and it was nothing like killing one of the Mieren. Tobazim felt the other's gift flare as it tried to protect him. Skin on skin, the sudden rush of power stunned him.

He let the man drop and stepped back.

Then he swayed as reality wavered and he was nearly drawn through to the higher plane with the warrior's departing shade.

He shook his head to clear it.

The leader of the intruders had thrown off Learon's bear hug. Now he sprang for Kyredeon. Unbalanced, Learon staggered backwards into Tobazim and they both went down.

Tobazim just had time to turn the long-knife so his choice-brother didn't end up with the blade between his ribs, but he couldn't prevent Learon from clipping his head on the side of a raised flower bed as they fell.

Trapped under his stunned choice-brother, Tobazim struggled to throw Learon off.

Meanwhile, Tobazim heard the sharp grunts and ragged breathing of vicious fighting. With a heave, he pushed Learon to one side and came to his feet, standing over his fallen choice-brother, ready to defend him.

But all the attackers were down.

Oriemn and Kyredeon straightened up. The pall of gift aggression hung on the still air, making Tobazim's heart race.

Hand-of-force Oriemn rolled one of the intruders onto his back. 'This one's dead.' He gestured to Tobazim. 'Get the lamp.'

Tobazim returned from the trysting bower in a halo of golden light. Oriemn took the lamp from him to inspect the dead T'En warriors.

Kyredeon had been bent double catching his breath. Now he straightened, unwound the blanket from his arm and tossed it aside. 'Who is it?'

'No idea.'

'Which brotherhood?'

'They're not wearing arm-torcs.'

Kyredeon spat in disgust.

Oriemn stepped over a body and rolled one of the intruders onto his back. On seeing the leader, Kyredeon tensed.

But Oriemn missed his all-father's reaction as he turned the last one over and looked up to Kyredeon expectantly.

'No idea,' the all-father said, and if Tobazim hadn't seen that flicker of recognition, he would have believed him.

Tobazim's legs felt as if they might give way. He took a step back and dropped to sit on the edge of a flower bed.

Learon groaned, as he sat up carefully.

Oriemn turned the lamp towards them. 'What were you two doing up here?'

Tobazim gestured to the nearby roof garden. 'We were exercising, when we saw–'

'Do you recognise any of them?' Oriemn asked.

'No.' Tobazim licked his lips. 'They were after the all-father.'

'What makes you say that?' Kyredeon demanded.

'One of them said, "these are not them," but their leader said to kill us anyway. This is All-father Kyredeon's private rooftop garden and his bower has been set up. Naturally, I thought–'

'No one asked you think.' Kyredeon cut him off. 'You should have reported to the hand-of-force, not come up here alone.'

'You're right,' Tobazim admitted. 'We only saw two of them and thought–'

'You would win stature,' Oriemn finished for him. 'You nearly got us all killed.'

Learon rolled to his feet, swaying a little. He was bigger than the hand-of-force and the other two stepped back.

'At first we thought they were Saskeyne's warriors, come to steal our banner,' Learon said, rubbing the back of his head. 'That's why we didn't tell anyone. But they were assassins.'

Kyredeon waved him to silence, turning away.

In the pause, Tobazim asked softly, 'How are you doing?'

'Head's thumping fit to burst. What about you?'

'Alive.' He glanced to the palace wall, about a bowshot away. The brothers on patrol were watching the lake, unaware of what had passed.

'What'll we do with the bodies?' Oriemn asked.

A thought struck Tobazim. 'Do you want me to search them, see if anything identifies their brotherhood?'

Kyredeon shook his head. 'No point. They took off their arm-torcs. They won't have anything to identify them.'

At that moment one of the *dead* men behind Kyredeon rolled to his feet, lifted his long-knife and went to stab the all-father between the ribs. Learon reacted instantly, catching him and diverting the strike.

Oriemn thrust his all-father aside and turned to deal with the attacker, but Learon already had him restrained.

'A gift-trick to mimic death,' Tobazim marvelled.

'Who sent you to kill our all-father?' Oriemn demanded. 'Was it Saskeyne? Dretsun? Hueryx?'

The assassin did not reply.

'You'll get nothing from him,' Kyredeon said. 'He's cut his hair. He's already dead.'

Tobazim realised they all had.

'Shall I kill him?' Oriemn asked.

'No. Put his eyes out and turn him out of the palace. Let our warriors hunt him for sport.' Kyredeon clearly relished the idea. 'That will deliver a message to those who sent him.'

Oriemn moved in, hands lifting to the assassin's face, thumbs ready to gouge out his eyes. Tobazim felt sick and Learon opened his mouth to protest. Taking advantage of Learon's momentary distraction, the assassin slipped free. He head-butted Oriemn and lunged between the two big warriors, heading straight towards Tobazim.

Before Tobazim knew what was happening, the assassin had grabbed the blade from him. Their eyes met and Tobazim looked into the face of death. He fully expected to die. But then he saw mercy in death's eyes.

The assassin darted past him, backing away, holding the long-knife ready.

Oriemn straightened up, sucking in his breath noisily. Kyredeon and Learon both moved to encircle the intruder.

'May your brotherhood wither and fade, Kyredeon. May you never sleep easy in your bed, Kyredeon,' the assassin said. 'May you die having looked long and hard into your own blighted soul, Kyredeon. May your shade be devoured by empyrean beasts, Kyredeon.' Then he lifted the blade and sliced his throat open.

It was the warrior's honourable suicide. He fell, making horrible choking noises, the blood bubbling from the wound.

Tobazim shuddered. At the same time, admiration warmed him. It was better to die whole and defiant, than maimed and hunted for sport by a rival brotherhood.

But questions remained unanswered. Who had sent the assassins, and why had Kyredeon pretended not to recognise their leader?

The hand-of-force rounded on them. 'Since you are so keen to fight for the brotherhood, you can relieve the guards on the ruined palace wall.'

Tobazim gulped. In Kyredeon's brotherhood you did not refuse an order. But tonight, he and Learon had killed several T'En. The warriors' shades would come after them and try to drag them onto the higher plane.

'They'll come for us,' he blurted.

'Don't worry. They won't be coming for you,' Kyredeon said and Tobazim realised the assassination attempt wasn't over. The shades of these warriors would try to drag the all-father onto the higher plane, where they might even sacrifice their own chance to reach death's realm, to ensure that Kyredeon's essence was devoured by empyrean predators. Now he understood the depth of the assassin's curse.

Tobazim glanced to Learon, who looked as though he had just reached the same conclusion. 'I see.'

'You see nothing.' Kyredeon's gaze fixed on him and Learon. 'You saw nothing. This never happened. Understood?'

They nodded.

'Swear on your brotherhood vow,' Oriemn insisted.

They knelt before Kyredeon and swore to silence.

'Now, go patrol the wall,' Oriemn dismissed them.

As Tobazim left the rooftop garden, everything felt unreal. He had fought alongside Kyredeon and his hand-of-force, but he had to wonder what had provoked the assassination attempt.

As Learon entered the stairwell someone hurtled at him. He caught his assailant and swung them up against the wall.

'It's me,' Paravia gasped.

Learon groaned and pulled her to him, wrapping her in his arms. She kissed him eagerly.

'I thought you were going to die,' she whispered. On tip toes, she planted kisses on his chin and throat. 'I thought I'd never hold you again.'

Learon lifted her off the ground the better to kiss her, his gift rising in reaction to the danger and the promise of trysting.

'Lear,' Tobazim protested. 'Not now.'

'Not ever,' Oriemn said, from the rooftop entrance to the stairwell. 'Get your hands off her.'

Tobazim felt cold as he realised who Kyredeon's new lover was.

'What business is it of yours–' Learon said, reaching for his weapon.

'Don't you dare draw your blade against me,' the hand-of-force said, although from his tone, there was nothing he'd like better. Oriemn let his gift rise, laced with threat and aggression.

'Lear...' Paravia caught his forearm. 'It's all right. I don't mind.'

'I should think not,' Oriemn said. 'It's an honour to be invited to the all-father's trysting bower.'

'You're his new lover?' Learon was shocked.

'It's all right,' she whispered, and cast Tobazim a look of mute appeal.

'Come on, Lear,' he said.

His choice-brother brushed off his hand, turning to Oriemn. 'Paravia's mine.'

'Is she your devotee?'

'No...' Learon admitted.

'Has she borne you a child?'

'No.'

'Then you've made no claim on her.'

'I'm making a claim now.' Learon turned to Paravia and Tobazim felt him gather his gift. 'Would you be my devotee?'

She opened her mouth to reply, but Oriemn cut her off.

'You're supposed to be patrolling the wall, Learon. Do I have to punish you for dereliction of duty?'

'I just need to–'

'You need to go to your post.' Oriemn was enjoying this. 'You can ask Paravia tomorrow. See if she still wants a mere adept, when she can have an all-father.'

Learon bristled.

Tobazim grabbed his arm. 'No, Lear. Come on.'

For one terrible moment, he thought Learon would brush him off and attack the hand-of-force. In his current state, Learon would grab him and segue straight to the higher plane.

'Go, do your duty, Lear,' Paravia told him. 'I'm going to do mine.' With that, she went out the door towards the bower, and all the fight went out of Learon.

In silence, they went to the chamber they shared with other young adepts, dressed warmly and strapped on their knives.

As they passed the infirmary, Ceyne came out and signalled Tobazim.

'Can't stop, have to report to the wall.'

Ceyne gestured to Learon. 'What's wrong with him?'

'Kyredeon's taken Paravia for his new trysting partner,' Tobazim said.

Ceyne shrugged. 'He's the all-father.' Then he gave Learon another look. 'I didn't know he was serious about her.'

'Neither did I,' Tobazim admitted. 'We'd better go. We're on patrol.'

Chapter Nine

ZABIER WOKE FEELING thick-headed. For a moment he didn't know where he was, and then he remembered he'd slept all day after being up all night. He felt awful. He recognised the signs; since leaving port, he'd had to be on alert, so he hadn't taken a decent dose of pains-ease – he needed a night in its arms.

'Good, you're awake,' Sorne said. 'Charald has called all the barons to his tent for the evening meal. We need to get dressed.'

'Why doesn't Charald rest?' Zabier grumbled.

'He cannot appear weak.'

'I know that. It was a rhetorical question.'

Sorne laughed.

'What?'

'You sounded like Oskane.'

'Well, he did have a hand in training me.' Looking back, Zabier realised the years in the retreat had been the best time of his life. Everything had started to go wrong when they returned to port.

'You'd tell me if something was troubling you, wouldn't you, Zabe?' Sorne asked.

'Of course.' Zabier answered, then listened to himself. Annoyance flashed through him. He was no longer Sorne's little brother. Had never been his brother.

'Good. Charald wants to see us first.'

Zabier dressed and they went into the next tent, where they found the king sitting at his table, with a manservant next to him.

'My food-taster,' Charald said. He gave the man a nod. 'Wait outside until the barons arrive.'

Zabier glanced to Sorne. He thought they had allayed the king's fear about poison.

'Come here.' Charald was dressed in finery, but there was a hectic flush to his cheeks and his eyes were overbright. The king had always carried his age well, but since last night, the flesh seemed to have shrunk on his big frame. He looked to be what he was: a True-man approaching sixty who had lived a hard life.

Charald leant close to Sorne, dropping his voice. 'You've survived a dozen assassination attempts. But they never tried to poison you. It's a cruel thing, poison. A pox on Nitzane and his ungrateful brother. I gave Dantzel a kingdom and made Nitzane the richest baron in Chalcedonia. Do I get gratitude?'

'But, sire,' Zabier said. 'We shared the food.'

'There are more ways to deliver poison. I'm going to be on my guard from now on. I can't trust anyone. Not the southern barons, not the Chalcedonian barons. I hear them whispering...'

The king gripped Sorne's arm. 'I thought I was going to die last night, and it made me remember how my father died on the battlefield. He left me a kingdom torn apart by greedy barons, but at fifteen, I was already bigger than most True-men. My son will be three in the spring and he's a cripple. You said I would have a healthy son. Where is he? I've tried asking the Warrior, but He won't give me a straight answer.'

Zabier waited to see how Sorne would wriggle out of this.

'In my vision you hugged a healthy boy,' Sorne said. 'This is what the Warrior showed me. How this comes about, I don't know. The gods move in mysterious ways.'

'The last two queens each gave me one son, then nothing but blue babies. Why? Why does the Warrior punish me? He must want something from me.' Charald's pale blue eyes darted about. 'When I conquered the kingdoms of the Secluded Sea, the Warrior rewarded me by returning the throne of Chalcedonia. Since then, two of those kingdoms have revolted. No wonder He's impatient with me. I could sail south to reclaim them, but the last time I left Chalcedonia, my son was killed and my cousin stole my throne. No, I must stay here. When I rid the land of Wyrds, the Warrior god will cure my crippled prince. He returned Sorne from the dead, so He can cure a club foot. That's it, isn't it?' He turned to them. 'That's the answer.'

Sorne hesitated.

'Do you want a sacrifice, sire?' Zabier asked. 'A vision to confirm your path?'

'Yes. Sorne will do the sacrifice.'

'As you say, sire.' Zabier looked down to hide his triumph. Sorne would risk his life, while he reaped the benefits of Sorne's vision.

Sorne hid his dismay. Another sacrifice? How could he live with himself?

Loud voices heralded the arrival of the barons, and Sorne stepped back to stand behind the king's chair. As they entered, the food-taster followed. The barons fell silent. They feared Charald. No one mentioned the straw man, the burnt banners or the king's rage.

The king's manservant tapped Sorne's arm then drew him into the private chamber of the tent, where he indicated the chamber pot. Sorne glanced down, not sure what he was looking for. The king's urine was... 'Red?'

'The colour of port wine.'

'Is it blood?'

'He hasn't been wounded.'

'Have you consulted the saw-bones?'

'He's good at sewing up wounds, but...' The manservant glanced around to make sure no one could overhear. 'The king's been talking to the Warrior all afternoon.'

Sorne shrugged.

'He's been getting answers.'

'Oh...' Sorne glanced towards the other side of the tent, where he could hear Charald holding forth. 'The king seems fine now.' He gestured to the chamber pot. 'Get rid of it. If this happens again, let me know.'

The man nodded and Sorne returned to his place behind the king's chair. The barons had ranged themselves around the table in their respective factions, southern barons down one end, with the Chalcedonian barons down the other.

The king was failing, but the barons would never follow a crippled prince... Sorne gasped. He was thinking like a True-man. The T'En could fix Prince Cedon. The healer hadn't been able to replace Sorne's lost eye because she needed something to work with, but the boy's foot was just malformed. If Charald brought the child here, they could... But no, Charald would never willingly hand over his heir to Wyrds. Not even if it meant the boy would be returned whole and healthy.

Or would he? Was his desperation for a suitable heir enough to make him overlook his hatred of the Wyrds?

'I've called you here because this insult cannot go unpunished,' Charald said. 'Last night proved the Wyrds cannot be trusted.'

The barons agreed. Not one of them questioned the king's logic. Sorne noticed how Kerminzto and several others lowered their eyes.

Charald named four barons, two southerners and two Chalcedonians. 'Each of you select a Wyrd estate and raze it. Bring me the trophy braids and several survivors. There will be a magnificent sacrifice. The ones we don't give to the Warrior, we'll string up on scaffolds along the causeway. The Wyrds will rue the day they crossed me.'

Sorne looked down to hide his horror. He'd seen Charald use these tactics before to break the spirit of besieged cities in the past. Back then, Sorne had done nothing; what could one man do against the King

Charalds of the world? This time they were his people, and he raged against his impotence.

Sorne despised the king. But he despised himself more for encouraging Charald to believe he was the tool of the Warrior. Originally, it had been Sorne's path to power, but now the king's delusion had power over them all.

Baron Eskarnor came to his feet. 'To King Charald, saviour of Chalcedonia!'

Everyone filled their goblets and stood. When the food-taster sipped Charald's wine, the barons noticed but made no comment. The toast was drunk and the goblets topped up. Sorne had seen far too many of these evenings. The barons would try to outdo each other, heaping fulsome praise on Charald.

'To ridding Chalcedonia of filthy Wyrds,' Eskarnor said.

'No.' Charald held up his hand. It trembled and he lowered it to raise his goblet. 'To ridding the *world* of Wyrds.' The king paused for effect. 'They'll never reach port. After I've pried them out of their city and they've loaded their wagons with riches, we'll surround their camp. We'll kill them all, right down to the last babe in arms.'

Stunned silence greeted this.

A buzzing filled Sorne's ears.

The king laughed. 'The Wyrds were never going to reach port. Do you think I want them sailing away to fester in one of my subject kingdoms? We'd just have to go through this all over again.'

As if released, the barons laughed and congratulated the king on his foresight.

Sorne's head spun. Why hadn't he seen this? He knew how ruthless Charald was. He'd been raised for the express purpose of ridding Chalcedonia of Wyrds. But he had thought that meant exile.

Murdering a whole race of people was... unthinkable.

Apparently not for King Charald.

* * *

ZABIER'S HEAD SPUN.

Killing all living Wyrds did not remove them from Chalcedonia. More half-bloods would be born. Look at Valendia. Her birth had driven his parents apart and broken up their happy home.

'What of the half-blood babies born to Mieren parents?' Zabier asked, before he knew he meant to. 'They'll keep coming.'

Charald laughed. 'Then you'll be kept busy, sacrificing them!'

In that heartbeat, Zabier's two worlds collided. Zabier the man who loved his sister confronted what Zabier the Father's-voice had done to protect her, and the impact rocked his world off its foundations. A lifetime of sacrificing half-bloods stretched before him; the thought revolted him.

Talk and laughter surrounded him. He took nothing in. A wave of nausea hit him.

Mumbling an apology, Zabier walked blindly out of the tent. Somehow Sorne was with him, supporting him.

He glanced to his choice-brother. Sorne's face revealed nothing. But then, Sorne had been raised for this. Zabier hadn't. Zabier pushed Sorne away, staggered several steps, fell to his knees in the snow and threw up.

When he was done, Sorne pulled him to his feet, drew him inside their tent and fetched him watered wine.

Zabier recalled the day Sorne had come to him, horrified by the rumours of Malaunje sacrifices. They'd just been to see Valendia, and when Sorne questioned him about the rumours, he'd denied everything. It had been the first time his private world and his public world had collided, and he'd rebuilt the walls. Now they lay in ruins.

As his choice-brother helped him take off his rich vestments, Zabier wondered: if Sorne had been revolted by the thought of Wyrd sacrifices then, was he hiding how he really felt now?

When Sorne tucked him into bed, Zabier caught his hand. He wanted to ask Sorne to help him escape from the king, but Sorne hadn't helped last time. He'd gone off with Charald to make his mark on the world and left him, a boy of thirteen, to serve King Matxin.

Besides, Sorne loved King Charald.

'What is it?' Sorne whispered.

'Nothing.' Zabier let him go. Sorne must despise him. After all, Zabier despised himself.

'Sleep.' Sorne smoothed his hair from his forehead. 'We can talk tomorrow.'

Tears stung Zabier's eyes and he turned away. Meanwhile, Sorne climbed into bed and the celebrations from the royal tent reached them.

Zabier lay in the darkness, heart racing, as everything he had ever done or failed to do while serving King Matxin came back to him. He could not bear it. He needed the release of pains-ease.

When Sorne's breathing became deep and regular, Zabier opened the chest and found the glass bottle. Normally he diluted the pains-ease and measured it carefully. Tonight, he took a mouthful, neat. It seared his throat on the way down.

He fought the urge to cough, tears streaming. Furtively, he returned the bottle and lay down.

Soon, he felt the warmth creep into his limbs as the sweet lies of pains-ease swept him away. Once he'd sought pains-ease in the belief it would bring him visions, and now he knew they were hollow dreams, but in his dreams, he was a hero, saving Valendia from King Charald. In his dreams, he saved the children and infants he'd sacrificed, because to do otherwise would kill him.

Funny... he thought it already had.

Sorne sat up cautiously. He'd waited as long as he could after Zabier took the pains-ease. Now he rolled to his feet and crept across to the bunk and listened to Zabier's deep, even breathing.

Imoshen needed to know King Charald's real plans. How much of the night was left?

He dressed warmly and slipped out of the tent. A light snow was falling from patchy clouds. Good, the snow would cover his tracks. He made his way through the camp, down to the lake's shore and along it, looking for a small boat to borrow. The cold was fierce. Finding what he was looking for, he slipped into the boat and rowed across the lake.

Getting into the city would not be hard. The brotherhood warriors would be eager to capture him. Convincing them he was Imoshen's agent was another thing entirely. After what Charald had said about him, the brotherhoods would want to kill him on sight.

But surely the fact that he put himself at their mercy would prove he was Imoshen's agent?

TOBAZIM GLANCED TO his choice-brother. Learon's brooding worried him. Their stretch of wall-walk backed onto the ruined palace and was bound by a tower at each end. They must have walked it twenty times in silence. Not that Tobazim blamed him. Every time he tried to come up with a topic of conversation, all he could think of was Paravia with Kyredeon in the trysting bower. The bower had been dismantled now, but he still saw it in his mind's eye.

When a patch of moonlight illuminated a man in a rowboat, it was a relief for Tobazim. He pointed. 'Look.'

'Could be another survivor from the estates,' Learon said. Malaunje had been arriving in small parties; exhausted women with small children, old men leading boys. 'Could be a Mieren spy.'

Tobazim and Learon watched as the oarsman came closer.

'He's using the causeway to hide him from the Mieren camp,' Learon said.

The oarsman rowed closer to the wall.

Tobazim leant over. 'Who goes there?'

The oarsman peered up at them. Tobazim couldn't make out his features, just the smudge that was his face.

'I have a message for the causare,' he called softly.

Tobazim glanced to Learon. 'What do you think?'

'Could be a Mieren ploy, but he's only one man.' Learon shrugged. 'If he gives us trouble we can handle him.'

'No. I meant should we take him straight to the causare?'

Learon hesitated, obviously torn. They had been raised to serve the brotherhood with unfaltering loyalty, but if they took him to Kyredeon, their all-father might use what he learnt for his own gain, rather than the protection of their people.

Learon came to a decision, straightened up and leaned over the wall. 'Go to boat-house gate below. We'll be right down.'

They knew their way through the ruined palace. Tobazim opened the gates and the oarsman rowed. As he secured the boat, his hood hid his features. He appeared to be unarmed, but there could have been anything under those furs. Tobazim and Learon kept their distance, hands on their knife hilts.

'Who are you?' Learon asked. 'And how do we know you speak the truth?'

Keeping his head down, he climbed up beside them. 'You aren't going to like who I am, but you must believe me, I'm Imoshen's spy and I need to see her.'

He pushed back the hood to reveal pure white hair and a face with one eye. Where the other eye had been was only smooth skin.

'The Warrior's-voice.' Learon reached for his long-knife. 'You sacrificed our people.'

Tobazim caught his arm. 'Think, Lear. He's here risking his life.'

Learon grimaced, but nodded.

'Take me to Imoshen. I must get back before dawn.'

Chapter Ten

IMOSHEN AWOKE INSTANTLY, to find Arodyti by her bed.

'We have the Warrior's-voice,' Arodyti said.

Frayvia gave a little gasp of surprise and sat up to light a candle.

'He claims he's your spy, Imoshen.' Arodyti sounded hurt and annoyed. 'I'm your hand-of-force. Why wasn't I told?'

Imoshen swung her feet to the floor. 'The fewer people who knew, the safer he would be.'

'I'm afraid quite a few people know now. He came up here with two of Kyredeon's warriors. I have him in your inner circle chamber.'

'Are Kyredeon's warriors here too?'

'Waiting at the sisterhood gate.'

'I'll get dressed.'

Arodyti left them.

'You asked Sorne to spy for you?' Frayvia whispered. 'How could you?'

'Just to let me know if his vision was likely to come true. Come on.'

They dressed and went through to the chamber. Egrayne was there, along with Sarosune, Arodyti's shield-sister, but no one else. Imoshen was grateful. She could tell Egrayne was hurt and angry. Imoshen should have consulted the sisterhood's voice-of-reason before sending Sorne out to spy.

He stood in front of the fire, sipping warm spiced wine. As soon as he saw her, he put the cup aside. She noticed how he glanced once to Frayvia, then away quickly. His emotions were close to the surface; she read him easily. He loved her devotee but never expected to share his life with her.

'You asked to see me?' She crossed the chamber.

He nodded. 'I have bad news, Imoshen. Really bad news.'

'Go on.'

His gaze flicked to the others.

'You can speak in front of them.'

'King Charald doesn't want to banish your people. He wants to wipe you out. When you ride out of here next spring, he'll wait until you've made camp, then he'll kill everyone.'

Arodyti swore.

'But why?' Egrayne asked.

Imoshen was not surprised. It fitted with her reading of the king. 'If he means to do this, why did he send his men to attack our estates? That makes him appear untrustworthy.'

'You have to understand how Charald's mind works. He thought you arrogant and took insult. He suspected you weren't seriously considering exile. Destroying those estates was his way of asserting himself. I've served him since I was seventeen. He's used the same tactics before to break the spirits of besieged cities.'

'He's a madman,' Egrayne whispered. 'Why would he massacre a whole race of people? That's... that's inhuman.'

'Charald always intended to rid Chalcedonia of the Wyrds. The T'Enatuath,' Sorne corrected himself. 'It's the only reason I wasn't murdered at birth. I was raised to infiltrate this city and discover your weakness. But I never realised he meant to wipe you out. It takes a certain kind of mind to contemplate such a thing.'

Arodyti had been whispering to her shield-sister, and now she turned to Imoshen. 'If we broke out and tried to fight a rearguard action all the way to coast, our warriors would be overwhelmed before we were halfway there. To reach port takes three days by fast horse, or five or six by cart, and that's when the roads are not choked with snow. Besides, we'd have no way of contacting our ships' captains.

'The only way any of us would survive is if, between now and spring, we sent out many small parties in different directions. It's the worst time to travel and, if we ran into the Mieren, they'd kill us on sight. Only the young, healthy warriors would stand a chance of escaping Chalcedonia. The children and old would be murdered or die in the snow.'

Egrayne, Arodyti and Sarosune all looked to Imoshen.

'There must be some way we can convince King Charald to let us leave Chalcedonia alive,' she whispered.

'There is,' Sorne said. 'Can Reoden heal a club foot?'

'The king's crippled son?'

'His heir.'

'He loves the boy that much?'

'Not the boy, the idea of founding a dynasty,' Sorne corrected. 'He's been trying for a son since he married Queen Sorna, thirty years ago. Three queens later and all he has is one crippled prince. Meanwhile, Baron Nitzane married King Matxin's daughter and produced a perfectly healthy son. That boy is Prince Cedon's heir. The war barons will not give their allegiance to a king they don't respect and fear. A king with a deformity cannot sit on the throne.'

Imoshen nodded. 'So we offer to heal the boy and—'

'No. Charald will never hand him over. As much as he wants a healthy heir, his hatred for your kind clouds his thinking. You'll have to abduct the boy.'

'Abduct him, then offer to heal him in exchange for safe passage to the sea.'

'Make the exchange on your ships, near the headlands.'

Imoshen nodded, but then she saw the flaw. 'But if Charald hates us so much, won't he reject the boy? Won't he think the prince tainted by association with us?'

'He should be grateful for his healed heir,' Egrayne muttered.

'If he were rational,' Imoshen agreed, her gaze on Sorne. She could tell his mind was racing.

'You're right, but...' He smiled grimly. 'While Charald would never hand the boy over, he might be persuaded to take him back. I told the king I'd had a vision of his healthy son ruling Chalcedonia. Belief in the Warrior is the king's flaw. He will rationalise anything if you dress it up in terms of religion.'

'But we don't believe in gods,' Egrayne objected.

'We don't have to believe in Mieren gods to be their agents.' Imoshen shared a wry smile with Sorne. She saw Egrayne didn't understand. 'The king knows T'En have visions. If the gods can speak to Sorne, they can send us visions.'

'Exactly,' Sorne said. 'It would please Charald to think you did the gods' bidding.'

Imoshen gestured to Arodyti. 'Fetch Ree.'

Her hand-of-force had almost reached the door, when Imoshen stopped her. 'Don't tell her what this is about. No one must know what King Charald intends. If the brotherhoods got wind of this, they'd do something rash. I can just see them choosing to die in a blaze of glory.'

Arodyti's eyes widened. 'It was Kyredeon's warriors who brought him here. The all-father must already know.'

'No,' Sorne said. 'They didn't take me to Kyredeon.'

'Why not?' Egrayne asked. 'Their loyalty is to their all-father, not the causare.'

'They brought me straight up here.'

Egrayne looked to Imoshen.

'Perhaps Kyredeon's own people don't trust him,' she said. 'At any rate, they won't be telling Kyredeon now. If their all-father knew they'd brought Sorne straight to me, it would cost them their lives.'

Arodyti nodded and left.

'At least we have hope,' Imoshen said.

'You think there's hope?' Sarosune whispered. 'The prince lives in the royal palace in Port Mirror-on-sea, surrounded by Mieren. How do we get into the palace? How do we get him out? How do we get him across Chalcedonia in midwinter, past King Charald's army and into the city?'

'We'll discuss this when we know if Ree can heal the boy.' Imoshen's mind raced.

While they spoke, Sorne had gone to the courtyard window to check the sky.

'You have to be back before first light?' Imoshen asked him.

He nodded, returning to the fireplace. 'I don't know if I can get away again. It was a combination of things that allowed me to escape tonight. Usually the Father's-voice doesn't drop his guard.'

'You're a prisoner?'

'Of sorts. The Father's-voice has my sister captive. If he suspected me of coming here–'

'You didn't find her? I'm sorry,' Imoshen said. She turned to her voice-of-reason. 'Egrayne, this is the injured Malaunje I asked Reoden and Ceriane to help heal. I didn't mention his true identity because...' Because she knew Egrayne would not approve. 'After we healed him, he told me he'd had a vision of Malaunje and T'En children being loaded into a cart by True-men. I didn't think our people's leaders would believe his vision, so I asked him to watch out and warn us if it looked like coming true.'

'But I couldn't,' Sorne said. 'I was drugged.'

'Did you sacrifice our people?' Egrayne asked, her voice cold.

Sorne exhaled, the pain of loss aging him. 'Just the once. I tried to save him, but–' He looked helpless.

'There's a chance we could reach the prince and get him out, if...' Sarosune turned to Sorne. 'Is there a secret way into the palace?'

'There's the crypts. They connect all the churches, but not the palace. It was only built in the last thirty years.

I suppose if it were possible to get maps of the crypts and maps of the palace dungeons, you could tunnel through. But–'

'Too complicated.'

Arodyti returned with the healer.

Reoden's eyes widened as she recognised Sorne. 'Are you sure we can trust him, Imoshen? The king–'

'He's just revealed King Charald's one weakness, Ree. I think we can trust him. Can you heal a club foot?'

'With time.'

'How much time?'

'It depends...' She made the leap of logic and her eyes widened. 'The king's crippled son. He's only two–'

'Three this spring,' Sorne said.

'How much time would you need?' Imoshen asked.

'I'd have to see how bad the malformation was. The bones must be encouraged to grow in the right way. The body must relearn how to walk. The mind must change its patterns of thought. The club foot is a deformity he was born with. It's not like encouraging an injury to heal itself.'

'But you can do it,' Arodyti said. 'All we have to do is work out a way to bring the prince here.'

'We can talk about that later. Sorne has risked his life to come here tonight. He should go now,' Imoshen said.

'There is one more thing,' Sorne said. 'Charald has ordered the barons to raze four more estates. He wants prisoners, and I have to perform a sacrifice. The rest of the prisoners will be hung on scaffolds along the causeway.'

Reoden moaned and sank into the other chair.

'He's retaliating for the burning of the effigy,' Imoshen said and Sorne nodded. She'd feared as much. 'Frayvia will escort you to the sisterhood gate.'

Arodyti gestured to her shield-sister. 'Saro can do that.'

'We need her here.' Imoshen turned to Sorne and took his hand. She could tell he was deliberately not looking at Frayvia. 'Thank you. Whatever happens, I hope you find your sister. If we all get out of this, you can bring her to us. We will accept her as one of our own.'

SORNE GUESSED IMOSHEN had read his longing for Frayvia but he didn't care; right then, he would have followed Frayvia anywhere. She led him into a dark chamber and pulled him into her arms, her lips seeking his.

When he could catch his breath, he whispered, 'I only have a few moments.'

'I don't care. We could all be dead tomorrow.'

It was like a madness took them both. Their love-making was intense and over far too quickly.

'Each time we do this, it gets harder to leave you,' he confessed. 'Last time, I meant to find Valendia and bring her back here. But now...'

Frayvia wriggled as she pulled her breeches up and tightened them around the waist. She shrugged into her knitted vest, tugging it down over her breasts, then pulled on her robe and slid her feet into her slippers. He watched, fascinated.

'What?' she asked. 'You didn't finish.'

He had no idea what he'd been saying.

She smiled and kissed his cheek. 'Valendia.'

'I hope abducting the prince will work, but the king is unpredictable and I don't—'

'Life is a gamble.' She held his eyes. 'But I refuse to give up hope. Imoshen has gotten us out of tight spots before.' She took his hand. 'Come on.'

Frayvia led him out of the chamber, out of the palace, to the sisterhood gate. Tobazim and Learon were still there, stamping their feet to keep warm.

They looked up with relief when they saw Sorne.

Frayvia pulled him around and kissed him. 'Don't do anything brave.'

He laughed.

She pushed him away.

The brotherhood warriors set off at a jog and he ran with them, down the causeway boulevard. They were clearly relieved when they reached the ruined palace and found their absence had gone unnoticed. They guided him through the ruined palace, right to his rowboat, and wished him luck.

AFTER SORNE LEFT with Frayvia, Imoshen sent for the sisterhood's gift-tutor. They explained the situation and discussed how to abduct the prince.

Finally, Arodyti held up her hand. 'This is how it stands. The lake's too big for Charald to patrol. We can get to the shore and we can travel across Chalcedonia. If we disguise ourselves, we can get into the city, and if we choose a feast day when the servants and guards are lax, we can slip into the palace. But once the alarm goes up and the Mieren are looking for the prince, we'll never get out alive.'

At that moment, Frayvia returned, and Imoshen beckoned her to join them. 'Sorry,' she said to Arodyti, 'go on.'

'I just don't see how we can bring the prince back here,' the hand-of-force said.

'I have a suggestion,' Imoshen said. 'We could use the gift-working technique of transposition.'

'Transposition?' Arodyti repeated. 'Why haven't I heard of this?'

'Because it's impossible,' Vittoryxe snapped. 'It's mentioned in the sagas. The stories were old when they were first written down. They tell of T'En moving from one place to another via the higher plane. There are even tales of them taking someone with them. But they're myths, nothing more.'

Imoshen knew Vittoryxe was going to hate her, but it had to be said. 'I've done it.'

The gift-tutor's eyes widened. 'Impossible.'

'The night the theatre burned.'

Frayvia gasped. 'That's why you appeared naked and smelling of smoke?'

Egrayne looked grim. 'I think you have some explaining to do, Imoshen.'

She had never intended to tell them about that night, and now she gave them only the bare bones. 'After the performance ended and everyone went home, I happened to get locked inside the theatre. When I realised it was on fire, I tried to get out. But I couldn't. I was trapped, and when I knew I was going to die, I felt my gift take over. It happened between one breath and the next. Before I knew it, I was back here with Frayvia.'

'Their link...' Reoden whispered.

Imoshen nodded. 'My gift took me onto the empyrean plane, but because I shared a deep link with Frayvia, I was drawn back here, straight to her.' She turned to the gift-tutor. 'You remember how I asked you about transposition the day after the theatre burned and you told me where to look it up.'

'Did she?' Egrayne asked.

Vittoryxe nodded, her reluctance clear. 'But this is madness. You're suggesting Arodyti grab the boy and transpose herself and him here, to Sarosune's side. She's had no training.'

'Neither had I,' Imoshen said. 'It was an instinctive reaction. Instead of going to the higher plane to gift-work, she passes through it to reach someone on this plane. But it has to be someone she shares a deep link with, like a devotee or her shield-sister.'

'I'll do it,' Arodyti said. 'At least I'll try to. The sooner we leave the better. It has to be a voluntary mission. Everyone who goes with me will be sacrificing themselves. The sooner Imoshen has the prince, the sooner she can negotiate with the king. When's the next Mieren feast day?'

'Midwinter's day,' Imoshen said. 'The next feast after that is spring cusp.'

Arodyti nodded. 'We might just reach the city by midwinter's day, but I don't know if–'

'I can't believe you're going ahead with this,' Vittoryxe muttered.

'Then give me an alternative,' Imoshen challenged. 'If there is another way, I want to know. None of the all-fathers have come to me with a workable suggestion.' When Vittoryxe had no answer, Imoshen turned to her hand-of-force. 'Prepare to leave.'

'I already know who I trust. I'll ask them.'

'Good.' Imoshen nodded once. 'Vittoryxe, can you find the passages on transposition?'

'You're forgetting one thing, Imoshen,' Egrayne said. 'If you plan to take an action against King Charald that can impact on all of us, you are supposed to call an all-council to get their approval.'

'I know. I've been debating whether to ask Saskeyne for a loan of his mind-manipulators, but–'

'How can you expect your hand-of-force to work with brotherhood warriors?' Vittoryxe protested.

'We are at war with a common enemy,' Imoshen reminded her. She turned to Arodyti. 'They could be helpful.'

'Only with Mieren who don't have natural defences,' her hand-of-force said then grimaced. 'Besides, I need to know I can trust the warriors who have my back. I don't want to give an order and have them refuse it.'

'And you'd be asking Saskeyne to send his warriors into almost certain death,' Sarosune added.

'You're right,' Imoshen conceded. 'I can't take this to an all-council. I'd have to tell the brotherhood leaders King Charald means to wipe us out. The hot-heads amongst them would do something noble and heroic. They could precipitate the destruction of all our estates, or even another attack on the city.'

'So you're not going to tell them,' Egrayne said.

'I think it's for the best. Besides, if we fail, we don't raise everyone's hopes.'

'What do we do if Arodyti fails to deliver the prince?' Reoden asked. 'We can't leave the safety of the city if we know the king means to massacre us on the road.'

Everyone looked to Imoshen.

She didn't want to contemplate this, but... 'We have around forty estates scattered across Chalcedonia. When the barons ride off to plunder them, we turn the brotherhoods loose on what remains of the army. While they are distracting the Mieren, the rest of us sneak out of the city and break into small groups to travel across Chalcedonia.'

'With every Mieren hand turned against us?' Egrayne protested.

'That doesn't give us much hope,' Reoden whispered.

'And that is why I cannot fail,' Arodyti said.

Chapter Eleven

SORNE REACHED CAMP just before the sentries changed over. He'd chosen the time with care. It was the end of their shift, and the night-watch would be thinking of their beds.

The barons had laid their tents out in rough lines, following the slope of the hill. As Sorne wove through the camp, the snow continued to fall; in places, the drifts had piled waist high. When he rounded the last bend and looked up towards the royal tent, everything appeared normal. A weight lifted from him. Now all he had to do was slip into Zabier's tent and get into bed before the first holy warrior reported for duty.

But when he approached the holy tent, it wasn't there. All he could see were lumps under a blanket of snow.

For a heartbeat his mind refused to make sense of it. Then he realised the snow had collapsed the tent. He made out a long lump where the desk stood, but everything else was indistinguishable. And Zabier had taken a hefty dose of pains-ease.

No time to waste.

Zabier's low bunk was to the left of the tent's entrance. Plunging his hands into snow, Sorne tried to find the tent fabric. His fingers scrabbled on the hard, frozen folds.

Digging deeper, he found his way under the fabric, lifted it, and thrust his head underneath. Snow fell down the back of his neck, making him shiver. The tent fabric pressed heavily on his shoulders. He wriggled further under the collapsed tent into the dark cold. Crawling on hands and knees, he forged on until his shoulder hit the edge of the bunk and he forced himself to kneel upright.

Feeling for Zabier with numb hands, Sorne thought he made out a head and chest. Sliding an arm under Zabier's shoulders, he hooked his hands around his brother's chest and tried to drag him off the bed. The combined weight of the tent, the snow and Zabier defeated him. His breath came in short gasps.

From outside he heard shouts.

The tent fabric jerked, nearly knocking him over.

He called for help.

It jerked again.

Then light hit him. He gulped fresh air as several of the holy warriors lifted the tent and peeled it back to reveal the end of the desk and Sorne crouching over Zabier as he tried to keep the tent fabric off him.

One of the holy warriors held a lantern and three more struggled with the heavy canvas. Their shouts drew others.

'Does the high priest live?' one of them asked.

Sorne lay Zabier's head and shoulders down on the bunk and pushed the hair from his pale face. With his eyes closed and his mouth relaxed, his brother looked terribly young.

Desperate, Sorne bent over Zabier's chest, listening.

He heard nothing. 'Give me a knife.'

Someone put a knife hilt in his hand. He held the blade to Zabier's mouth and nose, hoping to see condensation from his brother's warm breath.

Nothing.

Sorne pulled open Zabier's robe, placed his ear right over Zabier's heart and listened.

Nothing.

The king's saw-bones arrived.

Sorne lifted his head. 'Gretzen.'

'Anything?' The saw-bones asked as he knelt on the other side of the bunk.

'I... I don't know.'

Gretzen appeared to note his hesitation. The saw-bones pulled off his gloves, rubbed his hands together and felt Zabier's neck, searching for a pulse.

Sorne waited for him to lift his hand and say, *you were mistaken. He'll be fine.*

Instead, Gretzen took a funnel from his bag and put it over Zabier's chest, placing his ear to the top of the funnel.

Sorne held his breath. Zabier had to be all right. It couldn't end like this. Last night they'd seemed to be drawing closer. With time...

The way the saw-bones lifted his head told Sorne there was no hope. There would be no more time with his brother.

It could not be. He grabbed Zabier's shoulders and shook him, calling his name. Tears blinded him. He could not lose Zabier like this. It was so pointless...

But Zabier's skin remained pale and waxy. The only thing that seemed to have life was his brother's long fair hair. The lantern picked up ginger threads in the waves; it was the same shade their mother's had been.

Sorne released Zabier's shoulders and spread his hair out neatly on the pillow, so that it framed his still, cold face. Izteben was dead. Their mother was dead. If Zabier was dead, then all he had left was Valendia.

And only Zabier knew where she was. Sorne sank back on his heels, horrified. How would he find her now?

He stared at his brother's still face. He was sure Zabier had been about to reach out to him last night. With a little more time, he could have won his brother's trust. Together, they could have guided King Charald and made a pact to save Valendia.

Perhaps he would discover a clue as to Valendia's locaton in Zabier's notes.

Someone coughed. Sorne became aware of the saw-bones, Gretzen, and the whispering holy warriors.

He was a half-blood in an army of True-men intent on wiping out his race. He had to seize command now, or he'd be the next sacrifice.

Taking Zabier's hands, he folded them neatly on his chest and noticed Oskane's ring. A surge of hatred filled Sorne as he remembered having to kiss that ruby and thank Oskane for scourging him.

Now it was his.

When Sorne removed the ring, no one protested. After sliding it onto his little finger, he stood and lifted his head to look down on the sea of faces. He forced strength into his voice. 'I am the Warrior's-voice, returned from the dead, advisor to King Charald. Prepare the Father's-voice for burial.' His voice trembled, but he did not falter. 'I must see the king.'

He stepped over mounds of snow and gestured to the tent. 'Clean this up. When I come back, I want to see the holy tent restored.'

Now all he had to do was convince King Charald to reinstate him as his advisor.

When they'd returned to Chalcedonia after the Secluded Sea campaign, the king had believed Sorne's half-blood heritage was a liability. But Charald was no longer that man. Sorne had seen a vulnerability in him. It had always been the source of his rage. Now it was closer to the surface. The king was growing old, and for a man of war that was a terrible thing. There were always ambitious men ready to topple him.

Sorne found the king being shaved by his manservant.

'What was all the shouting about? I swear...' Charald ran down as Sorne showed him his hand. 'Oskane's ring?'

'My vision has come true,' Sorne said. 'Before the Warrior returned me, he showed me at your side, wearing this ring. The Father and the Warrior have long been rivals. The gods sent the snow to crush the holy tent. Only I lived. The Warrior is in ascendance. Your faithful service has ensured this.'

'I knew it.' Charald sprang to his feet. His manservant only just had time to wipe the last of the soap from his chin before the king pushed him aside. 'Now the Warrior will reward me for serving Him faithfully all these years.'

Once Sorne would have felt triumphant, but now he felt only self-contempt.

TOBAZIM'S GIFT WOULD not let him rest. Taking out his pen and ink, he began sketching. Ideas for rebuilding the ruined palace and incorporating it into Kyredeon's palace crowded his head, and he simply had to get them down on paper.

'There you are,' Ceyne said.

Tobazim came to his feet, wondering why the high-ranking brother had come to him.

The saw-bones shut the door, then checked that the bathing chamber and the bedchamber were empty. Tobazim watched with growing concern.

'Learon needs to keep his nose out of other people's business,' Ceyne said.

'If we hadn't stuck our noses into what happened last night, Kyredeon would be dead,' Tobazim protested.

Ceyne's eyes widened.

'You didn't know? But you're one of of his inner circle. He should have...' Tobazim took a step back. 'I swore an oath not to tell–'

'Too late, lad,' Ceyne said with a half-smile. 'You'll have to tell me now.'

'There were six assassins on the roof last night. Learon and I helped fight them off. Kyredeon should have told his inner circle.'

'You might have noticed, Kyredeon does a lot of things he shouldn't do and very few of the things he should.'

'So, if you weren't talking about the assassins, what were you referring to?' Tobazim asked.

'Yesterday, Learon objected to the way the adepts were teaching the initiates. He claimed the way he was taught was better.'

'Maybe it was.'

'Doesn't matter. He can't go around correcting the adepts who teach under Oriemn. He might as well correct the brotherhood's hand-of-force.'

It was true. 'I'll find him and talk to him.' But he hesitated; when they'd parted at dawn, Learon had gone looking for Paravia. By now the two would be inseparable.

'What is it?'

'Learon's with Paravia.'

'No, he isn't. I saw her run into another room, weeping.'

Tobazim felt a stab of fear. 'When and where?'

'Just now. Two floors directly below us.'

Tobazim thanked him and took off. He found Paravia hiding amidst the paper-making frames.

When she heard the door open, she shielded her face. 'Go away.'

'Paravia? What happened?'

'Tobazim!' She ran to him. Eyes red from weeping, she clutched his vest. 'You must find Lear. I'm afraid he'll do something stupid.'

'What happened?'

'I refused him.'

'Why? I thought you–'

'I do love him. I did it to save him.'

'I don't see how–'

'The all-father wants me for his own. I can't become Learon's devotee. If I did, it would infuriate the all-father. Go find Lear. Don't let him do anything stupid.'

Tobazim tried all the usual places: the weapons practice courtyard, the verandah where the young adepts watched for the Malaunje girls so they could flirt with them, and the rooftop garden, just in case Learon was doing his exercises. The longer it took, the more uneasy he became.

At length, he went back to the chamber they shared with other low-ranking adepts. Here he found Learon looking at his plans. 'Where have you been? I've been running myself ragged, trying to find you.'

'These are really very good,' Learon said. 'You know, I used to be jealous of you.'

Tobazim was flabbergasted.

'Our choice-mother loved you best. She gave you the silver nib.'

'She gave me that because you made me feel inadequate. My gift is only good for building. I'm not a great gift-warrior.'

'What did she say the day we left Silverlode Estate?'

Tobazim shrugged, but Learon insisted.

'She said, "It's easy to kill and destroy. It is much harder to build and grow."' Tobazim looked down at his ink-stained fingers, remembering the feel of her hands. '"The things you build will live on after you. Take pride in this."' He looked up at Learon. 'She also said to look after my little choice-brother.'

Learon grinned. 'Not so little.'

'Not so little then, either.' Learon was two small moons younger than him, and had left their choice-mother's sisterhood before he turned seventeen so they could join the brotherhood together. 'I hope she's all right.'

'Silverlode has stout walls.'

'And a productive silver mine. It will attract the greedy Mieren.'

'I'm not a scholar like you. I'm a warrior born. If I can't serve my all-father with honour, I have no purpose.'

'Lear...'

'They've denied us stature since the moment we arrived. They've belittled us. And now' – his gift surged – 'they've taken Paravia from me.'

'She's only trying to protect you.'

'Can you hear yourself? This is our brotherhood. We should not need protecting from our all-father and his seconds.'

He was right, but... 'Ceyne warned me. He said you needed to keep your head down.'

'Like he does? Can you see me standing back and letting injustice go unpunished?'

Tobazim shook his head. 'What are you going to do?'

'I'm going to appeal to the all-father. Oriemn must recognise my stature.'

'Kyredeon–'

'Paravia thinks I rank so low, she feels she has to protect me. Kyredeon's hand-of-force needs to give me the ranking I've earned. I saved the all-father's life last night. He'll listen.'

'Lear, I don't think it's a good idea.'

'I just came to let you know, in case...'

In case things went wrong. Tobazim's choice-brother was saying goodbye.

'I won't let you go.' He darted over to the door, pushing it closed. 'You don't need to do this. We can–'

'You never could stop me.'

He saw the blow coming but wasn't fast enough to avoid it. Learon's fist connected with his jaw. The back of his head slammed against the door. His knees buckled and he pitched forward. The world went grey.

THE SOUND OF running boots reached Tobazim as his sight cleared. He lay sprawled on the polished wooden floor, his face sticky. He touched his mouth, and his hand came away red with blood.

Running boots? Mieren attacking again? He rolled to his feet, feeling for the hilt of his knife. His head reeled and he staggered. For a moment, he didn't know why he'd been flat out on the floor.

Then it came back to him, along with the throb of his split lip.

Someone shouted in excitement. The running boots were not another attack, just high spirits.

He looked up and caught a glimpse of himself in a mirror. Blood stained his chin and teeth.

He might have to intercede on Learon's behalf. He couldn't appear before the all-father in this state. Slipping into the bathing chamber, he rinsed his mouth and wiped his face. Meanwhile, boots pounded along the corridor outside, coming this way. Tobazim turned towards the door even as Athlyn flung it open.

'Learon's in trouble. You've got to help him.'

Tobazim discovered his hand was on his knife hilt and had to force his fingers to relax. Violence would not save his choice-brother now. Diplomacy might not be too late.

Athlyn took in his split lip. 'What happened to you?'

'Where is he?'

'They're in the main courtyard.' Athlyn fell into step with him. 'You'll help him, won't you?'

'Did you hear the cause of the trouble?'

'They're saying Learon insulted Kyredeon's hand-of-force. The all-father won't let Oriemn kill him, will he?'

Tobazim did not answer.

By the time they reached the nearest balcony overlooking the main courtyard, the rails were crowded with adepts, initiates and Malaunje, and the air was thick with roused gift. Tobazim skirted a large group, heading for the far end where he could see down into the courtyard.

Learon stood alone, confronting the all-father and his inner circle. Oriemn and Kyredeon had their heads together with the voice-of-reason. Their words did not carry, but their sharp, concise gestures told Tobazim that his choice-brother's fate was being swiftly decided.

'What's going on?' Haromyr asked as he joined them.

'I don't know. I just got here,' Tobazim said.

At the sound of his voice, Ceyne pushed through the crowd to reach them. By rights, the old initiate should have been down in the courtyard with the rest of Kyredeon's inner circle. The saw-bones took in Tobazim's split lip, but did not comment.

'They say Learon insulted the hand-of-force,' Ceyne said. 'They say he refused to back down, then compounded it by offering a challenge.'

Tobazim bit back a protest. In any other brotherhood, it would not have come to this. Kyredeon should have listened to Learon and acknowledged the debt. The all-father should not have paraded their differences before the whole brotherhood.

Tobazim gripped the rail. 'Honour is everything to Learon. Trust to him to offer challenge.'

'Will it be a gift duel?' Athlyn asked.

'No,' Tobazim said. 'Learon's only been an adept for a little over a year, so the all-father wouldn't allow a gift duel. It'll be physical.' Which suited Learon. 'Probably unarmed.'

'I bet Learon wins,' Haromyr said. 'I've seen him at weapons practice.'

'Quiet. Kyredeon's made a decision,' Ceyne said.

The all-father nodded to Oriemn. At a signal from the brotherhood's hand-of-force, three of the warriors grabbed Learon, forcing him to his knees.

Tobazim waited to hear the terms of the duel, but Kyredeon did not speak. Instead, he lifted his left hand towards Learon's forehead.

A strangled sound of protest escaped Tobazim.

'What's he doing?' Athlyn asked.

'He'll drain his gift,' Ceyne said.

'But can't Learon stop him?'

'If he tried, Kyredeon would strip his defences and cripple his mind. He'd end up a lackwit.'

The whole courtyard went quiet.

'What'll happen to Lear?' Athlyn whispered.

Tobazim could not speak.

'Without his gift, he'll have no defences against Oriemn and the adepts. It will take days for his power to rebuild and, in that time, they'll–' Ceyne broke off as Learon reared up, but the three warriors forced him down.

Tobazim cursed and went to help his choice-brother.

'Don't.' Ceyne grabbed him. 'You'll achieve nothing. You tried to warn him.'

Tobazim felt Haromyr and Athlyn step in to each side of him.

'You're being watched,' Ceyne warned. 'Turn around and face the courtyard. If you protest or walk off, you're next.'

So Tobazim did nothing while Kyredeon feasted on Learon's gift. And he hated himself for it.

Finally, the all-father stepped back and Learon fell forward onto his hands and knees. Oriemn pulled him to his feet.

'What happens now?' Athlyn whispered, voice thick with horror.

Tobazim could not speak.

'Without his gift defences, Learon is as helpless as a Mieren,' Ceyne muttered. 'More helpless even than some of them, because they have natural defences. Oriemn's supporters will overcome his will and use him for their pleasure.'

The hand-of-force's gift swamped Learon's will in an instant, implanting a compulsion. Oriemn held out his hand, and Tobazim's choice-brother went to his enemy, eager for his lustful touch.

Every fibre of Tobazim's body revolted. He knew how Learon would feel when the compulsion wore off. Athlyn made a choked sound in his throat. Haromyr swore under his breath.

'They'll pass him around until they tire of him.' Ceyne sounded weary. 'His gift will rebuild itself eventually, but his stature will never recover. He'll never challenge Oriemn for hand-of-force.'

And Tobazim understood why Oriemn and Kyredeon had driven Learon into a corner.

Anger threatened to undo Tobazim's gift control. He grasped the rail, knuckles white as he noted who amongst his fellow initiates ventured down to the courtyard to share in Learon's humbling, and who slipped away, unable to watch. Ceyne turned to go.

'You're not staying?' Athlyn blurted. 'But you're inner circle.'

'I've seen it too many times, these last forty years. Each all-father has been worse than the last.' Ceyne looked very old as he walked off.

Athlyn turned to Tobazim, speechless.

'Out of my way.' Tobazim had to leave before he did something he'd regret and ended up like his choice-brother.

But it killed something in him to turn his back on Learon.

Chapter Twelve

TOBAZIM WALKED THE wall above the causeway gate. Today his body ached as if he had spent all yesterday at weapons practice when, in reality, he had spent all night warring with his instinct to go to Learon's aid.

It was a crystal clear winter's day. The causeway stretched before him, a narrow ribbon of stone set in the lake's azure waters. There was no warmth in the winter sun.

Beyond the lake, the town clustered along the shore and beside the road that eventually led to the port. Behind the town on the northern hillside were the tents of the besieging army. Smoke drifted up, hanging on the still air. It was so peaceful, it was hard to believe thousands of men-at-arms waited ready to kill his people.

Behind him booted feet charged up the stairs. Tobazim's stomach knotted as he turned to face the messenger – Athlyn again. 'What is it?'

'Learon wants us to open the gate.'

'What?' Tobazim left his post, running down the steep stairs to the winch room where Haromyr and three Malaunje warriors confronted his choice-brother. From his clear eyes, Learon had thrown off Oriemn's compulsion, but his gift would not rebuild for several days. Until then, he would be vulnerable.

He wore only a loin cloth and his arm-torcs. He carried one of the confiscated Mieren swords and a shield, rather than T'En long-knives. But what struck Tobazim was his hair. He'd cut his hair to his jaw. Normally, a warrior wore his hair plaited and wound around his head to cushion his helmet.

'What are you doing?' Tobazim demanded, although he knew the answer.

'Here, catch.' Learon pulled off his arm-torcs and tossed them to Tobazim. The silver was still warm from his choice-brother's body. 'I will not honour a brotherhood that has no honour.'

The others gasped. Tobazim's cheeks burned. Learon had been treated dishonourably, but this... 'Lear–'

'Today my mind is my own. I won't let them take it again.' His choice-brother looked straight through Tobazim. 'Let me out.'

'Lear, there's thousands of Mieren on the far shore–'

'Exactly. I seek an honourable death, and the chance to take a few of the enemy with me.'

'I've been ordered to let no one in or out.'

'Don't deny me this, choice-brother.' For a moment their eyes met, and Learon let Tobazim see the depth of his humiliation; he could not live with the dishonour.

Tobazim stepped aside and gestured to Haromyr. 'Open the gates.'

The other adept did not argue. He directed the Malaunje warriors to start the winch that raised the inner gate.

Tobazim stood silent, aware of his choice-brother beside him, gripping his weapons firmly, ready to die. How had it gone so wrong? What could Tobazim have done differently? He'd failed his choice-brother. 'I'm sorry, I–'

'You tried to warn me that we weren't dealing with warriors from the sagas,' Learon cut him off. 'I hold honour too high to live in these times.'

Did that mean he thought Tobazim was without honour? At that moment Tobazim felt he deserved Learon's contempt.

'When–' Learon's voice caught and he had to clear his throat. 'When it is done will you escort me to death's realm?'

Haromyr gulped and glanced to Tobazim.

'It will be my honour,' Tobazim said.

Without another word, Learon ducked under the still-rising gate and walked through the dark tunnel towards the outer gate and sunshine.

'Open the other gate,' Tobazim said.

As the Malaunje obeyed, he ran up the stairs with Haromyr and Athlyn on his heels. From the wall-walk they had a good view of Learon striding down the causeway.

IMOSHEN'S GIFT-WARRIORS WOULD leave tonight. They'd spent the previous day preparing for the journey and, since the mission was secret, saying goodbye to their loved ones without letting them know. Imoshen had hardly slept. She was torn. It seemed pointless to have the mind-manipulators and not use them, so she'd sought out Arodyti to broach the subject again.

She found the shield-sisters on the rooftop going through their exercises together; they moved in tandem with precision and skill.

Imoshen watched for a moment, then went over to the wall, to look at the besieging army. So many Mieren. And everything rested on Arodyti.

They'd done all they could to prepare Arodyti for transposition. Vittoryxe was still finding old scrolls with different version of the myths, and Imoshen wanted to do all she could to ensure her hand-of-force reached the port. Surely, if Saskeyne's warriors swore to obey her, Arodyti would reconsider taking them.

Once the shield sisters had completed their exercises, Imoshen turned to face them and argue her point, but Sarosune pointed. 'See, there. That's why we can't take brotherhood warriors.'

Imoshen turned to see a lone, near-naked T'En warrior walking towards the end of the causeway. 'What is he doing?'

'Winning glory, by killing himself. What else could it be?' Arodyti muttered. 'Too bad if this drives King Charald to retaliate.'

* * *

TOBAZIM STOOD ON the gate's defences, watching his choice-brother walk to his death. In opening the gates he had disobeyed his all-father, and he was proud of it.

Across the lake, he heard the first shouts of alarm. Half a dozen men-at-arms formed ranks at the end of the causeway; more came running.

Booted feet echoed up the stairwell behind Tobazim as more brothers joined him. Word spread fast. Soon the wall-walk was crowded. Tobazim suspected the sisterhoods would be up in their palaces watching from every vantage point.

'He goes to his death with honour.' Athlyn's voice shook with emotion.

'He wins stature for our brotherhood,' Haromyr assured the youth, squeezing his shoulder. 'Even if he has taken off his arm-torcs.'

Tobazim said nothing, too angry to speak. The arm-torcs weighed heavily in his hands. His choice-brother should not have been forced to do this.

Several Mieren ventured out to meet Learon. At this distance, Tobazim could not see the small signals that presaged their assault. He knew that battle was joined only when three of the men-at-arms attacked Learon. The scrape of metal on metal reached them on the gate.

Athlyn gasped as first one fell, then the second.

When Learon picked up the third Mieren, held him over his head and threw him into the lake, the watchers on the city walls cheered.

Learon struck his sword on his shield to signal his readiness. This time five Mieren warriors approached.

'He does us proud,' Haromyr said.

'Then your all-father must see this. Out of the way,' Kyredeon's voice-of-reason ordered.

Tobazim and his companions backed off, so that Kyredeon and his two seconds had the best view. Now

Tobazim had to crane his head to see over their shoulders. He heard his companions' sharp intake of breath, saw his choice-brother falter, falling to one knee, before rearing up again – the watchers cheered.

Tobazim's body flinched and jerked with each blow. It seemed Learon would be overwhelmed, but he cut his attackers down until he stood amidst a heap of fallen Mieren warriors.

'He's bested those five,' Kyredeon's voice-of-reason muttered. 'Will they send more?'

'No, they're backing off.'

'It's costing them too many warriors. They'll bring up the archers,' Oriemn said.

Someone obstructed Tobazim's line of sight. He thrust them aside in time to see Learon charge the knot of Mieren at the end of the causeway. The archers cut him down before he could reach them.

A hushed gasp filled the air, followed by shouts of anger.

'They'll defile his body,' Haromyr muttered. He pushed through the others to confront their all-father. 'We must negotiate for his body.'

'We ask the Mieren for nothing,' Kyredeon growled. 'Not even his arm-torcs.'

'I have them.' Tobazim offered the silver bands, head bowed. He feared if he lifted his head and met the all-father's eyes, Kyredeon would see how much he despised him.

He waited. Would the all-father see this as the insult it was intended to be, or would he interpret it as Learon preventing the torcs from falling into Mieren hands?

'Just as well,' Oriemn said. 'We don't want to give the Mieren any more trophies. I'll take those.'

Kyredeon took the arm-torcs. Tobazim's hands were lighter, but his heart was heavy.

'Learon died with honour,' Haromyr said. 'His shade will feast with the heroes in–'

'My inner circle will not be escorting him to death's realm,' Kyredeon announced.

Haromyr glanced to Tobazim.

The all-father's eyes narrowed. 'I did not give him permission to seek an honourable death. I forbid anyone to escort his shade.'

Tobazim fought the instinct to protest.

Oriemn caught Tobazim's arm, twisted it up behind his back and forced him to kneel before Kyredeon. It felt as if his shoulder was about to pop out of its socket.

'Do you understand?' Oriemn demanded. When Tobazim did not respond, he jerked his arm again making his shoulder scream in protest.

'I understand,' Tobazim ground out.

'Use his title.' Oriemn jerked Tobazim's arm once more.

'I understand, All-father Kyredeon,' he said, locking his fury down deep inside. He dare not object, not when he'd seen Kyredeon's idea of justice.

Oriemn thrust Tobazim forward.

Saving himself with his good arm, Tobazim came to his feet and gave obeisance as best he could before backing off. His death would not help Learon.

Nothing would help Learon.

Even so, he despised himself. If the winery had still stood, he would have asked permission to leave the city and serve the brotherhood there, but he was trapped. Trapped in the besieged city, and trapped in Kyredeon's brotherhood, until the day he died. His silver arm-torcs, once a symbol of pride, had become a symbol of imprisonment.

The full impact of his position hit him with such force that he staggered. Only Haromyr and Athlyn kept him upright. He was grateful they still stood by him.

When he returned to the bedchamber he shared with Learon and the other young adepts, he found all the Malaunje who had escaped from the winery waiting for him. No one said anything. Paravia stepped forward and sang Learon's favourite songs, one after the other.

There was nothing sad about those songs, but many wept unashamedly. When it was over, everyone left, until only Paravia remained with Tobazim.

He kissed her cheeks solemnly. 'Thank you.'

'Kyredeon sent for me last night.'

'I'm sorry.'

She shook her head. 'He didn't want me. He made me watch Learon's humiliation. He never wanted me. He wanted to get rid of Learon.' She caught his hand. 'Tobazim, what did you do to make an enemy of him?'

'Nothing. We only ever did what we believed to be right.'

Tears slid down her cheeks. 'Promise me you'll be careful.'

He nodded.

'I can't spend the rest of my life living under this allfather.'

'I know.' Tobazim was so tired, his head felt thick. 'One day someone will challenge him and we'll have a new all-father.'

'Not if he kills off all the adepts he sees as a threat.'

Tobazim flinched. 'Then I'm safe. I'm only a builder.'

'Oh, Tobazim.' She kissed him. 'Goodbye.'

He was too heartsore and tired to understand until the next day when they found her body.

She'd jumped off the tallest palace tower.

IMOSHEN GRIPPED THE stonework as the lone T'En warrior battled on the causeway. When he defeated the second group of Mieren, the brotherhood warriors cheered, their deep voices carrying up to the sisterhood palaces at the island's peak. Her heart soared with their voices. These were her people. She was so proud of this glorious, hopeless warrior.

At the same time, she was furious with him and his brotherhood.

'Such a waste.' Imoshen was surrounded by Malaunje and T'En now, all watching the battle. 'Why would an all-father send one of his warriors out to die like this?'

'Punishment?' Arodyti shrugged. 'Maybe it was his own idea, and he wants to impress his brotherhood and win stature.'

'Will the Mieren send more warriors against him?' a Malaunje boy asked. In his excitement, he had pushed in right next to Imoshen. 'Why do they hesitate?'

'Because they won't waste–' Imoshen broke off, wincing as Mieren archers cut down the T'En warrior.

The boy clutched Imoshen's arm. She felt his shock and pain clearly.

'Now they'll desecrate the body,' Arodyti said.

Sure enough, half a dozen of them picked him up and carried him off.

The Malaunje and T'En around Imoshen were subdued as they left to go downstairs.

Sarosune wiped the tears from her cheek. 'He was very brave and very foolish.'

Arodyti met Imoshen's eyes. 'This is how the brotherhoods behave after you ask them not to take action without approving it at an all-council. Now do you see why I won't take any of their warriors with me? Their values are not our values. They put honour ahead of good sense.'

Imoshen understood. She also realised she had a precedent for not taking her actions to the all-council for approval.

SORNE PUT ANOTHER sheaf of reports aside and rubbed his face. He was so angry with Zabier, if his brother had been here, he would have grabbed him and shaken him. How dare Zabier die and leave him with no clue as to Valendia's whereabouts?

He frowned at Zabier's travelling chest. There had been nothing personal in it, just piles of papers, all methodically tied with string. He would go through it all again, but at first glance there was no mention of a female half-blood, or a secret captive. There were, however, a lot of reports on Wyrd customs and gift working.

Maybe Zabier kept his personal papers in his travelling bag. Sorne picked it up and unpacked it. Right at the bottom, he felt something familiar wrapped in a knitted vest. With a growing sense of betrayal he took out his mother's torc. There it was gleaming up at him, the silver neck torc with the blue stone. Zabier had had it all along.

A shout made Sorne repack the bag.

He went outside to see a mass of men-at-arms heading his way. They waved their swords and shields in celebration, and they were making for the royal tent. Sorne found Charald standing outside, with several of his barons.

'What's happening?' Sorne asked.

As the men drew nearer, Nitzane arrived and edged around behind the group to stand near Sorne.

'First chance I've had to say I'm sorry.' His voice was cloaked from the rest by the cheering men-at-arms.

For a heartbeat, Sorne had no idea what he was talking about. Then he recalled, other than King Charald, Nitzane was probably the only one who knew that Zabier was his brother.

'Do you remember we had a sister?' Sorne asked. 'Did Zabier ever tell you what became of her?'

'No. Why?'

'She's missing.'

'If there's anything I can do...' Nitzane put a hand on his shoulder. Sorne had helped him find his mother.

The men-at-arms reached the king.

'What have you got there?' Charald asked.

They nudged one another, until one of their own stepped forward and bowed. 'A gift for you, King Charald.'

The men-at-arms parted to bring forward the body of a huge T'En warrior. He was naked and his chest was full of arrows.

As he lay sprawled in the snow at the king's feet, a dozen different men-at-arms began to tell the story, speaking over each other. According to them, he'd walked down the causeway, brazen as could be, and challenged them. Of course, they cut him down.

The men-at-arms tossed a True-man sword and shield on the snow next to his body, and complained about the lack of trophies: no silver braid, no arm-torc.

Now that Sorne had gotten over the initial shock, he recognised the warrior. It was Learon. He went cold with shock. Was this the poor fellow's punishment for letting him in to see Imoshen without telling his all-father? What had happened to Tobazim?

'What will we do with him?' Charald asked.

Eventually they chose a tree and tied him to it. Even slumped against the tree, he was taller than anyone, including Sorne.

King Charald ordered wine to be brought out and sent for the pipers. A fire was started. He distributed the wine to the men-at-arms who had delivered the Wyrd giant.

'This is what we are up against,' King Charald said. 'Giants, with powers that can steal your mind. This is why we must reclaim our land.'

They cheered. The pipers played, more toasts were drunk.

'He won't need these anymore.' The king hacked off the Wyrd's genitals and tossed them in the fire, amidst cheering.

Sorne did not blink; he did not dare. That could so easily be him tied to the tree, alive while they hacked him to pieces.

IMOSHEN HAD SPENT the rest of day finalising preparations for the journey. Now it was dusk and almost time to say goodbye to Arodyti and her warriors.

Frayvia slipped into Imoshen's private study. 'You were right. It was not a simple case of ambition for stature.'

Imoshen did not need their link to sense her devotee's distress. She stood up, opening her arms, and they hugged, touch making the sharing of emotion more powerful.

After a moment, Frayvia pulled away. 'It was one of Kyredeon's warriors. The all-father had drained his gift in retaliation for some insult, but no one could say what it was. Confronting the Mieren was the only way he could die with honour.'

'And Kyredeon drove him to it.' Imoshen shook her head. 'Keep your ears open. I have to work with these all-fathers. A tiny detail might give me an advantage.'

Frayvia nodded.

It wasn't supposed to happen, but messages did pass between the Malaunje of the brotherhoods and sisterhoods. As someone who had been brotherhood-raised and then made the change to a sisterhood, Frayvia was uniquely positioned.

Arodyti opened the door, saw Imoshen with her devotee and would have left, but Imoshen beckoned her, then sent Frayvia through to their bedchamber.

'All ready?' Imoshen asked.

Arodyti nodded and gestured to Imoshen's cabinet, with its many little nooks containing documents. 'All those treatises... I used to feel so sorry for you, always buried in your studies or madly drawing up breeding charts for Vittoryxe's birds. Then, the day we went to the spring festival, I noticed you observing everyone rather than joining in, and I realised you are happiest watching and observing.'

'I remember that day. You two dragged me along because you thought I was missing out.'

'We wanted you to have some fun.'

'I did.' Imoshen's gift flexed and she read intense purpose under Arodyti's casual conversation.

The gift-warrior ran her hand over the cabinet glass. 'I was convinced I'd never be the sisterhood's hand-of-force, because Vittoryxe didn't like me. But you became all-mother instead, and named me hand-of-force. Now...'

Someone tapped on the door.

'That will be Sarosune,' Arodyti said.

'Come in,' Imoshen called.

The shield-sister entered. 'Have you told her, Aro?'

'I was waiting for you.'

'Told me what?' Imoshen asked.

'Vittoryxe dug up more on transposition,' Arodyti revealed. 'What we learned this afternoon changes things.'

'It won't work with a Mieren?'

'It'll work. Turns out they're much safer on the empyrean plane. The beasts prefer us, with our innate power, to them. No... if one of the T'En tries to transpose, bringing a second person with them, the chances of them both successfully returning to this plane are neligible.'

Which meant she could be sending Arodyti to her death. 'You don't have to do this.'

'Of course I do.'

'Of course she does,' Sarosune echoed and the two shield-sisters exchanged looks.

Imoshen's heart sank. She would not only lose Arodyti, she'd lose Sarosune, too. The shield-sister bond was so deep that when one died, the other usually followed. 'There must be some way–'

'It's because of the amount of power they need to expend to bring the second person along,' Arodyti explained. 'It makes them shine like a beacon, attracting empyrean predators.'

'If Arodyti delivers the boy, she won't survive,' Sarosune said. 'So I'm going to the port with her. I want to be there, right up to the end. She can form a deep link with you to deliver the boy.'

Imoshen didn't want this. 'There has to be another way.'

'I'm ready, Imoshen.' Arodyti had rolled up her sleeve to reveal the fine skin of her inner arm.

Tears stung Imoshen's eyes.

'You made me your hand-of-force,' Arodyti said softly.

Imoshen exhaled and nodded. She pushed her sleeve up her arm to the elbow. 'I think it would be better if we kneel.'

They went over to the fireplace and knelt on the carpet.

Imoshen raised her left arm and Arodyti met it with her own. Their palms touched and their fingers entwined. Their skin pressed from elbow to wrist where the blood pulsed close to the surface.

'We already share the all-mother's link with her hand-of-force,' Imoshen said, her voice a little husky. 'We can build on that. Lower your defences.'

She lowered her own, so that her gift was exposed.

Imoshen found it was like seeing her friend in concentrated form, her essence refined and revealed by the nature and power of her gift – that sense of mischief, the passion and the determination. 'Lovely.'

'...S-strange.' Arodyti slurred her words as if drunk. 'Your gift feels more masculine than feminine. Sharp, impatient and a little w... wild.'

'It's because she was raised by covenant-breaking brothers,' Sarosune said.

Imoshen let her gift build then released it. Felt it roll over Arodyti. Her power came up against Arodyti's core and rolled back, empowered by the hand-of-force's gift.

The both swayed with the intensity of the sensation.

As Arodyti let her arm drop, she fell. Imoshen caught her, cradling her. She was sending her dear friend to die, and it broke her heart.

The light of mischief glowed in Arodyti's eyes. 'We could seal it with kiss. Saro wouldn't mind.'

'Yes, I would.'

Imoshen laughed. 'You are incorrigible.'

There was a tap at the door.

'Come in.' Imoshen released Arodyti and came to her feet. She had to steady herself on the mantelpiece.

Egrayne opened the door. She closed her eyes as she opened her gift senses, then met Imoshen's gaze. 'It is done.'

'Yes.' Imoshen's voice was thick with emotion.

'Time to go,' the hand-of-force said.

By the time they reached the sisterhood gate the snow had thickened, making visibility poor.

Arodyti studied the sky. 'We'll get down to the sisterhood's boat-house and out unnoticed.' She turned to Imoshen. 'Don't come any further.'

So they said their goodbyes. Sarosune and the others went first.

Tears stung Imoshen's eyes as she kissed Arodyti. 'I'll look for you on midwinter's day and spring cusp.'

'We'll make you proud of us.'

'I already am.'

Chapter Thirteen

SORNE PUT THE report aside and rubbed his face. The holy
tent was his alone now. It was midwinter's day and the
cold was fearful. If Imoshen's people snatched the prince
today, it would take anything up to ten days for the news
to get through to the king.

Even with the brazier right next to him, his breath
misted on every exhalation. He hated to think how
the men-at-arms were suffering. It was typical of King
Charald to stay in his tent, enduring the same hardships
as his men. His fortitude had been legendary on the
Secluded Sea campaign.

Sorne was once more advisor to the king, but it came at a
price, and he'd been dreading the return of the barons from
the Wyrd estates, with their trophy braids and sacrifical
captives. But since Zabier's death, winter had settled in
with a vengeance, making travel almost impossible. They'd
heard nothing from the four barons.

Sorne had devoted himself to sifting through Zabier's
papers a second time, looking for a clue as to Valendia's
whereabouts, but so far had turned up nothing.

What he had uncovered was a series of reports on Wyrd
gifts, their uses and limitations. When he found the notation
– *As confirmed by Oskane* – he realised the reports were
based on the information he'd left with Valendia for safe-
keeping when he'd set sail more than four years ago. This
information had been hidden in a chest, which must have
fallen into Zabier's hands. It explained Zabier's boast that
he'd set fifty priests to work researching the Wyrds.

Sorne's chest had contained the Wyrd scrolls, which had been written by True-men over three hundred years ago, before the Wyrds lived completely segregated lives. It had also contained Oskane's journals, which had been written during his years at Restoration Retreat.

As Sorne read the reports, he realised two things. Fifty priests might have read individual scrolls and journals, but only one priest, Scholar Igotzon, had collated the information, so only he knew the true limitations of Wyrd power.

And the man Sorne knew as Oskane had led a double life. Sorne had known about the she-Wyrd Oskane kept locked in the cellar. He and Izteben had visited the half-blood every day for years, to learn the T'En language. What Sorne had not known was that when Oskane visited Enlightenment Abbey, he had been pursuing his studies of the Wyrds by experimenting on living subjects.

It was the information revealed by Oskane's meticulous observations of Wyrds under torture that had confirmed or disproved the speculation as to the extent of Wyrd power in the scrolls, and it was this which had led Zabier to convince Charald he could defeat the Wyrds.

Sorne should have taken his chest with him when he sailed; then it would have been lost in his travels. Now True-men knew the limitations of the T'En gifts.

He sighed and rubbed his eyes.

From King Charald's tent, he heard laughter and singing and knew the barons had arrived for the midwinter feast. He folded up the notes and dressed in his formal robes.

Later, after the barons had left, Charald would sit and talk with him as he did every night. They'd discuss the cost to Chalcedonia of fighting to subdue the the revolts in Maygharia and Welcai. They'd discuss the king's war barons and how the southern barons deferred to Eskarnor. Charald had his doubts about the mettle of the Chalcedonian barons. He believed they weren't capable of standing up to Eskarnor. Their families had held their lands for hundreds of years and during that time they'd grown soft, unlike Eskarnor and the southern barons who were all self-made men, hard and ruthless.

It was just like old times, except in those days the king hadn't trembled when he was tired or overwrought. Charald had developed little tricks to disguise his infirmity. He'd place his elbow on the table and rest his chin on it to hide the way his head wobbled.

And, in the old days, you only had to tell the king something once for him to take it in. Now Charald repeated himself, often having the same discussion with Sorne two nights in a row.

It was surprisingly easy to fall into the old pattern of talking late after the barons had left. But Sorne never forgot that Charald had once ordered his death because it was politically expedient, and was perfectly capable of doing so again.

IMOSHEN SPENT MIDWINTER'S day in the sisterhood's sanctum, with her gift senses on alert, waiting for Arodyti to link with her. If the hand-of-force didn't reach the prince today, there was still spring cusp.

'I'm worried about Saffazi,' Egrayne confessed, then lifted her hands in apology. 'I'm sorry. This isn't the time–'

'No, go ahead. I thought she was looking a little pale.'

'She hasn't been herself since the Mieren attack. She turns seventeen soon and should start her initiate training. She spends far too much time with your choice-son. I told her we'd all grown up with lads we'd had to declare dead when they joined their brotherhoods. She gave a strange laugh and said what did brotherhoods matter when we could all be dead soon?'

Imoshen squeezed Egrayne's hand. 'You must admit, the rivalry between brotherhoods and sisterhoods does seem petty, when King Charald and his war barons sit outside our gates.'

'It is precisely because we are faced with this terrible threat that we must abide by our customs. Our customs are what make us what we are. If we discard them, our society will collapse.'

They sat through the day and into the night but Arodyti did not activate the link.

When Imoshen went to her chamber, she found Iraayel playing cards with Frayvia, while her infant daughter slept in the nursery. She knelt by the fire to join in their game. With the Mieren army at the gate evenings like this felt very precious.

After the game ended, Iraayel went back to the lads' chamber, and Frayvia packed up the cards. 'There is still time; we don't have to hand over the city until new small moon after spring cusp.'

'And if that fails, perhaps I will send someone to assassinate Charald. If the barons are battling for the crown, we'll stand a better chance of getting away in small groups.'

'That reminds me. Fifteen Malaunje, three T'En children and their choice-mother arrived while you were busy today,' Frayvia said. It had been worthwhile sending out messengers to warn their estates. Despite the worsening weather, small parties of refugees had been arriving steadily, making the last part of the journey across the icy lake on stolen boats or makeshift rafts at night. 'Reoden has welcomed them back to her sisterhood.'

'That's good.' Imoshen saw Frayvia hesitate. 'What is it?'

'Have you heard back from All-father Kyredeon? Will he take Iraayel into his brotherhood?'

Imoshen put out the lamp. She had not approached Kyredeon. By rights, he should honour Chariode's agreement to accept Iraayel, but.... 'I don't want Iraayel joining Kyredeon's brotherhood. Besides, Iraayel won't be seventeen until next winter cusp.'

Imoshen offered Frayvia her hand and pulled her to her feet. 'Perhaps the three of us should have gone to study with the Sagoras. Then Iraayel could belong to a brotherhood from a distance.'

'Looking back, I don't think the sisterhood had any intention of letting you leave,' Frayvia said. 'I think making you study the Sagoras' language was a delaying tactic.'

'You could be right.' Imoshen frowned, thinking of her Sagorese language teacher. 'I hope Merchant Mercai made it safely home.'

Frayvia laughed. 'Worry about us, not him.'

SORNE WAS ALONE with the king. The food-taster and manservant had retired for the night. Charald liked to talk, and most of the time Sorne just had to listen.

But this midwinter's night, Charald was silent as he cracked a nut and tossed the shell into the brazier. As long as his hands were busy, they did not tremble. And now that he looked, Sorne noticed white striations on the king's finger nails. He didn't remember them before. Maybe it was a sign of age.

'My ancestor was a fool. I've read accounts of that final battle. He had the Wyrds on the back foot. Yet he conceded and gave them that island. Why would he do that?'

Sorne shrugged. 'Perhaps segregation was his goal, not the destruction of a whole people.'

'I know you think it's impossible to rid Chalcedonia of Wyrds, but I will enact laws. Any woman who has a half-blood baby will not be allowed to have another child. Any siblings of the half-blood will not be allowed to marry. You see, I mean to wipe out the tainted blood.'

'And the father?' Sorne asked, keeping his voice even. It amazed him that Charald did not realise the irony: the king had been born with a half-blood twin and Sorne was his son.

'The father will get a second chance. After all, a man needs sons to carry on his name. If he produces another half-blood, he will not be allowed to have any more children. You see, I will eradicate the Wyrds. One day my son will rule over a kingdom of True-men.'

Sorne nodded. It was on the tip of his tongue to say, *If, by law, the siblings of half-bloods cannot marry, then Prince Cedon would not be able to marry. He is my half-brother, after all.*

But King Charald was happy to edit reality to suit himself, so Sorne held his tongue.

Chapter Fourteen

To SORNE'S RELIEF, the last half of winter was severe; they saw nothing of the barons who had been sent to raze Wyrd estates until ten days before spring cusp. Sorne joined the king to hear Baron Dekaitz's report.

'Where are my sacrifices?' King Charald asked. 'Where are the trophy braids for your banner?'

'The full-bloods had shorn their heads,' Dekaitz reported. 'When we arrived, the Wyrds were prepared. They'd dug ditches and planted stakes. I would have sat tight and waited them out, but you wanted sacrifices, so I sent my men to attack. Seven times they held us off. On the eighth attack we broke through. Our losses were terrible.'

Charald had sent the most troublesome of Eskarnor and Nitzane's supporters to make the second round of raids, and now Sorne understood why.

But the king just nodded gravely. 'Go on.'

'When we had them cornered, they fought until not one remained alive. We weren't too worried, because we thought we'd find the women and children hidden somewhere, but there were none. They must have sent them away before we arrived.'

'Sent them where?' Baron Nitzane asked. Dekaitz was one of his followers.

'To the city,' Charald said. 'It's impossible to guard the whole lake. If I told you to patrol the shore, you'd complain because you'd be spreading them too thin. I always knew a few Wyrds would get through. Doesn't matter. They'll suffer the same fate as the rest. But I'm disappointed in you, Dekaitz. We'll see how the other barons fare.'

Three days before spring cusp, another of the barons returned: one of Eskarnor's supporters, Baron Hanix. Eskarnor greeted him with a laugh and they embraced, Dacian fashion, slapping each other on the back.

Hanix had a similar tale to report.

'Heads shorn, all dead, no women and children, but I did find this one, hiding in the scullery.' Hanix signalled his man at the entrance to the tent, who left and returned with an aged full-blood female. They'd removed the tip from a spear and fashioned a noose on the end. She was led around with this. They drove her forward to stand in front of King Charald.

'She claims to be one hundred and thirty,' Hanix said. 'And looking at her, I'm tempted to believe it.'

She was certainly wizened. The barons drew nearer, peering at her, discussing her. They seemed both repelled and fascinated. So many of them crowded around her, the man-at-arms had to step back and lower his end of the spear.

'A hundred and thirty?' Charald repeated, eyeing the old woman. 'Prove it.'

'My grandmother saw King Charald the Peace-maker sign the accord. She said he had ice-blue eyes, like yours.'

There was muttering at this. The captive's gaze wandered over the gathering. When she saw Sorne, her mouth twitched with contempt.

'The Warrior doesn't value useless old women. She's not worth sacrificing.' Charald was dismissive.

Sorne felt the build up of power. The old woman swayed and reached out as if to steady herself, but those sharp old eyes were on the king and her claw-like hand was aimed at his forearm.

Sorne grabbed the back of Charald's chair and tipped him over. The king went sprawling on the ground.

The old woman staggered, collapsing against Baron Hanix, who went to push her away, but the moment his skin came into contact with hers they both disappeared. Their clothing dropped to the carpet.

Everyone drew back, horrified. They cursed and swore, drawing in shaky breaths.

Sorne helped the king rise.

'Treacherous Wyrds,' Charald spat. Sorne felt the king's hands tremble. 'The bitch tried to kill me. Bring wine.'

A servant ran out, and several of the barons poked the clothing and whispered. Sorne heard them speculating, and realised they had no idea what had happened. Even if Zabier had explained about the higher plane, where the T'En did most of their gift-working, the barons hadn't taken it in. They seemed to have grasped only the most basic concept of avoiding touch and, when presented with a "harmless" old woman, most had forgotten that.

With Zabier dead, only one person had read all the information in the Wyrd scrolls and Oskane's journals, and that was Scholar Igotzon. What if he should set himself up as an authority on Wyrds? Then the true limitations of the gifts would become general knowledge. Sorne needed to destroy Igotzon's reports, the journals and the scrolls.

Charald tipped half of his wine into another goblet and gave it to Sorne. 'The Warrior's-voice saved my life. I salute his quick thinking.'

The others echoed him, but Sorne noted the way Eskarnor eyed him. The two southern barons had been close. Sorne tensed, expecting accusations and anger.

'Why didn't Hanix's talisman protect him?' Eskarnor demanded.

Sorne realised he meant the malachite pendant. 'Was he wearing it?'

The men sifted through the baron's personal belongings. Sorne was getting ready to say it was Hanix's fault for forgetting to wear it, when they found the pendant.

They handed it to Sorne, and he felt the power the pendant had absorbed when the old T'En female had segued to the higher plane. Even though the power tempted him, Sorne tossed the pendant into a brazier. 'The talisman's protective power has been used up.'

'I didn't know they lost power with time,' Nitzane said.

Sorne nodded. The less they knew, the more powerful he became.

Nitzane removed his malachite pendant. 'Is mine still good?'

Sorne accepted it, felt precisely nothing and lied. 'I'll have to see if I can restore its protective properties.'

In no time at all, everyone had returned their pendants and he went back to his tent. As he dropped the pendants onto his desk, the tent flap opened. He turned to see Baron Eskarnor. Sorne felt the lack of his sword. In theory, the church's holy warriors would protect him, but Eskarnor could gut him before they answered his call.

Pretending a calm he did not feel, Sorne went around his desk and sat down. He was the man of learning, shielded by knowledge from the man of violence. But if need be, he could resort to violence. 'What can I do for you, baron?'

Eskarnor leant on the desk, looming over Sorne. 'You set that up. You got Hanix killed.'

Sorne laughed. 'If you believe that, you have an exaggerated idea of my abilities. I was as surprised as you.'

The southern baron eyed him, unconvinced.

'Hanix got himself killed. He underestimated the old woman.'

Eskarnor drew back, his mouth grim. Sorne expected bluster and threat, but the baron shook his head slowly. 'Why do you put up with the king? You might be his eldest son, but he'll never acknowledge you.'

Sorne went cold. He'd thought his identity a secret few knew.

'The others see an accursed half-blood,' Eskarnor said. 'I see a man who can make a king dance to his tune. I see a man who is not valued as he should be. The king is old and will not live much longer. When he dies, his subject kingdoms will all revolt and Chalcedonia will need to defend her borders. You should reconsider your loyalties.'

And he walked out.

Sorne's shoulders sagged. Eskarnor had been right about so much, but he was not right about Sorne's loyalties.

He bore Charald no love.

WHEN A THIRD baron returned empty-handed from attacking a Wyrd estate, Sorne was hopeful he would not have to sacrifice one of his own kind after all, but the very next day, the fourth baron returned with two shivering, skinny captives: an old Malaunje man and a little girl of about five. Her red-gold hair reminded Sorne of Valendia, and he couldn't bear to look at her. When she saw him standing behind the king's chair, she threw her arms around the old man.

'Is this all you bring me?' Charald demanded. 'No trophies, no silver braids for the new banners?'

'The Wyrds were prepared. The bodies of my men piled high in the snow,' Baron Ranzto protested. 'When we did break through, we found the Wyrds had shorn their heads. We captured these two wandering in the woods. They said they'd become separated from the rest.'

'You bring me scraps. Not worth sacrificing.' Charald was dismissive, but Sorne knew he was pleased. The king was whittling away at both the Wyrds and the barons who supported his rivals. 'Build me two scaffolds. Place them at the end of the causeway.'

'It will be done,' Ranzto said.

Sorne knew, unless Imoshen captured the prince and began negotiation, he would have to stand back and let these two die.

How could he?

His only consolation was the lack of wood to build the scaffold. The sap had frozen in the trees and the axes were blunted, but Baron Ranzto was resourceful and he would find the necessary wood.

'Get them out of here.' Charald gestured disgustedly to the old man and the little girl.

'If they spend another night in the cold, they'll both die before we can hang them,' Ranzto said. 'No True-man would share his tent with them.'

Anger rolled through Sorne, but he remained impassive.

Charald gestured to him. 'You deal with them.'

'Why me?' Sorne protested. They were prisoners. He was the Warrior's-voice. If the barons associated him with these two vulnerable captives... 'I don't want filthy Wyrds in my tent.'

The barons laughed, as he knew they would.

Pretending disgust, Sorne gestured to the captives. 'This way.' He swept out of the tent, leaving them to follow as best they could.

They struggled through the snow, falling behind him before he was halfway to his tent. Anger and urgency warred with pity inside him. 'Hurry up.'

Sorne ushered them inside his tent. A tray containing Sorne's half-eaten lunch sat on the table; he pushed it in their direction. The old man snatched the food. Tearing the flat bread in half, he gave some to the little girl, who wept with relief as she ate.

Sorne made a nest from spare blankets and draped two more around their shoulders.

The old man had been so intent on eating that he hadn't noticed what was going on. Now he looked up in surprise. Sorne held his finger to his lips. Exhaustion lined the old man's face. For a heartbeat, he simply stared at Sorne; then he dropped to his knees and threw his arms around him.

Those arms felt like chains. When Sorne freed himself, the man went to speak. Sorne signalled for silence, gesturing to the tent entrance. The man nodded and concentrated on sharing the remainder of Sorne's meal with the girl. Every now and then, he looked up at Sorne and bobbed his head in thanks. Tears slid down his grimy cheeks and he kept hugging the little girl. He thought they were safe now.

But Sorne was as much a captive as them. He could not reveal his true allegiance. At the same time, he could not stand back and let the True-men hang them.

Legs suddenly weak, Sorne went to his desk and sat down. Sick desperation welled up in him and he sank his head into his hands. He should send them both to the scaffold. To do otherwise could destroy him, but it went against everything he believed in.

How had Zabier borne this?

He hadn't. His mind had split in two. It was the only way he could carry out the sacrifices and protect his family. Sorne's heartfelt sympathy went out to his little brother.

A noise made him look up. The old man indicated they had to pee. Sorne felt an irrational urge to laugh.

It was spring cusp and their last chance to snatch the prince. Imoshen sat cross-legged in the sisterhood's sanctum, under the dome, waiting for Arodyti to activate their gift link. A scented lamp hung above her. As the day progressed, different members of her inner circle came and sat with her, keeping the vigil. They knew Arodyti had gone to lead a special mission, but not why.

Some chatted, some sat in silence.

It happened that Imoshen was alone when she heard talk from the hallway.

'...they're building two scaffolds, one each side at the end of the causeway.'

'Quiet,' Egrayne told them. 'The all-mother is in the sanctum.'

Egrayne came in and knelt beside her. 'You heard?'

'Yes. Charald must have some captives.' If Arodyti failed, could she sit back and watch him hang her people?

'Has Arodyti...'

Imoshen shook her head. 'How's Safi? I've hardly seen her.'

'Looking better. She's begun her gift training.' Egrayne's lips twitched. 'She says Vittoryxe...'

'Vittoryxe what?' the gift-tutor asked as she entered.

'Is an excellent teacher,' Egrayne said. Imoshen was certain Saffazi had said nothing of the sort.

Vittoryxe nodded, as if this was what she'd expected. 'I've been reading the myths...'

Imoshen felt her gift stir and concentrated as her link to Arodyti opened.

'...do you see any two-hundred-year-old T'En nowadays? Of course you don't.' Vittoryxe answered her own question. 'The myths are full of exaggeration. We—'

'What is it?' Egrayne whispered.

Imoshen licked her lips and had to remember how to speak. 'Arodyti is in the palace.'

'Quick, fetch the others.' Egrayne sent her devotee off.

'It's really happening. I don't believe it,' Vittoryxe whispered excitedly, then frowned. 'You ask too much of her, Imoshen. Transposition of herself, perhaps, but with the boy she'll shed too much power. She'll burn bright as a beacon. The predators won't be able to resist her—'

'She'll only burn bright for a heartbeat,' Imoshen said.

The rest of her inner circle must have been close; they arrived quickly and took their places on the cushions around the circular mosaic. By the light of the scented lamp, their wine-dark eyes looked huge, and all those eyes focused on Imoshen.

No one spoke.

Did they all agree with Vittoryxe? Was she sacrificing Arodyti in a hopeless gamble?

ARODYTI HATED HAVING to leave her shield-sister to fight six of the king's palace guards, but they'd reached the nursery.

As the men gave a shout and charged down the long gallery towards them, time seemed to slow. The warriors' boots thundered on the mosaics, and the many metal panels of their armour glittered like fish scales in the sun.

Silvery, late-afternoon sunlight streamed through the arched windows on her left. They looked out over the royal plaza, which was surrounded by the churches of the Mieren gods. Minarets, towers and domes as far as the eye could see – all inhabited by their enemy.

It was time to fulfil her promise to Imoshen. Time to say goodbye to Sarosune.

A rushing filled Arodyti's ears.

'Aro!' Her shield-sister caught her arm, swinging her around so that their eyes met. 'We knew it would come to this.'

Their companions were already dead. Doubtless raped, their sixth fingers souvenired and their distinctive, garnet eyes gouged out. Mieren were brutal with T'En captives, particularly women.

Arodyti couldn't bear to think of the Mieren desecrating her beautiful shield-sister. Sliding her hand around the back of Sarosune's neck, she felt the blunt ends of the shield-sister's shorn silver hair. The Mieren would not get the chance to make trophies of their braids.

Pressing her forehead to her shield-sister's, Arodyti opened her gift. Through their link, she reinforced her love. 'Saro, I–'

Sarosune silenced her with a fierce kiss, then shoved her away, rebuilding her defences. 'We cannot fail Imoshen. Go.'

She was right. With the heat of her lover's kiss still on her lips, Arodyti strode into the nursery chamber, swung the doors shut and slid home the bolt. Then she turned and looked for the boy prince.

The shouts of the king's guard had alerted the boy's wet-nurse. Small for one of her race, the Mieren woman stood trembling but defiant. Her eyes widened at the sight of a T'En warrior armed with a bloodied blade.

The harsh clatter of metal on metal came from the hall; the guards had reached Sarosune. Arodyti had only moments.

'Cedon,' the wet-nurse called the prince, sinking to her knees and opening her arms to him.

King Charald's heir ran towards her, his awkward gait evidence of the club foot that marked him as unfit to inherit the throne.

Prince Cedon reached for his wet-nurse's breast, pushing down the drawstring to bury his face in her pale skin. At almost three years of age, he would be considered too old to breastfeed by Arodyti's people, but she understood his instinctive need for comfort when confronted by a bloodstained T'En warrior.

A man screamed. The harsh clatter of metal on metal resumed, then stopped abruptly. The doors to the nursery shuddered as the king's guard tried to break them down. Sarosune was dead. She must not think of her shield-sister.

Arodyti strode across the chamber, intent on taking the prince. Desperate, the wet-nurse swept the boy up in her arms, and fled through to the balcony.

Arodyti broke into a run.

She found the wet-nurse had clambered onto the balustrade with the king's heir. Illuminated by the last rays of the setting sun, they stood etched against blue-black storm clouds. Seagulls circled the port's spires, their harsh cries carrying on the wind. Below the balcony, the palace wall dropped four storeys into a twilight-shrouded courtyard.

Glancing down once, the wet-nurse closed her eyes and stepped back, taking the boy with her.

Arodyti threw herself forward, just catching the boy's robe. Her knives clattered on the stones near her feet. She didn't remember dropping them. She grabbed the boy's arm and there she hung, half over the balcony, the boy and his nurse swinging in an arc. With a despairing cry, the wet-nurse lost her grip and fell away, her terrified face swallowed by shadows.

Arodyti hauled the prince up, barely registering his weight, and lifted him over the balustrade into her arms.

He clung to her, trembling.

So small and fragile.

Shouts and the thud of booted feet told Arodyti the guards had forced the doors.

The boy shuddered. She tucked his head into the hollow of her neck, making reassuring sounds. His white-blond curls reminded her of T'En children, but he had the ice-blue eyes of the Mieren. When he pulled back to look up at her, those eyes held confusion.

Boots thundered across the tiles.

Arodyti wanted to tell him everything would be all right, but she could not lie. If she failed, they would both die. The predators of the higher plane were swift and ruthless.

'There they are.' The first king's guard, a grizzled veteran, slowed and signalled the others to fan out as they stepped onto the balcony. They cast anxious looks to the balustrade, as if fearing she would throw the boy to his death.

'Put Prince Cedon down and we will let you live,' the veteran lied.

The boy reached out for the palace guard.

No more delays.

Arodyti opened her link to Imoshen and segued to the higher plane, taking not just their essences, but their bodies as well. It went against everything she had been taught, but it was the only way to achieve transposition and deliver Prince Cedon to Imoshen.

THE VETERAN KING's guard blinked in disbelief. The bloodied T'En warrior had simply vanished with the king's heir in her arms. He glanced to the others.

Stunned, they stared at the warrior's clothes and wicked long-knives. Steam rose from the discarded belongings on the cool balcony tiles.

The veteran cursed his bad luck.

The youngest of the guards started forward.

'Don't.' The veteran caught his arm. The others all turned to him, shocked by their failure to save the heir when it had seemed they had the T'En warrior trapped.

'I didn't know silverheads could vanish like that,' the youth protested.

'No one knew.'

'If they can vanish, why didn't they save themselves when the mobs burned their warehouses?'

All the king's guards looked to the veteran, but he didn't have an answer. He wished he did, for now he would have to report to King Charald, who would order his execution.

He deserved it.

He'd failed his king. Worse, he had failed the little boy who'd looked to him for help.

Chapter Fifteen

IMOSHEN CAME TO her knees as the tension built. No one spoke. Vittoryxe watched, eyes bright, ready to say *I told you so*. Imoshen was going to prove the gift-tutor wrong. She gathered her gift, preparing to anchor Arodyti.

Without warning, Arodyti's essence swamped Imoshen. Before her, in the centre of the circle, the naked T'En warrior appeared with a limp boy-child in her arms.

Real and solid, slick and warm, the boy fell into Imoshen's lap. She thrust the unconscious prince into Egrayne's arms and reached for Arodyti.

Too late.

Imoshen's fingers barely registered resistance as they passed through Arodyti's arm. Desperate, she threw herself forward, opening her gift to anchor her hand-of-force.

If Arodyti could return to this plane, she'd live.

Imoshen made Arodyti burn bright with power as she tried to anchor her friend, but at the same time the power summoned the ever-hungry predators, just as Vittoryxe had warned.

Refusing to give up, Imoshen channelled more power into the link, willing Arodyti to come through.

Exhaustion clouded Arodyti's mind. The hand-of-force had overreached herself to deliver the boy.

Imoshen tried to force Arodyti to focus, but there was not enough of her friend left. The act of transposing Prince Cedon had taken its toll.

The empyrean beasts attacked.

Imoshen felt them tear Arodyti to shreds, felt it as if it was her own body being devoured, and there was nothing she could do.

The impact of their savagery tore at Imoshen. Her sense of self dissolved and she felt the deep cold of the empyrean plane in her bones.

Something struck Imoshen's face. Shocked by the blow, she focused on her mortal body just as the calloused palm delivered another stinging slap. The impact rocked her head back and Imoshen tasted blood.

'Have we lost her, too?' Tiasarone whispered.

'I told her this was too risky,' Vittoryxe hissed. 'Sheer arrogance!'

Imoshen was not about to give the gift-tutor the satisfaction of being proven right. Concentrating, she opened her eyes. The worried faces of her inner circle wavered in front of her.

'Imoshen, can you hear me? Answer me,' Egrayne commanded.

'I'm all right.' She lifted a hand to her mouth. Her fingers came away stained with blood. Egrayne had been as determined to save her as she had been to save Arodyti.

But she'd failed. She'd been so sure she could hold on.

Furious with herself, Imoshen pushed Egrayne away and went to rise. Her voice-of-reason hauled her to her feet so rapidly that she nearly lost her balance.

'I told you, I'm fine.' Imoshen stretched. Her body ached as if she had pushed herself to her physical limit. Mentally, she felt flat and lifeless. Her gift was drained and her senses dull. Something important nagged at her mind... Prince Cedon. She turned to her voice-of-reason. 'The boy?'

'Alive. Stunned, by the look of it,' Egrayne reported. She gestured to Tiasarone. 'Turn around so we can see his face.'

The old woman shifted to reveal the boy. His head rested on her shoulder, pewter lashes forming crescents on his pale cheeks, lips parted. So small and vulnerable; a pawn in the games of adults. Imoshen felt for him. 'Take him straight to Reoden. Leave me now.'

The others went, all but her voice-of-reason.

'Arodyti's dead?'

Imoshen nodded. 'And Sarosune, and the others. Four of our best, lost.'

'You suggested transposition. I didn't believe it possible, but we have King Charald's heir. I only hope...'

'We can trust Sorne's judgement?'

Egrayne lifted her large hands in a shrug.

'The king is onto his third wife in his quest for a healthy heir.'

Egrayne unhooked the incense laden lamp. 'You'll signal the king?'

'Yes. We'll send a message tonight. Tell him we wish to talk tomorrow at midday.'

Egrayne nodded.

'We can show him the boy, but I don't know how long it will take for news of the prince's abduction to reach him. I doubt he'll believe his own eyes until his people confirm it.'

'When he does, you'll bargain for safe passage to our ships?' Egrayne asked.

'We'll keep the boy with us until we can make the exchange at the headlands.'

'Leave our home, leave Chalcedonia...' Lamplight sculpted Egrayne's strong features. Her shoulders sagged as though weary with the enormity of it. 'How can we abandon our heritage, Imoshen? How can you ask this of us?'

'The T'Enatuath is not the Celestial City, it is the people,' Imoshen insisted, fierce in her certainty. 'We'll take our heritage with us.'

Egrayne blinked, then hugged Imoshen. As she pulled back, her wine-dark eyes gleamed with tears. 'I was right to nominate you for causare.'

Imoshen was touched, and more than a little ashamed. She did not want this responsibility. 'Our sisters need to know how Arodyti and the others sacrificed themselves to bring us Prince Cedon.' She was so exhausted, she slurred his name. It was hard to think. 'We sent the boy to Ree. Her sisterhood–'

'I'll tell them. Go rest.'

Imoshen nodded.

'After all,' Egrayne's lips twitched, 'tomorrow not only do you have to bargain with King Charald, but you have to hold an all-council, reveal your plan for the prince, and eat humble pie because you acted without getting all-council approval.'

'GUARD DUTY AGAIN.' Haromyr complained to Tobazim. They'd been told to patrol the wall all the way from the causeway gate to Kyredeon's palace.

'At least we're in charge.'

'Only because it's a feast night and everyone else is celebrating. Oriemn's punishing you. And us with you.'

The hand-of-force had rostered on the Malaunje who had escaped from the winery with Tobazim and Learon, along with the warriors who had volunteered to help recover the trophy braids.

Tobazim's gaze was drawn to the Mieren, who had started building two scaffolds this afternoon. He leant his elbows on the stonework to watch. The builders were working by lantern light at the end of the causeway. Even from this distance, the construction made his gift stir, as he sensed the stresses and weights. The drop was not high enough to break the victim's neck. The urge to go down the causeway and make the necessary adjustments was very strong.

And completely irrational. 'Those scaffolds...'

'They must have attacked another of our estates and taken captives,' Haromyr whispered, voice thick with anger, gift rising. 'Then they brought them back here, just so they could mock us by hanging them at our city gates. What kind of people do that?'

'It's a calculated insult,' Tobazim said.

'You know...' Haromyr leant closer. 'They have to go to bed sometime. We could mount a sortie, burn the scaffolds.'

'That's the kind of talk that got Learon in trouble.' It still hurt to say his name.

A woman's voice called up to the wall-walk. They both crossed the city side of the gate defences to look down.

A T'En warrior stood directly below them, head tilted to look up. The distance was too great to make out the sisterhood symbol on her neck torc.

'Who's in charge here?' she asked.

'I am,' Tobazim said.

'The causare wants to meet with King Charald tomorrow at midday.'

Tobazim repressed a surge of fear at the mention of the causare. There had been no repercussions from the night they'd escorted Sorne to her, but it was always hanging over his head. On wrong word and Kyredeon would execute him.

'We'll send a message,' Tobazim said, turning away. 'Just in time. The scaffolds will be finished within a day.'

Haromyr handed him the lantern. He took it and signalled, until one of the builders ran off.

Soon, several men-at-arms ventured down the causeway in a pool of lantern light.

Tobazim gave the message to the men-at-arms.

'How can the causare save our people from hanging?' Haromyr whispered. 'She has to have something to bargain with.'

Tobazim suspected Sorne had given her something to negotiate with, although why it had taken so long he didn't know.

SORNE TOOK HIS usual place behind the king's chair. It was spring cusp and the scaffolds would be completed sometime tomorrow. As the barons talked about Hanix's death and how they hadn't expected an old woman to be so cunning or powerful, he realised he could save the Malaunje captives from hanging.

His mind raced. Before dawn, when the sentries were tired, he could lead the old man and child down to the lake and send them across in the same rowboat he'd used, then come back to his tent, hit himself over the head and let the holy warriors find him incapacitated. This would make it appear as if he had underestimated the old man, just as the barons had underestimated the old woman.

The True-men would mock him, but they would not be surprised. It would undermine his position in the camp, and it was a subterfuge he could only use once, but he would use it if he had to.

A sentry arrived with a message.

'Speak,' Charald gestured, as though he was the most reasonable of kings and had never ordered a man whipped because he didn't like the contents of a message.

'The Wyrds want to talk, tomorrow at midday.'

The king gave a bark of laughter. 'Knew the scaffolds would get to them. Now we watch them squirm.'

Had Imoshen captured the prince? Sorne looked down to hide his relief. Tomorrow, Imoshen would bargain for her people's survival and save the two captives.

'WHAT'S GOING ON?' Athlyn asked, pointing to the Malaunje dancing on the palace rooftop. The spring cusp festivities had been subdued, but within the last few moments the pitch had changed. People shouted and hugged. Laughter rang on the air. 'Has everyone gone mad?'

Tobazim cupped his hands and called across. 'Why are you celebrating?'

Half a dozen of them called back, drowning each other out. Tobazim looked to Athlyn and shrugged. A moment later a pretty girl ran up the steps to the wall-walk.

'Isn't it wonderful?' She threw her arms around Tobazim and kissed him.

'Much as I appreciate the kiss,' Tobazim said, putting her away from him, 'what's going on?'

She laughed. 'The causare has kidnapped the Mieren king's son, his only son. We'll be able to stay. Everything will be all right!'

She planted another kiss on his surprised mouth and danced away.

Laughter and music filled the night. Despite the celebrations, Tobazim saw the flaw in the logic. The king would turn on them as soon as they handed the boy back to him. But perhaps there was more to it than that.

After their watch finished, Tobazim sought the sawbones. He found him sewing up a cut on an initiate's forehead.

'Too much wine, not enough sense,' Ceyne told the youth. 'Now, go sleep it off.'

The initiate staggered away with his friends.

'What's going on?' Tobazim asked, gesturing to the door to the courtyard, where the celebrations were still going strong. 'Did the causare make an announcement?'

'Not that I've heard.' Ceyne packed his things away. 'Someone said they saw the sisterhood Malaunje celebrating. Said the causare had kidnapped the king's heir.'

'Even if she did, we can't stay here. The king would turn on us the moment we gave the boy back.'

Ceyne nodded.

'I don't understand.'

'It's been a sober, cold winter living under the threat of death. This is spring and we hear that the causare has kidnapped the prince.' Ceyne shrugged. 'It's a win for us. They're celebrating because they need to.'

Chapter Sixteen

IMOSHEN SLEPT LATE, exhausted by the battle to save Arodyti, exhausted because she had woken during the night with the realisation that Arodyti's gift essence had been consumed by empyrean predators, which meant Imoshen had sent her dear friend to the true death.

Today, Imoshen felt raw and fragile. She had barely dressed when Iraayel tapped on her door and entered without waiting for a reply.

'Is it true you kidnapped Prince Cedon?'

'Yes,' Imoshen said. 'And good morning to you, too.' She glanced past him. 'Where's Egrayne? I sent for her.'

'Saf told me Egrayne and the gift-tutor were up all night, trying to find the shades of the gift-warriors who died to get Arodyti into the palace nursery. They were trying to escort them to death's realm.'

Imoshen nodded and went to speak, but laughter and singing drifted through the window, echoing up from the courtyard two floors below. Imoshen frowned. The festival had been yesterday; why were they still celebrating?

Frayvia came in from the nursery with little Umaleni on her hip. 'What's going on?'

'They're saying we won't have to leave,' Iraayel gestured to the courtyard window. 'That you'll use the prince to get King Charald to sign the accord again. But he's broken it once already. As soon as you return his son, he'll break it again.'

'Yes, he would. But that's not why I've taken the prince.' Imoshen's head swam. What had Egrayne told the rest of the sisters? Knowing Egrayne, it hadn't been much, but clearly it had been just enough for rumours to spread. Annoyance flashed through Imoshen, stirring her gift.

'Imoshen?' Reoden came down the passage and saw her through the open door. 'We can't stay. King Charald still means to massacre us all. Nothing's changed...' She broke off as she swept into the room and realised Imoshen wasn't alone.

'What?' Iraayel whispered. 'Is it true?'

She nodded. 'Exile was never the Mieren king's goal. He wants to wipe out our people.'

'What kind of man does that?' Iraayel took a step back. 'And how could you lie to me?'

'I lied to everyone. Think it through, Iraayel. How could I reveal that King Charald planned to massacre us on the road to port, when we had no hope? People would despair. Now–'

'Now they think they can stay here.' Anger made Iraayel's gift rise.

'They can't stay here, and I don't know how the rumour got started.' Imoshen knew his anger wasn't directed at her, more their situation, but even so it made her uncomfortable. Umaleni whimpered and held out her arms. Frayvia handed the infant over to Imoshen. Meanwhile the celebration continued in the courtyard.

'They're not thinking clearly.' Frustration welled up in Imoshen. 'Why can't they see the logic flaw?'

'They're fooling themselves because they want to believe King Charald is a reasonable man.' Reoden shrugged. 'My people are the same. I worked on the prince, then fell into bed exhausted. When I woke up, I found all the sisterhoods celebrating.'

'I'll have to call the all-mothers,' Imoshen said. 'Then...' She looked up in horror. 'What if the brotherhoods–'

'All-mother?' Gift-warrior Kiane spoke as she came down the passage towards Imoshen's private chamber. 'The all-mothers have arrived. I put them downstairs in your formal greeting chamber.'

'Good. Tell my inner circle to—'

'And the all-fathers are at the sisterhood gate, demanding to see you.'

'That's bad,' Reoden whispered.

'No, it's good. I'll tell everyone, at once. Kiane, escort the all-fathers to the formal greeting chamber.'

'Bring them inside the sisterhood quarter?' She was horrified. 'No adult T'En man has stepped inside our gate in over three hundred years.'

'We haven't faced the destruction of our people in over three hundred years. Now, go. Tell Egrayne to come to me; I name you my hand-of-force.'

Kiane blinked.

Imoshen pressed her hands to her mouth, fighting an irrational urge to laugh. Taking a deep breath, she started again. 'I'm sorry, Kiane. But I have to meet King Charald at midday and I'm running out of time. Will you be my hand-of-force?'

'I would be honoured,' the gift-warrior said, but Imoshen could tell she was annoyed by the manner of her elevation. Kiane gave Imoshen the correct obeisance, then left to organise things.

In a very short time, Egrayne joined her and Imoshen took Kiane's oath. As they went down to the formal greeting chamber, Imoshen noted how quiet the sisterhood was. The arrival of a large group of powerful T'En men had startled Malaunje and T'En alike. She was aware of people watching from doorways, whispering.

'I don't understand why we couldn't meet the all-fathers and their seconds in the empowerment dome like always,' Egrayne whispered.

'Because that would have entailed sending them away and irritated them further. Because by inviting them into the sisterhood quarter, I've unsettled them. This is an extraordinary day, and I have taken an extraordinary action. Also, here in the palace, I have the advantage. Follow my lead.' Imoshen swept into the formal greeting chamber.

Late morning sunshine came through the tall, multi-paned glass doors, which stood open onto the courtyard beyond. The floor was white marble. The decorative cornices were picked out in silver, and silver sculptures gleamed in wall niches. The room had been designed as a backdrop for T'En colouring, and Imoshen had changed into a magenta robe to match her eyes and, other than her sisterhood torc, wore only silver and diamond jewellery.

The all-mothers and their seconds were down at one end of the chamber, with the all-fathers down the other. Imoshen could feel the pull of male power from the doorway and her gift surged as she read them. The brotherhood leaders were angry and confused, but also unnerved to find themselves inside the sisterhood quarter. Many of them had been raised here. They would be reminded of their childhoods and their choice-mothers, of when they deferred to females.

Imoshen waited in the entrance until the last whispered conversation ceased. 'Close all the doors.'

When no one moved, she crossed to the other side of the chamber to close the central pair of courtyard doors. Others moved to shut the rest of the doors.

Imoshen turned around to face the chamber. She ignored the formal raised dais where the all-mother was supposed to sit and sank to kneel on the marble floor. Early spring sunshine bathed her, but offered little warmth. The cold of the marble came through her silken pleated trousers.

After a heartbeat, Egrayne and Kiane settled beside and slightly behind her. Because this was her palace, custom decreed the others follow her lead. One by one, the brotherhoods knelt on her right and the sisterhoods on her left.

Imoshen could feel the men getting ready to accuse her of acting without all-council approval.

'I have a spy in King Charald's inner circle,' Imoshen said. 'He came to me with news I could not share until today. I took action without telling the all-fathers or the all-mothers, or even most of my inner circle, because the nature of his information was so dire.'

'What is this dire news?' Kyredeon asked, voice hard and brittle.

Imoshen met his eyes and waited a beat. 'King Charald wasn't offering us exile–'

'That's good, because we weren't going to accept his offer,' Saskeyne said, and there were a couple of chuckles.

'On our way to port, the Mieren king planned to surround our camp and massacre us all. I couldn't tell you this because I didn't want a panic–'

Several of the hands-of-force sprang from their knees to their feet in one fluid movement, startling her, and all the all-fathers and their seconds followed suit. Her gift rose and she had to bank it, while reminding herself never to underestimate the physicality of the men.

Outraged, the brotherhood leaders spoke of fighting and dying with honour. Powerful male gifts filled the chamber. When Kiane would have risen, Imoshen stopped her with a touch. The all-mothers took their cue from Imoshen.

Kyredeon confronted her. 'You knew this, and you didn't tell us. You didn't give us a choice!'

Even though every instinct told her to defend herself, Imoshen remained on her knees, with her hands resting lightly on her thighs. By her silence she made it clear the discussion could not resume until they were all seated.

The men had ceded power to the women, when they entered the sisterhood gate. And they had ceded power to her when they entered her sisterhood's palace.

Kyredeon's hands curled into fists. She knew he wanted to strike her, but the moment his skin touched hers, she would tear his essence from his body and send it to the empyrean plane, wounding him so badly he would not be able to escape its predators.

She thought of Reoden's murdered daughter, young Sardeon and the scryer both crippled by what they'd seen that day. If any of the brotherhood leaders deserved death, it was Kyredeon. And she let this knowledge seep into her eyes. If power was all the men respected, she could play that game.

He took a step back.

In that moment, she grasped the real reason the all-mothers had voted her causare. Certainly she was able to read people, but she was also willing to kill. They had used her to kill once before, when she had executed her father. They believed she could and would do so again, if she had to.

'You should have called an all-council,' Kyredeon said. He was still blustering, but he was talking and not using force.

Imoshen glanced to the other brotherhood leaders. About half of them were seated, and more knelt while she watched.

Soon Kyredeon realised only he and his two seconds remained standing. He turned to the all-fathers. 'She acted without the all-council's authority.'

Having said his piece, he returned to his place and knelt.

'I concede that I did not do what I asked all of you to do,' Imoshen said. 'But I had good reason to doubt the discretion of the brotherhoods. When I saw Kyredeon's T'En warrior make a stand on the causeway, I knew–'

Several all-fathers protested that this was Kyredeon's fault, while he insisted the gift-warrior had been acting alone.

'Someone opened the gate for him,' Imoshen countered. Kyredeon did not argue this.

'Besides,' she added, 'look how quickly the rumour about Prince Cedon spread last night. Imagine the panic, if our people learned King Charald planned to massacre us and there was no hope. Now that we have Prince Cedon–'

'Is it true you used transposition to snatch him from the palace?' Hueryx asked.

'Arodyti...' Imoshen could not go on.

'I claim stature for our sisterhood,' Egrayne said and named the gift-warriors they'd lost. While the others acknowledged this, Imoshen composed herself.

'I'm meeting King Charald soon. I'll negotiate for safe passage to the port, onto our ships and out of the bay.'

'Exile...' It was a communal exhalation of sorrow.

'For three hundred years we've lived segregated lives from the Mieren. In truth, we've been exiles in our own land, besieged in our city and estates. When we sail away, we'll find a new home, a sanctuary for the T'Enatuath.'

'You know this for certain?' the oldest of the all-fathers asked. 'You've consulted the scryer?'

Imoshen sent Reoden a silent apology. 'I can't consult the scryer, because the day Kyredeon's warriors killed Reoden's daughter, the scryer's gift was crippled. We have no scryer. We have no peace of mind, because we cannot trust each other. We cannot afford this rivalry – brotherhood against brotherhood, men against women. If we don't work together, we might as well open the gates right now and let King Charald's war barons ride in here and slaughter every last one of us.'

Imoshen found she was on her feet and didn't remember rising. Her gift was riding her. Everyone stared at her. 'I will do whatever it takes to ensure the survival of our people. You are either with me, or you're against me.'

No one spoke. She looked from face to face, reading the all-fathers and their seconds. They ranged from resentment to outright angry belligerance. She shouldn't have threatened the brotherhood leaders, but she meant it. There was not one amongst them who she trusted to lead their people to safety.

She clamped down on her power and turned to Reoden. 'Now I must see King Charald. We'll need the boy. I'd like to talk to him on the way down to the gate.'

*   *   *

SORNE HOPED HE'D done the right thing when he hadn't arranged for the old man and girl to escape overnight, because now the king insisted they accompany him to meet with the Wyrds.

'We'll let them see the copperheads up close,' Charald told the barons. 'More effective that way.'

Sorne beckoned two of his holy warriors. 'Go fetch the Wyrds.'

If he was to retain power, if he was to survive, the barons must not associate him with the victims. He must appear to be above all other Wyrds.

He went around, handing out the malachite pendants, and saying the Warrior's blessing, for all the good it would do.

'Are they working again?' Dekaitz asked.

'I've done the best I can with them. They've been exposed to a lot of Wyrd contagion,' he said. There, that should cover him if anything went wrong.

The king and his barons walked off. They were full of plans. By the new small moon, the Wyrds would be gone and the city would be theirs. Only another twenty-one days in the tents and they would be living in palaces.

As soon as the holy warriors approached with the old man and little girl, Sorne strode off.

He caught up with the king and his barons, who were inspecting the scaffolds at the causeway entrance. As Sorne approached the king, he avoided looking at the gallows. They made him sick. Everything about King Charald made him sick. If he stayed too much longer, he would become as corrupt as poor Zabier.

'They're already here,' the king crowed, gesturing to the Wyrds waiting halfway down the causeway. 'I knew the scaffolds would make them sit up and take notice.'

As a group, they stepped onto the causeway. It was midday, very early spring. The sky was clear and the sun held the promise of warmth. A slight breeze stirred the lake's surface, so that it danced with diamonds of sunlight. The glare made Sorne narrow his eyes.

Imoshen's pale hair seemed to attract the sun. Her gaze flicked to the old man and child, who Charald had positioned just behind him. Sorne wanted to whisk them both away. He feared the king would strike out in rage. He feared the king's rage would be the one thing that prevented this plan from succeeding.

When they were still a body-length from the Wyrds, Charald gestured to the old man and child. 'As you see, I have two of your copperheads, and...' He jerked his head, indicating the scaffolds behind him. 'I've prepared a little welcoming party. They're going to dance for me.'

The two men behind Imoshen stiffened, but did not speak.

Imoshen closed her eyes. When she opened them, they seemed to glow with the reflected light from the causeway and the lake. Sorne could feel her gift from where he stood. Now he feared her rage would impact on the negotiations.

But when she spoke her voice was calm. 'You have a son, who is nearly three. He has a club foot.'

'Yes.' Charald's response was wary.

Imoshen gestured behind her. 'Look atop the wall, above the gate.'

As she spoke, a boy was lifted up so that he sat on the stonework, legs dangling over the drop. His white-blond hair shone in the sun. One of the T'En held him around the waist. They said something to him and he waved.

'That could be any child.' Charald's voice held scorn. 'Why, from this distance it could be one of your own brats.'

'He has a club foot.'

'Not an uncommon ailment.'

'He calls himself Printh Thedon.'

Sorne saw the king flinch.

'Your king's guard are on their way here to report that the prince was taken yesterday afternoon, from his nursery.' Imoshen paused to let this sink in. 'He disappeared in the arms of a T'En warrior.'

'Why should I care? I have another heir.'

'King Matxin's grandchild? You would give your kingdom to the grandson of the man who stole your throne?'

Sorne could see the fury building in the king. His neck grew taut and his shoulders tight. Sorne glanced to the old man and child, trying to catch the old man's eye. They needed to edge away so the king's anger didn't find an outlet in them.

But to Sorne's amazement, Charald maintained his composure.

'The brat's a cripple. He'll never sit on the throne.' The king dismissed his son. 'The Warrior sent a vision. I'll have a healthy son who will rule after me.'

'We know. We've had the same vision. But you will have no more children. This is the son the Warrior intends to rule Chalcedonia. Prince Cedon will be whole. Once our healer straightens his club foot, he will be fit to take the throne.'

Sorne saw the king go very still.

The silence stretched. Bird cries carried on the breeze.

'The Warrior sent you a vision?' Charald was cautious, but hopeful. 'You can heal him?'

Relief made Sorne light-headed.

'We can. However, we are not gods, only the servants of the gods,' Imoshen said. 'The bones will have to be taught to grow the right way. We'll need until next spring to be sure.'

'Next spring?' Eskarnor muttered. 'I'm not spending another bloody winter in the snow.'

Sorne felt Imoshen's gift surge.

'Winter cusp,' Charald said.

'We cannot put to sea in winter,' she protested. 'The storms—'

'Winter cusp. That's my final offer.'

Sorne willed her to accept. The king could not afford to appear weak. Eskarnor was only looking for an excuse.

'Winter's cusp then. We want safe passage to the port, for all our people, including those on the estates. And' – she gestured to the captives – 'we want the old man and child, as a sign of your good faith. You have not kept your word before.'

'Have them. They're worthless.' King Charald caught the old man by the shoulder and shoved him forward. He stumbled. The child tried to help him. He recovered and drew her behind Imoshen, past the two men and behind the warriors.

'We'll make the exchange at the headlands on the first day of winter,' Imoshen said.

'Very well. But any Wyrds who remain in Chalcedonia after winter's cusp will be hunted down and executed.'

'So be it.'

Chapter Seventeen

TOBAZIM CLEANED HIS nib and studied his plans. He'd been awake since he'd heard the news about the prince last night. Even though he wasn't sure they were staying, he'd been driven by a rush of gift-inspired excitement. Since dawn, he'd been working on his plans to incorporate the ruined palace with Kyredeon's original palace and make the living spaces more efficient.

Buoyed by his gift, he felt nothing, not the cushion under his legs, not the hours spent at his kneeling-desk. Visions of a three-storey atrium swam in his feverish mind. He'd designed it to impress, and it needed a sculpture as the focal point: something innovative, something remarkable that would echo the daring of his design. He was only vaguely aware of Haromyr and Athlyn entering the chamber.

'How can you sit there scribbling when the causare is meeting with King Charald right at this moment?' Haromyr asked.

Tobazim shrugged, as Athlyn picked up a jade sculpture depicting two lovers in coitus on a galloping horse. After tilting it this way and that, he held it up. 'Is this even possible?'

Tobazim glanced to Haromyr and they both laughed.

Athlyn blushed.

One of the Malaunje who had escaped the winery with them opened the door. 'The causare returned with the two Malaunje King Charald was going to hang. The all-father wants everyone to the main courtyard. He has an announcement to make–'

'Exile?' a voice demanded in the hall outside. 'We face exile? You jest?'

'Exile or death,' someone replied.

'Exile?' Tobazim repeated, disappointed but not surprised.

'We won't know what's going on if we don't go to the main courtyard,' Haromyr said, practical as always. They headed out.

Tobazim pushed the kneeling-desk aside and followed them.

They joined the crowd, jostling for places on the many balconies and verandahs overlooking the main courtyard. The buildings were three and four storeys high, and every vantage point was packed. The courtyard contained a fountain down one end and several famous works by the High Golden Age sculptor Iraayel. These were the envy of the other brotherhoods.

The *Fallen All-father* took pride of place, its delicately veined marble gleaming in the sun. It depicted an injured all-father. His voice-of-reason and hand-of-force stood over him, ready to defend him to the death, and it never failed to move Tobazim. This was the essence of what the brotherhoods meant to him: to shelter and protect. Since Learon's death, he could not look on it without feeling angry.

Kyredeon stood with his two seconds and several of his inner circle.

'What's this talk of exile?' someone yelled from the verandah opposite Tobazim.

'Yes, what's happening?'

'What of the boy prince? Can't the causare renegotiate the accord?'

'I heard the Mieren king planned to kill us all.'

'Rubbish.'

'No, I heard it, too.'

'We'll be lucky to reach the ships.'

'We can fight. Why give up what's ours?'

There was a chorus of warriors ready and willing to fight.

Kyredeon held up his hands and the courtyard fell silent. 'It's true. The Mieren king meant to break his word and massacre us on the road to port. The causare has struck a bargain. In exchange for safe passage to the sea, we heal the king's heir and hand him over once we're on our ships. We leave the city, leave Chalcedonia by winter cusp. Anyone left behind will be hunted down and executed.'

This was greeted with disbelief and objections. Voices bombarded Tobazim from all directions. Even though he'd suspected the worst, now that it was real and they had a time limit, he could not imagine abandoning the city to the Mieren.

'Where will we go?' someone called out. 'There are Mieren everywhere.'

'King Charald conquered all the mainland kingdoms of the Secluded Sea and those that revolted are at war with him. We'll never be safe from him.'

'We'd be better off staying and fighting,' another person yelled.

'I can't imagine the all-fathers walking out of the city and handing it over to the Mieren,' Haromyr muttered.

'No. It's the all-mothers,' Ceyne admitted, joining them. 'They don't care about dishonour if it means saving the children.'

'It's not dishonourable to save the children,' Tobazim said, thinking of his choice-mother. 'Without them, we have no future.'

To Sorne, the king seemed to be back to his old self: alert and energetic. It made him realise how much Charald had faded in the years he'd been away.

Right now, the king stood in front of his tent, ordering the barons about. Nitzane and Eskarnor were to return to port with him. It was an old ploy – Charald would keep those he trusted the least close by him. The rest of the barons were to maintain the siege. This separated the two barons from their supporters.

Besides, Charald had to maintain the pressure on the Wyrds. The barons and their men were a visible reminder that the Wyrds would be handing over their city come winter cusp. Messengers were to be allowed out of the city, and Wyrds were allowed in.

'This has given him hope,' Nitzane whispered to Sorne. 'Perhaps now he'll leave my boy alone.'

'You don't want the throne for your son?'

'I used to think so. But seeing King Charald run himself ragged trying to keep ahead of Eskarnor convinced me it's not worth the trouble.' He grinned. 'When you're a king, there's always some greedy bastard trying to steal your throne.'

Sorne smiled. But the problem was, as long as Charald believed Nitzane was a threat, the baron was in danger. And, as long as Charald was distrustful of his barons, he was vulnerable. A king was only as strong as the barons who supported him. Today the king appeared well, but his mind and body were fading. Only Sorne and the king's manservant were aware of Charald's mental lapses, but his physical deterioration was evident to everyone.

Nitzane left to pack, and Sorne did likewise.

While returning the documents to Zabier's chest, he came across the bottle of pains-ease and realised he could absolve Nitzane of trying to poison the king by revealing Zabier's actions. Acting on impulse, Sorne grabbed the bottle and went to the king's tent. The public section, with its long table, brazier and rich fittings, was deserted. Going through to the back, he found Charald sitting on his bunk, hands across his knees.

He looked tired rather than triumphant, and his trembling had returned. So much for the illusion of good health.

'I've done it.' The king looked up. 'I've freed my kingdom of Wyrds and I'll have a healthy heir. I've finally given the Warrior what He wanted and He's rewarded me.'

'Sire, you were right to suspect poison.' Sorne showed him the bottle of pains-ease.

The manservant hurried over looking worried.

'Pains-ease?' The king read the label.

'Pure.'

'Never use the stuff. And it's not a poison.'

'I know. I found this in the high priest's chest. In its pure form, like this, it brings visionary slumber.' Sorne watched Charald closely. 'I think High Priest Zabier may have put some in your wine the night you thought you'd been poisoned.'

'But...'

'It can make people ill. We could test it if you like. If you took a few drops and it made you feel nauseous, we'd know it was the pains-ease that made you sick and Baron Nitzane was not trying to poison you.'

'Wait.' Charald frowned. 'The high priest drank the same wine and he didn't slumber like a baby.'

Sorne looked down, feigning shame. 'My king, the high priest was addicted to pains-ease in this form. He took a little every day. Did you ever wonder why his eyes appeared glassy?'

Charald swore. 'I never liked that fellow. Now I know why.' He thought for a moment, then beckoned his manservant. 'Bring me a glass of wine.'

The man provided one and the king opened the bottle.

'How much?'

'I don't know. I never use the stuff.'

'Don't want to make myself violently ill, but I need to take enough to test your theory.'

'If I may?' The manservant poured a small amount into the wine. 'My father was an apothecary and my brother learnt the trade.'

They waited. It wasn't long before the king went pale and began sweating. He cursed softly under his breath and rubbed a trembling hand across his chin. 'So now we know.'

Sorne took one more risk. 'Sire, I don't doubt for a moment that Eskarnor desires your throne, but I think you may have misinterpreted Nitzane's actions.'

'How so? He's been shoring up alliances with the Chalcedonian barons.'

'To defend you from Eskarnor and the southern barons.'

Charald's eyes widened. He looked ill and old, but he also looked hopeful.

'Nitzane's grandfather served you loyally all his life. His brother owes the kingship of Navarone to you and Nitzane owes his wealth and standing in Chalcedonia to you. If Eskarnor stole the throne, the first thing he would do is strip Nitzane of his estates and distribute them to his loyal men. It's in Nitzane's best interests to keep you on the throne.'

'You're right. I'm glad. I always like Nitzel's grandsons.' He rubbed his face and swayed.

'Lie back, sire. You look tired.'

'I am tired. Tired of warring.' Charald lay back on his bunk. 'Even in the years that I wasn't actually at war, I was watching the other kingdoms to make sure they weren't plotting against me. They've forced war on me. All I've ever done is defend myself and the throne. Oskane never told me it would be like this.' He lifted his head and looked around. 'Where is Oskane?'

Startled, Sorne met the manservant's eyes. The man wasn't surprised, and that worried Sorne.

'Oskane's dead, sire,' Sorne said gently.

'That's right. He's dead. Comes a time when all of a man's friends are dead and he even starts to miss his old enemies.'

Sorne sat by the king until he fell asleep. Then he beckoned the manservant and they moved away from the bunk. 'How often does he ask for Oskane?'

'Only when he's tired or stressed.'

'And that's when the trembling gets worse?'

The manservant nodded. 'And the pains in his stomach and back. But his urine hasn't gone that deep purple again.'

'Has he consulted the saw-bones?'

'No. The king doesn't trust him.' The manservant glanced over his shoulder; Charald was snoring. 'He's been getting worse this last year. The pains in his stomach and back are so bad, some nights he can't sleep and then he raves—'

'Madness?'

'No. He's afraid everyone is out to steal his throne. And he's right.'

Sorne winced. 'Has anyone else heard him ask for Oskane?'

'I think the high priest suspected.'

'When we reach the port, keep the other servants away from the king's private chambers. As long as you and I shield him, we can cover for him. He might be ailing, but if they knew his mind was slipping...' Sorne shuddered.

It was just one more thing for him to worry about. Instead of returning to his tent, he made his way to Nitzane's tent, where he found the baron drinking wine with his captain.

Nitzane greeted Sorne. 'You can settle this. Ballendin says Charald wants me with him, to keep an eye on me. I say it is because he doesn't see me and my son as a threat, now that his son will sit on the throne.'

'That's what I came to see you about.' Sorne kept his voice low. 'I've convinced the king his recent stomach upset was caused by a bad reaction to pains-ease. This puts you in the clear. He's always had a soft spot for you and your brother, because you're Nitzel's grandsons. You must seize the opportunity to prove your loyalty.

'This evening the king will dine with the barons. Charald is afraid he won't live long enough for his son to grow up and retain the throne. The last thing this kingdom needs is a civil war, with Queen Jaraile on one side and you on the other, in competition to set your sons on the throne. After you two have battled each other to a standstill, Eskarnor will step in and wipe out the winner. This is why you need to swear an oath to the king, promising loyalty to protect his son until the boy is old enough to defend himself. Speak to Baron Kerminzto, he's the queen's kin and he seems like a sensible man. Get the old nobility of Chalcedonia to make this oath. It needs to be done tonight, in front of the southern barons.'

'The Warrior's-voice speaks sense,' Ballendin said. 'Eskarnor can't seize the throne if you and Charald are united.'

'I'll do it. Then I can bring my boy home. I miss him,' Nitzane said. 'Send for the Chalcedonian barons, Ballendin.'

Sorne walked out of the tent with the captain. 'Nitzane shouldn't send for his son until after the Wyrds have sailed and the prince is returned.'

'Don't worry. I can curb his enthusiasm.'

'Good. You'll be in court?'

'I can be.'

'You should be. Nitzane...' Sorne hesitated.

'He's a good lad,' Ballendin said. 'But he's not his brother or his grandfather.'

'Yes.' Sorne was relieved.

He was even more relieved that evening when the Chalcedonian barons entered the royal tent with Nitzane in the lead. Someone, probably Ballendin, must have coached Nitzane, because he made a fine speech about loyalty and the benefits of continuity of leadership. He sank to his knees and swore, in the event of the king's death, to ensure the smooth running of the kingdom until the young prince came of age. Baron Kerminzto went next and the rest of the Chalcedonian barons took their turn.

With tears in his eyes, the king accepted their oaths.

Sorne glanced to Eskarnor. From the look the southern baron sent him, it was clear Eskarnor knew who was behind this cementing of alliances. Sorne had made a dangerous enemy.

Not to be outdone, Eskarnor sprang to his feet and gave the same oath. The southern lords followed suit, but no one was fooled.

Meanwhile, Sorne bided his time. As soon as he returned to port, he was going to visit the Father's church and ask for Zabier's assistant. Utzen would surely know where Zabier had sent Valendia.

IMOSHEN SAT IN front of the aviary with her infant daughter. Frayvia knelt beside them and threw a handful of grain through the bars. A flurry of birds swooped down, fighting over the food. Birds bred for their beauty, birds bred for their song – the aviary was a fluttering, fluting mass, each creature a work of art.

Umaleni squealed, her plump little legs kicking in delight. With her hands around Umaleni's chest, Imoshen could feel the excited racing of her daughter's heart. She opened her senses to the mid-morning sunlight sparkling on the tiles, the crisp air of early spring with just a hint of warmth to come and the feel of her daughter in her arms – perfect. She should really capture it for memory-sharing with Umaleni's father.

If he still lived.

Her arms tightened on their daughter. Ardonyx had to live.

'I can't believe we're sailing away, come winter cusp,' Frayvia marvelled. 'Where will we go? You spoke of finding sanctuary.'

Imoshen laughed. 'Don't rush me. I've only just got the brotherhoods to agree to exile.' In truth, she'd been thinking about it since the city was first beseiged. 'Of the five mainland kingdoms King Charald conquered, three are still ruled by his subject kings. Two have revolted, but he sent war barons to subdue them. We don't want to sail into a war. That only leaves the island of Ivernia.'

'The Sagoras?'

Imoshen nodded. 'They came from beyond the Endless Ocean three hundred years ago. For all we know, they were fleeing persecution like us. They've built their reputation as scholars. Hopefully, a people who value knowledge will be less likely to be afraid of us because we're different. I'll send a message.'

Umaleni gave a shrill of excitement, almost indistinguishable from the birds' cries. Imoshen laughed.

'Imoshen?' Vittoryxe's voice was rich with disapproval.

Imoshen bit her bottom lip and glanced to Frayvia, who sent her a look of sympathy. Schooling her face, Imoshen came to her feet and passed Umaleni to her devotee. She kissed her daughter's downy head.

With just the right touch of deference, Frayvia acknowledged the gift-tutor, then went inside.

Imoshen summoned a smile. Surely someone who bred such beautiful birds had some joy in her heart? 'We were just admiring your birds, Vittoryxe. They are a work of art.'

'A work of art?' The gift-tutor's gaze turned hard and glittering. 'Will there be a place for art when we are exiled? Or will we be reduced to grubbing in the dirt to feed ourselves?' Vittoryxe shook her head. 'We need to call the inner circle together. One of the initiates has gotten herself pregnant without permission.'

'Who?'

'Deyzi.'

'She's my age, almost an adept. Surely–'

'There's a right way to go about these things. She's taken a Malaunje lover, which means the baby could be a half-blood. We won't know until the pregnancy goes past the seven small moons and, even if she does carry the baby for the full year, it could be stillborn.' Vittoryxe's mouth grew thin with disapproval. 'We don't want her gift corrupting because she's broken-hearted. That's why all pregnancies have to be approved by the inner circle. I know you've ignored our practices and gotten away with it, but our customs are there for a reason. To keep us safe.'

Vittoryxe paused as if waiting for Imoshen to argue, but she'd had an idea. Later, she sought out Reoden.

'Why can't you ensure all our T'En babies are healthy?'

'I wish I could.' The healer poured spiced wine for them both. 'But it's not a simple healing, like urging flesh to knit. The baby will either grow right, or it will have malformed organs that eventually kill it. This wrongness is embedded deep in every fibre of the growing infant. I don't have that level of skill.'

PART TWO

Chapter Eighteen

RONNYN NUDGED HIS sister. 'Race you to the top of the next dune.'

He took off, imagining himself the leader of a great brotherhood and his sister, a warrior from a rival sisterhood. His mother's stories filled his head with visions of honour and courage, empowering his pounding heart. His feet speared through the fine dune grass, sinking into soft, white sand. He made it through the valley between the dunes, leapt a patch of snow and started up the other side. His thigh muscles protested as he put everything he had into beating Aravelle.

And this time he did.

He made it to the top of the dune ahead of her, hardly able to believe it. They both bent double to suck in deep breaths, and then straightened up. That was when he realised he was taller than her. At thirteen, she was a year and a half older. Today's victory was sweet indeed.

Ronnyn couldn't help smiling.

Aravelle's eyes narrowed and she shoved him so hard he lost his balance and fell backwards, sprawling on the soft, powder-fine sand. His protest died on his lips as she frowned past him.

'Is that a body?'

He scrambled around on his knees and shaded his eyes. It had stormed the night before, but today the wind had blown the clouds away. Now the setting sun gilded the dunes and the shallows of the secluded beach.

Ronnyn peered west into the glare, trying to make out the object that lay on the sand, exposed by the tide.

The stranded dark shape could be one of the rocks that protruded from the beach, but he didn't think so. They'd crossed the island, aiming for this particular inlet because this was where debris from the storms washed in. They'd been hoping for something useful, never thinking to find a body.

'Come on.' Aravelle ran down the far side of the dune with him at her heels. Breaking free of its plait, her long copper hair streamed behind her and her bare feet flashed, kicking up spurts of sand.

They slowed to a walk as they reached the hard-packed sand where the sea had retreated. Between them and the body, the beach seethed as a multitude of tiny azure crabs scurried for safety. If six-year-old Vittor had been with them, he would have chased the crabs, chortling with glee.

But Ronnyn was glad their little brother was not with them today.

The dead man had been a fisherman, by his clothes.

He wore a wet-weather sealskin vest just like their father's. His hair was the colour of damp beach sand. The wind had dried long tendrils that stirred as though they had a life of their own.

'One of the Mieren?' Ronnyn had never seen their people's ancestral enemy.

'Must be,' Aravelle whispered. 'Probably washed overboard during the storm.'

'It's possible. We haven't found any wreckage.' Ronnyn stepped closer and dropped into a crouch. His weight collapsed crab tunnels beneath him, and bubbles rose from the saturated sand. The wind blew wisps of his white hair into his eyes and he tucked the strands behind his ears.

Aravelle perched beside him then reached out tentatively, rolling the dead man onto his back.

A moan escaped him.

They both jumped with fright. Ronnyn lost his balance and he fell on his backside. Cold seawater seeped through his breeches. The tide was creeping in.

Aravelle's alarmed mulberry eyes met his. Her vivid red lips parted in surprise. She sprang to her feet. 'We must get help.'

'Wait.' Ronnyn scrambled to his feet, gesturing to the sea. 'Tide's on the turn. We don't want him to drown before we get back.'

His sister took the fisherman's arms, while Ronnyn took his legs. The man was full grown, but not much bigger than them. Together, they carried him beyond the seaweed that marked the high water line.

They were out of breath by the time they lowered him onto the soft, dry sand. Blood had dried on his forehead. A three-day growth shadowed his jaw, but under the chill of the evening air there was still warmth in his skin.

'He should be safe here,' Aravelle said. 'Come on.'

They ran up over the dunes, then through the spindly pines where twilight had already claimed the path. At last, they came to the crest of the final dune, and looked down on their secluded inlet. A single column of smoke told them dinner was cooking. This was their world. They'd come in from the north and the curve of the small beach stretched out on their left. The sea lay flat and glassy, reflecting their father's fishing boat as it rested at anchor.

On their right, the lagoon lay behind the dunes, surrounded by a flat area of arable soil. There was the vegetable patch, the smoke house and chicken coop. The billy-goat lifted his head and gave voice.

Nestled in the middle was their cottage. Made mostly from wreckage and driftwood, their home was silvered by the weather, but its shingle roof had protected them from many a winter storm.

Their mother stood at the front door, laughing as their father chased the three little ones across the beach. He advanced on them, his copper plait flying. First he caught plump little Itania who was only just walking. She squealed with delight as he lifted her high in the air, swinging her around. Laughing, he kissed her red-gold curls.

Then he tucked her under his arm and chased down Tamaron. The three-year-old ran across the beach, white hair streaming, determined to get away. Tripping in the soft sand, their little brother surrendered with a squeal of mock terror. Tamaron's peals of laughter carried up the dune to Ronnyn and Aravelle.

'Da!' Six-year-old Vittor sang, dancing just out of reach. 'Can't catch me, Da.'

Laden with two little ones, their father could not catch him, no matter how hard he tried. Ronnyn felt a smile tug at his lips and glanced at Aravelle. Like him, laughter illuminated her face.

Their mother shaded her eyes and waved to them on the dune. It was just like any other evening, but today they had news.

'There's a fisherman,' Aravelle called.

'Washed up on the beach,' Ronnyn shouted, wanting to share the excitement. 'He's alive.'

'What?' Their father put Tamaron and Itania down, then strode towards the dune. Their mother also ran to meet them.

Aravelle and Ronnyn plunged down the dune, legs sinking calf-deep in the cold, soft white sand. When they reached their father at the base, he steadied them.

'We dragged him up beyond high tide,' Ronnyn said. 'Come see.'

'I wanna see too,' Vittor cried.

Their parents exchanged looks. Their mother caught Vittor by the shoulders, drawing him close so that the back of his head rested against her abdomen, his white hair bright against the dark material.

Tamaron and Itania trotted over. They tugged on their mother's robe, wanting to be picked up.

'Come on, Da,' Aravelle urged. 'We'll show you.'

Again, their parents exchanged loaded looks.

'Where?' their father asked.

'Driftwood Beach,' Ronnyn supplied. Eager to be gone, he backed up the rise. 'Come on, Da.'

'Asher?' their mother whispered.

Their father turned a grim face to Aravelle and Ronnyn. 'You two stay here.'

'But Da–'

'But nothing. Do as you're told.'

Ronnyn was surprised and hurt. Their father never snapped at them. Stung, he watched their parents hug and kiss. Their copper hair mingled in the breeze, their love a bright shining thing that warmed his worried heart.

'Douse the fire, Sasoria,' Asher said. 'And keep the children inside. There might be more than one.'

Ronnyn caught Aravelle's eye. From her expression it was clear that she didn't understand either. They had been warned to run and hide if anyone came to the island, but this was different; the fisherman was injured and needed their help.

As their father set off, their mother turned towards the cottage, saying, 'Come in, now. Dinner time.'

Ronnyn and Aravelle protested vehemently, Vittor less so. He was used to being excluded.

'Ronnyn, bring Vittor and Tamaron,' their mother ordered. 'Vella, bring Itania.'

Aravelle picked up their little sister, while Ronnyn took both his brothers' hands.

The cottage was dim and smelt of oregano and chicken. Only this morning, father had killed a belligerent young rooster that had pecked Itania. Roast chicken was a treat. The aroma made Ronnyn's mouth water and his stomach rumbled.

His mother hurried to the fire, throwing sand on the hearth to put out the flames. 'Close the shutters, Vella, then light the lamp.'

Aravelle put Itania down and reached for the fish-oil lamp. The moment the toddler's feet touched the reed matting she made for the door.

Aravelle thrust the lamp into Vittor's hands and ran after Itania. Ronnyn followed. They caught their baby sister just outside the door. Itania laughed and wriggled, delighted with the game.

Ronnyn ignored his little sister's giggles, fixing on his big sister's face. 'We were the ones who found the man. We should go help Da.'

Aravelle nodded. She deposited Itania inside the cottage and shut the half-door.

'We're going to help Da carry the man back,' Aravelle announced through the opening, and they took off.

Their mother called them, but they ignored her. Ronnyn had never disobeyed his parents in his life. It made him uncomfortable but, at the same time, he was determined. He felt the fisherman was his responsibility, his and Aravelle's.

They took familiar paths, running from one side of the island to the other in the growing twilight. By unspoken consent, they did not to try to catch up with their father, but paced themselves, jogging for a bit, then walking briskly.

Ronnyn was sure Da would see reason. He'd need their help to carry the man back, and it would be dark soon. For the second time that evening, they ran through the pines and negotiated the dunes on the far side of their island.

Only a sliver of sun hung above the horizon by the time they neared the top of the last dune. The sky had been scoured of clouds and, behind them in the east, the first stars had already appeared along with the eager small moon.

'Wait.' Aravelle caught Ronnyn's arm. 'Let me handle Da.'

He nodded. Now that they were here, he felt nervous.

At Aravelle's signal, they knelt just behind the lip of the dune where they could watch the beach unseen. Their father wasn't tending to the injured man. Instead, he paced up and down, running his hands through his hair, which had worked loose from its plait.

'What's Da doing?' Ronnyn whispered.

Aravelle nudged him and pointed. 'Lucky we moved him.' The sand where they'd found the fisherman was under water now.

As though he'd made a decision, Asher turned and strode over to the injured man.

'Now he'll help him,' Aravelle murmured.

Their father sank to kneel in the sand beside the fisherman. He placed his hands around the man's throat and put his whole weight into throttling him.

Unable to believe his eyes, Ronnyn reached for Aravelle. They watched in horrified silence as their father killed a defenceless man.

ARAVELLE FELT HOT, then cold, then sick. She didn't recognise the stranger who'd just strangled an unconscious fisherman. This killer was not the gentle, laughing father who'd taught her to mix inks so she could capture the line of a wind-bent tree in a single brush stroke.

The stranger, who wore her father's face, released the dead man's throat and sat back on his heels, staring blankly at what he had done.

'Why?' Ronnyn whispered, tears falling down his cheeks. He turned to her as they crouched behind the crest of the dune. 'Why, Vella?'

She had no answer.

A sob escaped Ronnyn. She slid her arm around his shoulder and pulled him close. The movement attracted their father's gaze. He lurched to his feet and strode up the dune towards them, his expression thunderous.

Stunned, Aravelle could only stare as he bore down on them.

'I told you not to come. Why did you follow me? *Why?*'

He hauled them to their feet, although they were almost as tall as him now. Aravelle twisted out of his grasp and darted away.

When Asher released Ronnyn, her brother fell to his knees and flung his arms around their father's waist. 'I'm sorry, Da.' A sob choked him. 'I'm sorry.'

With a groan, their father knelt and hugged Ronnyn. As they wept in each other's arms, tears blurred Aravelle's vision. Asher lifted an arm, beckoning her, but she shook her head, unable to reconcile the fisherman's murderer with the man she knew to be her father.

'I don't understand.' Ronnyn drew back to search their father's face. 'Why did you kill him?'

'He was one of the Mieren,' Asher said, as if that explained everything. 'He would have betrayed us. I had to protect my family.' Asher came to his feet as though fighting a great weight. 'We must bury the body. Can't leave it for the wild dogs.' He gestured into the hollow between the dunes. 'Dig a grave down there.'

And he strode down the other side of the dune to retrieve the fisherman's body. Ronnyn went to dig the grave.

Aravelle followed, but she felt disconnected from reality. A noise like the crashing of the waves filled her head, drowning all sounds. The strange sensation did not ease as they dug the grave with their bare hands and tipped the man's body in.

As their father carefully arranged the dead man's limbs, the wrongness of it made Aravelle hot and furious. Again tears stung her eyes. 'Why honour him in death?'

'He was someone's father, someone's son.'

Aravelle stared down at the husk that used to be a person. She'd helped her mother pluck the rooster for dinner. It worried her that once life was extinguished, people were just so much dead meat.

'But why kill him?' Ronnyn asked. 'We could've asked him not to tell anyone about us.'

'Mieren can't be trusted,' Asher stated. 'Why do you think I sail to another island to trade the sea-boar ivory? I don't want the trader knowing where we live. He makes a big profit on our ivory because he knows I don't dare take it to anyone else. Only greed keeps his mouth shut. No...' Asher gestured to the dead man. 'Greed would've opened the fisherman's mouth. Someone would've paid him to find out about us. Then word would've reached our old brotherhood and, before long, we'd see a boatload of silver-haired warriors come to take us back to the city. They'd punish your mother and I for running away. They'd send you boys to a sisterhood to rear because you're pure T'En.' His breath left him in a sigh of defeat. 'It's why we ran in the first place. So we could keep you, Ronnyn.'

Asher pulled him close and hugged him.

'I'm sorry, Da,' Ronnyn whispered.

Their father drew back, hands on Ronnyn's shoulders, face earnest. 'Nothing to be sorry for, son. It's not your fault you were born T'En. It's not your fault your mother couldn't bear to give you up and I couldn't bear to see her hurt. It's no one's fault that Vittor and Tamaron were also born pure T'En. And now this new baby, who knows what it will be...' He rubbed a trembling hand across his mouth. 'So no one must know about us.'

Ronnyn nodded.

They could not go back. They'd always known this. That was just the way it was.

Righteous indignation filled Aravelle. No one would break up her family, not while she lived. A fierce love and determination filled her.

But, at the same time, her father had killed a defenceless man and that was wrong.

Asher studied the sky. 'Getting dark. We must bring rocks to stop the wild dogs digging up the body.'

So they collected rocks. It took four trips before their father was satisfied. All the time, the evening's events kept going around and around in Aravelle's mind. Try as she might, she could not see an alternative. Her parents' old brotherhood must never find them; Mieren could not be trusted. Their father had to protect them.

Yet... 'Doesn't feel right to kill a helpless man,' she muttered.

Their father stacked the last rocks on the grave, then stood up and wiped his forehead. 'You know I grew up with Mieren before going to the city, but I never told you why I left. When I was thirteen, the people of my village broke into our house. They killed my parents and set fire to the cottage. I would have burned to death, but I jumped out the attic window, fought my way through them and ran across country to the city.'

'Oh, Da...' Ronnyn whispered.

'These were people I'd known all my life, yet they turned on us. You can't trust True-men.' He grimaced. 'It's late. Time to go home.'

By the time they reached the far side of the island, both moons were up, bright enough to cast shadows. With all the shutters closed, their cottage was a dark shape against the silver sand. Unless a fishing boat came into the little inlet, they would not spot it, or their father's boat.

Asher stopped. 'Vella, Ronnyn, promise me you won't tell the little ones what happened today. I don't want them growing up in the shadow of fear.'

'I promise,' Ronnyn said immediately.

'Of course.' Aravelle found it easy to make the promise. She wished the fisherman had never been washed up on their island, or that he'd been dead when they found him; anything to relieve her father of the burden that stole the laughter from his eyes.

'Good.' He hugged them both, but she remained stiff in his arms.

She couldn't help it. For all that she understood the necessity of killing the injured man, she couldn't accept it.

When she pulled away, Asher did not comment.

Six-year-old Vittor must have been watching; he threw the door open. 'You're late. Ma made us wait and I'm starving.'

He laughed, stepping aside to reveal the dinner table. The roast chicken sat on the feast day plate and a gift sat in front of Ronnyn's place. 'Ronnyn's twelve today!'

Aravelle blinked. How could she have forgotten? The little ones shrieked with excitement and ran over to hug Ronnyn.

Their mother laughed and looked to their father. But Aravelle noticed how Sasoria's expression sobered when she saw their father's grim eyes.

Unaware of this, Vittor led the little ones back to the table and helped them onto their seats.

'Wash up. Then we can have dinner.' Sasoria pointed to the back door and the rainwater barrel.

'We've already washed,' Ronnyn said.

'Your voice.' Concerned, she touched his forehead. 'You're not hot. Is your throat sore?'

'His voice is breaking.' Asher smiled proudly.

Their mother laughed and caught Ronnyn by the ears, pulling his face down to hers to kiss both his cheeks. 'Silly me. Of course it is.'

Ronnyn grinned at Aravelle, his forehead crinkling in a way that could be earnest and endearing but which tonight she found annoying. He was pleased with himself, as if he'd done something clever.

She sniffed. It wasn't like any of them had control over what they were – male or female, Malaunje or T'En.

Ronnyn unwrapped his gift – one of Da's shirts made down, and a fish-gutting knife of his own. Ma and Da hugged him, then she and their mother served up the evening meal.

It was all very normal, and all very subtly wrong.

Nothing was said about the fisherman. The little ones were tucked into bed and the kitchen cleaned, and still nothing was said.

Their father waited while she and Ronnyn climbed up the ladder to the loft above her parent's bed, and then he doused the light. There was no point in burning precious lamp oil unless there was work to do, but Aravelle wished she could have sat up; she could not sleep.

She lay awake for a long time.

At last she heard her father's low voice as he told her mother what had happened. His harsh sobs carried clearly, along with their mother's reassurance.

'You did the right thing, Asher, the only thing.'

'I know. But... sometimes I wonder if *we* did the right thing, breaking the covenant. What will we do when–'

'Hush.'

Restless, Aravelle pushed the down-filled quilt aside and crawled to the window, set in the sloping roof. She opened the shutter, welcoming a shaft of moonlight. It illuminated Tamaron and Vittor's sleeping forms, and reflected in Ronnyn's watchful eyes.

Silently, he joined her at the window. There was enough moonlight to see his features clearly.

Without a word, they slipped out onto the shingles and crouched there, balanced against the steep pitch of the roof, hugging their knees. For a while they said nothing, letting the slight breeze lift their hair and play with their nightshirts.

The double full moons illuminated the bay and sands. Moonlight silvered Ronnyn's white hair, reminding her that when his gift started to manifest, his hair would darken to silver. And then he would be different from her, more than her.

She'd been born Malaunje like their parents. It hadn't mattered when they were growing up, but now that she thought about it, she resented it fiercely. According to their mother, no one knew why the majority of their race were born Malaunje and only some were pure T'En, heirs to the gifts. But this divided them, and it had driven their parents to run away.

'Da had to do it,' Ronnyn said. 'I'd do it to protect us from the Mieren.'

Aravelle knew he was imagining himself the leader of a great brotherhood, protecting his people. All their lives they'd played games based on their mother's stories of the T'Enatuath – games of honour and bravery – but, since she turned thirteen last winter, the games had grown hollow as it dawned on her that one day she was not going to meet her warrior over the next dune.

Would she ever know the love their parents shared?

'Do you think we should tell Vittor about the hide?' Ronnyn asked. Their father had built a hiding place, in case the Mieren came to their island. 'What if we were captured and he was left–'

'If he was left alone on the island...' Vittor would not survive. She couldn't bring herself to say it, so she started again. 'If we were captured, I'd want all of us to be together.'

'You're right.'

Aravelle heard the catch in Ronnyn's voice, and knew he'd understood what she'd left unsaid. 'You notice Da didn't tell us to run to the hide if the brotherhood's T'En warriors come.'

Ronnyn went very still.

'Because they'd find us.' Aravelle could not hold it in. 'They'd sense us with their gifts. We'd have no protection from them.'

'Perhaps it would not be so bad if the brotherhood found us,' Ronnyn said slowly. 'Perhaps they wouldn't be angry with our parents.'

Aravelle glared at him.

He shrugged. 'Hueryx didn't sound so bad. He was kind to Ma.'

'How can you say that? Even if he's nice, the brotherhoods are bound by the covenant. They'd have to give you, Vittor and Tamaron to a sisterhood to rear, and I wouldn't see you until you were all grown up. By then you'd be proper T'En, and you'd refuse to acknowledge me...' Hot tears stung her eyes, strangling her words. The tears she hadn't shed over the dead fisherman cascaded down her cheeks. Horrible, harsh sobs wrenched at her chest.

'I'll never forget you, Vella. Never.' Ronnyn hugged her, his voice thick. 'I didn't mean it. I don't want the brotherhood to find us. I don't even know why I said it.'

But she knew why. Like her, he wanted more than endless days of working to put food on the table. They lived the lives of struggling Mieren, when they were heirs to all the beauty and knowledge of the Celestial City.

She was so angry, her head hurt. Impatient, she thrust him away.

'I said I was sorry,' Ronnyn protested.

'I'm not angry with you.' How could she tell him that she was angry with their parents, with their people, with the Mieren? With life. 'I'm not angry with you. I'm just... angry.'

'You're always angry about something.'

'I know. I can't help it.'

'Vella.' He offered her his hand.

After a moment, she took it and held on.

Chapter Nineteen

AFTER ARRIVING IN port, Sorne went straight to the Father's church, taking time only to change. Now he wore the too-short rich vestments of a high-ranking priest, borrowed from Zabier's wardrobe. Perhaps he would start a fashion for calf-length robes. But fine robes could not hide the fact that he was a Wyrd and his kind had been exiled. The whispers and looks both here and back in the palace reminded him that he was a half-blood in a world of True-men, and they could turn on him at any time.

Priests scurried and penitents scattered as he strode the familiar corridors. He was sure they were running to the person who had stepped in to fill the void when Zabier left with the king.

Sorne headed for the high priest's private chambers, where he found a round little True-man wearing the robes of high priest.

Despite having only a few moments' warning, the True-man greeted him at the door and led him into the formal chamber. Several curious assistants watched through the doorway, but Utzen was not amongst them.

'Warrior's-voice.' The plump True-man's gaze avoided his missing eye and dropped to the ruby on Sorne's six-fingered hand. First Oskane had worn it, then Zabier. This new high priest had to be wondering if Sorne intended to claim the role. 'We did not have word the king was returning.'

'No, it was a sudden decision. The siege has been successful. The Wyrds are to be exiled by winter cusp. I see

you have moved into the high priest's private chambers.'
Complete with hidden stair and apartment for his mistress
or, in Zabier's case, secret family.

'Yes. We were all deeply saddened when we received
word of High Priest Zabier's death, but someone had to
ensure the smooth running of the church. The people of
Chalcedonia rely on us for spiritual guidance.'

'Of course. You are lucky High Priest Zabier left his
assistant behind. Where is Utzen?'

'Ah. Unfortunately, he disappeared the first night of the
riots.'

Sorne remembered the riots: burning buildings, mobs in
the street and the bodies of Wyrds strung from shop signs.
If Zabier had tried to send Valendia to safety that night,
Utzen might not have made it out of the city. Had she
been killed and her body thrown in a nameless grave? Fear
cramped Sorne's belly, but he schooled his face to betray
nothing.

He focused on the high priest, who was watching him
intently. For all that this man reminded Sorne of someone's
jolly uncle, he had to have political acumen to have risen to
this position. 'I'm sorry, I don't know your name.'

'High Priest Faryx. I have served the church, man
and boy, for forty years. Please take a seat. I'll call for
refreshments.'

Sorne recognised the ploy. Faryx was treating him like a
guest. The True-man was determined not to give up power.
That suited Sorne. He knew what was involved in running
an organisation this size, and did not want the task. As
long as he found Valendia and ensured Imoshen and her
people reached the ships in safety, he was happy.

When he sank into a chair, Faryx relaxed a little. After
sending an assistant to bring the refreshments, the new
high priest took the seat opposite. Sorne remembered
how, when King Charald returned to Chalcedonia, King
Matxin's daughter had claimed sanctuary in this very
room. She had been a plain speaker.

'Let me be plain,' Sorne said. 'I am the king's advisor. You are the high priest of the Father's church, greatest of the Seven. I am sure we can help each other. The king has given me the task of ensuring all Wyrds are rounded up and exiled by winter cusp.' He hesitated, because he did not know if Faryx was aware of Zabier's secret family, or his relationship to Sorne. 'I have heard rumour of Wyrds being kept in the Father's church–'

'Here? Oh, no.' Faryx shook his head, drawing back a little. 'We have nothing to do with tainted blood.'

'High Priest Zabier carried out Wyrd sacrifices in his capacity as Father's-voice.'

'He did.' The corners of Faryx's mouth turned down in disgust. 'But that was between him and the king. It was not approved of by the established church.'

This came as a surprise to Sorne. He picked his words with care. 'During King Matxin's reign, I was in exile with King Charald. I was told the church condoned sacrifices.'

'During King Matxin's reign, the church did what it had to, to survive. Everyone did.' The high priest hesitated, then seemed to make a decision. 'You have been frank with me. Let me be frank with you. Our parishioners like ceremonies that consist of beautiful music, incense and singing. No one likes ceremonies that go horribly wrong, where people die. At King Charald's last sacrifice, fifteen people died, including one baron, the Warrior's-voice and four of his priests. Charald called them martyrs and we managed to smooth it over, but if the king intended to continue this practice, we...' He ran down as if aware he had been about to deliver an ultimatum. Faryx lifted his hands in a shrug. 'He is the king.'

'He is unpredictable.' Their eyes met, and Sorne was aware they had come close to speaking treason. 'But King Charald is infinitely preferable to Baron Eskarnor of Dace. Eskarnor fancies the crown. Baron Nitzane has united the Chalcedonian barons behind him and sworn loyalty to the king and his young heir. As long as Charald has Nitzane's support, Eskarnor can't make a move. That's why Charald invited them both back to the palace.'

'You're telling me this because...'

'You sit in the centre of a web that stretches across Chalcedonia. Your priests hear things and these things reach you. If Eskarnor's supporters attack Nitzane's estates, you'll hear.'

'Why should I let you know?'

'Eskarnor is from Dace. He has no respect for Chalcedonian gods. If he came into power, he would disband the church, steal its lands and wealth, and install Dacian gods and priests loyal to him.'

Faryx's eyes widened.

'Ask what happened in Navarone at the abbey.' Sorne shrugged. 'Then, if your priests notice Eskarnor's men-at-arms slipping into the city, let me know.'

'King Charald is lucky to have such a loyal servant,' Faryx said.

At that moment a penitent arrived with a tray of refreshments.

When the door closed Faryx turned back to Sorne. 'We heard the silverheads snatched Prince Cedon from the palace nursery, simply disappeared with him. How is this possible?'

'No one knows. The Wyrds have promised to return the boy with his club foot healed. King Charald believes the Warrior is acting through them to give him a healthy heir.'

Faryx's eyes widened, but all he said was, 'The king is very devout.'

'Very,' Sorne conceded. 'And he has appointed me to facilitate the Wyrd exile. I have reason to believe High Priest Zabier sent his assistant away with a half-blood female the night of the riots. She needs to be collected and exiled along with the rest of the Wyrds.'

'I know Utzen left with a cloaked woman, but I don't know what became of them. I'll make enquiries.'

Sorne thanked him. 'And I will advise the king against making sacrifices.'

'Excellent. Wine?' Faryx offered.
Sorne accepted.

RONNYN RAN ACROSS the dunes, feet spearing into the sand.
At the top of the dune he looked down across the beach
and saw Mieren boats, two of them. They'd come for
revenge. They'd come to kill his family. He had to warn
them. Had to get them safely into the hide.

But no matter how hard he tried, he couldn't run fast
enough. It felt like he was forging through waist-deep
surf, like nothing he could do would save himself or his
family.

'Ronnyn, wake up.' Aravelle shook him softly.

He came awake on a gasp, heart racing.

She drew him close. He relished the warmth of her
skin through the much-washed nightshirt. She rubbed his
back, uttering soft crooning noises, and he let her, too
grateful to protest.

'I was having a nightmare.'

'I know. You cried out in your sleep.'

'It was so real. The Mieren were here, coming after us.'
He felt her go still.

'Was it a vision?'

'No. I don't... my gift isn't moving yet.'

'A bad dream, that's all.' She sounded relieved. 'How
will you know when your gift starts manifesting itself?'

'I... I don't know.' He frowned. 'I don't think Ma and
Da know. Malaunje aren't privy to T'En secrets.'

'So how will you know?' she persisted.

'I don't know.' The thought both annoyed and excited
him. And he felt himself harden.

She pulled away.

'Sorry, I can't help it.'

'Roll over.'

So he did, giving her his back. She cuddled up to him.

'I'm sorry. It just happens.' More and more, recently.

'That'll probably be what it's like when your gift comes on you,' she whispered. 'It'll just happen.'

And he wouldn't have any control. That was why T'En children began their training when they were empowered, between thirteen and fourteen. Only he wouldn't get the training he needed. How would he know what to do? What if he hurt someone?

'You're thinking too hard.' Aravelle's gruff voice made him smile. 'Go to sleep.'

'You go to sleep.'

'Don't tell me what to do.'

'I wouldn't dare.'

He felt her chuckle, her chest pressed to his back.

Everything would be all right. No one knew they were here; they'd dealt with the fisherman. They'd been safe for twelve years.

But what about his gift?

'You're thinking again.'

'How can you tell? You gifted now?'

But this time his banter made her turn away.

He rolled over and sat up on one elbow. 'Vella?'

No answer.

'Vella?'

Silence.

'I didn't ask to be born T'En.'

Still no answer.

His parents' answer had been to run away. But what if that was the wrong answer?

He tensed. Their parents loved them and would never do anything to hurt them.

As he stretched out on his back, a small voice chipped away at his certainty. What if his parents had been wrong to run away? What if he lost control and hurt someone?

He'd never forgive himself.

The gifts were powerful. The T'En trained from the age of thirteen for twenty years to become an adept. What made him think he could manage on his own?

But surely his parents would have thought of this? They wouldn't put the others at risk if his gifts were dangerous. Look how quickly his father had acted, killing the injured fisherman to hide their family.

Then why did it take twenty years to become an adept?

Perhaps he should go back to the Celestial City?

And leave his family? It would tear him apart.

Tears burned his eyes as he faced the very real possibility that he would have to leave. It would break his heart, but if it meant keeping his family safe, he'd do it.

He'd do it in a heartbeat.

There. Now he had his answer, he was able to sleep.

'WHAT IS THIS?' Imoshen asked as Egrayne dropped the message in front of her. She picked it up, regarding the royal seal with some misgivings.

Egrayne sank into the seat opposite. It was late. They were tired. Between them lay a pile of scribbled notes, the logistics of exile – messages to outlying estates, messages to their ships. They'd been at it all evening, balancing the challenge of reaching port in time to set sail by winter cusp, while delaying as long as possible to bring in the harvest on their estates, since they didn't know when they would be able to grow their own food again.

Egrayne gestured. 'Open it.'

Imoshen broke the seal and unfolded the heavy paper. She scanned it quickly, then laughed and handed it to Egrayne. 'Sorne has been appointed to ensure our exile goes smoothly.'

Egrayne smiled. 'He's a clever one. You should–'

Iraayel thrust the door open. 'It's Saf. She's up to something, and I... you should come now. Both of you.'

Imoshen glanced to her voice-of-reason. Saffazi's fragile beauty hid a strong will and an equally wilful gift. They sprang to their feet, tiredness forgotten.

Iraayel led them out into the corridor up a floor and around to the scriptorium. It was dark. Imoshen tensed as soon as she stepped into the room, her senses alerted by gift-working.

Iraayel cursed. 'She promised to wait!'

'What is that girl up to now?' Egrayne muttered, striding past Imoshen. Egrayne was no longer responsible for her – she had begun her initiate training – but a mother never stops worrying about her children.

Fear prickled across Imoshen's skin; the gift-working felt too powerful for an initiate to be in control.

Iraayel took off at a run, weaving through the shelves.

'Wait.' Imoshen darted after him. 'Whatever you do, don't touch her.'

Imoshen reached the lamplit alcove in time to see her choice-son confront a Malaunje youth no older than him.

'What happened?' Iraayel demanded.

'She went ahead. I was supposed to drop my defences, but it didn't feel right.'

'Saf?' Iraayel knelt, reaching for Saffazi, who lay unconscious on the cushions.

'Don't!' Imoshen cried.

Too late.

The moment he touched her, he toppled like a puppet whose strings had been cut. At their side, the kneeling Malaunje youth reached out instinctively.

'No.' Imoshen grabbed him by the shoulder.

With a moan, Egrayne sank to her knees next to their two choice-children – beautiful youngsters on the verge of life, lying like discarded toys.

Fatal accidents while learning to harness the gifts' power were rare, but they did happen.

'Saf complained that Vittoryxe was holding her back,' Egrayne whispered. 'Why didn't I listen?'

Imoshen took in the little nest they'd made for this illicit gift-working. They'd chosen a secluded alcove that looked out onto the aviary balcony. They'd placed cushions and bedrolls on the floor. And they had invited this Malaunje youth to join them. What were they up to?

'Look at me.' Imoshen fixed on the youth's face, trying to place him. His gaze slid past hers, fear written in his features. He knew they'd been breaking the rules. His cheeks still had the roundness of a boy. Pale skin, mulberry eyes, vivid dark-red lips and hair, a crooked little sixth finger. She placed him. 'Redraven. What's going on here?'

'Saffazi offered to dream-share with me, all-mother.'

'Dream-share with a Malaunje?' No wonder he looked guilty.

'This is not dream-sharing,' Egrayne said.

Without a word, Imoshen knelt over Iraayel and Saffazi, not touching, trying to sense if their essences were still on this plane. Cold fear seized her. 'She's dragged them both onto the higher plane. Iraayel's unprepared and she's inexperienced.'

'We should send for Vittoryxe.'

'That will take time and–' Imoshen broke off. They both knew the sisterhood's gift-tutor would use this breach to belittle their choice-children and undermine their leadership.

'I'll bring them back,' Imoshen decided. Arodyti's death throes flashed through her mind, making her stomach clench with terror.

'No, I'll go,' Egrayne insisted. 'We can't afford to lose our causare.'

'Anchor me.' Imoshen dropped her gift-walls and reached for her choice-son before Egrayne could stop her. The moment their skin touched, she let herself go and segued to the higher plane.

She'd been prepared for conflict, but not for this.

Mieren overran the palace, rampaging through the halls, tearing the paintings off the walls, overturning statues and furniture. She could hear their howls and the smashing of glass. For a heartbeat, Imoshen wondered if Saffazi had done the impossible and performed transposition through time.

Then one of the Mieren rounded the corner and she looked into his eyes and knew he was no mortal man.

Everything fell into place. The higher plane had taken form from Saffazi's mind. The city was all she knew, and the night the Mieren stormed the palace had been the most terrifying night of her life.

Until tonight.

Every time the beasts destroyed a painting or smashed a vase, they tore a piece from Saffazi's essence and devoured it. When they had shredded enough of her, she wouldn't be able to maintain her concentration and they'd feast on her.

All this passed through Imoshen's mind in a flash as the predator approached her. Stripped of the illusion, she saw it for what it was: a scraeling, a scavenger. It was not strong enough to tackle her alone, but soon more would come. To defend herself from them she would have to expend power, and that would draw the more dangerous predators, the ones she did not want to test herself against.

Lifting her arms, Imoshen confronted the scraeling as if it were a vicious dog. On this plane, her body was her own creation and she willed a sword and shield into being. The beast dropped back, but did not slink away.

Where were Saffazi and Iraayel?

Imoshen opened her senses and cast about. Felt the lure of power being expended and ran in that direction. The scraeling loped after her. Others joined it.

Rounding a bend in the balcony, she found Iraayel and Saffazi making a stand at the top of the stairs, just as they had done in real life. Iraayel had formed the sword he had used the night he held the steps against the Mieren. At his back, Saffazi fought with the two long-knives. She was an adept of both armed and unarmed combat. They made a beautiful pair.

Iraayel forged towards Imoshen, drawing Saffazi with him. Fingers outstretched, Imoshen reached for Iraayel, who held onto Saffazi. The instant Imoshen touched her choice-son she sought Egrayne through their sisterhood link, felt her voice-of-reason's presence and followed it back to the earthly plane.

She came to herself lying on the floor amidst the cushions. From where she lay, she watched Egrayne roll Saffazi over.

Despite her ordeal, the initiate was conscious and unharmed.

'Ma?' Saffazi sounded seven, not seventeen.

Egrayne hugged her choice-daughter.

Imoshen struggled upright, fighting nausea as she looked for a sign that Iraayel was unharmed. He blinked, staring blankly. Blood seeped from several wounds taken on the higher plane. The moment she touched him, intelligence returned to his gaze.

She hugged him fiercely, shaking with relief. Behind her, she could hear Egrayne assuring herself Saffazi was unharmed, in mind, body and gift.

Egrayne's tone changed, growing sharper as anger overcame her relief. 'What were you thinking? You could have been killed. What were you trying to do?'

Saffazi glanced to Iraayel, and Imoshen read her. Saffazi thought he would lie for her. This shocked Imoshen. Until this moment, she'd believed she had Iraayel's complete loyalty.

'I had to bring them, Saf,' Iraayel said, coming to his knees. His hands trembled as he wiped blood from his eyes. 'I told you this was dangerous. You shouldn't have tried it.'

'And I told you that I could handle it.'

'You were not handling it when I found you.' Imoshen's voice shook with anger. Her gift spiked, almost slipping her control. 'The empyrean plane was devouring you!'

Saffazi flinched.

Imoshen looked down, clenched her hands in her lap, closed her eyes and reeled in her gift until she had regained complete control. When she looked up, her gaze settled on Iraayel and she took in the gash on his forehead. Pressing her sleeve to his head, she muttered, 'I should've sealed those wounds on the higher plane, now they'll have to heal like ordinary injuries.'

He brushed her hand away. 'I'm all right. I heard your warning. I chose to go after Saf. I knew what I risked.'

But he didn't. That he'd managed to hold his own against the lesser beasts of the higher plane was due to the strength of his will alone. That he'd managed to forge a weapon from his gift showed innate ability. Egrayne had identified him as a gift-warrior when she empowered him.

'Only luck preserved your lives long enough for me to bring you back.' Imoshen turned to Saffazi. 'As for you. You dragged Iraayel through to the higher plane and he has not even begun his training there. You could have killed him.'

'I didn't mean to.' Instantly contrite, Saffazi's lower lip trembled. 'We were supposed to be dream-sharing.'

Iraayel reached for her, his hands cradling hers with exquisite tenderness.

Imoshen's heart sank. He loved her, but he was destined to spend his life in a brotherhood. As a mother she would do anything for Iraayel, but she could not protect him from his own emotions.

Imoshen looked away from them, into Redraven's face. Adoration suffused his features. Him too? What was it about Saffazi that elicited such devotion?

'This Malaunje youth trusts you,' Egrayne said. 'You could have killed him. That you didn't was due to his good sense and excellent gift affinity. Unless you have great control, dream-sharing and memory-sharing must only be done with someone of equal strength, otherwise your gift will swamp them. We don't want any more devotees.'

'You both have devotees,' Saffazi protested.

'Roskara became my devotee by accident.'

'Frayvia also became my devotee by accident,' Imoshen said quickly. She believed Gift-tutor Vittoryxe was partly to blame for hoarding knowledge and doling it out with irritating condescension. No wonder Saffazi wanted to explore her gift on her own.

When her gift first started to manifest, Imoshen had been in a similar position. Deliberately kept ignorant by her captors, left to discover what she could do by trial and error, she'd been lucky not to get herself killed.

Imoshen was aware of Redraven, still as a mouse, witness to T'En mysteries forbidden to all Malaunje but devotees; and even they were kept ignorant of the deeper mysteries. His ignorance had nearly cost him his freedom, or even his life.

The secrecy surrounding the gifts was dangerous. There were so many things Imoshen wanted to change. If the leaders of the T'Enatuath knew their causare's true agenda, they would have been horrified.

'I stole Frayvia's freedom the night my infant son died,' Imoshen revealed. 'Like you, Safi, I didn't mean to involve her in my gift-working. It happened when we tried to escape Lighthouse Isle. It was almost midwinter, very cold. We ran down to the beach and climbed into a rowboat. They tried to stop us. My bond-partner fought off the attackers, but they tipped our boat over. My newborn was strapped to my chest. It was deep water. I tried to keep his head above water, but one of the attackers sought to drown me. I got away, swam to a rowboat and climbed aboard. The current had taken Iraayel and Frayvia. By the time I dragged them aboard, between the cold and the water, there was no spark of life left in my newborn. I tried to pluck his life essence from the higher plane to restore him. But—'

'That's traduciation, Imoshen!' Egrayne gasped. 'Absolutely forbidden.'

'I didn't know. I was crazy with grief. Frayvia was nearby when I segued onto the higher plane. By accident, I dragged her essence with me. She had no protection from the predators. I had to link with her to save her life. She's been bound to my gift ever since.' Imoshen's voice hardened. She wanted to impress the desperation that had driven her to make this mistake. 'It is not something attempted lightly, as a dare or for stature, Saffazi.'

The three young people looked down, guilt written large on their faces.

'This is why I speak of private T'En matters before Redraven. He must know what he risks. To become a devotee is to be linked for life. You–' Imoshen broke off as she realised the silly boy was so lovesick it probably sounded like a good idea to him.

Egrayne cleared her throat, sending Imoshen a wry look, but the voice-of-reason was all business when she spoke. 'The creation of a devotee has gone out of favour. If you die, your devotee dies. It is a selfish act.'

There was silence for a moment, as the youngsters digested this.

'You are dismissed, Redraven,' Imoshen said. He did not need to be told twice. Springing to his feet, he gave a deep obeisance, hands going to his heart to signify love and then to his head to signify duty, before leaving.

'I know, I disappoint you,' Saffazi said to Egrayne. 'But the gift-tutor is holding me back. I can't stand–'

'She's holding you back for your own good.'

'But...'

Imoshen caught Iraayel's eye and they both slipped away.

As they walked in silence, Imoshen wondered if she dared broach the subject of Iraayel's feelings for Saffazi.

'Have you heard anything from the all-fathers?' Iraayel asked.

'I hear nothing but complaints and accusations from the all-fathers. At least now they are resigned to exile. But to answer your question, no one has offered you a place in their brotherhood.' It infuriated her; they were taking out their hatred of her on him.

They paused where the passages diverged.

Iraayel said, 'I'm sorry to be a burden to you–'

'Don't say that. You were never a burden.'

'I was four years old the night your baby died, but I remember your heartbreak. I lived while he died. I wish–'

'No.' Imoshen hugged Iraayel as hard as she could, tears stinging her eyes. She pulled back. 'Never say that. Never!'

Tears of love glistened in his wine-dark eyes, and Imoshen recalled a long-lost memory of her mother. She hadn't seen her since she was five. Iraayel was the son of her mother's sister, and there was a family resemblance. Grateful, Imoshen hugged Iraayel again, her gift close to the surface.

Iraayel sensed it. 'What's wrong?'

'Nothing.' She pulled back.

A Malaunje hurried past. Word of the causare and her choice-son embracing in the corridor would spread, reaching Vittoryxe's ears, and Imoshen would be in for a scolding.

As long as the gift-tutor did not hear of Saffazi's daring.

'I should go,' Iraayel said softly.

'You saved Safi's life tonight. If you'd touched her without me there to bring you back, you'd both be dead.'

'I know.' But his tone told her he would still have risked his life for Saffazi. No wonder he wanted to stay with the sisterhood.

'Off you go.'

Feeling fragile, Imoshen waited for Egrayne. They walked back through the deserted corridors, silent until they entered Imoshen's chambers.

Egrayne sighed. 'She is the last of my choice-daughters, the only one who still lives. I have such hopes for her.'

'Don't blame Safi. It's Vittoryxe. She hoards knowledge. I'll speak with her.' As soon as Imoshen said it, she knew it would be the wrong move.

'I'll speak with her,' Egrayne said quickly. 'I should tell the gift-tutor about Safi's indiscretion.'

'No need to invite trouble.'

Egrayne took Imoshen's shoulders in her hands and kissed each cheek. 'Your choice-son is wise beyond his years.'

'He's in love with your impetuous choice-daughter.'

Egrayne chuckled. 'So is the Malaunje youth. Ah, what will I do with her?'

Chapter Twenty

RONNYN COULD NOT take his eyes off the great sea-boar. Safe behind a rock, he marvelled at the creature's size. The biggest he'd seen so far, its body was covered in glossy blue-black skin. Whiskers grew from its snout and each flipper ended in a needle-sharp prong. Then there were the tusks, each was as long as a full grown man's fore-arm and as thick; they reared up from each side of the sea-boar's jaw.

Hearing his father's tales had not prepared Ronnyn for the reality of these magnificent beasts. He glanced to Aravelle to see if she was equally impressed. She frowned, pushing tendrils of wind-blown copper hair out of her eyes. Between them lay the sack of tusks they'd already gathered. Wind whipped in from the sea, driving sand before it, stinging their bare legs and arms.

Ronnyn ignored the discomfort, concentrating on their father. The boars were surprisingly fast over short distances. The tusks their father hoped to collect lay on the beach not far from where the sea-boar sunned itself on the sand. During mating season, the males often gored each other to death. Only the strongest set up a harem of females. The scavengers picked the carcasses clean, leaving the bones and tusks.

It was difficult to decide when to come to Sea-boar Isle. In the autumn, while the mating battles raged, the shores rang with the bulls' roars, and now that the pups had been born, the females jealously guarded their rush-lined nests, staking out patches of sun-warmed dune.

But all Ronnyn and Aravelle wanted were the discarded tusks, left amidst the bleached bones on the sand.

'Don't worry,' Aravelle squeezed his shoulder. 'Da knows what he's doing.'

At that moment, Asher crept out from behind a rock, making his way down the dune towards the ivory. Ronnyn held his breath. The sea-boar male did not stir. The six females continued to groom their pups.

A seagull cawed overhead, hanging effortlessly on the wind. Ronnyn glanced up at the bird, and missed the moment the largest female spotted his father. Her warning bellow echoed across the beach.

'Quick, Da,' Aravelle breathed.

The female gave another call. The male reared up and charged down the sand, as the female charged in from the other direction.

'He's trapped.' Aravelle jumped to her feet.

Their father weighed his chances, then dashed behind the female. She was too quick. Changing direction, he tried to run between the two but tripped on a bone, sprawling in the soft sand. He was up instantly, but the female had cut him off.

Now he turned to face the sea-boar. The big male lunged in, goring his thigh, tossing him high in the air. His body spun end-over-end like a toy, falling to the sand in a heap. Ronnyn stared, unable to believe his eyes.

'Save Da,' Aravelle ordered, even as she leapt over the rock and raced across the beach.

Stunned, Ronnyn was three strides behind her by the time he jumped over the rock. His heart raced. In disbelief he saw Aravelle run behind the female, which was about to inspect their father as he lay in an ever widening circle of bloodstained sand.

'Over here,' Aravelle cried, dancing perilously near the other females.

Fierce admiration burned in Ronnyn's chest.

Both the male and female charged Aravelle. She ran along the beach, away from the nest, away from their injured father.

Right into the path of another bull.

Ronnyn froze. Time seemed to slow. Fear stole his breath. He was too far to help.

His sister's legs faltered. A surge of determination took him. She must get past. Everything became incredibly clear and sharp.

A gust of wind whipped up the sand right in front of the male, flinging it in the creature's face, into its eyes. It reared back.

Aravelle leapt past the sea-boar, and kept right on running.

Ronnyn darted over to his father, hooked his arms under Asher's shoulders and dragged him along the beach.

Only when he had his father safely behind the rock did he look back. To his relief, there was no sign of Aravelle's body on the beach. The rest of the females had begun the weaving motion they took up when threatened. The biggest female and the male were out of sight, presumably chasing his sister.

As long as she didn't trip, she could outrun them.

Turning his attention to his father, he rolled Asher onto his back. So much blood, and that open wound, right down to the bone.

The sight of it made him sick with fear.

Drawing his fish-gutting knife, Ronnyn cut the torn breeches away, making strips to bind the long, deep wound. Ronnyn tore off his vest and pressed it to the gash. He strapped the bandage as hard as he could. He'd glimpsed things inside his father's leg that weren't meant to see the light of day.

Blood still seeped through his jerkin. What should he do? Behind him, something crunched on the sand. He spun, knife lifted.

Aravelle glanced to the knife and grinned.

He put it away.

'How is he?' she asked, dropping to her knees. Her cheeks were flushed, hair wild.

He had never been so glad to see her. 'We must get him back to the boat. I've slowed the bleeding, but not stopped it.'

Between them, they carried their father down the beach and around the headland. Neither mentioned the other unconscious man they had carried like this.

The boat was anchored in the shallows, and it was hard getting their father aboard. Ronnyn had to rig the net as a sling. Their rough handling worsened the bleeding.

'That wound needs to be sewn,' Aravelle said. 'Best do it now, before he wakes up.'

Their mother had sewn Ronnyn's hand after he cut it with Da's fishing knife. It had hurt so much he'd cried, even though he tried not to.

They used their mother's brindle-berry wine to clean the needle and then the wound. That woke their father. He cursed and struggled to sit up. Ronnyn tried to hold him down.

'Your leg's bleeding real bad, Da,' Aravelle said. 'We're going to sew it up.'

Asher's expression cleared and he nodded. 'Do you want me to do it?'

Ronnyn caught Aravelle's eye.

'No, I'll do it,' she said. 'I can see what I'm doing.'

Ronnyn was glad he didn't have to.

She used the finest of the sail-mending thread. Ronnyn helped hold his father's leg still. It jumped around as the muscle spasmed. It was easier when their father passed out again.

Finally, Aravelle stood up, looking pale. Her hands shook and the front of her shirt was covered in blood. Ronnyn was so glad she was with him.

They studied their father. There was a worrying sheen to his skin.

'We should sail for home right now,' Aravelle said. 'I'll go back for the ivory bag. You get the boat ready.'

But first they carried Asher down to the single bunk in the cabin and strapped him in. Then Ronnyn packed everything securely away and drew up the anchor. The tide was coming in. Aravelle ran back through the shallows with the ivory bag. When he hauled it over the side it was heavier than he expected.

'You went back for the tusks?' he guessed.

She nodded, scrambling up to join him. 'Let's go.'

He couldn't believe her daring; he wished he was as brave.

Before setting off, they checked on their father. His skin felt hot.

'Fever,' Ronnyn whispered. 'That's bad.'

'Ma will know what to do,' Aravelle said.

As they came out onto deck, Ronnyn caught his sister's arm. They'd never sailed the boat on their own, and never been to the trading isle. There were so many things they didn't know, Ronnyn realised they'd never manage without Asher. 'If Da dies, our family will have to go back to the brotherhood. Won't we?'

Aravelle blinked and frowned, as if she was about to tell him not to be silly. Then she nodded slowly and he knew his father's wound was as bad as he'd feared. But he was also pleased, because it meant she acknowledged he was old enough for the truth and they were in this together.

Once the wind filled the sail, Aravelle took the tiller. She knew the way back through the island channels. It fell to him to sit with their father and, even though it was mid-afternoon, he was exhausted. The tiredness was like a great, smothering grey blanket creeping over his mind.

He fought it, but the waves of weariness kept returning, inevitable as the incoming tide. Each time he drove it back, it rolled over him. In the end, he picked up the curved needle and pricked his skin repeatedly to stay awake.

As long as Aravelle was on duty at the tiller, he had to be alert at their father's side. It was the least he could do.

* * *

IMOSHEN DIDN'T WANT to be here, but she had no choice. She'd known Bedutz since he and Iraayel first became friends. As a child, Bedutz had smiled trustingly up at her when she told the boys stories. Today he was seventeen, and Vittoryxe would send him to his brotherhood.

Imoshen didn't want to be here, but as leader of the sisterhood, she had to witness the ceremony. While the Malaunje played a solemn dirge, she lit the ceremonial candles. Their scent of bitter almonds reminded her of other deaths, both real and symbolic.

The candles sat in their niches, illuminating the underside of the sisterhood gate. It was that grey time before dawn, when babies are born and the elderly die.

Schooling her face to betray nothing, Imoshen stood to one side while Vittoryxe plaited Bedutz's long hair. As his choice-mother, Vittoryxe had done his hair since it grew long enough to braid and now, in their last moments together, she braided it again.

Some of the females chose not to touch their choice-sons, preferring to distance themselves. Imoshen was surprised to see Vittoryxe do Bedutz's hair, but the gift-tutor was nothing if not devoted to T'Enatuath ritual.

After completing the braid, Vittoryxe wound the ceremonial leather around Bedutz's plait at shoulder height. Then she took the scissors and cut his hair off above that point. While cutting his hair, she was also cutting the shallow gift link that all T'En mothers shared with their children.

Lifting the severed braid to show the sisterhood, Vittoryxe said the words to complete the ritual. 'My choice-son, Bedutz, is dead. This is all I have to remember him by.'

The sisters moaned in sympathy.

Imoshen's heart raced as her gift tried to break free of her control. She would not declare Iraayel dead. She would not turn her back on him. She would not...

Be able to do otherwise, because her sisterhood would refuse to acknowledge him. Even as she thought this, Bedutz walked past the long row of sisters and each one symbolically turned their back to him.

When he came to Imoshen, she refused to look away. With tears in her eyes she met the gaze of the boy she had grown to love.

For a heartbeat his chin trembled, then he clenched his jaw and turned away from her.

Would that be Iraayel on his seventeenth birthday?

Seething with fury, Imoshen watched as the Malaunje stripped Bedutz so that he stood naked on the cold paving stones. Seeing him like this, there was no denying he was an adult man, but this did not mean he was their enemy.

Turning him out and forcing him to give his loyalty to an all-father – that was what turned him into their enemy. It was all so wrong.

Pale-skinned and perfectly formed, Bedutz went through the sisterhood gate and out of their lives.

Hueryx's gift-tutor and four adepts waited to escort him to his new home. At least he was not going to Kyredeon's brotherhood.

The gift-tutor placed a cloak around Bedutz's shoulders, symbolically cloaking him with the protection of the brotherhood. Then the warriors strode off with him in their ranks. He did not look back.

Imoshen watched until she could see him no more. Other leave-takings had not caused her so much pain. She knew it was because her time with Iraayel was running out, but even knowing this she could not armour herself against the loss.

Blinded by tears of impotent fury, she walked home with the women of her sisterhood, her back stiff and straight. She did not blink, for fear the tears would fall. Some sisters sobbed softly. Not Vittoryxe; she walked in front of Imoshen, head held high, Bedutz's plait cradled in her arms.

No one spoke. After today, no one would speak his old name, Bedutz Choice-son Vittoryxe. He would be Initiate Bedutz of Hueryx's Brotherhood.

Vittoryxe stumbled on the palace steps. Her devotee tried to help, but the gift-tutor brushed her aside.

They finally stopped outside Vittoryxe's door, and each of the women came forward to kiss the gift-tutor's cheek, offering her the words of sympathy to formally acknowledge her loss.

Imoshen waited until last. She leant forward, letting her lips brush Vittoryxe's cold, dry cheek. In the past she had been able to say the appropriate words. Today they stuck in her throat. She could not offer false coin.

She thought it wrong to drive these boys away. She feared if she opened her mouth all her private thoughts would come tumbling out, that or tears. But not to say the words insulted Vittoryxe's loss, so she tried to force her tongue to move. 'I... I–'

'You? You make a mockery of everything we believe. You were raised by covenant-breaking males.' Vittoryxe's voice rose dangerously. 'You don't value our sisterhood's great heritage. You think the division into brotherhoods and sisterhoods is wrong. You don't deserve your raedan gift. You perform transposition by accident, then laugh at my gift lore. You don't deserve to be causare!'

And the gift-tutor's hand lashed out in a slap that Imoshen could have blocked. But she chose not to, because everything Vittoryxe had said was true. If Imoshen had her way, she would dismantle the covenant and so much more.

The slap rocked her head.

Even though her gift rose to defend her, she did not react.

Infuriated, the gift-tutor raised her hand again.

'Enough.' Egrayne caught Vittoryxe's. 'Dretsune, Ysattori.'

The warrior-turned-scholar and her shield-sister stepped between them, blocking Vittoryxe's view of Imoshen.

The rest of the sisters stood in stunned horror. If Imoshen and Vittoryxe had been brotherhood warriors, this insult would have meant a challenge at dawn, or an apology of such magnitude it would cripple the attacker's stature.

'Vittoryxe?' Egrayne's voice was heavy with meaning. But Imoshen did not want a feigned contrition. Vittoryxe had meant every word she said.

'No, Egrayne,' Imoshen said, even as her gift tried to break free to protect her, even as her right cheek burned and tears poured down her cheek. 'Our gift-tutor's heart is breaking. As a mother, I understand and take no offence.'

Then she turned on her heel and walked off.

That afternoon, Imoshen sat at her desk and turned over the latest message to inspect the seal. Not from the Sagoras. She was disappointed, but there was still time to hear back from them.

When exile had been confirmed, she'd sent messengers to all the T'Enatuath's estates. Some had returned promptly to report estates burned to the ground, or inhabited by Mieren with no sign of their original inhabitants. But there was good news, too. Some estates planned to bring in their harvest early, then trek to the coast to meet up at Port Mirror-on-sea. Like this one.

She smiled, put the reply aside and crossed another estate off her list. More of her people safe, or safe once they reached the port.

Her hand settled on the last message from Sorne. When the brotherhood and sisterhood warehouses had been burned in the riots, records of the merchant shipping fleets' whereabouts had been lost. Sorne was having trouble tracking the ships down.

Although Imoshen had grown up on Lighthouse Isle and was used to fishermen, she did not know a lot about long sea voyages. She wished the last all-mother hadn't sent Captain Iriane to find a route through the ice-floes to the far-east. The sisterhood had sent Iriane north in an attempt to beat Captain Ardonyx, who was trying to find a route south through the Lagoons of Perpetual Summer. The first to reach the far east would establish a trade agreement and bring riches to his or her brotherhood or sisterhood. Now Imoshen could have used Iriane's knowledge of the sea. If not Iriane, then her bond-partner Ardonyx. She wished Ardonyx was back safe. He did not even know that she'd fallen pregnant and delivered a healthy sacrare daughter.

'Have you eaten, Imoshen?' Egrayne asked from the doorway.

'No...' She hid a surge of fear, for her mind had been unguarded. None of the sisters knew the identity of Umaleni's father, not even Egrayne.

'I thought so. You'll wear yourself into the ground.' Her voice-of-reason came in to peer at the papers on Imoshen's desk. 'Have you had bad news? What troubles you?'

'I've been thinking about the logistics of taking our people into exile,' Imoshen said. Hopefully, Egrayne would put her sorrow down to leaving the city. 'If only Iriane hadn't been sent to find a northern passage.'

'Poor Iriane...' Egrayne whispered. 'She's in for a nasty surprise when she returns.'

Imoshen nodded. 'But there's nothing we can do. At least she didn't take the sisterhood's flagship. With a little crowding, we should be able to fit the whole—'

'I don't see how we can transport everything. See that painting? It's a Tamattori original.' Egrayne pointed to an oil painting of Imoshen the Covenant-maker's meeting with the all-fathers. 'It's a true record, painted by Tamattori, who memory-shared with one of the surviving gift-warriors whose mother had been a young initiate at the time. I hate the thought of leaving it for the Mieren.'

'We won't. It will be safe in the hold of our sisterhood's flagship.'

'And what if the ship sinks?'

'If our ship sinks, the fate of a painting will be the least of our worries,' Imoshen muttered, then saw Egrayne's expression. Her mind raced. 'We'll make copies of all the great artworks so every ship has one, and we'll spread the originals across the fleet. That way we lower the risk. And it will give our Malaunje craftsmen and women something to do while they wait for exile.'

'And what of the sculptures? Some of them are twice as tall as a full grown man.'

Imoshen's head swam.

Egrayne squeezed her arm and headed for the door. 'Promise me you'll eat something?'

Imoshen nodded and went back to work.

A few moments later, Frayvia came in with Umaleni.

'Uma's walking,' her devotee announced.

'Of course she is. You're holding both her hands.'

'She walked without holding on a moment ago.' Frayvia slipped her hands free from Umaleni's, then backed off. 'Come on. Walk to me, Uma.'

'She's not one yet,' Imoshen said with a smile.

'She's not far off.' Frayvia held out her hands. 'Come to me.'

Umaleni stood there and did nothing.

Imoshen laughed, but came out from behind her desk anyway and opened her arms. Umaleni took three steps, then fell forward. Imoshen caught her, and swept her up for a cuddle.

If only Ardonyx could see his daughter. 'I wish...'

'Has there been no word of him?'

'Nothing. If his ships return after winter cusp, Charald will have him and all his crew executed.' Imoshen hugged her daughter, drawing comfort from her. Umaleni rubbed her eyes.

'She's ready for her nap,' Frayvia said.

They carried her into the nursery, sang her to sleep and then closed the connecting door.

'What of your link?' Frayvia whispered. 'Can't you reach–'

'Too tenuous. The distance is too great and we haven't reinforced it since the night Uma was conceived.'

'Could you contact him through the higher plane?'

'Only if he was also gift-working on the plane at the same time.' Imoshen tried to rub ink off her finger.

Frayvia covered her hands. 'My stomach churns with your frustration and fear. At this rate you'll wake Uma.'

'I'm sorry. It's just... Ardonyx knows the sea, and we are going into exile. I trust his judgement. I need him. I miss him.'

Frayvia gestured to the bed. 'Would it help?'

'You don't mind?'

Frayvia laughed softly. 'They're your memories.' She went to the bed, patting the spot beside her. 'And they are such happy moments.'

'I know.' Imoshen smiled through her worry. 'I chose the best ones for you to keep safe for Uma, in case I—'

'If you died, I would die.'

'According to gift lore. But I'm not convinced.' She went over to the bed and sat with one leg tucked under her so that she faced Frayvia. 'If I am killed, I need you to hold onto life for Uma's sake. No one loves her like we do. They all see her as a sacrare, a powerful tool who'll serve the sisterhood. Only we see her for herself. Oh, Fray, don't cry.' Imoshen cupped her devotee's cheek as tears stung her own eyes. 'These things have to be said, my love. If Ardonyx and I are killed, then I want you to watch over Uma. When she is big enough, tell her about the memories. They are my legacy to her. It may be the only way she knows her mother and father.'

Frayvia nodded through her tears.

Imoshen pulled her close, cradling her as she stroked her devotee's hair.

After a moment, Frayvia sat up, wiped her cheeks and summoned a smile. 'Which memory do you want to share? How you met?'

Imoshen laughed softly. 'At Merchant Mercai's? I was so angry when Ardonyx turned up for my language lessons, but he wasn't there to spy on me. He didn't even know who I was.'

'For him, you were someone sent to learn the language of the wise Sagoras.'

Imoshen nodded. 'He hadn't even been in the city when I executed Rohaayel.' After twelve years, it was still too painful to recall that day.

Attuned to her sorrow, Frayvia touched her arm in sympathy.

Imoshen covered her devotee's hand. 'I sent a message to the Sagoras, but I haven't heard back. If they don't give us sanctuary, I don't know where we can go.'

'Mercai won't let you down. You became more than teacher and pupil, you became friends.'

'As much as one of the Mieren will accept one of the T'En,' Imoshen conceded.

'You know him. You spent years studying his language–'

'It was worth it, to meet Ardonyx.' Imoshen squeezed Frayvia's hand. 'He was so angry when he discovered who I was that he sailed off, but he could not stay away. I want to remember when his ship returned. We both wore the Sagora veils as a courtesy to our teacher. When he saw me, he took his off, revealing his face. He knew I could read how he felt. We...'

She reached for Frayvia, stretching out on the bed with her devotee in her arms. The warmth of Frayvia's soft cheek pressed against the hollow of her throat. Their breathing synchronised and she opened her gift, drawing on the memory Frayvia had held in safe-keeping. It had been laid down the very day it happened, so it was as fresh and sharp as the event itself and each time they revisited it, it became stronger, more firmly implanted.

But as wonderful as reliving the memory was, it was also a torment; she knew it would only make her miss Ardonyx more.

* * *

TOBAZIM SLOWED AS he heard the name of his choice-mother's estate.

'...Silverlode?'

He increased the length of his stride to walk behind the two high-ranking adepts, as they all headed to the dining chamber.

'Are you sure?' Ceyne asked. 'When did you hear?'

'Just this afternoon, I sent one of my Malaunje to the free quarter to the jewellers. I swear everyone has the same idea. They all want precious stones. Easily transportable wealth. The prices–'

'You were saying, about Silverlode Estate?'

'Yes. My servant overheard a sisterhood Malaunje talking about the massacre.'

'Everyone at Silverlode Estate was killed?' Ceyne asked.

'After the warriors died defending the gate, the Mieren herded everyone, even the children, onto the wall. They were thrown over the cliff.'

Tobazim knew that wall. In winter when the winds blew in from the north, you could not stand upright. In the summer you could see the whole of Chalcedonia laid out below.

A rushing filled his head and his vision went grey. Staggering, he stepped into a doorway to hide his weakness.

Memories swamped him – afternoons spent under the orchard trees reading, Learon chasing him up the tower stairs as they pretended to be great warriors, his choice-mother and her sisters sitting by the fire on cold winter nights, singing to the children.

Gone. All gone.

He wanted to find Learon and tell him.

But his choice-brother was also gone. Nothing was left, not Learon, not Vanillin-oak Winery, not Silverlode or his choice-mother...

The door opened behind him and he almost fell.

Haromyr steadied him. 'What's wrong? Are you sick?'

'Silverlode Estate was overrun by Mieren. Everyone's dead.' He had to tell someone. 'My choice-mother's dead!'

Haromyr looked shocked.

Tobazim regretted his slip. He was not supposed to mourn his choice-mother's death. She should have died to him the day he left the sisterhood. 'Forget it, I–'

Haromyr pulled him into the chamber.

He was vaguely aware of artworks, some carefully wrapped, some damaged, and recalled Haromyr saying he'd wanted to train as a sculptor, but had been advised to take the warrior's way. 'What were you doing?'

'Trying to think of a way to save our precious works of art from being desecrated by the Mieren.' Haromyr shrugged in apology. 'I'm sorry about–'

Tobazim went to the window, which looked out over a courtyard. On the verandah opposite Malaunje women sat at their looms, singing while they worked. They reminded him of childhood winter nights around the fireplace. 'I must tell Athlyn. We shared the same choice-mother. He'll take it hard.' He turned and noticed Haromyr's troubled expression. 'What's wrong?'

The adept glanced to the door. 'I heard that Kyredeon sanctioned that sacrare girl's murder–'

Tobazim's choice-mother had hinted as much. 'But he executed the warriors responsible, strangled them with his own hands.'

Haromyr nodded. 'He had to. They botched it.'

'Why would he have her killed?'

'She was a sacrare gift-wright, able to reach into a T'En and cure or cripple their gift.'

Tobazim's knees went weak and he sank onto the window seat behind him. 'Sanctioning the murder of a T'En child. That's–'

'You think Kyredeon would not do it?'

Tobazim thought Kyredeon would, and that terrified him. 'We're sworn to serve him until we die.'

'Or until he dies.'

Tobazim looked up, startled.

'Don't tell me you haven't thought about offering challenge.'

'He's powerful, and so are his two seconds. And he has his inner circle's support. It would be suicide.'

'I know. But the alternative...' Haromyr shuddered.

Tobazim swallowed. 'Have you spoken to anyone else?'

'I only told you because you hate him as much as I do.'

'Speak of this to no one. No one. You understand?'

'Can you go on living like this?' Haromyr whispered. 'We're sworn to obey our all-father. What if he asks you to murder Imoshen's sacrare child?'

Chapter Twenty-One

SORNE OFFERED QUEEN Jaraile a strawberry, grown in the palace's very own hot-house.

She thanked him, but the smile didn't reach her eyes, which focused off into the distance. 'You're so kind.'

His kindness was motivated by guilt. When he'd suggested Imoshen kidnap the prince, he hadn't considered Jaraile's feelings. Desperate with worry, the queen had grown pale and thin since her son was taken.

'You must eat.'

She picked up a strawberry, took one nibble then seemed to forget it. They sat at the king's table in his private dining room. Charald was down one end playing cards with Baron Nitzane. The baron was losing and the king was having a great time. It was clear Charald preferred Nitzane's company to the queen's. And now that the Wyrds were to be exiled, his son would be returned hale and hearty, and the Chalcedonian barons had pledged to serve the king's heir under Nitzane's leadership, Charald had no fears. He had no more use for Sorne.

In the tent, Sorne was the king's advisor and confidant. In the palace, he was an embarrassment.

'He doesn't like thunderstorms,' Jaraile said, her mind on the prince. 'They frighten him. I hope the she-Wyrds are kind to him.'

'They are very kind. I've been corresponding with Causare Imoshen. Prince Cedon is with their healer. She'll take very good care of him.'

She nodded, but she didn't believe him.

He'd told her the same thing every day since arriving in the port. Now he added, 'It's in the Wyrds' best interests to make sure he is returned safely.'

'But things can go wrong. To the Wyrd leaders, my little boy is only a means to an end.'

'True. But in this case, the leaders of the T'Enatuath are women, not men.'

'How strange.' She turned to him, her eyes alert for once. 'Does that mean they aren't afraid of their husbands?' Then she heard what she'd said and sprang to her feet. 'It's late. I'm tired. Good night, Sorne.'

Jaraile went around the table and dutifully kissed the king's cheek. He waved her aside without looking up from his cards. She drew back and turned to bid the baron good night.

'You win, sire.' Nitzane threw in his hand. 'I swear I have no luck tonight. Queen Jaraile must shuffle the cards to bring me luck.' He gathered the cards.

'Bring you luck?' Charald poured himself more wine. 'She never brought me any luck. All she ever gave me was a crippled son and a stillborn. I've had to make all my own luck by serving the Warrior.'

Jaraile flinched. Nitzane frowned, then presented the cards to the queen.

She shrugged. 'I don't know how to shuffle. I've never played cards.'

'Never played? Why ever not?' Nitzane asked.

'My father didn't think it was a suitable game for a young girl.'

'Didn't think you'd understand the rules, more like,' Charald said, nudging the baron.

'I'll teach you,' Nitzane offered. 'Let me show you how to shuffle.'

'Not now,' Charald protested. 'Hurry up and deal. I'm on a winning streak.'

So Jaraile retired for the night and the men resumed their game.

Restless, Sorne stood and stretched. The balcony doors faced west, looking out over the bay. Something caught his eye, a glow where there shouldn't be one.

He went onto the balcony from where he could just make out a ship's sails burning. The vessel was nowhere near the wharf that the harbour-master had put aside for the Wyrds.

Satisfied, Sorne went inside to find that Charald and Nitzane had started another game. Loud laughter and the clump of boots echoed down the hall, interrupting them.

'Eskarnor and his men are back early,' Nitzane said. Both barons had come to court with a dozen-strong honour guard. Eskarnor preferred a night on the town to a night playing cards with the old king. Captain Ballendin and his men were more comfortable keeping the king's palace guard company of an evening.

Nitzane discarded two cards, took another two, and grimaced.

Charald chuckled. 'Your face betrays you. Now, your grandfather, he could keep a straight face. I never knew what he had in his hand.'

The belligerent laughter came nearer. A high voice yelled something. The men laughed louder. Sorne tensed at the tone. Charald and Nitzane put their cards down.

'Dacians,' Charald muttered.

'All southerners are barbarians,' Nitzane agreed.

The door swung open and Eskarnor strode in. He'd been drinking, but he was by no means drunk. Sorne stepped back into the shadows.

Eskarnor looked around the room and spotted him. 'Just the man, or should I say Wyrd, I want to see. Look what we found being harangued by a mob.' He gestured to his men, who had remained out in the hall. 'Bring him in.'

Two men came through the door, dragging a Malaunje boy of about ten between them. Sorne made sure his face revealed nothing. The boy writhed and kicked, and cursed in five languages. He was bloody, muddy and ferocious.

Why had Eskarnor saved him? Certainly not out of the goodness of his heart.

The lad glared, saw Sorne and went very still.

'Here.' The baron shoved him towards Sorne. 'Another one for exile.'

The boy glanced to Eskarnor, then back to Sorne, clearly confused.

'Go on.' Charald gestured to Sorne. 'Get him out of here.'

'Yes, get him out of here,' Eskarnor echoed. 'The king's dining room is no place for a Wyrd.'

The implication stung Sorne. He stepped around the table and directed the boy to go ahead of him, but that meant approaching Eskarnor. The lad hesitated.

'Wait...' Eskarnor looked Sorne and the boy up and down. 'Seeing you with the lad's made me think of something. Sire, you've ordered us to execute all Wyrds who remain here after winter cusp. Does that include this one?' He gestured to Sorne.

From the king's expression, it was clear he had not thought that far ahead. Charald came to his feet, his mouth working as he chewed this over.

'The Warrior returned Sorne from the dead,' Charald said. 'I was there. I saw it.'

'The god returned him to rid the country of Wyrds,' Eskarnor said. 'Once he's done that, he's nothing but another Wyrd.'

'That's right.' The king was relieved. 'The god returned him to get rid of the Wyrds. That means he's only the Warrior's vessel as long as the god needs him.'

'So he's to be exiled with the rest?' Eskarnor spoke to the king, but his eyes challenged Sorne.

'Yes. He's served his purpose.'

Sorne fought a surge of anger. He made himself turn and bow to the king. 'You appointed me your agent to make sure the Wyrd exile goes smoothly. Until then, I will serve you, sire.'

He turned to leave.

The baron smiled and stepped aside so slowly it was an insult. His men parted to let Sorne and the boy through. Sorne felt the boy tremble as he guided the lad with a hand between his shoulder blades.

Laughter echoed up the corridor after them. Sorne seethed; tonight, Eskarnor had manipulated them all.

Back during Charald's conquest of the Secluded Sea, Eskarnor had seemed to be simply a successful war baron. But, Sorne realised now, Eskarnor couldn't have been more than nineteen when Charald rode across Dace plundering the kingdom. The youth had turned and sworn to serve the invader. He'd taken a handful of survivors from his father's estate and forged it into a company of loyal followers. Then, like Sorne, he'd had years to observe how King Charald played men off against each other. Now Eskarnor was in his late twenties and was not just a simple war baron. He was both capable and cunning.

Sorne shut the door to his chamber and turned to the boy.

'You're not one of them,' the lad said. 'You're a prisoner, like me.'

Sorne grimaced. 'What were you doing running around port? Don't you know you have to stay on the Wyrd wharf?'

'I don't know any Wyrd wharf. I'm Captain Ardonyx's cabin boy, and the Mieren stole our ships and cargo. They started a fire. While we tried to put the flames out, they snuck aboard, hacked up the crew and went for the captain.' The boy's chin trembled. 'I don't know if he got away.'

Sorne rubbed his mouth. 'Why would they attack your ship for the cargo, when they've let others berth at the Wyrd wharf?'

'We've just returned from a voyage to the Lagoons of Perpetual Summer. In the hold, the spices were knee deep. Each sack was worth much more than its weight in gold.'

Sorne let his breath out, went to his desk and took out paper, pen and ink. 'Give me the names of the ships. I'll take this complaint to the harbour-master tomorrow.'

'The harbour-master told us where to berth.'

So far, the harbour-master had smiled and nodded and done everything Sorne requested, while ensuring he turned a profit. Sorne had come across the type before: petty officials who used their position to feather their nests. The harbour-master would back down once he realised Sorne knew what he was up to. 'Tell me anyway. Then go have a bath. I'll take you to the Wyrd wharf tomorrow.'

'I'm awful hungry.'

Sorne smiled. 'Don't worry, you'll be fed.'

ARAVELLE HUDDLED IN front of the hearth, so weary she could hardly think straight. Sailing back with Ronnyn had been nerve-wracking. There was the dread that she would mistake the channels through the many islands, and the constant gnawing fear for their father. But they had made it home this morning with him alive, if feverish. Seeing her mother's reaction to the wound had confirmed Aravelle's worst fears.

They'd carried their father in, placed him on the bed, and then cleaned the wound and bathed his body to reduce the fever. Even the little ones had known it was serious. They'd been subdued all day and gone to bed early, without complaint.

Now, Aravelle and Ronnyn sat at the table by the glow of the fire and a single fish-oil lamp. Their mother took the pot of honey-tea off the hearth and poured three cups.

'Will he be all right, Ma?' Ronnyn whispered, ignoring the tea.

Sasoria sat opposite and took their hands in hers, her mulberry eyes fierce. 'He's strong. Vella did well, stitching him up. I could not have done better. What we have to watch for now is inflammation of the wound. But I have the herbs to purify the blood.' Sasoria squeezed Aravelle's fingers so hard it hurt. 'I won't leave his side.'

And she understood that if her mother could make this happen by sheer will alone, she would.

Ronnyn nodded, but there was uncertainty in his wine-dark eyes, and worry gnawed at Aravelle's stomach. Before this, their father had seemed invulnerable. Now...

'Father won't be the same, will he, Ma?' Aravelle pressed. 'He won't be able to do the things he could.'

'It will take a while for him to recover,' their mother conceded.

'But he will recover?' Aravelle insisted. 'We won't have to go back to the city?'

Sasoria looked a little startled. After a moment, she rallied. 'We'll make no decisions tonight, or any night soon, Vella.'

Aravelle smiled and sipped her honey-tea, but she had not missed her mother's concession. Return to the city was a possibility and, once there, her parents would be punished and her family torn apart. She could not bear the thought of losing her brothers to the sisterhoods. Somehow, she and Ronnyn would have to do all the things their father couldn't. She was reasonably confident about things on the island, but she feared her knowledge of the sea would let her down. She had no idea where Trade Isle was and the islands were like a maze. There were things they needed from the trader. Would Asher be well enough to guide them, if they sailed the boat? Would he be well enough to conduct the trade?

'We've only got half the usual amount of ivory. What will we trade?' Ronnyn asked.

'Don't worry.' Sasoria's mulberry eyes gleamed. 'Scholar Hueryx provided us with something to ward against a day like this.'

'Why would he do that?' Ronnyn asked, sitting up. 'I thought you ran away from him.'

'So we did. But he was free with his gifts before that.' Their mother laughed at their expressions. 'Get the cards out, Vella.'

Aravelle knelt in front of the fire and removed the hearth stone to reveal the safe-hole where they kept their most treasured possessions.

She took out the pouch that protected the cards. How she loved the brotherhood cards, with their intricate, elegant lines, the rich coloured inks and exquisite gold-leaf work. Each card depicted a beautiful T'En man. They ranged from the brotherhood's three leaders, through the scholar to the warrior, and the Malaunje cards: warriors, women and children. On the back of every card was a symbol of the snake swallowing its tail.

Ronnyn knelt beside her, ready to help.

'Look under the matting,' their mother said.

Aravelle handed the pouch to Ronnyn and reached into the shadowed cavity. Until now she hadn't been aware that the safe-hole hid more than the cards. When she removed the reed mat base, this revealed a wooden floor to the safe-hole.

'Slide your fingers in, lift it,' her mother advised.

She discovered that what she'd thought was a wooden floor was actually the lid of a shallow wooden chest.

'Tricky,' Ronnyn whispered in admiration.

Aravelle took the chest out. It was surprisingly heavy and there seemed to be no catch. She looked to her mother, who held out her hands.

They returned to the table where Sasoria ran her fingers around the chest's smooth edge until she found something, then released it, sliding out a tray. Inside, on a bed of red velvet, lay a flat circle of golden plates linked by tiny chains. The plates were embossed with snakes in the same eternal circle as on the cards, and their eyes gleamed with gems.

Aravelle had never seen anything so beautiful.

'A golden necklace,' Ronnyn whispered, awed.

'An electrum torc,' their mother corrected. 'Scholar Hueryx gave this to me when... It was one of many things he gave me, but the only one I brought with me.'

By the light of the lamp, they saw that six of the gems had been removed. Sasoria tapped the empty spaces. 'These we bartered to aid our escape and buy our boat.' She tapped the remaining yellow gems. 'With just one or two of these citrines we can get what we need even at the prices the trader charges. So, you see, we don't need to rush back to the brotherhood.'

She returned the torc to Aravelle. 'Put it away now and go to bed.'

Aravelle did as she was told, but it was only as she drifted off to sleep that she wondered why Scholar Hueryx had given her mother, a Malaunje scribe, jewellery fit for a sisterhood leader.

THE FOLLOWING DAY Sorne took a horse from the royal stable, lifted the boy up before him and rode down to the Wyrd wharf. He passed trading houses, sail-makers and taverns before entering an area where the buildings almost met overhead.

When he'd asked the harbour-master to put aside a wharf for the Wyrds, he hadn't realised the man would see this as an excuse to raze the worst slum in the wharf district. According to the harbour-master, the area he'd torn down and burned was a den of iniquity, vice and disease, and the good folk of his district had wanted to be rid of it for years. Sorne suspected the harbour-master and his partners intended to divide the land between them. It was in a prime position.

But the inhabitants of the rats-nest had to go somewhere and they had moved into this area. Now it was overcrowded, insanitary and filled with the dangerous and the desperate. Cruel-faced Mieren watched them ride past.

After they came out the far side of the new slum, they crossed an area of charred timbers and blackened stone about a bow-shot wide, where the worst of the slums had stood.

Ahead of them, a rubble barricade had been erected. It ran from the cliff on the right to the edge of the wharf on their left. This barricade was defended by the harbour-master's strongarms. Apparently, the good folk of the port district had also claimed they could not sleep in their beds unless they knew the Wyrds were contained. About a dozen strongarms lined the barricade and clustered around the gate.

The gate swung open and Sorne rode in. Only two ships had made it into port so far, and the Wyrds remained on board. Sorne delivered the boy, who protested because both ships were sisterhood ships and he was from a brotherhood.

Then Sorne went to see the harbour-master to complain about the attack on Captain Ardonyx's ships. The man had an excuse for everything. The ships should have been sent to the Wyrd wharf. He blamed a clerk for the misunderstanding. As for the brigands, there were always men who would seize an opportunity; he would make enquires. It was clear to Sorne there was no hope of recovering the cargo. He left the harbour-master with the impression the king would not tolerate another such incident.

Next, Sorne called in on the Father's church. High Priest Faryx was waiting for him in the greeting chamber. An assistant delivered a tray of wine and sweet pastries. It had become a ritual now, and Sorne was coming to understand why the high priest was so plump.

'I asked about this Baron Eskarnor,' Faryx revealed. 'In Navarone, after the surrender, an abbey was attacked. The priests were massacred and their abbey stripped of all valuables.'

'Nothing could be proven,' Sorne said. 'There were no survivors.'

'The gold and sacred religious relics?'

'Gold melts down. Religious relics can be sold to the pious.' Sorne shrugged. 'Have your priests heard of any trouble out on the estates?'

'Nothing.' Faryx nibbled on a sweet pastry, then licked his fingers like a satisfied cat. 'So far there's been no news of the missing she-Wyrd.'

'You wrote to Restoration Retreat?'

'That's right. I meant to tell you. There is no Restoration Retreat. It's been empty since Oskane returned to port.'

Sorne was beginning to think his sister had died the night of the riots. His heart felt heavy. He'd failed her. He'd gone to warn the city, then diverted to save Graelen. Only Grae had died, and he hadn't been in time to warn the city. He'd succeeded in turning a massacre into exile, but that was small compensation for what he'd lost.

Later, as he was leaving, he stopped a penitent and showed him two of the reports on Wyrds. 'I came across these. I think they belong to someone called Scholar Igotzon. Where can I find him?'

'Follow me.'

The Father's church was huge, covering several blocks. It wasa maze of wings and courtyards set behind high walls. Sorne realised he was being taken into one of the old wooden sections. The windows were smaller, the ceiling lower, and the stone floor had been worn down by hundreds of years of pious footsteps. The penitent opened a door to a long room that was almost a passageway. There was a desk up this end, a chest to one side of the fireplace and a wall of deep niches, housing scrolls.

No one was about.

'That's all right,' Sorne said. 'I'll wait.'

The penitent hesitated, then shrugged and headed off.

After closing the door, Sorne checked the desk's neat stacks of paper. Igotzon was very organised. Good.

He wanted to find Scholar Oskane's journals. They contained Oskane's observations of his childhood. If Valendia was dead, as he feared, they were all he had in the world.

The T'Enatuath had accepted exile, but he suspected King Charald's plans to prevent more Wyrds being born were unworkable. The church officials, very wisely, had decided costly sacrifices were wasteful and dangerous. So the Wyrd population would gradually build up, and one day the True-men could turn on them again. Which reminded him, he should really remove the reports Igotzon had written. They were the most dangerous, distilling the information from both the Wyrd scrolls and Oskane's journals.

But the length of the chamber and the number of scrolls was daunting. There had to be a system. He began taking scrolls out at random to see if he could detect a pattern to their storage.

He'd only reached the third column of niches, when an alarmed voice asked, 'What are you doing? Some of those are hundreds of years old.'

Sorne returned the scroll and turned around slowly. 'You have an amazing collection here.'

The man stiffened. He was not much shorter than Sorne, and thin to the point of being emaciated. 'I know who you are.'

'And you are Scholar Igotzon.' Sorne strode back and offered the reports. 'These are yours, I believe.'

Igotzon took them from him, looked at them, then up at him thoughtfully. This close, Sorne realised he was younger than he appeared.

'Were these all you found?' Igotzon asked.

'There were some more, but the tent collapsed and everything on the high priest's desk was water-damaged. I had to throw them out.'

'That's all right, I have the originals. And I remember everything I've ever written.' He spoke as if this wasn't a boast, but a simple fact.

Then he peered at Sorne curiously. 'You're the one Scholar Oskane studied, aren't you? I've read your life story. It's a pity I have to report to the head historian right now, but you must come back. I have so many questions. Walk with me so we can talk.'

As Sorne answered Igotzon's questions, he wondered if the scholar cared that the reports he'd so meticulously written had been used to hound the Wyrds into exile. Sorne suspected Igotzon had not made the connection. There was something almost childlike about him.

In his travels, Sorne had met many True-men. Most hated him because he was a half-blood, while a few could see past his tainted blood to who he was. Igotzon did not see his tainted blood *or* who he was; he saw only that Sorne knew things he did not, and was hungry for that knowledge.

When Sorne returned to the palace, he found King Charald in his chamber of state working with the law scholars. Based on the king's rough ideas, the scholars had drafted laws to prevent half-blood births. Now they were polishing the wording. Rain drummed against the windows, making it hard to hear their conversation.

Sorne did not disturb them. Instead, he went looking for Nitzane and Jaraile. He found Eskarnor and his men taking a late lunch, but there was no sign of the queen or Nitzane.

The southern baron looked up from his plate and saw Sorne in the doorway. Ever since he'd convinced Charald to send Sorne into exile with the Wyrds, he'd taken delight in baiting him. Eskarnor gestured impatiently, as if to say, *what?*

'I'm looking for the queen.'

'She's playing childish card games with Nitzane in the solarium.'

Sorne went to leave.

'Have you noticed how as soon as the Wyrds accepted exile, the drought broke?' Eskarnor's eyes gleamed with contempt. 'It's as if the gods are rewarding us for ridding the country of Wyrds.'

His men responded with similar observations, but Sorne didn't bother to stay and listen. The drought had broken. It had to break some time. Trust Eskarnor to make something of it. Doubtless he'd made this observation to the king, who would see it as a sign from the gods.

Sorne found Nitzane and Jaraile in the solarium, just as Eskarnor had said. The rain had ceased and sunlight filtered through the many windows, making the water droplets glisten.

As Sorne entered, the baron laughed and laid down his cards. 'There, you beat me. I only had a pair. I told you you'd be good at this.' Nitzane noticed Sorne in the doorway and he gestured to the queen. 'She's a quick learner.'

'Where's Captain Ballendin?'

'I sent him to my principal estate. One of my neighbours tried to lay claim to the Wyrd vineyards. Remember, I told you they've been burnt out? Since the lands were originally part of my family's estate, I sent Ballendin to make sure they were returned to me.'

'He's coming back?'

'When it's all sorted.'

Sorne had to be satisfied with that.

Jaraile sat with her wrist turned up to reveal her cards, also revealing the bruises on her pale skin. Someone with large, strong hands had gripped her wrist until they left marks.

Nitzane's gaze dipped to her wrist, then up to Sorne again with significance, but all he said was, 'Give me your cards, my queen. I have another game I can teach you.'

It struck Sorne that Jaraile was luckier than his mother had been. Poor Queen Sorna had been fifteen when she'd married, given birth and been murdered. Not her father or her kinsman, High Priest Oskane, had stood up for her, when King Charald ordered her killed to make way for another wife.

Jaraile's father had shielded her until he died, and now Nitzane had taken her under his wing. Even Sorne felt duty-bound to protect her.

Chapter Twenty-Two

For Ronnyn, life had never been the same since Sea-boar Isle. To begin with, it had looked like their father would die. Delirious with fever, Asher had raved on and off for days. He believed the brotherhood warriors were coming for them. They'd steal his family, and strip him of his mind and memories as punishment.

As spring unfolded into summer, Asher had slowly improved, but his leg would never be the same. He had to walk with the aid of a cane. Some days he only made it from the bed to the kitchen table. All the heavy work had fallen on Ronnyn and Aravelle.

Every few days, the fever came back. Last night Asher had hardly slept. He was in bed now, too weak to move.

Ronnyn had been replaying the sea-boar attack in his mind. The more he thought about it, the more it seemed to him the sand had swirled up into the sea-boar's eyes at just the right time to save his sister. He suspected... *hoped* it had been caused by his gift. He'd tried to move things since, but nothing worked. Perhaps it had been luck that had saved his sister, after all?

He needed to know what to look for when his gift manifested. But he didn't want to ask his mother about it in front of Aravelle. It seemed bad manners, when his sister would never have a gift of her own.

As soon as Aravelle took the washing basket across to the line, he finished chopping wood and headed over to the cottage to join his mother at the back door, where she watched the little ones. Standing beside her made him realise the top of her head only came up to his nose. When had she become so small?

'What?' she asked with a fond smile.

'You're getting smaller.'

She laughed. 'You're getting bigger.'

It was the perfect moment to ask about the gifts.

And he clammed up. He didn't know where to start. In fact, he discovered he didn't want to, almost as if talking would make them real and the reality might be that he was imagining things.

What if she laughed at him?

She'd mean it kindly, but he couldn't bear the thought. This was all too new and private.

So he folded his arms and leaned against the doorjamb.

On their left, the lagoon sparkled in the sun. The tide was out right now, revealing wet sand. Itania trotted after Tamaron as he headed down the path, intent on some big adventure.

When Ronnyn was small, this had been his whole world – the vegetable patch, the smokehouse, the chicken coop and the pen where they kept the goats at night. Which reminded him, he'd spotted a big stink-badger's tracks earlier. They often hunted in packs and loved chickens, so he needed to check the coop was secure.

On the far right, the clothesline stretched between two pines. He could see Aravelle's bare feet as the washing flapped around her.

He glanced to his mother. Since spring, a little pucker of concern had taken up residence between her eyebrows. The frown remained even when she smiled, and he could not blame her. Here she was, pregnant, with a parcel of children and, some days, their father couldn't even walk to the outhouse.

His mother pressed the pads of her fingers into her eyes. She'd been up all night nursing Asher.

'You should go lie down. Vella and I can watch the little ones.'

'You're a good boy. I don't know what I'd do without you two.'

Vittor's sing-song voice carried to them. Ronnyn had let the goats out and now Vittor began to drive them up the slope on the far side of their little valley. Since the drought had broken, the grass had grown deep and green. Vittor saw them watching and waved.

Ronnyn glanced back to his mother. She smiled, but the frown still pulled her brows together. If he admitted he thought his gift was manifesting, he would add to her worries. He decided to ask only general questions about gift-working.

Aravelle came out from between the lines of washing and began to fill the last line. Time was running out.

'How does it feel when the gifts come on?'

His mother laughed. 'I'm Malaunje. How would I know?'

'You served the T'En scholar, Hueryx.'

'As his scribe.' Sasoria glanced to him. 'Don't worry, you won't be thirteen until next spring cusp and they don't empower T'En children until after that, and then only when their gifts are beginning to manifest. You have a while yet.'

She sounded so certain. Had the sand flicked up into the sea-boar's eyes by pure chance?

His mother lifted her hand. 'Over further, Vittor.'

He moved the goats on.

Ronnyn tried again. 'What kind of gifts are there?'

'That's T'En lore, not for Malaunje to know,' she said, but her eyes, so like Aravelle's, crinkled at the corners as she gave him a mischievous look. 'But we know things. There are some rare gifts that only surface once in a generation or even less—'

'Like seers?'

She nodded. 'Men are seers. The female equivalent is a scryer.'

'What's the difference?' he asked, leading up to his real question. 'Other than the name?'

'There is...' She broke off as she shaded her eyes, watching the goats, then waved to signal Vittor that was far enough. 'The gifts manifest differently for males and females. I'm not sure how exactly. The T'En do love their secrets.'

'So the men–'

'Are nearly always noets of some kind, able to manipulate the mind and create illusions. This is not always much use with Mieren, some of whom have natural defences. The women are generally more powerful than the men, particularly if they have birthed a sacrare child.'

'Sacrare?'

'Born of two T'En parents. They have great gifts, and somehow this enhances the mother's gift as well.'

Aravelle had almost finished. No time for subtlety. 'What about a gift that moves things?'

'Real things?' She laughed and shrugged. 'Most gift-working is done on the higher plane. It exists alongside this plane and it's dangerous. When your gift comes, you must promise not to go to the higher plane.'

'Of course. But I meant moving things here, in the real world.'

'Not possible, except maybe for a sacrare.' She was looking distracted again, her gaze on Itania and Tamaron, who had almost reached the lagoon. If they got into the damp sand it would mean more washing. Sasoria raised her voice, beckoning. 'Tam, Tani, come back now.' She did not relax until they began to make their way up the path that curved around the vegetable patch.

She returned to his question. 'A noet could make you think he'd moved something, but it would still be there. Illusion, Ronnyn, that's what mind-manipulators are good at.'

So it had been pure good luck that drove the sand into the sea-boar's eyes. He should be grateful, but he was disappointed. Ronnyn didn't expect to be the first seer in two hundred years. From what his mother said, he would be a mind-manipulator.

So be it. He would focus on harnessing his gift and try to create illusions. And he'd train himself, since there was no one to train him. But who should he practise on?

Not his parents. That left Aravelle.

Which made him wonder. 'Do Malaunje have defences from gift power?'

'Of course, otherwise we'd be slaves to the T'En. That's another thing, sometimes...' Sasoria broke off. She frowned. 'What are they up to now?'

The two little ones had come halfway back to the cottage and opened the gate to the vegetable patch.

'Probably looking for sweet young carrots,' Ronnyn said. 'You know how Tam likes to...'

He broke off as Tamaron used a stick to prod something that lay hidden under the broad leaves of the butternut pumpkin vine.

'Probably found a frog,' Ronnyn decided, more interested in their discussion. He glanced over to the clothesline. Aravelle was headed back and so was Vittor, although he had further to come. Better get his questions in quickly. 'What were you going to say? Father was saying not to touch–'

'Most gifts require touch, but...' His mother broke off, all her attention on Tamaron and Itania. They'd both crouched down to get a better look at whatever was hiding under the pumpkin leaves. His little brother poked it again.

'Could be a snake,' Sasoria said. 'Quickly, Ronnyn, go see what they're up to.'

Worried now, he headed towards them. But before he got far, something darted out from under the leaves, going for Tamaron. Itania squealed. He caught the flash of a long body, short muscular legs, powerful shoulders, and dark fur, with white markings behind the neck.

A stink-badger!

Ronnyn ran. Grabbing the axe as he passed the chopping block, he vaulted over the vegetable patch fence and ran through the bean trellises.

Luckily for Tamaron, the stink-badger's attack was only a warning. It let him go and the three-year-old stumbled back. Too shocked to react, he just stood there, blood pouring from his face.

Itania stared at him, equally shocked. Just as Ronnyn came up behind them, she let out a shrill scream. She didn't run. Neither did Tamaron. The three-year-old didn't even try to stop the bleeding, just stood there and wailed.

They were both so terribly vulnerable.

Where was the stink-badger?

As soon as Ronnyn reached them, he shoved both the little ones behind him. 'Go back to Ma.'

He scanned the pumpkin patch. The stink-badger had retreated. If it was the one that made the tracks, it was a big male. They were lucky it hadn't gone for Tamaron's throat.

He'd have to kill it.

His mother darted through the gate, calling Tamaron and Itania, who ran down the path and into her arms.

Ronnyn caught movement in the corner of his eye. He spun around. It was Aravelle. She didn't bother to go to the gate, just put her foot on the bottom rung of the fence and swung her weight over, jumping to the ground.

'Stay out of the pumpkin vines,' he warned, before she could disturb the creature. 'Come 'round this way, to me.'

'What is it?' she called.

'Stink-badger. A big one.' He glanced back in time to see his mother struggling to stand, with Itania in her arms and Tamaron clinging to her, weeping and bleeding.

Movement. This time it was Vittor running back to join them. He passed out of sight behind the smokehouse and chicken coop on his way around to them.

'Everyone stand back,' Ronnyn ordered. 'Vella, pick up Tam. I'm going to try to drive it towards the corner and trap it.' Where the chicken coop and smokehouse formed a right angle.

'I can help,' Aravelle insisted.

'Help by picking up Tam.' He didn't take his eyes off the vines. He'd spotted movement under the leaves.

'I'll take Tam,' Sasoria said. 'Get the rake, Vella. Help Ronnyn.'

Vittor ran through the gate and up the path, taking a position on Ronnyn's right. Along the way, he'd grabbed the hoe and Aravelle had the rake. But all of them had bare feet and legs, and the stink-badger could easily knock Vittor over.

'Make noise. Scare it,' Ronnyn told them. 'Walk on each side of me, slightly behind me.'

They did, advancing with him across the pumpkin vines. He saw the way the leaves moved; the stink-badger was weaving from side to side as it backed away into the corner.

The beast made a break for it, trying to get past Aravelle on the left.

Ronnyn went that way, cut it off and drove it before him. They could see it clearly, with its big body, sharp teeth, and scars from fights with the wild dogs.

They'd trapped it now.

'Stay back.' Ronnyn stepped in.

The creature reared up on its hind legs and bared its teeth. A pungent stench hit the back of Ronnyn's throat. It made him gag. He went to swing, but another stink-badger came at him from the left, past Aravelle. It sank its teeth into his forearm, and he felt the muscle tear. The creature hung off his arm, nearly unbalancing him.

Seizing its chance, the first stink-badger came at Ronnyn. Vittor swung the hoe, clipping its rear leg as it leaped.

On his left, Aravelle brought the rake down hard, slamming it onto the other stink-badger's eyes, forcing it to let Ronnyn go. She'd freed his left arm, but he'd dropped the axe, and when he bent down to grab it, his fingers wouldn't work.

Vittor whimpered. Ronnyn looked up to see that the first stink-badger had aimed its foul spray at his little brother and Vittor was bent double retching. Defenceless.

Nothing could be allowed to hurt his family.

He grabbed the axe with his right hand. Time slowed. Everything became totally clear and sharp. Bringing the blade around in an arc, he struck the creature's flank before it could attack Vittor. Hot blood sprayed him, seemed to empower him.

Holding the edge of her smock over her nose and mouth, Aravelle dragged Vittor out of danger.

The second stink-badger gave a horrible yowl as it came at Ronnyn again.

He slammed the axe down into the beast. Blood arced up.

Even mortally injured, the first stink-badger went for him again.

Ronnyn struck over and over, until both beasts had stopped moving. He was bathed in hot blood. Bright beads of blood gleamed like jewels on the broad green leaves.

He'd never felt more alive as he stood, gulping for breath.

From far away, he heard Itania whimper.

When he turned to the others, he found Vittor and Aravelle had backed off to join their mother and the little ones. They all stared at him as if they didn't know him. As if they were afraid of him.

Then Vittor gave a whoop and a cheer.

Ronnyn glanced down to the two stink-badgers. They were mangled beyond recognition.

'Vittor, come here.' His mother's voice sounded odd, or it might just be his ears. Everything, even the chickens' familiar squawking, sounded far away. 'Vittor, strip off those clothes. I'll have to burn them. Then help me get Tam inside. His face needs stitching. Vella, go help Ronnyn.'

As his mother returned to the cottage with Itania in her arms, Vittor struggling to carry Tamaron beside her, Aravelle came closer.

She stopped a little way from him. 'You can put the axe down now.'

He did, but it was hard to make his right hand unclench.

She pointed to his left arm. 'You need stitches.'

His forearm was a mess. Strips of meat hung in tatters and he could see bone. The sharpness he'd felt during the attack left him as suddenly as it had come.

Aravelle pulled off her smock, revealing her knitted under-vest. Taking his injured arm, she wound the smock tightly around it and tied it off. 'Hold your arm up high against your body.'

He did as he was told. His mind felt slow and thick, like honey on a winter's day.

'Don't you faint,' Aravelle warned. 'I can't carry you.'

He knew he should be indignant, but he couldn't seem to get annoyed. 'I'll be all right.' He slurred his words.

Aravelle picked up the rake and prodded what was left of the two stink-badgers. 'You really made sure they were dead.'

'Couldn't let them hurt you or Vittor.'

She looked him over. Her knitted vest and breeches revealed the curves of her body. Funny, they were both bigger than their mother, but she still dressed them like children.

'You stink something awful, and you're covered in blood,' Aravelle said. 'It's all through your hair. You need to wash up.'

He nodded. And just stood there.

She frowned and put the rake aside to guide him towards the cottage. She walked on his right side, her arm around his waist.

Ronnyn turned towards the cottage and the water barrel, but the world kept turning and he went down, vaguely aware of Aravelle trying to support him.

The next thing he knew he was inside, on the floor in front of the fire, stretched out on a blanket while Aravelle knelt next to him. She frowned in concentration as she bandaged his arm.

'You're awake, good.' Aravelle was all business. 'I rolled you onto a blanket and dragged you inside. Ma's already sewn you up. Tam and Itania wouldn't stop crying, so she climbed into bed with them and Da.'

He listened. It was quiet behind the partition. 'Sounds like they're all asleep.'

'They are.' Aravelle finished bandaging his arm. 'There. Vittor, take this bowl and tip it out.'

As the six-year-old took the bowl of dirty water away, Aravelle poured hot water from the kettle into another bowl, then checked the temperature.

Ronnyn shifted. Was he naked? He felt the much-washed material of the feather-down quilt on his bare thighs. Had Aravelle stripped him? He flushed at the thought. He wasn't a boy any more.

'Let's get that blood off your face,' Aravelle said as she wrung out the cloth and turned back to him.

He caught her arm with his good hand. 'How's Tam? I wasn't quick enough to get to him. Is he–'

'Ma sewed up his bottom lip. He'll have a scar, just like a real brotherhood warrior.'

'You were like a warrior,' Vittor said from the doorway. He came over to kneel next to Ronnyn. 'You were ferocious. The way you swung that axe!'

Ronnyn grinned and glanced to Aravelle. Her mouth had pulled into a tight line of disapproval.

'I had to kill them, Vella. Had to protect you and Vittor. They would have hung around and stolen our chickens. I–'

'I know. You did the right thing.' She sponged his face clean of dried blood. Her touch was gentle, but her eyes would not meet his.

Ronnyn tried to catch Aravelle's eyes. 'Vella?'

She glanced around as if looking for something to do. 'Vittor, go fill the kettle. We could all do with some honey-tea.'

He jumped to his feet, eager to help. He grabbed the kettle and went to fill it, only to discover the water bucket was empty, so he took it outside to the rainwater barrel.

Ronnyn pulled himself up onto one elbow, then sat up, resting his back against the chest beside the hearth. 'Vella, what's wrong? Look at me.'

'Nothing's wrong.' But her gaze slid away from his.

'I had to kill them.'

'I know. It's not that.'

'Then what is it?'

She bit her bottom lip, sharp white teeth indenting the red curve.

Was she scared of him? He lifted his uninjured arm. His hand felt clumsy as he cupped her cheek. 'I'd never hurt you.'

'I know that. It's just... I let that stink-badger get past me.' She gulped back a sob and tears raced down her cheeks. 'And it made a mess of your arm. You could be crippled for life because of me!'

And she sobbed as if her heart would break.

He pulled her down against his chest, felt the heat of her tears on his bare skin. With his good hand, he rubbed small circles on her back while she sobbed. It was not like Aravelle to let him comfort her, and he discovered he enjoyed it.

Too soon she pulled away, wiping her wet cheeks.

'You still smell pretty bad,' she said. Blowing her nose, she pushed damp hair from her red-rimmed eyes. This time, when she met his gaze, hers was determined. 'I'll work with you every day. I'll massage the muscle. I'll help you get the movement back in your fingers.'

He nodded. He didn't really believe he'd be crippled. He'd get better, he always had. 'And in the meantime, I can learn to use my right hand.'

Vittor came back. When he saw Aravelle's tear-ravaged face, he put the bucket down and rushed over, demanding to know what was wrong.

'Nothing.' But fresh tears slid down her cheeks.

Vittor's chin trembled and he shuddered as he drew in a breath. A sob escaped him.

'Silly boy,' Ronnyn said fondly, pulling him close.

As if this was a signal, Vittor succumbed to a storm of tears. Ronnyn smiled, as his little brother wept on his chest. He felt strong and powerful, protective. This must be what it felt like to be a man. 'It's over, and you were very brave.'

Aravelle put the kettle on. Soon the water was boiling merrily and the familiar smell of honey-tea filled the cottage. His injured arm throbbed with each beat of his heart, but Ronnyn felt good. He didn't care what it cost him to protect the people he loved. And in that instant, he understood what had driven his father to kill the fisherman.

No price was too high to keep his family safe.

Chapter Twenty-Three

Tobazim patrolled the ruined palace's wall-walk. As the sun dipped towards the west, frustration drove his steps. It was midsummer's eve, and over the next eight days, everyone would be celebrating, indulging in sanctioned trysting – and a fair amount of illicit trysting, from what he gathered.

But not him. The hand-of-force had done it again, sending the Malaunje warriors from the winery, along with the same dozen T'En adepts and initiates, to patrol the walls of both palaces. It was far more than they needed. Why, back when the city had first been attacked, he and Learon had...

The pain hit him, and the guilt.

He turned and gripped the stone, until he could control his gift.

Chariode's palace came into focus. The exterior appeared fine, but inside it was ruined, like Kyredeon's brotherhood.

The all-father had complained that he'd won Chariode's brotherhood, but all he had to show for it was half a dozen young initiate warriors, a ruined palace, estates he would have to abandon, a missing shipping fleet, and over two dozen Malaunje non-combatants, who he had to shelter and feed, for which he blamed Tobazim.

But Tobazim didn't care. He was glad he'd saved the women and children.

Now he understood why a high-ranking male like his old gift-tutor served out his days on a distant winery instead of taking his place in his brotherhood's inner circle. His gift-tutor had chosen to banish himself. Sometimes exile was the best path.

The realisation surprised him.

Unfortunately for him, he no longer had the option of voluntary exile from Kyredeon's palace. He was stuck in the city. What he needed was a shield-brother, someone at his back who he could trust with his life. Their gifts would augment each other, making them both more powerful. More power would protect them both from Kyredeon, but it would also attract his ire. It was a two-edged sword.

Taking a shield-brother was not something to be done lightly. It was for life. Sometimes when one died, the other died with him. And, as much as Tobazim needed to know there was someone he could place absolute trust in, he could not imagine binding just anyone to him. The bond of shield-brother, like the bond of devotee and T'En, was sacred and not to be entered into lightly.

All of which brought him back to this. He was alone in a brotherhood whose vindictive leaders had singled him out as a threat.

Just then Athlyn, Eryx and Haromyr joined him. Tobazim gestured to the free quarter, where they could hear singing and laughter.

'If you associate with me, you'll never rise in the brotherhood ranks. All you have to do is deny me and you could be taking part in the festivities.'

'Tobazim...' Athlyn whispered, hurt that he would even suggest it.

He could have kicked himself. If these brothers thought life impossible, they'd do something stupid and symbolic like Learon.

'Just look at the city.' Eryx gestured, changing the subject. 'Have you ever seen anything more beautiful?'

Tobazim looked up. The white towers and domes climbed all the way to the sisterhoods' palaces on the peak. Bathed in the setting sun's rays, they appeared to be made of gold. No wonder King Charald and his barons wanted to capture the city. It was so perfect it took his breath away and made his gift stir. To build and create, that was his purpose.

'I can't believe we're going to hand it over to the Mieren,' Haromyr muttered.

'We can build somewhere else,' Tobazim said. 'We can build a better city. A better T'Enatuath.'

'That's why we don't deny you,' Eryx said. 'You give us hope.'

How could he, when he had none himself?

'Tobazim?' Maric called.

He crossed to the other side of the wall-walk.

The Malaunje warrior pointed across the lake, burnished by the setting sun. Tobazim sighted along Maric's arm. He frowned. Was that a log coming this way? He narrowed his eyes against the glare. It was definitely being propelled by something.

'What is it?' Eryx asked.

The log continued to glide towards the city wall. It wasn't heading just anywhere along the city wall, but specifically aiming for Chariode's boat-house. When the log drew nearer, he spotted at least seven people hanging onto the side of it.

An arm signalled.

Tobazim waved back. 'They're probably from some distant estate and don't know that we've reached an agreement with the Mieren king. If they've come here, to this section of wall...' They would be from Chariode's brotherhood, and they were in for a rude shock. He turned to the others. 'Eryx, hold the wall. Athlyn and Haromyr, come with me.'

He led them down the steps, through the connecting courtyard to the boat-house. It was the longest day of the year and there was still enough light to see the lake beyond the grille, but inside the boat-house was dark.

Tobazim lit the lantern and swung the gate open.

The log edged closer until it bobbed gently against the city wall. One by one, the refugees let go and made their way in, past the moored barge to the steps, where Athlyn and Haromyr helped them out of the water.

Tobazim counted five Malaunje and two T'En. He didn't recognise any of them. They all smelled of lakewater and looked exhausted, shivering in their wet, ragged clothing. One of the T'En was a big male, almost as tall as Learon, but the other T'En was their leader.

Tobazim swung the gate shut and bolted it, then came back to the steps. As he returned, the leader's gaze swept over Tobazim, then Haromyr and Athlyn.

Clearly suspicious, he moved in front of his men. 'Who are you? And what are you doing in All-father Chariode's boat-house?'

Tobazim hesitated, but could think of no easy way to say this. 'Kyredeon claimed Chariode's brotherhood.'

The big adept bristled. 'Impossible!'

But the older one looked shaken. 'For that to be true, our all-father and most of his high-ranking brothers would have to be dead.' He searched Tobazim's face, reading the truth there, and his lean cheeks blanched. 'Do any still live who can vouch for me? I'm ship's captain Ardonyx, returned from a two-year voyage of exploration. This is Adept Ionnyn and five of my sailors.'

'When the Mieren stormed the city, Chariode's brotherhood bore the brunt of the initial attack. All the high-ranking T'En died—'

'What of the women and children?' one of the Malaunje asked. 'Where are they? Surely the Mieren didn't...'

'They killed...' Tobazim remembered the bodies and could not go on. He swallowed. 'Around two dozen women and children were rescued off the roof.'

'So few?' the sailor whispered.

There was silence for a moment as they digested the news.

Then Athlyn asked, 'Why did you come in by the lake, when you could have walked down the causeway?'

'Walked down...' Ardonyx's voice grew thick with anger.

'When we landed nine days ago, we didn't know anything was wrong. We'd sailed as far as the Lagoons of Perpetual Summer, surviving both storm and shoal. The last thing we expected was to be attacked in our home port. There was no warning. They set one of my ships alight. While we were distracted, they cut us down. This' – he gestured to the others – 'is all that's left of two ships' crews. Since then, we've travelled by night, avoiding everyone. When we got to the lake, we saw the tents and realised the city was besieged, so of course we approached by stealth.'

'You shouldn't have been attacked in port,' Tobazim said. 'Since we've agreed to exile–'

'Exile?' Ionnyn repeated, shocked.

Ardonyx nodded to Tobazim. 'Go on.'

'Since we've agreed to exile, messengers can leave our city and refugees from the outlying estates are still trickling in. You would have been safe travelling on the road.'

'I thought my ships were safe in the harbour.'

Tobazim conceded his point. Taking into account the weathering of sea life, Ardonyx was no more than ten years older than him, perhaps a little taller and of a slighter build. There was something faintly foreign about his manner, as if he'd been too long in strange lands.

'Where are our women and children right now?' the same Malaunje sailor asked. 'I must know if my family survived.'

'Of course.' Tobazim sympathised. 'Come this way. But first, I have to deliver you to the all-father.'

He led them out of the boat-house, through the ruined palace. When they saw the extent of the damage, they were shattered.

'You said the Mieren came in through our brotherhood's palace?' Ardonyx walked beside him. 'Surely someone heard the fighting. Why didn't anyone come to our aid?'

'It was winter's cusp, a feast night. No one realised Chariode's brotherhood was under attack until it was too late.' Tobazim was ashamed to admit the truth.

He led them out onto the street, along to the entrance of Kyredeon's brotherhood, where the courtyard was bright with lanterns. Laughter, music and song echoed down from the windows and balconies, contrasting with the sober attitude of Captain Ardonyx and his surviving crew.

Tobazim felt for Ardonyx. Not only had he lost his friends, men he had known since he joined the brotherhood at seventeen, but he would now lose his ranking and have to work his way up again. He must have been well-respected to lead a voyage of discovery.

'You say the Mieren confiscated your ships?'

'And my cargo. Exotic spices, never seen this far north before.'

'What were they like, the Lagoons of Perpetual Summer?'

'Bluer than a summer sky, warm and so shallow you could see our ships' shadows on the white sands below us.' Ardonyx spoke slowly at first, his voice gathering strength. 'Strange creatures crawled on the seabed and fish swam in schools, darting about like beautiful birds. The sandy shores of the islands were so white they shone in the sun. And each island was crowned with tropical forest. There were palms, fruit growing wild for the taking, flowers larger than my hand across, and birds colourful as jewels.'

'Sounds like paradise.'

'It was. But everywhere we went there were Mieren. We were lucky, the islanders had never heard of Wyrds and were happy to trade. Both my ships' holds were filled with spices more valuable than gold.' His mouth tightened with anger. 'Now the port Mieren will grow rich on the blood and sweat of my crew.'

'What're you doing here, Tobazim? You're supposed to be on the wall.' Kyredeon's hand-of-force had been drinking, but not enough to make him amiable. It never was. He gestured to Ardonyx. 'Who is this?'

'Hand-of-force Oriemn. These are relics of Chariode's brotherhood, returned from a voyage to the Lagoons of

Perpetual Summer. They are all that survive of two ships' crews.'

Oriemn frowned. 'Bring them.'

Tobazim escorted the captain and his crew into the palace's main courtyard. Lanterns illuminated two dozen Malaunje dancers, who scattered as Kyredeon's hand-of-force dismissed them with a wave. The musicians faltered to a stop.

Marble statues gleamed, decorated with garlands of summer flowers. The flowers' heady scents competed with the smell of seasoned roast pork cooking on spits. The city might be under siege, but they had not stinted on the feast. It was an all-father's duty and honour to provide for his people.

The gathering fell silent as Oriemn knelt and reported to his all-father. Kyredeon lay on a couch with his voice-of-reason.

Oriemn rose and stepped to one side. Kyredeon beckoned Ardonyx, who approached, gave obeisance and then sank gracefully to his knees. Ionnyn followed two steps behind. The five Malaunje sailors also dropped to their knees.

Kyredeon's voice-of-reason whispered something to the all-father, and his eyes narrowed.

'I know you, Ardonyx,' Kyredeon said. 'You were part of Chariode's inner circle. You'll never be part of mine, not when you swore undying loyalty to him. Give me one good reason why I should not have you executed.'

The five Malaunje moaned and whispered.

Ionnyn lifted his head. 'Permission to speak, all-father?'

'Speak.'

'Captain Ardonyx saved our lives.'

'Your lives are not in question. Go.' He dismissed Ionnyn and the Malaunje with a wave of his hand. 'Go.'

The sailors exchanged looks, then gave obeisance and backed out. Tobazim did not blame them.

Ionnyn remained on his knees at Ardonyx's back. Tobazim admired him for this, and admired Ardonyx for earning such loyalty.

Kyredeon frowned at Ionnyn, then turned his attention to Ardonyx. 'Now, tell me why I should not turn you both out and let my warriors hunt you down for sport.'

'A ship's captain could be useful,' Tobazim said, before he knew he meant to. 'Thanks to the causare–'

'Causare?' Ardonyx repeated. 'We have a causare again? Who is it?'

'Imoshen the All-father-killer,' Kyredeon said. 'First she births a female sacrare and her sisterhood votes her all-mother, then she wins the causare vote!'

Ardonyx went very still.

Tobazim snatched this chance to speak. 'When we sail into exile, an experienced ship's captain will be of great service to our brotherhood. Our lives could depend on his skill.'

'Who asked for your opinion?' Kyredeon sprang to his feet and his voice-of-reason also rose as the tang of gift readiness filled the air. It made Tobazim's heart thunder and his gift respond.

'To the sanctum.' Kyredeon signalled his hand-of-force. 'Bring the two relics. As for you' – he turned to Tobazim – 'get back to your duties.'

He had no choice but to leave.

Much later that night, when Tobazim had finished his watch, he returned to the chamber he shared with the other young adepts to find them drinking and playing cards with the two new arrivals. He was surprised and relieved, as he'd prepared himself for news of the captain's death.

'So, Ardonyx, you're one of us now.' Tobazim sank to his knees at the low table, and poured a glass of wine. 'How'd you manage that?'

Ardonyx discarded two cards, selected two more and smiled sweetly. 'Oh, I just asked Kyredeon to be reasonable.'

Tobazim gave a bitter laugh. 'I'd love to know how you did it. I've done nothing but irritate the all-father since I arrived. At this rate, I'll be ninety before I know the touch of a T'En woman!'

'There's always unsanctioned trysting,' Haromyr suggested, ever-resourceful.

Tobazim shook his head. As curious as he was, he was not going to risk Kyredeon's rage. He indicated the cards. 'Deal me in.'

'Too late.' Ardonyx met his eyes as he lay down his hand. 'I claim the brotherhood.' And he laid out his winning hand.

The others laughed, throwing down their cards.

'This must be your lucky night,' Haromyr said.

'Hope it holds out tomorrow, then. I've asked to meet the causare.' Seeing their stunned expressions, Ardonyx shrugged. 'The Mieren stole my ships and cargo, and murdered all but six of my crew. King Charald has promised us safe passage to the sea, but I doubt he can deliver. Who knows how many of our people the Mieren have killed since we accepted exile? Somehow, the causare must ensure those stranded on isolated estates get to port safely.'

Shame filled Tobazim. He'd been thinking only of himself and how much he hated serving under Kyredeon, while their new brother thought of the T'Enatuath.

As IMOSHEN HUGGED her daughter, Umaleni patted the jewels around her neck, making happy little bird noises. The sisterhood had gathered on the rooftop garden under a festive tent to celebrate her daughter's first birthday.

The only sacrare child of the T'Enatuath, Umaleni had been showered with gifts and attention all morning. The fuss had surprised Imoshen, and she vowed not to let them spoil her daughter. When Umaleni grew up, she would need to be strong and hard-headed.

The toddler wriggled and Imoshen put her down, so she could join Tancred, who was playing with the blocks at Imoshen's feet. Today, the geldr was the mental equivalent of a five-year-old. Seeing Tancred always saddened Imoshen. He was the same age as her, but he would never go to live with the brotherhoods. His T'En mother had been so desperate for a daughter that she'd tried to ensure her child would be born female, and had ruined him.

Laughter carried across the rooftop garden. The women of the sisterhood were excited, their gifts barely contained. Traditionally, midsummer was a time of celebration. Over the next eight days, poets' reputations would be made or broken, playwrights would parody events and polarise opinions, artists would exhibit their work, and the salons would be filled with debate.

But the most eagerly anticipated event was tonight's masked carnival, where Malaunje and T'En alike mingled in the park, in the eateries and in the dance halls that opened off the lantern-strung streets of the free quarter. This evening, under cover of masks, those who dared could indulge in unsanctioned trystings.

Meanwhile, there were the sanctioned trystings to organise. The status, gift and temperament of both individuals had to be considered. The man and woman would come away with their gift enhanced by the experience, but for this to happen, they had to lower their defences, which left them open to attack. It was a delicate balance: the higher the adept, the more dangerous but rewarding the trysting.

Which reminded Imoshen... it was two years since she'd seen Umaleni's father. A year from conception to birth, and a year since their daughter was born. He'd sailed to find a southern passage to the far-east. For all she knew, he was dead.

She mustn't think like that; he would return.

'Midsummer's day.' Egrayne's sharp mulberry eyes studied Imoshen. 'A propitious time for a birth.'

Imoshen's gift surged, and she realised Egrayne was trying to guess the identity of Umaleni's father.

All around them, the sisters nibbled delicacies and spoke of the coming midsummer celebrations. Meanwhile, Malaunje musicians played and the sisterhood's poetess composed rhyming couplets about the trysting prowess of various T'En men.

'I have been watching you, Imoshen,' Egrayne said softly. 'And I have not been able to identify the adept you chose for Umaleni's father. Was it one of the all-fathers I recommended?'

Imoshen only smiled and shook her head.

'Keep your counsel, then, but beware. You let your gift defences down once with him. He'll seek to breach them again to gain advantage over you, especially now that you are causare.'

Ardonyx wouldn't, of that Imoshen was certain, just as she was certain Egrayne would be horrified if she realised Imoshen had made the deep-bonding. Egrayne saw the T'En men as enemies. But for every male like Kyredeon, there were males like Ardonyx and her choice-son.

'Time to see the all-fathers,' Egrayne said.

They set off down the causeway road to the free quarter. The Mieren shops were all boarded up, and had been since winter cusp.

When they reached the park, the T'En males were waiting near the steps of the bower building, eager gifts barely contained. Imoshen and her seconds climbed to the top floor and went along the arched verandah. They passed other bowers, where all-mothers were already negotiating trystings over wine and fruit.

Imoshen's bower had been decorated for the festival. Gauzy drapes hung from the ceiling. Ripe fruits, scented flowers and summer wine sat on the low table, surrounded by velvet cushions. The chamber radiated life and fecundity, just as it should.

Imoshen knelt at the low table and checked her pen. 'Send in the first all-father, Egrayne.'

Her voice-of-reason returned at a run. 'It's Kyredeon.'

'Ah.' Imoshen had every intention of refusing all his trysting offers.

Kiane stepped to one side to announce the men as

they entered. She ended with, '...and Adept Ardonyx, formerly of Chariode's brotherhood.'

It was all the warning Imoshen had. Ardonyx appeared older and thinner. The world contracted until there was only his presence. Her gift tried to break free, seeking his. A rushing filled her ears. She felt light-headed and insubstantial, yet at the same time more alive than ever.

Kyredeon gave an abbreviated bow, dropping to kneel opposite her. 'My new adept has disturbing news.'

'Causare.' Ardonyx made the formal obeisance, sinking to his knees.

Meanwhile, Imoshen scrambled to collect her wits. 'Ardonyx, the sea captain?' she asked, as though searching to recall him. 'What is your news?'

Kyredeon answered for him. 'Mieren killed all but six of his crew and impounded his ships. As his all-father, I demand compensation.'

Imoshen glanced to Ardonyx. There was the slightest hint of cynical amusement in his wine-dark eyes.

'Your ships carried great wealth, captain?' Imoshen's voice was neutral, but her gift thrummed under her skin.

'Both holds were waist-deep in spices from the Lagoons of Perpetual Summer. Spices worth more than their weight in gold.'

She hid a smile. No wonder Kyredeon was eager for compensation.

'I'll contact King Charald's agent, but this is larger than the fate of two ships,' Imoshen said. 'This means the Mieren are not honouring the king's word. Our people on the outlying estates may have trouble reaching port.'

'There is a way to make the Mieren's greed serve us,' Ardonyx said. 'The causare could offer a reward for live T'En and Malaunje. A few silver coins would be a year's earnings to most Mieren.'

Imoshen smiled. 'Very good. I'll send a message to King Charald's agent.'

'And it suits his purpose,' Ardonyx said. 'As much as it suits ours.'

She smiled. She had to force herself to look away and rein in her gift.

'I propose a toast.' She poured a glass of wine for each of them and, as a sign of her approval, let her power imbue the wine with gift-essence. Lifting her own glass, she said, 'To the greed of Mieren serving us.'

They echoed her words. Egrayne gave a little gasp of surprise as she sensed the wine's gift essence. Kyredeon and his two seconds drained their goblets in one gulp.

'You honour us, causare.' Ardonyx sipped his wine slowly, savouring her generosity.

'Exile draws near.' Imoshen's mind raced. 'We need to form an exile-council, made up of representatives from each sisterhood and brotherhood. They need to bring a variety of skills to the table. For instance, Ardonyx knows ships, the sea and the Mieren.'

'I would be honoured to serve.'

'Excellent.' This meant she would see him often, but if she did not lie naked in his arms soon, her power would escape her control. Already she could feel the tension in the bower rising, as the others responded to her gift readiness.

'Egrayne...' – Imoshen had to clear her throat – 'make a note to send messages to each brotherhood and sisterhood, requesting a representative for the exile-council.'

Egrayne nodded and dipped the nib in ink.

'There is also the question of trystings,' Kyredeon said. 'Have your sisters requested any of my brothers?'

'I'll check in a moment.' Egrayne kept scribbling.

Imoshen bit into a strawberry, aware of Ardonyx's eyes on her. She had to remember how to swallow. If only she could officially tryst with Ardonyx, but his stature was too low and she must not single him out. If Kyredeon discovered he had her secret bond-partner in his power, she shuddered to think what the all-father would do.

In the past, they'd met at their language lessons, but Merchant Mercai had returned to Ivernia, leaving the Sagora house empty. For a moment her heart leapt, before she remembered that the foreign quarter lay outside the causeway gate. But there was still the Sagora shop in the free quarter.

She glanced to Egrayne, who was pretending to check the trysting list.

Imoshen picked her words with care. 'Much has changed since you left us to make your voyage of discovery, Captain Ardonyx. The foreign quarter is empty, and all the Mieren shops in the free quarter are closed. You may wonder why we still celebrate the traditional midsummer festivities. In such dark days, ritual is important. It brings us together.'

Would he make the connection? With the masked carnival, it would be easy to slip away from her sisters this evening, and meet him at the Sagoras' shop.

'The bond of ritual is important,' Ardonyx agreed. As his knowing eyes met hers, she felt a surge of excitement mingled with admiration.

'I'm sorry, All-father Kyredeon,' Egrayne said. 'Your brothers are not on our list.'

'This is the seventh midsummer in a row that my brotherhood has been slighted by your sisterhood.' His angry, hungry gaze went to Imoshen. 'The causare sits there, enticing me with her power. I demand she acknowledge my rise in stature with a trysting.'

The bower went utterly still.

'You forget yourself, Kyredeon. All-fathers do not demand, they gratefully accept.' Egrayne sounded calm, but her gift had risen. She sent Imoshen a warning look.

The last thing Imoshen wanted to do was take Kyredeon to her bower. The problem was that, despite his tone, Kyredeon was correct. He had saved the women and children of Chariode's brotherhood; this should be acknowledged. And she was causare.

'I would honour your rise in stature, Kyredeon,' Imoshen

said sweetly, 'but I've taken a vow of celibacy to make no formal trystings until our people are safely at sea.'

'That reminds me,' Ardonyx said. 'When I was escaping the port, I discovered Chariode's warehouse had been burnt to the ground.'

Kyredeon was diverted. 'I want compensation for the warehouse and its contents.'

Amused, she met Ardonyx's eyes. How could she wait until this evening?

Chapter Twenty-Four

IMOSHEN STOOD AT the window watching the sun set. When her sisters went to dress for the evening's masked carnival, she'd complained of a headache and retired for the evening. Now her heart raced and her gift prowled within her body, making her skin tingle. All she could think of was seeing Ardonyx.

'Ready?' Frayvia asked, entering the chamber.

'Uma sleeps?'

'Worn out from too much fun. You're wearing that?'

'Doesn't matter. I'll be wearing a cloak and mask.'

'At least let me do your hair.'

'Nothing too fancy. I go out tonight as a simple sister, not an all-mother or the causare.' Imoshen sat in front of the polished silver mirror.

'Down in the Malaunje chambers, they're talking of him,' Frayvia said. 'They say he saved five of his Malaunje crew at the risk of his own life. Only one other T'En escaped. They say he is more than fair.'

'High praise indeed, from the Malaunje,' Imoshen teased. 'What do they say of me?'

Frayvia's eyes gleamed. 'They say nothing in front of me.'

'What about behind your back, when they think you can't hear?'

'They say you are surprisingly fair.'

'Is that good?'

Frayvia nodded. 'There.'

She had threaded a crownlet of zircons through Imoshen's hair and left the rest free down her back.

As she came to her feet, Imoshen's hair fell like a cloak to her knees, but it was not really fashionable. To be truly elegant, her hair should be long enough to walk on. Imoshen grimaced. She'd always resented the time it took to dress her hair and the weight of the jewelled headdresses she had to wear.

Frayvia fetched a plain cloak and mask. As the devotee settled the material over her shoulders, she hugged Imoshen, revelling in the gift-readiness that came off her skin.

Imoshen did not mind; it was part of the bond between a T'En and their devotee. With a fond kiss, she left Frayvia and the sisterhood.

Choosing the right moment, she fell in with the happy crowd heading down to the free quarter, where lanterns hung from every post and doorway, casting a friendly glow. As Imoshen passed a lane, she heard eager laughter and sensed the urgency of passion unleashed by carnival licence.

The women, both Malaunje and T'En, who were looking for trysting partners wore the traditional pleated silken pants with no centre seam and a topless bodice. Most rouged their nipples, just as they painted their eyes and lips. Tonight, all wore their hair free, threaded with semi-precious stones.

The men looked just as fine, with their breeches slung low on their hips, their chests bare the better to display their scars, and their eyes and lips painted.

Music hung on the warm air; laughter, song, the scent of jasmine, delicious aromas drifted from the eateries – tonight sounded and smelled just like any other carnival night, but there was a feverish intensity. This was their last midsummer in the city before they sailed into danger.

Imoshen found the Sagora shop. Last winter cusp, the Sagoras had closed the shop at the end of trade and bolted the shutters, never dreaming they would not be back the next day.

The shop's sign was the Sagora symbol: the scroll and the nib. They prized knowledge above all else, which was why Imoshen had approached them for sanctuary. Surely people who prized knowledge would not fear those who were different?

Imoshen slipped down the lane between the shops and into the tiny back yard. There was no sign of Ardonyx, but the door hung off one hinge.

She shifted the door, leaning it against the wall. A patch of moonlight revealed the glint of scattered silver coins, presumably left by a looter who'd been disturbed when the Mieren were routed. The small back room was a mass of overturned supplies.

Inside the shop it was darker still. Imoshen took a moment to gift-enhance her sight. This used to be her favourite shop and it distressed her to find the stock thrown about, scrolls in heaps and maps torn from the walls.

Opening her senses, she searched for Ardonyx, but there was no sign of him. No one had been here for a long time. The air felt still and flat, and everything she touched was covered in a layer of dust.

Unable to stay still, she paced towards the front door.

He would not come.

Now that she was causare, her stature far outstripped his. Most T'En men would resent this. What was worse, now that he'd sworn fealty to Kyredeon, his life would be forfeit if the all-father found out they'd made the deep-bond.

When she reached the shadows near the front door, she heard a shriek, then muffled laughter, from the street. She envied the revellers their light-hearted dalliance. It could never be like that for her. Where she gave her heart, she gave everything, and she'd never expected to find that same quality in a brotherhood warrior.

For them both it was all or nothing.

She leaned her forehead against the wooden door. Deception had allowed their love to flourish, and deception had kept it safe; and her second sacrare child had come from their union.

Did he know that their child thrived?

He wouldn't come. It was too risky.

'Imoshen?'

She spun around to see him silhouetted in the open door. Joy coursed through her body, rousing her gift.

He removed his mask, revealing a face both intense and intelligent, and beloved to her. 'Imoshen?'

'Here,' she said and he strode towards her. 'You shouldn't have come.'

'I know.' He met her halfway. 'I can't stay.'

She cupped his face. 'We have a sacrare daughter.' Then she opened her link and memory-shared – precious moments, saved just for him. She let him feel Umaleni in her arms, a hot, slippery newborn, let him feel the tug on her nipple as the babe fed and the rush of milk hardened her breasts, let him feel her joy as Umaleni's brilliant, mulberry eyes shone with intelligence, let him hear their child's delighted laugh, let him experience her own glow of pride as Umaleni took her first steps unaided.

He gasped and almost staggered.

Imoshen moved to support him, but then it was him supporting her, him holding her close as they kissed. She tasted the salt of tears on his lips.

Tears stung her eyes. Her lips moved against his. 'You cannot stay. It's not safe.'

'I know.' His breath brushed her face.

Through their link, she felt how much he wanted her, and her body responded as something deep inside her clenched. His hands tightened on her waist. They were moving. She felt the door at her back. Shadows so deep they were like black velvet enveloped them. Lost in sensation, she welcomed the dark, the better to concentrate on touch. Her hands slid inside his breeches, felt the vibrant life and urgency in him.

Her knees trembled as he slipped his hand under her clothing to hold her. Then he was lifting her onto him, with the door at her back. She lost track of where she finished and he began. For a heartbeat it was a relief to feel him in her, and then that wasn't enough. His ragged breathing delighted her. She knew her power over him, but it was a two-edged sword. She gasped, grasping his shoulders, and let down her gift-defences to ride his passion.

An eternity later but still far too soon, sanity returned. As she pressed her forehead to his, both gasped, both were elated and renewed. He let her gently down and her sandals touched the floor. She felt his seed slide down her thighs, slippery as hot silk. Still linked, she knew he felt the sensation and marvelled.

Her heart beat like a great drum, reverberating through her body, and her gift pulsed beneath her skin. He ran his hands over her, the lightest of touches on her flesh, revelling in her power.

'Your brotherhood will sense me on your skin,' she warned. 'They'll know you've been with a powerful T'En sister.'

He shook his head. 'I'll overlay it with a brotherhood trysting.'

'He'll know. He'll give us away.'

'He's never trysted with a T'En woman. It will happen so fast he won't know what's going on. I'll be safe. We'll be safe.'

'We'll never be safe, never be together...' And to her horror, she burst into tears.

He laughed, hugging her, whispering nonsense.

Imoshen brushed his hands aside, fighting for control. Rebuilding her gift-defences, she shut down the intimate depth of their link. 'If I didn't know better, I'd say run away with me.'

'There's nowhere to run. There are Mieren everywhere,' he said.

She caught his face, kissing him again. 'I thought you were dead.'

'So did I, more than once.' He captured her hands, kissing her palms. 'I can taste my gift on your skin. What'll you do?'

'Slip back into my chambers, bathe. And if that isn't enough, gift-infuse my devotee before dawn. She'll think herself lucky.'

He pressed his forehead to hers. 'I must go. I'm being watched. Kyredeon doesn't trust me.'

She drew in a shuddering breath. 'We can't see each other again. Not like this.'

He said nothing.

Imoshen bit her bottom lip. 'I couldn't bear it if anything happened to you–'

'Why did you become causare?' Anger radiated from him as he gripped her shoulders. 'It's made you a target.'

Surprised by this sudden change of topic, she had no answer.

He released her. 'The leaders of the great brotherhoods are all eyeing the causareship and plotting how to wrest it from you.'

'I had no choice. We needed a causare to deal with King Charald the Oath-breaker. The all-mothers couldn't bear the thought of our fate resting in the hands of a brotherhood leader. They thought I was the only all-mother with enough stature to win a vote and keep the all-fathers in line. I couldn't say no.'

He pulled back a step. She felt his frustration and fear, even though their link was closed and they no longer touched.

She reached for him, trying to re-establish the link to siphon off some of his distress. 'Don't be–'

'I'm not angry with you. It's...' He gestured towards the Mieren army, camped on the shore. 'It's them and it's...' He rubbed his jaw. 'Coming back to find Chariode and everyone dead...' His voice broke. She would have hugged him, but he held her off. 'The very last all-father I'd choose to serve is Kyredeon.'

'I know. He's dangerous.'

His expression was bleak.

'If he's dangerous, someone should challenge his leadership. You were on Chariode's inner circle.'

'Exactly. I'm new to the brotherhood, and the others don't know me. Kyredeon has spies reporting on his own people. His hand-of-force is a thug who runs a pack of bullies. Everyone's afraid to stand up to him.'

'Is there no one the brothers would unite behind?'

'No one of high enough stature. Not yet, anyway. And, from what I gather, Kyredeon gets rid of anyone who looks like a potential threat.'

Imoshen nodded, remembering the big warrior who died on the causeway. 'I don't like to think of you having to give your loyalty to him. He doesn't deserve it.'

Ardonyx laughed and kissed her. 'I must go.'

Since they'd made the deep-bond, the raedan aspect of her gift no longer worked on him. It had worked on her first bond-partner, but they'd both been so young. Ardonyx was an experienced adept with a powerful gift of his own. No wonder Kyredeon feared him. 'I asked you once before, if what they said about the playwright Rutz was true. Could he imbue words with power and sway us without us realising?'

'Rutz is dead, killed when the Mieren attacked.'

She grinned. 'If Rutz is dead, you won't be able to write any more plays.'

'I doubt we'll have time for plays in exile.'

'If Rutz could imbue words with power, he could have swayed Kyredeon.'

'If Rutz had that gift...' Ardonyx shrugged. 'He never did and he never wanted it. His friends and lovers would never know if he was swaying them with gift-imbued words. Forget it.'

Imoshen tried to recall the point she'd been leading up to. Something about... 'The all-council. So far I've used my raedan gift to choose the right moment to call for a vote, and the all-fathers have voted the way I'd hoped. But even with the extra vote I get as causare, the all-fathers outnumber the all-mothers. We're going into exile. It's crucial I control the all-council meetings. If you took over Kyredeon's brotherhood, I'd know I had one all-father vote I could count on.'

'Even if I could take over the brotherhood, my vote would follow my conscience, not your lead.'

'I wouldn't have it any other way. I need your voice on the all-council. You've seen the world. I value your insights. I don't want to put you in danger, but... I need to know there is one all-father I can rely on. Is there no way–'

'There is one adept,' Ardonyx admitted. 'He escaped when the Mieren massacred his winery, and arrived in the city with his choice-brother and a dozen Malaunje. He's the one who saved Chariode's Malaunje women and children. About a dozen young initiates and adepts have gravitated to him. But Kyredeon crippled him, by provoking his choice-brother into–'

'The big warrior who confronted the Mieren on the causeway?'

Ardonyx nodded. 'Besides, Tobazim is too young. He's only been an adept for a little over a year.'

'I'm younger than him.'

'You have stature. You're a raedan. You executed Rohaayel and the brotherhoods' best gift-warriors. Tobazim doesn't have enough stature to get the numbers to challenge Kyredeon. And the all-father is just waiting for a chance to send him into danger, or accuse him of disloyalty and execute him. And when that happens, he'll purge half the brotherhood, me included.'

'Can you protect this Tobazim? Cultivate him?'

'I'm going to have to, if we want to kill Kyredeon.'

Imoshen's stomach cramped with fear for him. If the all-father knew they stood here, planning...

'I hate it that you are in danger.'

He laughed. 'You're in more danger than me, causare.

Kyredeon has been known to use assassins. Lucky for you, his best assassin went missing just before winter cusp. Otherwise, I don't think you would have survived this long. He'd have sent Graelen after you.'

She wasn't worried about herself. 'I will never reveal that you are my bond-partner. If Kyredeon or any of the all-fathers move against me, don't risk yourself for me. If I die, my sisterhood will raise our daughter, and my devotee adores her. It's you I worry about. And Iraayel. Since All-father Chariode died, he has no brotherhood. I've made formal requests, but none of the all-fathers will take him, and he turns seventeen just before winter cusp. The sisterhood will declare him dead and send him out the gate the day he turns seventeen. With no brotherhood to protect him–'

'Imoshen... we won't be here for that to happen.'

'Of course, I wasn't thinking. It's just... I don't know how to keep him safe.'

'None of us are safe.'

She loved his wry smile.

'I should go now.'

She nodded.

He lingered.

She brushed her fingers across his lips, sensed his defences drop, felt her body clench and his respond.

With a groan, he took a hasty step back. 'Don't–'

'You're right. I'm sorry.'

'This time I really am going.' His voice held raw regret.

'Yes, go. Go quickly.'

He did, heading out the door at a run. It was a wrench to see him go.

She turned and pressed her forehead against the cool wooden door, felt the grit and the dust, felt her heart beat an uneven tattoo against her ribs.

Finally, she turned around and faced the world. Before she went anywhere, she had to rein in the joyous tolling of her gift. It rang through her body like the pealing of festival bells. Such a pity not to experience this every day.

When she thought she could pass within touching distance of another T'En without them feeling the overflow of her power, she pulled her hood up, and went to leave.

Then she remembered the mask. Where was it? She finally found it amidst a pile of scrolls. Luckily it wasn't crushed.

Replacing her mask, she headed back to the sisterhood's palace.

TOBAZIM PULLED THE covers over his head as someone entered their sleeping chamber. An eager, cajoling male voice was answered with a delighted laugh. By the scent of gift power on the air, Tobazim guessed it was one of the young adepts, eager to tryst with a Malaunje woman.

His own gift tried to surface. Annoyed, he rolled off his bed, startling them both. Wordlessly, he apologised and stepped into corridor, closing the door after him.

He'd left Haromyr and the others wandering the boulevards, masked and hopeful, painted and bare-chested. And that annoyed him. Tonight, everything annoyed him.

Why had King Charald made it his life's work to rid Chalcedonia of the T'Enatuath? Why did he, Tobazim, have to be promised to this particular brotherhood? If this one, then why had Kyredeon won the leadership and not some other, more reasonable man, one Tobazim could have served with honour?

Why did Learon have to die? What was the point of going on?

Striding along the corridor, he came to the end and back again. He looked into the communal chamber. Empty. Everyone else was out drinking, dancing, flirting. Trysting.

In frustration, he pulled his plans from the cabinet and unrolled them. Sheets of intricate lines and calculations.

Visions of beauty swam in his mind's eye, buildings that would never be built.

What a waste!

Furious, he stoked up the brazier, watching the sparks rise as the flames built. His gift flared to life, ready to protect him. He did not bother to suppress it.

'What are you doing?' Ardonyx asked from behind.

He didn't answer.

'What are you doing, Tobazim?'

He shoved the plans into the flames. He wished he could consume his gift as easily, so that it did not drive him to produce visions that demanded to be built.

Ardonyx plucked the plans from the flames before they could do more than singe.

Tobazim registered Ardonyx's scent and the tang of power that came off his skin: it was rich and exotic, and it called to him.

Ardonyx held up the plans between them. 'What's wrong with you tonight?'

'Nothing.' Tobazim reached for the plans.

Ardonyx stepped back, taking the plans out of reach. 'I'm not letting you–'

Infuriated, Tobazim swung at the new brother. His fist collided with Ardonyx's jaw with a satisfying crunch. Ardonyx staggered. The plans went flying, scattering across the parquetry.

Ardonyx shook his head as blood seeped from his lips.

Tobazim shoved past Ardonyx, heading for the plans. They were his to destroy if he chose.

Ardonyx jumped him and they careened across the chamber, through the doorway into the bathing chamber. The tiles were hot and damp, slippery with scented oils and soaps. Water steamed in the huge sunken tub. His brothers had been too focused on preparing themselves for trysting to empty it. Ardonyx's weight unbalanced Tobazim and he lost his footing. The new brother released him as he fell to the tiles. He registered the impact but felt no pain.

He turned on one knee.

Ardonyx offered his hand. Behind him was the sunken bath, big enough for a dozen.

Tobazim sprang forward, tackling him. They fell, and scented water closed over them.

Tobazim grappled, didn't care if he drowned; if they both drowned.

They came up for air. Tobazim's eyes stung. He was glad the bathwater hid his tears. Furious with himself, he tried to shove past Ardonyx to get to the far steps.

Ardonyx caught him by the shoulders, pinned him against the edge of the bath and kissed him.

The fury that had been empowering Tobazim instantly turned to desire. Ardonyx tasted of blood, of violence and a gift essence that was exotic; its heady lure called to him.

The heat, the scented oils and the pounding of his heart all overwhelmed Tobazim. He felt desire rise and knew it was driven by his craving for Ardonyx's gift, but did not care. He let his gift free while his body went along for the ride and his mind switched off.

MUCH LATER, ARDONYX studied his plans. 'I've overseen the building of ships. I know plans. These are really very good.'

'But useless, since we're not staying.' Bitterness made Tobazim's voice tight. 'How can I use my gift? I need to be doing something useful.'

Ardonyx returned his plans. 'The causare is forming an exile-council. I've been asked to represent the brotherhood, and I'll need an assistant.'

Tobazim looked up startled. 'You're asking me?'

'Only if you want to.'

Of course he wanted to. But should he? By serving on the exile-council, Ardonyx would earn stature for the brotherhood, which should protect him from Kyredeon's ire. But the higher he rose, the more of a threat he presented to Kyredeon.

Tobazim stood up and returned his plans to their niche. He'd keep his distance because he wasn't just risking himself – he was risking Athlyn, Haromyr and all the others, who had aligned themselves with him. 'I'll serve on the committee with you, but this... what happened tonight. It was a mistake.'

Chapter Twenty-Five

RONNYN WENT OUT to the wood heap. Now that his mother had removed the bandages, he wanted to inspect his left arm in the bright light of day. What he saw dismayed him.

Fresh scar tissue. Lumpy, misshapen muscles.

Feeling slightly sick, he turned his bad arm this way and that. Truly, it was an ugly thing.

No point in feeling sorry for himself. The wood wouldn't chop itself. Come to think of it, the wood heap was getting low. Seventeen days had passed since he'd killed the stink-badgers. He reached for the axe with his left hand, his bad hand, but the moment he tried to close his fingers around the wooden handle, lightning bolts of pain shot up his arm. He gasped and clasped his arm to his chest.

'Ronnyn, are you alright?'

Before turning to face Aravelle, he blinked to clear the tears from his eyes. 'We need more wood.'

'Don't bother with the axe.' Aravelle gestured to the large reed baskets. 'We can collect driftwood instead.'

That meant going to Driftwood Beach. Neither of them had been back there since spring when they had found the fisherman.

Now they didn't mention him and avoided the hollow where he was buried. The bay looked much the same. Driftwood had piled up in the usual spots. They placed the baskets on the sand and began loading them up. There were some big pieces; he should have brought the axe. He tried cracking them over rocks, using his right arm. It had grown strong with constant use.

When his basket was full, he forgot and went to pick it up with his left hand. Bolts of fire shot up his arm and he ended up gasping as his arm spasmed.

'Still bad?'

He didn't bother to answer.

'Now that the bandage is off, I want to try something.' She led him over to a patch of shade where the trees met the sand, and they knelt. 'Show me your arm.'

He didn't want to. Before the bandages came off, he'd had some hope. Now he knew the worst. 'It's–'

'It's not going to get better if you don't use it. Show me your arm.'

She took his hand, turning it over to inspect the way the scars ran up his arm. Satisfied, she placed his palm on her thigh and pulled a jar from her pocket. When she opened it, he smelled their mother's rosemary ointment.

'You came prepared.'

'I told you I'd help you get better. Did you think I'd forgotten?'

He shook his head, grateful that she had looked on his arm without flinching; he could barely do that himself. The smell of the rosemary ointment was strong, but it was a good smell, pure with the promise of healing, or so he hoped.

Aravelle rubbed the ointment on her hands then began to gently massage his arm, starting from his elbow down. Despite the care she took, the muscles twitched and clenched painfully.

Ronnyn bit his bottom lip and concentrated, breathing through the pain. And that's when the smell of the rosemary became much more intense and sounds became sharper as he felt his gift rise. It was the same sensation that had come over him when the stink-badger went for Vittor – everything became more intense. The power thrummed through his body, making his heart race, helping him cope with the pain. He almost asked Aravelle if she felt it too. But he didn't want her to know; she'd made it clear she resented his gift and he didn't want it coming between them.

Aravelle was bent over his arm, concentrating as she worked on the knotted tendons of his hand. Her tongue peeped from between her lips as she gave each finger the same careful attention.

If he was a mind-manipulator, he should be able to catch a glimpse of her thoughts. Ronnyn opened his mind and tried to listen in to hers, but sensed nothing.

Eyes closed, he tried harder. Still nothing. Yet he could feel his gift and the need to use it.

'Try using your hand now.'

To amazement, his fingers had a little more movement than before, although the pain still shot up his arm.

'See?' She sounded pleased. 'I'll do this every day. And every day you'll get a little better.' She rocked back on her heels and sprang to her feet, aglow with delight.

He couldn't tell Aravelle that his gift was moving. His mother thought he had another year before his power began to trouble him. He feared if his parents learned it had manifested early and he couldn't focus it, he'd have to go back to the city to train. With father unable to work, his family needed him more than ever.

No one must know.

IMOSHEN STOOD ON the balcony, overlooking the palace's grand staircase. This was where Iraayel had held off the Mieren attackers. He'd been barely sixteen that night and so brave, yet none of the all-fathers would have him. She'd do anything to protect him, but...

Frustration drove Imoshen's gift and her vision shifted. She saw Iraayel at the top of the stairs, the night of the attack, saw him save Bedutz's life as one of the Mieren tried to gut him.

She hadn't seen that happen. How could...

Unnerved, Imoshen went in search of the gift-tutor. Even though it was day three of the midsummer festival, she found Vittoryxc in the gift-training chamber hard at work. Light streamed in through the tall windows, illuminating the mahogany tables and cluttered shelves.

'This is impossible...' Vittoryxe indicated a large pile of gift treatises down one end of the table. 'How can I choose what to take and what to leave behind? All of them are important.'

'Then you should take them all.'

Vittoryxe gestured to the rows of shelves that went up to the ceiling. 'All of them?'

'Oh...' Imoshen sat down.

Vittoryxe kept sorting, muttering to herself, growing steadily more upset.

Imoshen watched for a moment then asked, 'What is remembrancing?'

'Remembrancing is the calling up of a powerful event associated with an object or place,' Vittoryxe said. 'The gift is innate, unlike memory-sharing or dream-sharing, which both spring from the intellect.'

'Then remembrancing is not something I could do,' Imoshen asked, certain she had.

'You're a raedan, isn't that enough for you?'

Imoshen said nothing. At empowerment, a T'En child's gift was revealed, and then he or she was trained to be proficient in it. Like an unused limb, other nascent gifts withered. Perhaps T'En training traditions were too restrictive; she suspected culling the gift treatises would be a good thing.

Laughter and running footsteps reached them. The gift-tutor sprang to her feet and charged out the door. Imoshen followed. She was in time to see Vittoryxe catch the oldest of four T'En boys. Imoshen recognised Dragazim, the gift-tutor's own choice-son.

The other boys apologised and left.

'What have I told you, Dragazim?' Vitttoryxe asked.

'Forgiveness, choice-mother. We were just–'

'I don't care what you were doing. If you've got nothing to do, you can review your lessons.'

His face dropped. 'But it's a feast day.'

'I don't care. Go inside.'

'Yes, choice-mother.' Face flushed, Dragazim gave obeisance and entered the gift-training chamber.

Imoshen's heart went out to boy. 'Must you be so hard on him?'

Vittoryxe turned on her. 'What would you know? You've only ever raised one choice-son, and you were too soft on him. Dragazim is a male about to come into his gift. He's going to be a danger to himself and others. Once the power starts manifesting...' She shuddered. 'The gift surges in the first few years. It drives even sensible boys to do stupid things. Some of them never get it under control. I'm only thinking of him. The harder I am on him, the harder he will be on himself when the gift rides him!'

'But Iraayel–'

'Iraayel? You should never have been made his choice-mother.' The gift-tutor's thin lips pulled back from her teeth in a grimace of frustration. 'I don't know why I bother.'

Vittoryxe went into her chamber and slammed the door.

WHEN SORNE RECEIVED Imoshen's latest message, informing him of the reward for live Wyrds delivered either to the port or to the city, he went straight to High Priest Faryx, who agreed to spread word through the churches. It was the fastest way to reach the people of Chalcedonia, and the bounty should help to ensure the safety of Wyrds travelling to port.

Then he went to see the harbour-master to let him know about the reward and to the Wyrd wharf, where he informed the strongarms. If any Wyrds were delivered to the port, he was to be contacted and he would pay the bounty. Lastly, he rowed out to the largest of the sisterhood ships to see a certain cabin boy.

He found Toresal at lessons. The boy was glad to escape, and bounded across the deck to join him.

'So how are you settling in with the sisterhood Malaunje?' Sorne asked.

'They're not so bad.' His face brightened. 'The ship's cat has had kittens. Do you want to see them?'

'Not right now.' Sorne smiled. 'I have good news. Captain Ardonyx made it to the Celestial City.'

'He's safe? What about...' He rattled off half a dozen other names.

'Sorry, all I know is that the captain and some of his crew made it to the city.' Sorne noticed this ship's captain heading this way.

'Good,' the cabin boy muttered. 'I'm glad the Dacians didn't get him.'

'Off to your lessons,' Sorne said, moving to meet the captain, who was Malaunje like him.

'Good news,' Sorne said, by way of greeting. 'Captain Ardonyx reached the city safely.'

'He might be safe, but there's no still sign of his two ships. If we're not careful, someone will sail off with them. Then we'll never track them down.'

'I'll follow it up with the harbour-master,' Sorne said.

The Malaunje captain gestured to the shore. 'This is our home port, but we might as well be in a foreign kingdom. My people have to get permission from the harbour-master's guards to go into port, and even then they're escorted.'

'It's for their own good,' Sorne said. 'I was here during the riots. The Wyrd warehouses were burned, and—'

'That's another thing. We're only allowed to buy our stores from certain merchants. And the prices they're charging...'

Sorne wasn't surprised. 'I suspect the harbour-master is channelling Wyrd gold into his supporters' pockets. Anything else?'

'Where are the rest of our people's ships? I know of two captains who should have returned by now.'

'Messages have been sent to the harbour-masters of all the major ports along the Secluded Sea. As soon as a Wyrd ship docks, they are supposed to tell them to make all haste back to this port.'

'And what if they don't give them the message? What if cut-throats slip aboard at night, murder the crew, steal the cargo and sail off with the ship? How would we know? It's not like our people can go into a tavern and hear news of our exile. They're confined to their vessels.'

Sorne's head spun. He'd been concentrating on getting the Wyrds across Chalcedonia to the port. 'What do you suggest? Would a reward for the return of Wyrd vessels help?'

The dour ship's captain grimaced. 'Why should they accept a reward, when they can take a ship and make a living from it?'

'I'll write to the causare.' Truth be told, he didn't see what any of them could do.

Chapter Twenty-Six

As ARAVELLE LIT the scented lamp, she savoured the exotic perfume. It reminded her of other season cusps, going right back to when she was small and there had only been her brother and her parents.

Tonight, as she prepared for the spiced wine ceremony, she concentrated on doing everything just right. She selected the spices: cinnamon, vanilla bean and cloves. Then, because it was the autumn ceremony, she added lemon rind and a diced apple. She stirred it all into the wine as it simmered over the heat.

In the centre of the table was a sea-boar tusk, which Father had carved to illustrate how she and Ronnyn had saved his life. The story was told in a spiral, in bas relief, rising to the tip. Instead of the usual poem painting, they used the carved tusk as a focal point for their meditation, while she prepared the spiced wine to give thanks.

On the right-hand side of the table, Vittor, Tamaron and little Itania watched. Their wide mulberry eyes sparkled with excitement. Her parents sat on the left side of the table, with Ronnyn closest to her. His skin was flushed from hard work and the scrubbing he'd given himself in the lagoon. His long white hair was bound in a damp plait. Their father's shirt was tight across his shoulders and short in the sleeve.

He looked distracted, as if he was hearing music no one else could hear, and it worried her. She kicked him under the table. His eyes flew to hers.

She didn't let them connect. Instead, she poured a little water into a bowl and sprinkled lemon-scented leaves into it. First she presented the bowl to her mother, who dabbed a little on her eyes and lips, then her palms, in the ritual cleansing; then her father did the same, moving slowly, with painful care. The injury had turned him into an old man before his time.

Ronnyn watched closely. Today would be the first time he took part in the spiced wine ceremony.

A surge of resentment stung Aravelle. She'd had to wait until she was thirteen for this honour. But their parents had decided to acknowledge Ronnyn's hard work and bravery by elevating him early.

And now his gift was manifesting. He thought she didn't know, but she wasn't stupid. When she massaged his arm, it felt like the sensation of an impending summer storm. Wonderful, and yet frightening. Just thinking about it made her heart race and her skin tingle.

One day, the storm would break. Then what would their parents do? If they went back to the city, it would tear their family apart, but it also would mean her father and brother could be healed. And Ronnyn needed to study under a gift-tutor.

She knew he worked at controlling the gift as assiduously as he'd worked at regaining the use of his left hand. She wasn't about to betray him, but...

His gaze met hers across the steaming wine.

She looked down to where the wine swirled as she stirred it over the heat, lamplight gleaming on its silky surface.

If she was absolutely honest, she wasn't about to reveal his experiments with the gift because the sensation made everything more intense, colours brighter, scents stronger and life richer. She didn't want to give it up.

Judging the spiced wine ready, Aravelle poured it into the cups. There were only two proper glass cups with brass handles. She presented the first to her mother, with the handle turned to her mother's left. Then she went to present the second to her father.

Sasoria shook her head. 'Your father and I will share. You two use the other, take turns.'

Their mother raised the cup, her eyes on their father. 'I give thanks for the safe delivery of my bond-partner, Asher, my love. And I give thanks for our fine strong children, who have worked so hard.'

Sasoria took a sip from her cup, then offered it to Asher. He deliberately turned the cup so that his lips touched where hers had been, then took a sip. All the while, his eyes never left hers. Their love illuminated their faces, illuminated their lives.

Vittor gave a sigh of happiness.

Aravelle smiled. But she wished she could rid herself of this burning envy. She couldn't help thinking it was because Ronnyn was T'En, that their parents honoured him early. To make up for these unkind thoughts, she offered the second cup to him. 'I give thanks. You killed the stink-badgers to protect us. I should have been quicker to save your arm. I failed you.'

'No...' He gestured for her to go first. 'You risked your life so I could drag Father away from the sea-boars. You sewed up his wound, then you brought the boat home safely. You should go first.'

Warmth filled her, dissolving the kernel of jealousy.

Feeling lighter of heart, she bathed her face and hands, then lifted the spiced wine to her lips. The wine was sweet and tart, and warm. And it slipped down her throat like the fire of life.

A gasp escaped her.

Ronnyn's lips lifted in an uneven grin and his forehead crinkled in that familiar endearing way. She offered him the cup. He took it, raised it to salute her and sipped.

His eyes watered a little, but he swallowed and took another sip. This one went down smoothly.

Then he looked to her over the cup, and his hard gaze held her.

This was the new side of him, the side which kept challenging her. Was he daring her to reveal the gift games he'd been playing? He had to realise she wouldn't, but did he guess why? Shame made her cheeks flush, and she looked down.

'Arm wrestle, Ronnyn?' Asher suggested.

Their mother rose from her seat, graceful despite the swell of her belly. That was another thing: if the baby was going to be Malaunje, it would come by the next new small moon. The longer her mother was pregnant, the more chance the baby would be T'En.

Ronnyn swung one leg over the bench and offered his bad arm to Father. While recovering from the stink-badgers' attack, he'd been arm wrestling with Asher every night. And every night Vittor watched and cheered, then insisted on arm wrestling Father, who let the six-year-old test his strength, sometimes letting him win. Even little Tamaron insisted on having his turn, taking his place with a great seriousness that told Aravelle, in his mind, he was already a fearsome warrior.

Tamaron's face had healed, but he would always have a scar on his bottom lip and chin. Every time she saw his scarred face, she felt guilty. She should have protected him. And she knew Ronnyn felt the same way.

Vittor crowed with delight; Ronnyn was holding his own. In fact, as she watched, he forced Asher's hand past the vertical. She glanced to their father's face. He was not making it easy; he strained to keep his arm upright.

She bit her bottom lip, willing Ronnyn to win.

There could be no doubting the effort both of them were putting in. They concentrated, knuckles white, forearms corded. Ronnyn's mouth formed a tight line of pain. Then his muscles spasmed and their father slammed Ronnyn's arm down on the table before he could help it.

Aravelle winced in sympathy.

While Asher made sure he hadn't hurt Ronnyn and Vittor assured Ronnyn he had nearly beaten their father, Sasoria beckoned Aravelle. 'Time to bring out the zither, Vella.'

As soon as Ronnyn's injury started to heal, their mother had begun coaching him to relearn to play the instrument. Arm wrestling for brute strength and the zither for fine coordination – their parents were doing everything they could for Ronnyn.

Everything, short of taking him back to their people. The thought surprised Aravelle. It made her feel disloyal.

TOBAZIM GIFT-ENHANCED HIS sight as he stood on the wall-walk. He'd chosen a cloudy night to cloak their actions from the Mieren on shore. Above him, the winch took the strain of the statue's great weight.

The thought of their ancestral enemy inheriting the Celestial City was bad enough, but the thought of what the Mieren would do to their works of art had eaten away at him until he found a solution. He'd suggested they make small copies of their largest statues to take with them. Meanwhile, they could sink the originals in the lake to preserve them. Down in the depths, the marble statues would be safe from wilful destruction. The sawbones had put the idea to Kyredeon, who had approved Tobazim's plan.

Tonight was the first test of the winches he'd designed. His gift told him everything would work, and he'd also calculated the stresses and double-checked his figures, but this was the true test. Would the winch support the statue, or would the marble plummet onto the barge, injuring the Malaunje workers below? He gripped the rail, worried he'd overlooked something, or his gift had led him astray.

Beside him, Ardonyx and Haromyr watched the procedure.

'Steady...' Ardonyx whispered, as Malaunje guided the statue into place on the barge. It landed with a solid thump and the barge settled, but remained afloat.

Tobazim breathed a sigh of relief.

Originally he'd seen his suggestions as both a solution to the problem and a way to gain stature for his non-martial gift, but now all he felt was relief.

He noticed Ardonyx's grin and realised the new brother understood. This both annoyed and fascinated him. Since midsummer, he had accompanied Ardonyx to the exile-councils. Only two brotherhoods and one sisterhood owned merchant shipping fleets, and the others had had to negotiate with them for ships. It had been fascinating, watching the interplay of power as each T'En dealt with the logistics of exile, while trying to maintain their own stature and that of their brotherhood or sisterhood. The only two who were not worried about their stature were the causare and Ardonyx and, paradoxically, this enhanced their authority as they spoke with quiet confidence. Ardonyx knew so much about the larger world beyond the T'Enatuath, even the causare deferred to him.

With a non-martial gift, Tobazim had never expected to mix in the company of such high-ranking T'En.

'Do you want to try for the second statue?' Haromyr asked, recalling him.

'Yes.' If the barge could take these two medium-sized statues, it should take the weight of Sculptor Iraayel's *Fallen All-father*.

Tobazim gave the signal, and the Malaunje retrieved the ropes and pads and began securing the second statue.

Then he studied the sky. A storm was coming. He hoped to be finished before it struck. 'As soon as the second one is loaded, we'll set off.'

They had a quite a distance to row, as the lake stretched back towards the mountains. They needed a deep spot. Malaunje fishermen had explained there was a whole hidden landscape of valleys and hills under the water. Tobazim found the idea fascinating.

'Soon the other all-fathers will be following your lead, secreting their largest statues to protect them from the

Mieren,' Haromyr said. 'Why, I wouldn't be surprised if the causare sent for you to do the same for the sisterhoods!'

Tobazim hid a smile. That would be sweet indeed. To think he had been worried about gaining stature because of the nature of his gift.

'Can I come out on the lake with you?' Haromyr asked.

Tobazim hesitated. 'Lowering the statue in the dark is going to be dangerous. We could tip the barge and swamp it. I'll go alone, with the Malaunje for this first attempt.'

But, when the time came, Ardonyx simply stepped onto the barge and Tobazim said nothing. They set off across the dark water.

With the stars and moons cloaked by cloud and only the occasional flash of lightning, the night was very dark. Tobazim relied on the Malaunje fisherman to judge their position; even with his gift-enhanced sight, he could only make out the faintest line where the surrounding hills met the sky. A flash of lightning illuminated the clouds and Tobazim recognised the shore line.

After a while, one of the Malaunje fisherman reported, 'We're here.'

'Do a depth sounding,' Tobazim said.

The Malaunje hurried off. Tobazim heard the slither of weighted rope falling away, and the rhythmic movements as the fisherman pulled it up, then called the result.

'Right,' Tobazim said, keeping his voice low. Sound carried over water. He did not want curious Mieren sailing out here to investigate after his people were exiled. In theory this part of the lake was too deep for anyone to dive, but Ardonyx had told him of pearl divers he'd seen on his southern voyage, who could hold their breath to amazing depths.

'Prepare to lower the first statue.' Tobazim had calculated the stresses and weights for this, too. Even so, he tensed as the operation began.

Ardonyx strolled over to join him, his expression hidden in the darkness. He said nothing as the winches creaked and their braced arms swung out over the lake.

'In position,' the Malaunje called.

'Go ahead and lower it. But gently.' Tobazim did not want a splash to attract attention.

'It's submerged.'

'Release the ropes.'

He waited for the slither of the ropes that told him the statue was sinking, and felt the barge lift under his feet, felt his gift make the adjustment that told him where the centre of weight lay and where the stresses were.

'One safely away,' Ardonyx said softly.

'Move the barge over a little, then prepare the next statue,' Tobazim said. While this was done, he waited for Ardonyx to broach what was on his mind. Since midsummer, he'd come to regret the necessity of keeping the sea captain at a distance.

'Do you think our people will ever come back here?' Ardonyx asked. 'Or do you think other people will discover our treasures perhaps a thousand years from now, when the exile of the T'Enatuath is a myth? Do you think they'll wonder why we hid our greatest statues?'

Tobazim realised he'd been so intent on saving their heritage from Mieren he hadn't thought that far ahead. Now his mind raced, grappling with the idea.

'They'd need a sealed vessel, one with fresh air and lights, and a manoeuvrable arm that could put slings under the statues.' Even as he said it, he began to conceive plans, discarding them one after the other as flaws appeared. 'Metal would make the best ship, but the weight, the propulsion...' His gift stirred and his skin prickled as excitement pumped through him. He wanted nothing more than to go back to his desk and start on the plans.

Ardonyx drew closer, attracted by the surge in his power. And, as Tobazim felt his gift respond to his new brother's, he realised he admired Ardonyx's vision.

'We're ready,' the Malaunje called.

Tobazim cleared his throat. 'Go ahead.'

'You have won stature for yourself and for our brotherhood,' Ardonyx said.

Tobazim grimaced. 'Stature is only worthwhile if it allows me to do things like save our heritage or build my visions.' And even as he said it, he knew it was true. When he'd come to the city, it had been specifically to win stature, but his values had changed. Disconcerted, he reached out to steady himself, felt Ardonyx accommodate him, and his gift reached for Ardonyx's.

Tobazim reeled it in, but did not pull away. Ardonyx could see further than him. Admiration stirred in him, along with longing. Nothing in Kyredeon's brotherhood was pure and good. Nothing, except Ardonyx.

'We'll be leaving for the port soon,' Ardonyx said softly.

Leave the city and their land... Tobazim found it hard to believe.

After the second statue was sent to join its brother they rowed back across the lake towards the Celestial City, which floated like a glowing vision, balanced on its own reflection.

'Our home is a beacon in a dark world,' Tobazim said. 'And soon our home will be a fleet of sailing ships, precious little protection from violent Mieren and the untamed elements.'

'That's where we differ,' Ardonyx said. 'I love the sea. Certainly, she's a harsh mistress and she punishes fools. She can be capricious. But she can also set us free.'

And Tobazim knew, if he ever took a shield-brother, it would be Ardonyx.

Chapter Twenty-Seven

SORNE FOUND KING Charald in his chamber of state. Official documents had been spread across the polished mahogany table, but the king was asleep in his chair, snoring. It was so unexpected, Sorne nearly laughed. Then he noticed how aged the king was looking. Ever since the attack on the Wyrd city, and his reaction to the pains-ease, Charald seemed to have shrunk in mind and body.

Rather than disturb him, Sorne went to back out of the room, but the king jerked awake, sat up and assumed an alert expression like a player assuming a role.

'Ah, it's only you.' He relaxed. 'Didn't I tell you the Warrior would be pleased when I rid the land of Wyrds? It looks like we'll have our best harvest in ten years.'

Afraid of betraying his contempt, Sorne looked down. Just then the law scholars arrived with another draft for King Charald's approval.

'How goes the preparation for exile?' the king asked Sorne, as the scholars took their seats and opened their leather folders, removing sheafs of paper.

'The Wyrds complain that many of their ships are missing.'

'I can't be responsible for sea-vermin.'

'I happen to know that in other kingdoms, some ships have been confiscated when they arrived in port,' Sorne said.

Charald shrugged. 'I can't be held responsible for what happens in other ports.'

'What does happen in other ports?' Eskarnor asked, entering the chamber.

Sorne saw Charald stiffen slightly, but the king waved a casual hand. 'Wyrd ships have been impounded.'

Eskarnor shrugged as if to say, *what do you expect?* 'Have you heard back yet?'

'Heard back about what?' Charald asked.

'The sickness in the camp besieging the Wyrd city. You said you'd send the court saw-bones.'

'I said nothing of the sort. In fact, I don't remember discussing this.'

Eskarnor looked troubled. 'It was twelve days ago, just after autumn cusp, in this very room.'

'Rubbish,' Charald said fimly, but his head trembled slightly. He sat forward and cupped his chin in his hand. The action appeared casual, but Sorne had been observing the king and knew it was a deliberate ploy to hide his infirmity.

'I... I must have been mistaken.' Eskarnor backed out.

The law scholars exchanged glances, and Sorne realised they believed Eskarnor and not King Charald. Curious, he stayed while they read the new laws for the king's approval. It soon became clear Charald was having difficulty concentrating. The scholars would explain something and get the king's approval then, a little later, he wouldn't remember what he'd agreed to. Charald grew frustrated and dismissed the scholars before they were done. No wonder the new laws were taking so long to draft.

Troubled, Sorne went to see the king's manservant.

He found Bidern dozing before the fire in the king's chamber. At the sound of the latch opening, the fellow sprang to his feet.

'Don't bother.' Sorne closed the door and sank into the chair opposite. They'd known each other since Sorne had accompanied the king on his Secluded Sea campaign, at the age of seventeen. 'Do you remember our discussion back when we were besieging the city? Have there been any more incidents? Will the king agree to see the court sawbones?'

'He hasn't trusted any sawbones, since Baron Etri. I watch over him.'

'Has he had any more conversations with the Warrior?'

'No. But his tremors are worse and some nights he can't sleep.'

'And his memory?'

'He can remember things in the past in great detail, but he forgets what he had for breakfast.'

Sorne nodded and came to his feet. 'Send for me if his urine changes colour or if he does anything that worries you.'

Then he went looking for Nitzane. Eventually, he found the baron strolling around the royal plaza with the queen. A few autumn leaves skittered across the flagstones. The facades of the seven great churches of Chalcedonia glowed in the afternoon sun. It had rained earlier, and everything, including the sky, had been washed clean.

When Nitzane first took an interest in the queen, Sorne had been relieved; it had saved him the trouble of reassuring Jaraile that Prince Cedon would be returned safely. But now, as Sorne approached them, Nitzane bent his head to listen to something Jaraile said and Sorne knew by the tilt of his head that the baron was in love with her.

Not again.

He'd fallen for King Matxin's daughter, when she'd taken sanctuary in the Father's church and Charald was hounding her to marry him. What was it about women in trouble that appealed to Nitzane?

Marrying Matxin's daughter had irritated the king and provided an alternative heir, but Sorne had managed to smooth it over.

Falling in love with Queen Jaraile...

'I'm glad I found you.' Sorne stepped between them. 'Have you noticed the king becoming absent-minded of late?'

Nitzane shook his head, but Jaraile looked up quickly and Sorne had his answer.

'What have you noticed?' Sorne asked her.

'He hardly speaks to me, so I couldn't say if he's becoming absent-minded, but he hasn't been his usual self. The simplest thing used to drive him into a rage. He hasn't had one since he came back. At first, I thought it was because he was happy about Prince Cedon being healed and the Wyrds being exiled. Then I realised he still got peeved, but didn't seem to have the energy to get upset. Lately, I realised he lacks the concentration to work himself into a rage.'

'Now that you mention it, he doesn't want to play cards anymore either,' Nitzane said.

'His health has declined quickly in the half-year since he came back,' Jaraile said. 'The trembling is getting worse.'

'That trembling...' Nitzane muttered. 'Has he spoken with the sawbones?'

'That would mean admitting he's growing old,' Jaraile said, with a twinkle in her eye.

They smiled at each other; it was very sweet and quite inappropriate.

Eskarnor would be happy to use this relationship to drive a wedge between the king and Nitzane. As long as Charald had Nitzane and the Chalcedonian barons' support, the southern baron could not move against the king. Sorne suspected everyone was aware of the king's tremor, and his rages were legendary, but other than himself and the manservant no one knew of the king's hallucinatory conversations with the Warrior, and his absent-mindedness had been noticed only by those closest to him and the law scholars. What would the Chalcedonian barons say if they knew Charald's mind was failing? It could all unravel so easily...

'...you, Sorne?' Nitzane asked.

He found he'd reached the palace steps with no idea what the baron had just asked. 'Have either of you said anything to the king about his health?'

Both of them shook their heads.

'Someone is going to have to speak to him while he can still make decisions.'

They looked at each other, clearly reluctant to broach the subject.

'The king is an old man,' Sorne said. 'His mind is going and he's not going to live to see Prince Cedon grow up.'

'He's only just decided to trust me again,' Nitzane said. 'I don't want him thinking I plan to steal his throne.'

'He despises me,' Jaraile said, 'he always has. Could you speak to him?'

RONNYN FINISHED FILLING his firewood basket and sat with his back against a tree trunk, waiting for Aravelle to join him. She'd massaged his arm every day since the bandages came off. His range of movement had improved, but he'd still had to use his right hand for most things. Sometimes he caught himself reaching for objects with both hands, as though his body didn't know which to use.

Aravelle put her basket next to his. Either she'd grown or the smock had shrunk. It barely brushed the top of her thighs now. Their mother would have to make her a new one.

As she turned towards him, he felt his gift rise. It was easy now. At least, calling the gift was easy and forcing it down had become second nature. He still had no luck guiding it to do anything useful.

Aravelle joined him in the shade, folded her legs under her and rubbed rosemary ointment on her hands. He loved the smell.

As she reached for his arm, he reached for his gift. From his mother's stories, he knew touch enhanced the gift. Surely this time he would sense her thoughts.

But as Aravelle continued to massage his arm, he met resistance; no matter how he tried to slip around it, he could not get even a glimpse of what she was thinking.

Was his gift so weak? It didn't feel weak. At times it felt so strong it threatened to overwhelm him. Maybe it was him. Maybe he had no control...

A lightning arc of pain shot down his arm, making his fingers jerk. He pulled his arm away. Driven by pain and frustration, he jumped up and paced.

'I'm sorry.' Aravelle scrambled to her feet. 'I didn't mean to–'

'You didn't.'

'I hurt you.'

'It's me. I hate feeling useless.'

'Your arm is getting better every day,' she assured him, misunderstanding the source of his frustration. 'Do you want to try again?'

Did he? Did he want to try to breach her natural defences, and fail again? What if he succeeded and she realised what he'd done and hated him for it?

He felt like laughing at his own stupidity. All this time he had been trying to sense her thoughts, ignoring the fact that if he succeeded he'd drive her away.

'Ronnyn?'

'That's enough for today.'

'But...' She flushed and looked down. 'I haven't finished.'

He wanted to try again. His gift crawled under his skin, driving him crazy. 'Do you think it's still warm enough to swim?'

'Not really. But I'm sure all this swimming's been good for your arm. Come on.'

She helped him lift his firewood basket, then slid the straps over his shoulders. He stood, feeling his thigh muscles take the weight, and tucked the axe through his belt. He watched as she arranged her own basket. She walked ahead of him. As she climbed the rise, the muscles of her calves and buttocks flexed, firm and strong. He looked away, concentrating on where to put his feet.

When they reached the cottage, he spent ages chopping wood until his gift was exhausted by hard work. Then he took a dip in the lagoon, scrubbing his skin clean with fine white sand. Some days it felt like he was scrubbing the top layer of skin off, but he scrubbed and scraped away every trace of his gift-enriched sweat.

SORNE COULD HEAR the king shouting from the end of the corridor. Had they tried to discuss his deteriorating health? Charald was a proud, arrogant man; he would not welcome talk of his decline. This was why Sorne hadn't broached the subject of his son's future. So far, the right moment had not come along. And now...

The words 'ungrateful' and 'conniving' reached Sorne. Half a dozen servants lined up in the hallway, wringing their hands or listening with interest. Sorne fingered the Khitite soothing powder he carried with him. As soon as they'd returned to the port, he'd located an apothecary and made sure he had a supply. He was prepared to slip it into the king's wine and talk him to sleep if need be. But he was tired of cleaning up after King Charald. There were other things he should be doing. He'd just been down to the wharf to pay for another delivery of Wyrds but, according to Imoshen's latest message, she would be sending someone to manage the Wyrd wharf soon. Then he could hand over to them and try one last time to find Valendia. If that failed, he'd have to conclude she'd died the night of the riots and go into exile with the T'Enatuath.

This reminded him – before he left port he should give Jaraile the soothing powders so she could handle the king.

His heart sank when he entered the chamber to find Baron Eskarnor at one end looking pleased with himself, the king striding back and forth ranting, and Jaraile and Nitzane down the other end.

'You're here.' The king turned to him. 'I found these two in the solarium.'

'We were playing cards,' Nitzane protested. 'Nothing more.'

Charald flung an accusatory hand at Jaraile. 'She was laughing. She never laughs for me. All I ever get is long-suffering sighs. Besides' – he gestured to Eskarnor – 'the baron tells me he saw them kissing.'

Sorne laughed. 'And you believed him?'

The king looked to Sorne with hope.

'When did this kiss occur?' Sorne asked the king.

'Three days ago, the afternoon I was meeting with the law scholars.'

'Ah, that explains it. It would have been right after I gave the baron this message for the queen. I wouldn't be surprised if Jaraile had kissed Nitzane.'

Sorne offered Charald the latest message from Imoshen.

The king took it and unfolded it.

'Second paragraph down,' Sorne said. The king frowned and Sorne realised Charald's sight was going. 'The handwriting is cramped. I'll read it.'

He retrieved the message and found the line. '*You can tell Queen Jaraile I saw her little boy yesterday. His foot is almost completely corrected. He showed me how he exercises it every day to build up the muscles. By winter's cusp, we expect him to be able to jump and run, and get into mischief.*'

Forgetting that she was supposed to have already heard this, Jaraile clasped her hands to her chest, eyes filled with tears of relief.

Sorne gestured to her. 'Never doubt your queen's love for your son, King Charald.'

As Sorne put the message away, he looked over to Eskarnor. The man's eyes glittered. Sorne allowed himself the slightest smile.

The southern baron turned on his heel and walked out.

Charald beckoned the queen. Nitzane followed. As they reconciled, Sorne noticed the way the king reached for both Jaraile and Nitzane and he realised Charald felt vulnerable.

Since Sorne had discovered he was King Charald's unwanted half-blood son, he had both loved and hated this man. He'd admired the king's tactical brilliance and physical strength, and the way he managed his war barons. He'd despised his blind rages, and his reliance on a fictitious god to justify his campaigns.

Now, for the first time, Sorne felt pity.

Leaving the king with Jaraile and Nitzane, Sorne headed for his chamber. Eskarnor stood watching him from the end of the long gallery. Without his men around him joking, blustering and posturing, the baron seemed more threatening rather than less.

All Eskarnor had to do was bide his time. Jaraile was sweet and kind-hearted, but she was not King Matxin's daughter; Marantza could have ruled a kingdom. As for Nitzane, he wasn't a natural leader of men like his brother or a cunning diplomat like his grandfather. He was just a good-hearted, impulsive man who happened to have been born into a position of power.

When Sorne went into exile with the Wyrds, Eskarnor would make his move. Sorne told himself it was none of his business. All he had to do was ensure the Wyrd exile went smoothly and make one last attempt to find Valendia.

He was hoping his sister had made it out of the city the night of the riots. He was hoping Zabier had lied to him and re-opened Restoration Retreat without the church administration knowing. He was hoping Valendia was safe there.

If it was at all possible, he would save Valendia and set her free.

Chapter Twenty-Eight

RONNYN FELT LIGHT-hearted. He'd been released from the chores and released from their island. For the first time ever, both he and Aravelle had accompanied their father to Trade Isle. Before sailing, their father had taken him aside and revealed it was not uncommon for Malaunje women and girls to be kidnapped off the street by the Mieren. He'd made Ronnyn promise to protect Aravelle.

She would have been furious, if she knew.

The chill in the air held the foretaste of winter. He blew on his hands and pulled the sailor's knitted cap down over his head to hide his white hair. They could never pass for Mieren – even if their six fingers and toes escaped notice, their distinctive wine-dark eyes would give them away – but Ronnyn could pass for Malaunje if he hid his hair. 'How do I look, Da? Good enough to fool the trader?'

'Good enough.'

'And me?' Aravelle asked. She wore a pair of Ronnyn's old breeches and a seal-skin vest that hid the curves of her upper body. Like him, she wore a fisherman's cap, but wisps of copper hair peeped from its rim. 'Do I pass for a Malaunje boy?'

Ronnyn felt a grin tug at his lips as Father shook his head.

'What's wrong? What's giving me away?' Aravelle demanded.

'You're too pretty,' Ronnyn said.

'No, it's not that,' their father said. Then, seeing her expression, he smiled. 'You're just as lovely as your mother, Vella, but that's not what's giving you away. It's your manner. You're too feminine. You tilt your head, you use your hands.' He mimicked her.

The sight of their father pretending to be a girl was too much for Ronnyn. A laugh bubbled out of him and he couldn't stop.

Without warning, Aravelle jumped him, caught him in a headlock and mock-punched his face. He was laughing too much to fight back.

'Yes, that's better, Vella.' Asher applauded. 'Much more boy-like. Although I think we'll call you Araven. And you, Ronnyn, will have to be Ronaric. It's a Malaunje version of your name.'

When Aravelle released him, Ronnyn rescued his cap, which had come off in the scuffle, and straightened up. He expected her to grin at him. But she was staring at their father. Without warning, she threw her arms around Asher, hugging him with all her might.

Ronnyn couldn't see what had prompted her. But their father seemed to understand because he hugged her back just as hard and, when they pulled apart, his eyes were bright with unshed tears.

Aravelle glanced to Ronnyn, her features suffused with love, willing him to share the moment.

She was so beautiful she took his breath away. No wonder Mieren coveted Malaunje women.

'Right.' Asher cleared his throat. He studied their boat, which was moored in the shallows, and then the sky, judging tide and time. 'Come on. Trader's been meeting me in the same clearing ten days after autumn cusp since we escaped. I suspect he's in league with the sea-vermin who live on the far side of the island, so I don't like to linger.'

Ronnyn sobered at the mention of the ruthless predators. He'd seen their sails skimming the sea, like dragonflies on a pond. Luckily, the sea-vermin hunted fat-bellied merchant vessels with packed holds, not lone fishing-boats like theirs.

As Ronnyn and Aravelle each took some spare sacks and the sacks containing the sea-boar ivory, their father limped on ahead. Once they were over the rise and onto harder ground, he leaned heavily on his cane.

'This is a chance for you to practice your Chalcedonian. Trader usually comes alone, but he sometimes brings a youth to help with the load.' Asher bent and scooped up a couple of distinctive, smooth white stones. 'If he's not there, I leave these in a circle, that way he knows I want to trade.'

Ronnyn realised Asher was telling them all this in case he died and they had to come alone in future. For all that Ronnyn had been doing the work of a grown man, he wasn't ready to take on his father's role. Not when the decisions he made could mean the difference between his family eating and starving.

'Ronnyn?'

He looked up, saw Asher and Aravelle were waiting for him, and hurried to catch up.

Shadows had gathered under the pines and Ronnyn was sweating by the time they reached the clearing, where an old, white-haired Mieren waited.

This was the first time Ronnyn had seen one of the Mieren on his feet, eyeing them with wary intelligence. So this was the face behind all the stories about Mieren turning on his people. The trader's wiry white hair was barely long enough to tie back, and his jaw was covered in a salt-and-pepper beard. His ice-blue eyes were almost unnaturally pale, but it was clear he saw well enough when he straightened up as they approached.

A small goat-drawn cart stood on the far side of the clearing, carrying the trader's wares. There were metal tools and implements they could not make without a forge, and the little luxuries that so delighted their mother.

'Saskar.' The trader greeted their father, with a brief nod. Ronnyn met Aravelle's eyes. Their father hadn't mentioned that he used a false name.

'Trader Kolbik,' Asher said, in Chalcedonian.

'You brought help this year?' Kolbik gestured to Aravelle and Ronnyn.

'My sons, Araven and Ronaric.'

'Fine strapping boys.' He gestured to their father's bad leg. 'What happened?'

'I was gored by a sea-boar.'

'Then you're lucky to come out of it with nothing worse than a limp.' He gestured to the cane. 'Can I see?'

Asher crossed the clearing to pass the cane to him. Ronnyn did not like the way the trader watched his father's lopsided walk, or the calculating look he cast over both himself and Aravelle, noting their beardless cheeks.

Trader Kolbik studied the cane, and the fine carving on the handle, the snake curling around itself. He cast Asher a swift look. 'How much?'

'Not for sale.'

Kolbik shrugged and returned the cane, much to Ronnyn's relief. 'Let's see the ivory.'

Asher signalled Ronnyn and Aravelle, who emptied the sacks onto the dark leaf-litter.

The trader prodded the ivory with his boot, then sucked at his teeth. 'Not much here. You won't get what you ordered–'

'We can pay.' Asher limped over to the cart to inspect the load.

Ronnyn noticed a sturdy pick.

Asher assessed the cart's contents, putting a pile of them to one side. 'You're missing the glass window.'

'Glass is a luxury item. Hard to get.'

'We'll take what you have.'

'And what'll you be paying with? Not this ivory alone.' Kolbik rubbed his bristly jaw. 'Even if you threw in the cane, I wouldn't consider it.'

'Stack the ivory on the cart, lads. Put the things in our sacks,' Asher said.

'Hold on,' the trader protested. 'I haven't...'

Asher reached into his vest and drew out a small leather pouch. He loosened the drawstrings to pick through it, pulling out two small citrines. 'This more than covers your goods.'

Kolbik's eyes lit up, and he cast their father a calculating look.

Meanwhile, Ronnyn moved fast, stuffing things into the sacks. He had a bad feeling about this, but the trader did not object as they finished loading up. Ronnyn swung the pick over one shoulder, carrying his sacks in the other hand, and they set off. He found it heavy going, tramping back across the island. The pick dragged on his shoulder. He'd deliberately taken more of the load than Aravelle but, even so, they both struggled with the pace their father set. Asher's limp became more pronounced. He stumbled several times, each time righting himself with more effort. He'd be stiff and sore tomorrow.

Aravelle gave Ronnyn a worried look.

Ronnyn studied the sky between the pines. Low clouds with blue-grey bellies promised a storm; already they'd delivered an early evening. Normally their father wouldn't put out to sea until the storm had passed, but tonight would have to be an exception.

Relief lightened his load as they breasted the dune overlooking the beach. Clean white sand stretched out to the shallows where their boat rocked on its moorings. The tide had come in farther than they expected.

'Looks like we'll be getting our feet wet,' Asher muttered, face grey with exhaustion.

Ronnyn wished he was old enough to manage the trade alone. He'd suggest it next time. They needn't have worried about the trader recognising him for T'En.

'Come on.' Asher headed down the dune and they followed him.

A shout made Ronnyn turn. Four Mieren ploughed down the dune to their left. They rode short-legged, shaggy-haired ponies which were hardly hampered by the soft sand. Ronnyn recognised Trader Kolbik, accompanied by three strangers.

'Run!' Asher cried.

They plunged down the dune, sending cascades of sand ahead of them. Ronnyn could hear his father grunting with pain every time his bad leg took his weight.

Ronnyn cast a glance back to the Mieren, judging their distance and speed. Already the ponies were only a stone's throw away. They wouldn't make it back to the boat. The sacks thumped on his back and the heavy pick threw his stride off balance. His heart hammered. He paced himself; he didn't want to leave his father and Aravelle behind.

Asher stopped where the soft sand started to harden.

'Vella. Go to the boat, pull up anchor,' Asher ordered, between gulps of air. 'We'll delay them.'

'I won't leave you.'

'Go. Ronnyn's bigger and stronger.'

A rush of pride warmed Ronnyn.

Aravelle hesitated only for a heartbeat, then turned and ran into the shallows, sending up sprays of water. One of the ponies peeled away to cut her off, and the other three headed for Ronnyn and his father.

He felt his gift pulse and try to rise. Useless thing. If he couldn't influence minds, it was nothing but a liability. Savagely, he forced it down.

Ronnyn dropped his sacks and swung the pick off his shoulder. Its sturdy weight felt good in his hands. Now, when he could not afford to falter, he used his right hand.

His father just had the cane and his fish-gutting knife. Razor sharp, it was only good for close fighting. Ronnyn didn't want the Mieren to get that close.

The nearest man jumped from his pony, slid a cudgel from his saddle and approached. He weighed them up as he decided who to attack first. He had the same odd sky-blue eyes as the trader; they all did. His hair was the colour of wet sand, and shoulder-length. A beard covered his lower face, making it hard to read the expression around his mouth.

A second man jumped down from his pony. He was armed with a nasty-looking sword, the metal nicked and stained. The two were so alike they had to be brothers.

Looking at the Mieren, Ronnyn realised that he stood taller than either of them. No wonder their attackers watched him carefully. The one with the cudgel edged around to confront Asher. The swordsman drew nearer to Ronnyn, caution in every step.

Meanwhile, Trader Kolbik clambered down stiffly. 'Hand over the pouch, Saskar, and we'll let you go.'

But even as he spoke, one of the Mieren lunged in to attack Asher. Ronnyn only caught a flurry of movement in the corner of his eye; he was still watching his own opponent, who did not move to attack.

A grunt of pain made Ronnyn glance around in time to see his father go down, clutching his bad leg. Now both Mieren faced Ronnyn.

One lifted the cudgel, the other swung his aged sword in a wide arc. Ronnyn dodged, blocking with the shaft of the pick. He couldn't leave his father, who struggled onto one knee, bad leg extended, hand clamped to his thigh, which was bleeding again. He'd need help to get to his feet.

Ronnyn cast a quick look over his shoulder. The fourth man was trying to drive Aravelle back towards the beach. He didn't like to think what they'd do to her, if they realised she wasn't a boy.

The swordsman struck. A heartbeat later, the other swung the cudgel.

Ronnyn aimed the pick at the swordsman, who deflected with his ancient weapon. The sword snapped at the same moment as the cudgel hit Ronnyn's forearm. The strength went out of his fingers, and the pick flew from his grasp. He bent double, gasping with pain.

But he didn't go down. He regained his balance, to stand over his father. For the moment his right arm was useless. He pressed it to his chest and drew his fish-gutting knife with his left.

Both Mieren eyed him warily.

He watched the one with the cudgel. If the man got in one good blow to the head, his wits would go. And then who would save his father and Aravelle?

The cudgel wielder swung. Ronnyn ducked.

The other one came in from the side; his fist caught Ronnyn a glancing blow to the head. Ronnyn's ear rang. He shook his head, blinking hair from his eyes. Both Mieren backed away, making the sign to ward off evil. Ronnyn realised he'd lost his cap.

'A silverhead!' the swordsman cried. 'Ya bastard, Kolbik. Ya didn't tell us they had a full-blood Wyrd!'

The trader cursed.

The way the two closest Mieren eyed Ronnyn was almost funny.

'Help me up.' Asher held out a hand.

Ronnyn sheathed his knife, offered his left hand and pulled his father to his feet. For once, his bad arm didn't betray him.

Asher leaned heavily on him, breath rasping with pain. Ronnyn wondered where the cane was, then spotted it a few steps away.

'He's only a boy,' the trader said. 'His hair's still white. He doesn't have any power. Take him down.'

The swordsman drew a knife and exchanged looks with the cudgel wielder. They fingered their weapons as they closed in.

'Here, this is what you want.' Asher pulled out the leather pouch. Ronnyn had to steady him, as Asher tipped the pouch's contents into his hand. Two more citrines from his mother's torc. It wasn't fair.

'You can have all six stones,' Asher lied. 'Just let us go.'

The trader and his companions went very still.

'There!' Asher threw the stones over their heads onto the soft sand.

The two nearest Mieren turned and raced back to where the stones had landed. Falling to their knees, they began sifting through the sand, looking for six stones where there were only two.

Trader Kolbik glared at Asher and joined his companions in the sand. A pony charged past Ronnyn as the fourth thief went after his share.

'Ronnyn, my cane.' His father pointed.

He scooped it up and then grabbed the sacks. His right arm was working again, if a little sluggishly. Luckily nothing was broken.

They headed for the boat, with his father limping badly. Aravelle reached it first, tossed her sacks over the side and levered her weight up. She went straight to the anchor.

Ronnyn threw his things over the side, saw his father was in difficulty. Without waiting to be asked, he hoisted Asher up and into the boat.

By the time Ronnyn was aboard, Aravelle had hauled in the anchor. Ronnyn tugged on the rope to raise the sail. It swung, catching the wind that drove the storm their way. His father grabbed the oar and limped to the bow where he pushed them out into deeper water. Ronnyn went to help him.

The storm hit, wind driving cold rain. Ronnyn hauled the oar in and glanced back to the shore. The four Mieren were still madly scrambling through the sand. Even as Ronnyn watched, the three younger ones stood, turned on the trader, struck him down and searched his clothing. No honour. They were scavengers; sea-vermin.

Ronnyn didn't know whether to laugh or cry. 'That was so clever, Da.'

But his father didn't answer. He crumpled in a heap.

Aravelle could not leave the tiller. Her frantic eyes met Ronnyn's. He knelt next to their father, who was grey and unconscious. Asher's heart raced under Ronnyn's hand and his right leg was drenched in blood.

Cursing the Mieren, Ronnyn carried their father into the cabin and placed him on the bunk, where he packed the wound and wrapped it tightly. Seeing it bleed again made him feel guilty. He should have protected Asher, should have used his gift.

To do what? He didn't know how to guide the power. It was like reaching for the pick with his bad left hand. It was much safer to use his right when he needed to be sure of his grip on the weapon.

The boat wallowed in a trough, before lifting to meet the crest of a wave. They'd come out past the headlands now and were taking the full brunt of the storm.

He pulled the blanket up and strapped his father in. Then he went out on deck to help Aravelle. The boat bucked as it fought the sea. He had to halve the amount of sail, and even then, it was too much for Aravelle to hold the tiller.

He tried to take over.

She resisted, shouting into the driving wind, blinking rain from her face, her features illuminated by a flash of lightning. He crowded her, taking the tiller in spite of her protests.

In the aftermath of the thunder, his ears felt raw. Despite the pain in his forearms, he fought to hold the tiller and keep the boat's prow pointed into the waves.

She glared at him, braced against the rise and fall of the deck.

'Go inside,' he shouted. 'See to Father.'

She hesitated, her head silhouetted against clouds illuminated from within by lightning.

'Go.'

For the first time, she didn't insist she knew better. He braced his legs and admitted it was a struggle to hold the boat on course. How Aravelle had managed, he did not know.

Then he just concentrated on holding the prow into the waves.

SORNE WATCHED SCHOLAR Igotzon scribble madly.

'After the Maygharian king surrendered, then what happened?' The skinny priest didn't even lift his head.

Sorne had been describing King Charald's Secluded Sea campaign. It had taken eight years to conquer the five mainland kingdoms; Sorne was sure he could string out the story long enough to discover where Igotzon was hiding the Wyrd scrolls, Oskane's journals and the reports. So far they had covered the conquering of Maygharia, and already he knew where the Wyrd scrolls were kept.

The bells rang for prayer.

'Is that the time?' Sorne came to his feet. 'I must go.'

'I know Charald forced the Maygharian king to part with his son as a hostage.' Igotzon was still scribbling.

'That's what Charald thought, but the Maygharian king never intended his son to sit on the throne. The youth was a wastrel. The king had been grooming his daughter all along. When Charald insisted the Maygharian princess marry Baron Norholtz and the baron was crowned his puppet king, neither of the Chalcedonians realised Norholtz would be dead within a few years and the daughter would be the sole ruler.'

'That's right, King Charald sent you to quell the Maygharian uprising.'

'Which I did, but Norholtz was a fool. He threw away the victory and the throne.'

'How?'

'That's a story for another day,' Sorne said, then smiled. 'It feels strange. You know so much about my life.'

'Well, I have read Scholar Oskane's journals.' Igotzon glanced to the chest beside the fireplace. 'And I keep up with events. It's my goal to write the history of our time.'

'I don't think I've come across anyone with that goal before,' Sorne admitted. Now there was just the reports to uncover. 'I must go. The king's expecting me.'

'The king...' Igotzon frowned. 'I plan to start the history at the beginning of King Charald's reign. Your insights would be invaluable.' He dipped his nib and tapped off the excess ink. 'I'll make up a list of questions.'

He set to work and Sorne left.

Back at the palace, Sorne heard the king's voice coming from his chamber of state. He found Charald alone with a map of the known world on the mahogany table.

The king looked up as Sorne entered and spoke as though they'd been in the middle of a conversation. 'My father left me a kingdom in chaos. The treasury was empty and the war barons were on the march. They thought they'd whip me and force me to form some sort of council, like the Wyrds have, where every baron had a vote. That's no way to rule a kingdom. Oskane said...' He looked around. 'Where is Oskane?'

Sorne shut the door, came over to the table and put a hand on the king's shoulder. 'Oskane groomed me to replace him. You were fifteen when your father died. You had Oskane and Baron Nitzel to advise you. Your son will be four next spring. The Chalcedonian barons have united behind Baron Nitzane, who has sworn to serve Prince Cedon until he reaches his majority, but the southern barons are not men of honour. They'll see a small boy and try to steal his throne. What will happen to your son, if you are struck down suddenly?'

For a heartbeat, he thought the king would bluster and refuse to face his own mortality.

Then Charald gestured to the map. 'He'll be high king of the Secluded Sea, with a full treasury. But you're right, he'll need men I can trust to govern the kingdom and groom him to rule.'

'Exactly. Who will those men be? Have you spoken to them? Have you had your law scholars draft a formal decree giving them this authority?'

Suspicion sharpened Charald's pale eyes. 'You want to be one of those men?'

'Me? No, I'm exiled with the rest of the Wyrds, remember? I'm thinking only of your son and the future of Chalcedonia. Have I ever done anything but serve you loyally?' *When it suits me?*

'That's true,' Charald muttered to himself. Then he looked up, head trembling. 'You do it. You draft the decree.'

Relief made Sorne's legs weak, and he realised he'd been troubled by the thought of leaving Jaraile and Nitzane with the floundering king, while Eskarnor circled with his pack of wolves.

Sorne took a sheet of paper from the writing desk, quill and ink, and prepared to write. 'Who do you trust to guide the prince?'

'Not Nitzane,' Charald said. 'He's not the man his grandfather was.'

Since Nitzane's grandfather had arranged for his son-in-law to be murdered so his widowed daughter could marry the king, Sorne saw this as a recommendation. He tapped the nib on the ink-well as if thinking. 'While Nitzane might not be a ruthless politician, he has a good heart and he's honourable. He would bring those qualities to the prince's upbringing, and he listens to Captain Ballendin, who is a good strategist and judge of men.'

Charald nodded once and Sorne wrote Nitzane's name on the top of the list.

'If you are looking for someone who is a good judge of men and has the political acumen, you could not go past High Priest Faryx.'

'Of the Father's church?' Charald looked doubtful.

'Like High Priest Oskane,' Sorne said.

'Very well, one man of heart, one man of learning.'

Sorne added the priest's name. 'And one man of war. But who? You need someone who is a good strategist, but places loyalty ahead of personal ambition. Why not appoint the commander of the king's guard? It would be in his best interest to ensure the prince reaches his majority.'

'Do it. And I want Jaraile's cousin, Baron Kerminzto, too. He's good with men and he's related to the boy.'

'That's four advisors,' Sorne said, writing their names. 'You need a fifth to have the deciding vote. How about the queen?'

Charald blinked. 'A woman?'

'She has the prince's best interests at heart.'

'Can't hurt.'

Sorne added the queen to the list, then showed the king. 'So you are agreed?'

Charald nodded and Sorne offered him the quill. The tremor showed in his signature, but all his decrees looked like this now.

Chapter Twenty-Nine

ARAVELLE HUNG THE last smock on the line. She was tired, bone tired. She'd felt tired since the run-in with Trader Kolbik five days ago. Between them, she and Ronnyn had brought their father home, but he'd been feverish on and off and their poor mother was run ragged, what with nursing their father, being heavily pregnant and looking after the little ones.

The rest of the workload fell to Aravelle and Ronnyn. Cooking, cleaning, washing, chopping firewood, repairs, preparation for winter... They lived like the poorest of Mieren.

Today Father had woken clear-headed and had managed to walk as far as the kitchen table.

Itania shrieked with joy as Tamaron chased her. At least the little ones were not worried. Even six-year-old Vittor wasn't old enough to realise how serious things had become.

Feeling lighter of heart, Aravelle headed back to the cottage. The shutters were open and her mother's voice carried clearly.

'Do you regret running away?' Sasoria asked.

There was silence. Aravelle imagined her father holding out his hand as he sat by the fire. She imagined her mother going to him and cradling his head.

After a moment her father said, 'You know I don't regret our time together. You are my world.'

His voice was raw, and Aravelle's throat grew tight with emotion. She desperately wanted to be someone's world.

'But we have to face facts. The trader could come after us.'

'You said the islands are like a maze.'

'They are. But eventually, he'll find his way through the maze. More pressing is Ronnyn. He's twelve, and his gift will start manifesting in a year or two. Once that happens, he should be empowered and begin his training. We should go before his gift starts driving him.'

'The sisterhoods will take him, and Tam and Vittor, too. It'll tear my heart out. And now there's–'

'There's a reason the T'En keep their distance from Malaunje. When Ronnyn's gift comes to him, it will affect all of us–'

'I'll teach Vella how to maintain her gift shields.'

'Yes, you do that. After all, the defences worked so well for you,' he said, and his tone made Aravelle's cheeks burn.

'My defences held,' her mother insisted. 'He never made a devotee of me.'

'No, but you liked playing with fire. Don't deny it.'

Aravelle's heart raced. The term 'devotee' was new to her, but she had her suspicions.

'We have to think of Ronnyn,' Asher said. 'His arm is as good as it's going to get. Healer Reoden could help him.'

'I know... She could help you, too.'

'Don't fool yourself, Sasoria. The brotherhood won't petition her to heal me. They're more likely to punish me.'

'I was selfish to ask you to run away with me,' Sasoria said, voice tight with emotion.

'No, I was selfish. I wanted you all to myself, and now we have to face the consequences. There's something else we have to face. You've already defied the odds and birthed three beautiful, healthy T'En boys. This new baby...'

Aravelle backed away, her hand covering her mouth. She'd forgotten. They'd been lucky with the three boys, but so much more could go wrong with a T'En baby. What if the new baby was stillborn?

She ran past the chickens and the little-ones, past the smoke-house. She ran to the clotheslines and stepped between the lines. The wind blew the sheet against her body, hiding her from prying eyes.

There she wept angry, bitter tears. It wasn't fair. Because of the gifts, they had no control over their lives.

'Vella, what's wrong?'

She looked up to see Ronnyn standing at the end of the washing line, visible between the flapping sheets. He'd been out cutting the trees for timber to reinforce their chicken coop and goat pen, and sweat made his much-washed shirt cling to his body. When had his shoulders grown so broad?

'You're crying.' Concerned, he tucked the axe in his belt and came down between the washing lines. As he drew nearer, the wind picked up tendrils of his white hair, swirling it around his face. She stared up at him. Her eyes were level with his nose now, and his hair was darker at the temples. It was only the slightest difference in tone, but it was evidence of his gift starting to manifest.

'Is Da all right?' he asked.

She nodded, wiping her cheeks, furious with herself.

He laughed and hugged her.

That did it. She couldn't stop the tears. Sobs shook her shoulders. He hugged her tighter, and she felt his gift stir. It was intoxicating. As her senses sharpened, everything became more intense.

She craved the sensation.

Furious with herself, she pulled away, flipped the washing over her head, ducked under the line and headed for the cottage.

She hadn't moved three steps when he caught up with her, grabbed her arm and swung her around easily. Gone were the days when she could outwrestle him.

'Vella? I don't–'

Signalling him to keep his voice down, she glanced over to where the little ones were still playing. There was no sign of their parents. 'I overheard Ma and Da talking about going back to the city.'

'I can look after us.'

'I know. This isn't about you providing for us.' She didn't want to say it, but she knew she should. 'It's about your gift. You need training.'

His forehead crinkled earnestly. 'I'd never hurt—'

'Not on purpose.'

'What did they decide to do?'

'They think we have another year or two. If we go back, there's a T'En healer who might be able to fix your arm, but the brotherhood will punish Da and our family will be torn apart.' She felt the tears threaten again. 'It's not fair.'

TOBAZIM HAD NEVER been particularly fond of horses, and they weren't fond of him; but the T'En were expected to ride. So he ended up riding through the causeway gate with Ardonyx beside him at the head of their party. Back at the exile-council, when they'd volunteered to be the first to go to port and organise the exile, it had seemed so far away.

Now it was almost full small moon and they were leaving the Celestial City. Only one more small moon and it would be winter cusp and time to leave their home forever.

Looking over his shoulder, Tobazim saw people waving from the wall and the brotherhood palace roofs. There were even people on the sisterhood palaces.

'So many,' Tobazim said.

Ardonyx shrugged. 'We're the first to leave the city. Our departure makes it real.'

'I've only ever lived in the sisterhood's estate, the winery and the city. I've never been outside of Chalcedonia. I've no idea what to expect.'

'You have more idea than most. The majority of them have never left the city. Exile is going to be a shock.'

'It doesn't worry you?'

'The whole reason I went to sea was because I couldn't stand being confined.'

His tone made Tobazim glance to him. There was so much he did not know about Ardonyx, and now they were riding to port together. Behind them rode around twenty T'En warriors. Haromyr, Eryx, Athlyn and the rest, plus Ionnyn and the few T'En survivors of Chariode's brotherhood. About three dozen Malaunje crowded onto four wagons, most of them women and children. If he'd had a choice, he would not have brought so many non-combatants but, when they started putting the party together, people just kept coming up to him, asking to join in. He'd tried to explain they were the advance party and he didn't know what conditions they would find in port, but they were adamant.

Athlyn caught up with them. 'I'm surprised Kyredeon let us bring such a large party.'

Ardonyx glanced to Tobazim, a half-smile on his lips. 'Will you tell him, or will I?'

Tobazim grinned. 'Kyredeon thinks good riddance to us. He hopes we'll be attacked en route by Mieren brigands–'

'I thought we had safe passage to the sea.'

'In theory, we have safe passage,' Tobazim said.

'In theory, my ships were safe in port,' Ardonyx added.

Tobazim felt the tug of like to like. In many ways he had more in common with Ardonyx than he'd ever had with anyone, even his choice-brother.

They reached the end of the causeway and the chatter. The barons and their men had lined up to watch them go.

As Tobazim looked up the hill, he saw heavy black storm clouds. They were going into danger, into the unknown, yet he embraced the challenge.

Sorne welcomed the high priest. 'Take a seat.'

Nitzane, Jaraile and Halargon, commander of the king's palace guards, were already seated on the far side of the table. Sorne hadn't sent for Baron Kerminzto; he wanted to get the decree signed without delay.

Also present were two law scholars to act as witnesses. Sorne could not witness a legally-binding document thanks to his tainted blood, and Jaraile's signature was not legally binding as a woman.

Of course, a legal document was binding only as far as you had power to enforce it. But in this case, the most powerful church, the most powerful baron, the prince's kinsman, the queen and the commander of the king's guard had a vested interest in seeing it honoured.

'This undertaking will ensure the stability of the kingdom until Prince Cedon turns fifteen,' Sorne said. 'Then he can choose his own advisors, but if you do your jobs well, I'm sure he will continue to turn to you. I've sent for the king... Ah, here he comes now.'

Charald strode in, took a look around the table and turned to Sorne, glowering with suspicion. 'What's this?'

'Everyone's ready to witness you sign the decree, sire. Remember how we discussed Prince Cedon's future?' Sorne spoke quickly, before Charald could say something that revealed how much his mind was slipping. 'In this very room, six days ago, you spoke of how your father died and left you with Nitzel and Oskane to advise you. You told me you were worried about...'

Charald took a step back, shaking his head.

Sorne's heart sank. 'You asked me to draft the decree.'

He eyed them all. 'You're conspiring against me.'

'Perhaps this will help.' Aware of the high priest and two law scholars regarding him with distrust, Sorne shuffled through his papers. 'Here. This is the list we made together. You signed it, sire.'

He placed it on the table and everyone peered down at it.

'I don't remember signing that,' the king said.

Aware that Charald's sight was not what it had been, Sorne picked up the paper to bring it closer. 'Take a good look, sire. It's your signature. This is why you had the discussion with me. You were worried about your memory.'

The king's eyed narrowed. 'Eskarnor warned me you were up to something, but I didn't believe him. You're trying to steal my throne. I–'

'What of Prince Cedon?' Jaraile pleaded. 'Who will look after our son when you're dead?'

Sorne winced.

'Yes, you'd like that, wouldn't you? Then you could marry your lover.' Charald stabbed a finger at Nitzane.

The high priest and law scholars looked shocked.

'Hold on.' Nitzane sprang to his feet. 'You can't cast aspersions on the queen's honour. If you weren't an old man, I'd–'

Charald bristled. 'This old man could best you–'

'Think of our son, not yourself, for once!' Jaraile rounded on the king, colour high, eyes blazing. 'He's only a boy. It's your duty to protect him.'

'Duty?' The king spluttered. His skin reddened with fury, and he burst into a tirade, shouting a string of bitter accusations at the queen, about duty, and her lack of it.

High Priest Faryx had never witnessed one of Charald's rages, and he made the mistake of trying to talk sense. The more they confronted the king, the more adamant Charald became, and the less rational. In the past, his rages had terrified staff and courtiers. Now, it became clear to Sorne, the king's anger sprang from fear; his voice became querulous. His tremors became worse and, when he started calling for Oskane, everyone fell silent.

'Where is he?' Charald demanded, tears streaming down his cheeks. 'How dare he go off when I need him? Where's Oskane?'

Jaraile sank into a chair, hand to her mouth, stricken. Nitzane blinked in dismay, went to say something, then stopped.

They all turned to Sorne, who approached the king. 'Oskane sent me, sire. He told me you needed to rest. Let me fetch your manservant.'

'What?' Charald looked at him, blinked, then the fragile belligerence left him. 'Yes, get Bidern.'

Relieved, Sorne sat the king down opposite Jaraile and summoned a servant to fetch the manservant. Then he went to the sideboard, poured a cup of wine and slipped in two of the soothing powders.

'Drink this, sire.'

Charald accepted the cup, took a mouthful and stared across the table. 'All you had to do was give me a suitable heir.'

'But he will be healthy,' Jaraile protested.

His gaze shifted to her. 'I wasn't talking to you.'

Jaraile gasped. Everyone went very still.

The king tossed back his wine then appeared to be listening. 'I know.' He put the empty cup down. 'He's the best of the lot, but they'd never accept him.'

The door opened. Sorne drew the manservant inside, then went to the king. 'Here's Bidern, sire. Time to—'

'Mind your tongue, boy, I'm talking to your mother.'

Sorne baulked. The manservant made a strangled sound in his throat. Sorne recovered and helped the king to his feet. His hands were gentle. He didn't trust himself to speak.

The king wandered out on the manservant's arm.

Sorne closed the door and turned to face the others. He felt shattered. Without a word, he went to the sideboard and brought the tray with the wine and cups over to the table. He poured them all a drink, his hands shaking very slightly. Was he developing his father's ailment? He'd kill himself before it took his mind.

He drained his cup.

As if this was a signal, everyone spoke at once, their voices hammering at him.

'What were you thinking, trying to pass him off as fit to made decisions?' the older of the two law scholars asked. 'We cannot witness an agreement if he's not of sound mind.'

'More to the point, he cannot rule if he's not of sound mind,' High Priest Faryx said. 'We—'

'He's never been like this before,' Jaraile protested. 'I'm as shocked as you.'

'He has grown a little forgetful,' Nitzane admitted. 'But his mind has been sound.'

Sorne was tempted to say the king had *never* been of particularly sound mind, but he restrained himself. 'He was of sound mind the other day and he will be again. This has happened before.'

'What?' Jaraile turned to him.

'When?' Nitzane asked.

'During the siege,' Sorne admitted. 'It seemed to be triggered by an illness. This time I think it was the rage that triggered it. What happened here must not leave this room. He will come good again.'

Sorne saw they did not believe him. He drained his wine. 'Come with me. I can prove it is a medical condition.'

The two law scholars exchanged looks.

'Yes, I want you to come too. Everyone who was here today must see this.'

And he left the chamber with the others in tow. When they entered the king's outer chamber, Sorne told them to wait and slipped into the bedroom. The manservant was folding the king's clothes. Charald lay in bed, snoring with his mouth open.

'What was in that wine?' Bidern whispered.

'Soothing powder from Khitan. I've been giving it to him for years to help control his rages. Please tell me his urine has changed colour.'

Bidern nodded and glanced to the bedpan. 'When I saw the colour I left it there.'

'I don't know what's wrong,' Bidern said. 'The medicine seemed to be working, but–'

'Medicine? I thought he didn't trust the saw-bones.'

'No, but he trusts me. My father was an apothecary, and my brother has continued in the trade. I've been dosing the king since the middle of last year on arsenic powders. When he took ill in camp, I doubled the dose.'

'Arsenic?' Sorne repeated. 'But that's the royal poison.'

'It's prepared as a medication.'

'Stop dosing him. Stop everything.'

'But–'

'Sorne?' Nitzane peered in and whispered. 'The others are getting restless.'

'Tell them to be quiet. The king is sleeping.' Sorne brought the pan out to them. The urine was deep purple-red.

'Is that blood?' Jaraile asked.

'No, that's the colour the king's urine goes when he has one of these fits.'

'It looks like port wine,' Captain Halargon muttered.

'So you see, it is a physical problem,' Sorne said.

'What has the saw-bones said?' the older of the law scholars asked.

'The king won't see one,' Sorne admitted. 'He's afraid word will get out and his enemies will move against him. Besides, saw-bones are mostly good for setting bones and stitching up wounds. This...' – he gestured to the urine – 'this is beyond their skills. This is why we must protect the king. The longer he can sit on the throne and his enemies believe King Charald the Great is a threat, the longer the kingdom is safe and the more time his son has to grow up.'

No one spoke. Captain Halargon looked grim.

Sorne looked around. 'For the sake of the kingdom, for the sake of Prince Cedon, I ask you to keep silent.'

'He'll be back to normal in a day or two?' the older law scholar asked.

'Yes.' Sorne sincerely hoped so. 'When the moment is right, I'll send for you and the decree can be signed.'

'What of Eskarnor?' High Priest Faryx looked dubious. 'If he realises–'

'Between us,' Sorne gestured to the baron, the queen and the captain of the guards, 'we'll keep Eskarnor away from the king.'

Chapter Thirty

TOBAZIM PAUSED WHEN he sensed the build up of male gift aggression behind him. He turned to see Haromyr and Ionnyn jostling each other on the bottom step of the harbour-master's building, tussling over who should go up next. If they'd been dogs, they would have been growling. It had been like this ever since they entered port. Everyone was on edge.

'Io,' Ardonyx said.

Ionnyn glanced to him, then away.

'Haromyr.' Tobazim held his eyes until the other lowered his gaze. With that, he and Ardonyx turned and went up the steps.

Everything felt wrong. Even the stairs were built for Mieren legs; the treads were just a fraction too small and the risers too low, making him take the steps two at a time. And all the while, his gift thrummed through his body, reverberating like the skin of a beating drum.

Ardonyx walked out of the stairwell into the harbour-master's office, with Tobazim one step behind. Tobazim took in the room at a glance. Built on the fourth floor, the office overlooked the bay. The sun was setting behind the bay's huge sandstone headlands. Five Mieren worked at desks.

From up here, Tobazim could see the whole port laid out. The ships nestled against the wharves like piglets sucking at a sow's belly; countless more dotted the bay. Their masts stretched like a forest sprinkled with fallen stars, as the lanterns were lit. He'd had no idea there were so many ships.

Tobazim had felt a sense of dislocation upon entering the fortified port. There were tenements five and seven storeys high, all packed with laughing, fighting, crying, singing Mieren. The weight of their unguarded emotions meant he had to concentrate to maintain his defences. Now he understood why King Charald had no trouble raising an army of ten thousand and gladly sacrificed a thousand warriors to make a point.

It was all so different – he just wanted to climb aboard Ardonyx's ship and surround himself with familiar T'En things, which he could do soon if this harbour-master would just lift his head and be civil.

Instead, the man continued to write, bald head bent over his desk even as they stood before him. Tobazim bristled on Ardonyx's behalf. The harbour-master's four scribes didn't move.

Finally, the harbour-master pushed his sheet of figures aside and looked up. For a moment his shallow, pale blue eyes met Tobazim's, then they skimmed past in a dance that was fast becoming familiar.

'Master Hersegel, I greet you.' Ardonyx spoke Chalcedonian with the fluency of long use. 'Today we meet under very different circumstance. I have come to reclaim my ships.'

The little man lifted his hands. 'An unfortunate misunderstanding. If I'd realised, I would have sent you to the Wyrd wharf. Your ships are there right now.'

'What of my cargo?'

'Gone, I fear. Stolen.' The harbour-master shrugged. 'You know how I detest dockside thievery. I fight an uphill battle to keep it under control.'

Ardonyx dropped his voice, speaking T'En to Tobazim. 'With a percentage going into his pocket. The man's a rogue.' Ardonyx switched to Chalcedonian. 'And where is the Wyrd wharf?'

Stiffly, the harbour-master came to his feet. From his bent shoulders and drooping jowls, Tobazim would have said he was past ninety; as a Mieren, he was probably nearer to fifty.

Standing only as high as Ardonyx's chest, the harbour-master was almost as wide as he was tall, and he rolled from side to side as he walked to the windows. Once in position, he pointed towards the nest of wharves and ships. 'There.'

Ardonyx joined him, keeping a good arm's length between himself and the man. Tobazim tried to make out which wharf he meant, but there were too many.

'It's not big enough,' Ardonyx objected.

'This is a busy port, I can't spare another.' It was not an apology. 'I've hired strongarms to guard the entrance. You go in and stay there. I don't want your people wandering around the city, causing trouble.'

'Are we forbidden to leave the wharf?'

'Did I say that?' He looked far too pleased with himself for Tobazim's liking. 'Leave, if you must. But I cannot be held responsible for what happens to Wyrds wandering the port alone. There are brigands in town, especially down near the docks. They see your rich garments, your silver arm-torcs and...'

Ardonyx's eyes narrowed. 'We will have to come out to order supplies. Your merchants won't want to miss out on our custom.'

The solid little man considered this. 'Very well, but you don't come out without my strongarms' permission, and no more than four of you at a time.'

'And the other T'Enatuath ships? The causare sent a list to the king's agent.'

Hersegel searched his desk, uncovered a piece of paper and ran a blunt-tipped finger down the list of names. 'This one, she was sunk. Her, I don't know. She was confiscated, then the new owner sailed off. This one, I don't know. This one, confiscated—'

'Those ships which were confiscated must be returned to my people, by the order of King Charald.'

The harbour-master lifted his head. 'As I told the king's agent, I've sent messages to the other ports around the Secluded Sea, but...'

Ardonyx looked grim. 'Remember, Hersegel. We can't sail without ships, and your king wants us to sail.' With a curt nod, he went to leave.

'I've already had a delivery of Wyrds,' the harbour-master said. 'I told them to wait in the warehouse. I was going to send a message to the king's agent, but since you're here, you can pay the bounty.'

'We'll do that,' Ardonyx said. 'Meanwhile, please let the agent know we are here.'

As they'd hurried down the stairs, with Ionnyn and Haromyr behind them, Ardonyx muttered, 'He's a heartless thief. They all are. The Mieren merchants are going to rob us blind.'

Down in the street, they joined their companions and mounted their horses. Twilight had claimed the valley between the buildings. Without street lamps, the only light came from the open doors of businesses and unshuttered windows. Respectable establishments closed up for the night, as bawdy houses opened and taverns did a roaring trade. But Tobazim's party travelled in a pall of silence. Conversation fell away at their approach, and once they were past, a wave of comments picked up behind their backs.

Passers-by gave the T'Enatuath party a wide berth, the well-dressed holding handkerchiefs to their faces and averting their faces. There seemed to be a fashion for malachite jewellery; everyone wore it. And everywhere Tobazim looked, blue eyes slid away from his gaze.

'Soon you'll see my ships.' Ardonyx seemed cheered by this thought. 'The *Spring-cusp* is a sturdy vessel, reliable, quick, five masts, three decks. The *Autumn-moons* is a beauty, lovely lines, seven masts. There are ships more richly appointed, but I know every creak, every whisper. My ship, she talks to me.'

Tobazim felt the pieces of the puzzle fall into place. This was why Ardonyx's gift had felt exotic. It was tied to his ships, and the sea was a foreign country to Tobazim.

Now Ardonyx led them through a narrow street only just wide enough for their wagons. The buildings almost met overhead. The way sloped down into a hollow where boards rattled over fetid water. There was no sign of the stream itself; houses had been built over it, so that the water travelled in darkness to the sea. It struck Tobazim as obscene. He was glad he had grown up under open skies with the mountain at his back and the whole of Chalcedonia laid out at his feet.

Here, surly denizens inhabited the shadows. From narrow doorways, lean, hungry-eyed children watched them. Tobazim was shocked by how ragged and thin they were. If Mieren could treat their own young like this, no wonder they did not balk at murdering the children of Wyrds.

As a boy, his choice-mother had taught him that Mieren callousness and cruelty arose from their lack of the T'En gift or Malaunje gift affinity. They could not feel the pain they caused one another. Even so, the Mieren disregard for each other evident in the faces of these starving children shocked him.

He was relieved when they emerged from the street of top-heavy hovels. An area of open land dotted with charred rubble lay ahead of them.

'Ah, that explains why hatred burned so fiercely in those Mieren,' Ardonyx said, gesturing to an area of blackened rubble ahead of them. 'The harbour-master flattened half their homes, poor rats.' He saw Tobazim's expression. 'That's what they call this quarter, the rats-nest.'

'The Mieren call their own people rats?'

Ardonyx jerked his head back the way they had come. 'Their nest is a den of filth. If you hadn't been shielding so heavily, you would have felt it. Enough cruelty, greed and desperation to make you physically ill. The harbour-master used us as an excuse to knock down a few blocks of the worst of it, to isolate the area where he's quartered us. Here we are.'

They'd come to a barricade, defended by the harbour-master's hired thugs. About a dozen of them lined the barricade and clustered around the gate. At his party's approach, the strongarms stiffened, reaching for weapons. Once inside that gate, Tobazim's people would be prisoners.

A lantern hung from a poorly-constructed barricade. A second lantern was hastily lit and raised on a pole and hung from the gate tower – a rickety platform. One of the strongarms sauntered out to meet them. He was not the largest, but the light of cunning burned in his pale eyes.

'Harbour-master Hersegel said you were to answer to us now,' Ardonyx bluffed. 'We're in charge of the wharf.'

The guard glanced to his men, and they shuffled aside, but did not open the gate. It was a blatant insult. Tobazim contained his anger, turned in the saddle and signalled the nearest Malaunje. One of Ardonyx's sailors jumped down from the cart and opened the gate. As they rode through, Tobazim was aware of unfriendly stares.

The sky still held the afterglow of the sun but night had claimed their wharf. A jumble of dark buildings, some of which tilted alarmingly, spread out before them. There was just enough ambient light to make out the nearest one on their right: a warehouse with a dull glow coming from its open door.

Tobazim thought longingly of hot food and getting off this torture device they called a horse. Two ships were tied up, one on each side of the wharf. Another two ships were moored further out.

'The two ships anchored near our wharf are sisterhood vessels.' Ardonyx guided his mount closer. 'The two moored here are mine. My defiant little *Spring-cusp*' – he gestured to the ship directly ahead of them, then to the one on their left – 'and the *Autumn-moons*. Aren't they beautiful?'

Tobazim hid a smile. To his landsman eyes, the *Autumn-moons* looked like a row of terraced houses, with a taller building at each end. No lights glowed in the ships' windows.

'The sails burned when the Mieren attacked our ships. They'll have to be replaced,' Ardonyx said. He reached out to take Tobazim's forearm. 'But you should see them when we're at sea.'

Tobazim's vision blurred and he saw the sails illuminated by the setting sun. They looked like a dragonfly's wings. They were so beautiful an aching joy filled his chest.

Ardonyx's hand dropped and Tobazim's vision returned to normal. Memory-sharing was an intimacy that revealed trust. Tobazim was honoured.

Just then, Ionnyn and Haromyr caught up with them.

'What's that foul smell?' Tobazim had noticed it as soon as they approached the wharves. 'Some kind of fish?'

Ardonyx laughed. 'Seaweed, you landsman. It's low tide.'

Tobazim felt his face grow hot. He was going to be out of his depth for a while, and he didn't like it.

A man shouted from the door of the warehouse.

'What now?' Haromyr muttered.

'The unwanted Wyrds?' Tobazim guessed.

Ardonyx dismounted, handing his reins to one of his sailors. Tobazim stepped down and turned to find Maric ready to take his horse.

'What do we do, Captain Ardonyx?' the sailor asked. 'Unload the carts and stow the stores aboard ship?'

'Not yet.' Ardonyx spoke absently, studying the man who came towards them. To Tobazim, he looked underfed, wiry, and ambitious.

'You've come from the queen of the Wyrds?' the man asked.

'We represent the causare, our leader,' Ardonyx corrected.

'Good. These women and their brats are eating our profits. You're welcome to them.' He led them into the warehouse.

It was large and high-roofed and the far end was lost to shadow. Tobazim caught glimpses of stars through cracks in the roof. The place had a stale smell that was a mixture of damp, unwashed bodies and mice. His gift stirred, roused by the Mieren threat and the warehouse's state of disrepair.

Gathered around an open fire and a single lamp were ten rough-looking Mieren who came to their feet, radiating threat. Huddled at the far end, in the dark, several women tried to keep about a dozen children quiet. Even so, a small child cried, as if he had been crying for a long time and would soon fall asleep from exhaustion.

When Ardonyx and Tobazim entered, the women came to their feet, whispering hopefully. As far as Tobazim could tell, they were all Malaunje.

'This lot have come from their queen,' the man told his companions. 'We'll finally get our reward.'

This was greeted with relieved muttering to the effect that it was about time, but the Mieren did not take their hands from their weapon hilts.

'You're in charge here?' Ardonyx asked the first man.

'I am,' the leader said, as he eyed their silver belt buckles and the brotherhood torcs on their arms. 'We've got fifteen Wyrds for you, all copperheads, so that's fifteen silver coins you owe us.'

Ardonyx ignored this. 'Bring them into the light.'

'Over here, you lot,' the man bellowed. 'You heard me. Hurry up.'

An old woman and two young ones called the children, picked up the toddlers and hurried across. They gazed on Ardonyx and Tobazim with a fierce hope. That they did not defer but met Tobazim's eyes outright told him how desperate they were to return to the protection of the T'Enatuath.

'Are you sisterhood or brotherhood Malaunje?' Ardonyx addressed the old woman in T'En.

The Mieren leader spoke before she could answer. 'A couple of them are knocked around a bit – they wouldn't do as they were told – but they'll heal up all right. We didn't spoil their looks.'

Tobazim studied the two young Malaunje women. One had a split lip, the other a black eye. Now that there was hope of release, they blazed with fury.

'I am Lysarna of All-father Tamaron's brotherhood.' The old woman spoke T'En. 'Ours was a small estate far to the north. We knew nothing of the attack on the city. One day, while our men were out hunting, these Mieren came. They said our people had been exiled and they'd come to confiscate the estate. Old scholar Vittor did not believe them. They–'

'Don't listen to what she's saying,' the man spoke over her. Tobazim suspected he was worried by her tone. 'We've fulfilled our part of the bargain. We just want our silver.'

The old woman kept speaking. 'Scholar Vittor tried to stop them, but they cut him down.'

'Here, what're you telling them?' the man demanded.

'They dragged us out of our home–'

'Shut up!' The man raised his hand.

Ardonyx caught it mid-arc and held it, without apparent effort. 'Let her finish.'

The other Mieren moved closer, their hands going to their weapons. The women put the children behind them, and edged away.

Lysarna gestured to the two young women. 'They raped–'

'She's lying. Whatever she says, it's all lies!' the man shouted her down.

Ardonyx twisted his arm up behind his back and thrust him aside; he staggered and turned on his toes, his hand going to the hilt of his weapon.

'What's going on, Ardonyx?' Ionnyn asked, coming in with Haromyr. Several more T'En stood in the doorway.

The Mieren strongarms looked them over, clearly calculating the odds.

'If any of them makes a move, Ionnyn, kill them,' Ardonyx said in T'En. Then he continued in Chalcedonian. 'I was just paying these Mieren for their service.'

'Paying them?' Tobazim objected in T'En. 'You heard what they–'

'If we don't pay them, others like them will hear of it and they'll consider our people worthless,' Ardonyx said. His words were reasonable, but his hands shook with fury as he pulled out his pouch and counted out fifteen silver coins.

The leader of the Mieren watched Ardonyx put the pouch away.

'There you are,' Ardonyx said, dropping the coins into the man's worn hands.

'What about the cost of food?' the man objected. 'You can afford it.'

'You're lucky to get out of here with your life,' Tobazim told him, voice tight with anger.

The man glanced from him to Ionnyn and Haromyr, then signalled his companions. With bad grace, the Mieren packed their travelling kits.

The moment they left, the old Malaunje woman dropped to her knees. 'Adept Ardonyx, we are in your debt.'

'No. The T'En swore an oath to protect all Malaunje. I am sorry we could not have done more,' Ardonyx said.

'They need food and decent shelter,' Tobazim said. 'This warehouse is a fire trap, and it's about to fall down.'

Ardonyx nodded. 'They can sleep onboard one of my ships.' He took the old woman's hands, helping her up. She lifted her face to him, surprised and honoured. 'Soon, you will have warm food and clean beds, I promise.'

The others crowded them, thanking them, weeping with relief. The children plucked at Tobazim's robe, trying to find bare skin to touch, needy for the reassurance of his gift. He felt overwhelmed.

'Wait here by the fire,' Ardonyx told them. 'We have to inspect the ships.'

Eagerly, they came over to the fire, some running to fetch the few belongings they'd managed to bring with them.

Ardonyx turned on his heel and marched out. Tobazim strode by his side and Ionnyn dropped into step behind them. Three Malaunje sailors waited with lanterns to light their way.

'The *Autumn-moons* first.' Ardonyx headed straight for the gang plank. 'They're fine vessels, crafted from strong oak timbers. You'll find this interesting, Tobazim. Each deck is divided into compartments which can be sealed, so that if one part of the hull is breached, the ship will not sink.'

Tobazim followed, adjusting his weight as the wooden gang plank bounced with their steps. The ship's intricacies fascinated him, and he wanted to see Ardonyx in his natural element.

On board, he found the high deck at the front of the ship could be reached by a set of stairs, one each side. The rear of ship had two higher decks, one set back further from the other, so that from here it looked like a two-storey building with a large balcony.

Near him, on the mid-deck, were hatch covers and water barrels. Although the ship was long, he could cross the deck in six strides. At least now he understood why Ardonyx thought of the safety of the whole T'Enatuath, rather than an individual brotherhood. He had seen the larger world, and with so many Mieren ranged against them, it was clear to Tobazim that they had to put aside old rivalries.

'Ionnyn, take three sailors and go below, check for traps and sabotage,' Ardonyx ordered. He gestured to one of the older Malaunje. 'Harkar, go to the fore-deck cabins and make a list of what's been stolen and what needs to be repaired.'

They nodded and divided up the lanterns.

Ardonyx ran lightly up the stairs to the first rear deck, going to the door. Tobazim followed, holding the lantern.

As soon as Ardonyx opened the door the smell hit them. Not dead bodies, excrement. The hall stretched before him, three doors opening from it, a single door at the far end. They held their cloaks over their noses, but it made little difference.

Ardonyx nodded to the far door. 'My cabin.'

Tobazim tried not to gag.

When Ardonyx swung the door open, Tobazim raised the lantern. The cabin had been stripped; not a stick of furniture remained. Human waste was smeared across the floor, the windows and the bunk base.

'Barbarians! How could they do this?' Ardonyx ran to the far window, thrusting it open to vomit into the sea. Tobazim followed, dry retching. The cool night air was a relief. Tobazim welcomed the honest smell of seaweed. Ardonyx raised his head, tears streaming down his face. He wiped a trembling hand across his mouth.

'We need to get out of here,' Tobazim croaked.

Ardonyx nodded. He opened all the windows before he left, and the smell followed them out onto the deck.

'Curse the Mieren,' Ardonyx muttered. 'Not content with stealing a king's ransom in cargo, they've stripped my girls and defiled them!'

In a matter of moments, the others joined them, reporting much the same thing. Deeply indignant, they were eager to begin cleaning the ship that very night.

'Open all the windows and doors to let her air overnight. Check the *Spring-cusp*, I don't doubt they've defiled her, too.' Ardonyx said. 'Tomorrow's soon enough to clean them. Tonight, we'll make do in the warehouse.'

But he seemed shaken and deep in thought when they returned to that rickety building and their people, who were disappointed to hear the ships could not be used. They had to pack the T'En and all the Malaunje, those who came with them from city, and All-father Tamaron's people into the dilapidated warehouse.

Ardonyx was distracted, so Tobazim divided the building into areas for Malaunje and T'En. He asked Paravia's friend, Tia, to make sure the fire was built up and the women and children from the other brotherhood had enough blankets and food.

Meanwhile, the sailors set up private alcoves for the T'En initiates and adepts in a corner, using stacked stores to make partitions. They unpacked the provisions for the night. Soon they had the small travelling braziers fired up, and the smell of sizzling onion, lamb strips and beans filled the air.

When this was done, Tobazim went out to check on the wharf. There were half a dozen ramshackle buildings, all in worse order than this one. The horses had been quartered in one. The sea flanked the wharf on two sides, a cliff cut off the third, and on the fourth, the harbour-master's strongarms maintained a vigil at the barricade. It was not perfect, but it would have to do.

He noticed someone on the deck of the smaller sisterhood ship. If more Malaunje arrived before Ardonyx's ships were ready, he'd have to ask the sisterhood for help housing them all.

Tobazim returned to the warehouse, where he told Ionnyn and Haromyr to select five men and take the first watch.

'Wake us for the midnight to dawn watch. I'll feel safer when we are aboard the ships.'

Chapter Thirty-One

TOBAZIM PULLED HIS cloak more securely around him and walked the wharf in the pre-dawn chill. Despite his lack of sleep, he felt amazingly alert. He hadn't used his gift for days; it had built up. He tapped into it now, to enhance his sight, but it was like picking at a scab, more pain than pleasure.

There was just enough light to discern the uneven ground and ramshackle buildings. He made his way through the abandoned sheds towards the point where the barricade met the cliff, then he walked the perimeter. Each time he passed one of his people he stopped and spoke softly with them, before moving on.

When he came to the point where the cliff met the wharf, Ardonyx was waiting. Stairs went down here to a floating jetty. There was another set of stairs and floating jetty on the far side of the wharf where the barricade met the sea. Tobazim felt exposed: despite the barricade on one side, there were too many points of access to make the wharf defensible. They headed back towards the warehouse.

As they reached the end of the building, they heard a soft shuffle and a murmur. They both hesitated.

Tobazim was in the lead. He crept to the corner and looked up the side of the building towards the barricade. Three of the harbour-master's men were coming this way.

Tobazim placed a hand on Ardonyx's arm and gift-shared what he'd seen. Then he crept around the corner and down the side of the warehouse. He pressed his back against the wall, risking a quick glance around the corner. At least thirty Mieren had gathered between the warehouse and the barricade, near the building's entrance. Tobazim's gift surged as it tried to come to his defence; he forced it down.

'Quiet now,' someone warned. Tobazim recognised the voice of the man they'd paid for the Malaunje women and children. 'I've sent some of my boys to deal with their sentries. The ones inside will be sleeping. We'll cut their throats, remove those silver arm-torcs, buckles and knife hilts, throw their bodies in the sea and divvy up the goods.'

'And if we're asked, we didn't see a thing,' another of the Mieren added. Tobazim recognised the leader of the harbour-master's men.

Tobazim and Ardonyx drew back, crept down the side of the warehouse and around the corner.

'We should warn the sentries.'

'They're supposed to be on guard. We have to warn our people inside the warehouse,' Ardonyx whispered. 'But the Mieren block the only door.'

Tobazim's gift rose. 'There's another way in.'

He ran to the far back corner of the warehouse. Drawing his knife, he placed it between the loose boards and levered them apart. Rotten wood crumbled.

He tore off several more boards and was about to slip inside, when Ardonyx grabbed his arm. 'You make sure the Malaunje women and children get out safely. I'll lead the defence.'

His instinct was to fight alongside Ardonyx, but they had a duty to protect the Malaunje.

Inside the warehouse, it was very dark. The fire had burned down to coals. The Mieren could open the door any moment, creep in and start cutting throats.

Ardonyx headed towards the far end, where the T'En slept near the entrance. Tobazim stepped over a sleeping child and shook the shoulder of the first adult he could find. His gift was riding him, and the young woman woke with a gasp.

He covered her mouth and whispered, 'The Mieren have come back. Wake the children quietly and come with me. Hurry.'

She sprang to her knees, leaning over two sleeping children to wake her companion. Tobazim woke the the next adult he could find. 'Get up. Keep quiet. We're in danger. Bring the children.'

He heard the soft urgings of the women. The children obeyed as quietly as they could, but with so many, there was whispering and stirring. A toddler whimpered and was quickly silenced. If he didn't get the women and children out before the fighting started, they'd be underfoot. He'd seen the aftermath of a massacre; he didn't want to see it again.

Tobazim could hear soft scuffling and weapons being unsheathed as Ardonyx prepared the warriors at the far end.

'What's going on?' Tia asked.

'Cut-throats. They'll attack any moment. Come.' Scooping up a small child, Tobazim headed for the opening. 'This way.'

A muffled shout and the rasp of metal on metal told him the attack had begun. The women and children surged forward, pouring through the gap.

More quickly than he expected, they all made it out. Tobazim found he was surrounded by a sea of frightened children and women carrying infants. Some of the older youths had stayed to help defend the wharf.

Thuds, curses and the clatter of metal on metal came from inside the warehouse. He fought the instinct to go back himself and help.

'Come.' He led around forty women and children through the dilapidated buildings towards the nearest sentry, only to find a body in a pool of blood.

As he made for the next man, Maric came running towards him.

'The Mieren—'

'I know. Alert the other sentries, then go help Ardonyx.'

'What about the women and children?'

What about them? They'd be trapped between the sea and the cliff, if Ardonyx failed to hold back the Mieren. 'The sisterhood ship will take them. You go.'

He went.

'This way.' Tobazim led them to the end of the wharf where it met the cliff. He beckoned Lysarna and Tia. 'Take them down the steps to the floating jetty. Signal the sisterhood ship from there.'

He left them, running back through the sheds towards the warehouse. As he rounded a corner, he ran into Maric and several others. They were heading for the warehouse entrance.

'No, this way.' Tobazim led them towards the gap in the back wall.

From the warehouse, he could hear only muffled shouts and thuds. It was an oddly quiet fight, compared with the night the Mieren had invaded the city.

With the others just behind him, Tobazim ducked into the warehouse. Some of the stores were alight. Illuminated by leaping flames, he saw a jumble of struggling bodies. In the confusion, he couldn't spot Ardonyx.

Frustration made his gift surge. He forced it down, drew his long-knives and charged, yelling at the top of his voice, with the others at his heels.

The arrival of reinforcements startled the Mieren. Finding themselves attacked on two fronts, many made a dash for the front door. Tobazim ignored them, concentrating on finding Ardonyx.

He slashed and cut, feeling meat and bone part beneath his blade.

The fight had abruptly gone out of the Mieren. Cutting throats while people slept was more their style. Now they just wanted to get out with their skins. The last five turned and ran. His people gave chase.

Tobazim shoved past Ionnyn, to find Ardonyx slumped and bleeding. Seeing him injured made Tobazim's gut tighten.

Ardonyx frowned. 'What are you doing here?'

'Saving your skin.'

Ardonyx grinned then toppled forward.

Horrified, Tobazim dragged him into their makeshift quarters and placed him on a bedroll, then lit the lamp. The worst of the injuries was a wound in Ardonyx's belly, and they had no sawbones.

His first thought was not what would the brotherhood do without Captain Ardonyx, but what would *he* do without Ardonyx?

IMOSHEN DREAMED OF fighting Mieren. Fierce, snarling faces lunged at her. She blocked and swung, then blocked and failed. A stabbing stomach pain woke her.

Rolling out of bed, she bent double. When she pulled her hands away she expected to find them covered in blood. Nothing.

'What is it?' Frayvia whispered, coming over to join her.

For an instant she couldn't make sense of her dream. Then... 'Ardonyx is hurt. Mieren must have attacked his party.'

Frayvia guided her back to bed. 'Can you reach him?'

She tried. 'The distance is too great. Besides, he's wounded. His focus will be turned inward.'

Ardonyx wounded... she hunched over in pain. It would be too cruel if he was killed now. What would she do without his cool head and knowledge of the sea?

TOBAZIM CURSED AND covered Ardonyx's wound with a blanket, applying pressure to slow the bleeding. 'Athlyn!'

The youth came running.

'Keep pressure on his wound.'

Springing to his feet, Tobazim strode out. In a matter of moments, he had fresh lamps lit and had ordered Malaunje to patrol the barricade. He sent Eryx to ensure the women and children were safe on the sisterhood ship and to find out if either ship had a sawbones on board.

Then Haromyr and Ionnyn revealed the captives. Two Mieren huddled in a corner near the door. Both were injured. One would not last out the day. The other watched him fearfully.

'Shall I slit their throats?' Haromyr asked.

Tobazim was tempted.

'No, we don't want more Mieren deaths on our hands.' He hadn't killed anyone tonight, merely driven them off with wild blows and intimidation, and he wasn't going to start killing now. He didn't want the angry shades of dead Mieren trying to drag him onto the higher plane. Not when the shades of those Mieren his men had killed would already be coming for them. Weakened by his wound, Ardonyx was in no state to defend himself. Tobazim would have to protect them all.

Haromyr still waited for orders.

'Take these two outside. They can keep their dead company.'

Cold and furious, he went over to survey his party's dead: two of his Malaunje, both inexperienced warriors. One of the young initiates had a head wound that made him see double, but he would be fine in a day or so. The rest of their injured were still able to function.

Tobazim went outside into the cool grey of dawn.

Here Ionnyn and Haromyr had laid out the bodies of the dead Mieren, six in all. One was the leader of the harbour-master's guards. That pleased Tobazim. He had a bone to pick with Hersegel. The injured man who was still conscious pressed his hand to his side and winced. Blood seeped through his fingers. His companion managed to rouse himself enough to moan for water.

'What would you have us do?' Haromyr asked.

'Bind the injured Mieren's wounds. Give them both water.'

He returned to the warehouse, where he met a Malaunje sawbones, and a boy he assumed was her assistant. He took them in to see Ardonyx, who was pale but conscious.

'Toresal,' Ardonyx said. 'You're safe.'

'Cap'n.' The boy threw himself on Ardonyx's chest, weeping with joy.

'Here.' Tobazim peeled the lad off his captain. 'Give the healer room to work.'

While the lad asked after his shipmates from the *Autumn-moon*, Tobazim watched the saw-bones work. Tonight had made several things clear to him. They could not trust the Mieren; he would have to make the wharf secure himself. And he could not face life in Kyredeon's brotherhood without Ardonyx at his side. But he wasn't sure if Ardonyx felt the same way.

When she was done, the healer came to her feet. The boy remained by Ardonyx's side, holding his hand. Tobazim thanked the sawbones, and walked her and the lad to the warehouse door. Mist clung to the wharf, illuminated by shafts of dawn sunlight. 'How is he?'

'He won't be dancing for a while, but he'll live. Send for me if he develops a fever.'

He thanked her and told Eryx to escort her back to the sisterhood ship, then sent the lad to join the sailors, who had begun to clean the ships.

Finally, Tobazim knelt next to Ardonyx. 'How do you feel?'

'Wonderful.' Ardonyx rolled his eyes. 'What's been going on?'

Tobazim began to outline the situation, but Ardonyx passed out before he was halfway through.

Cold fury gripped Tobazim. This should never have happened.

Unable to sit still with his gift riding him, he sprang to his feet and strode outside. 'Hitch up a cart. I'm going to see the harbour-master. Ionnyn and Haromyr, come with me.'

They threw the bodies of the dead into the cart, helped the injured man climb up, then placed his unconscious companion in his arms before setting off.

Almost no one was stirring in the narrow lanes of the rats-nest. In the more prosperous trading quarter, shopkeepers' apprentices were opening shutters and sweeping door steps. The smell of fresh bread made Tobazim's stomach knot in hunger.

By the time they reached the harbour-master's building, it had clouded over. As soon the cart stopped, Tobazim jumped down. 'Haromyr, bring the injured one.'

He sorted through the dead until he found the leader of the guards and threw the body over his shoulder. He turned to Haromyr. 'Ready?'

'Ready.' The injured Mieren shook so badly he could not stand, and Haromyr had to carry him.

Empowered by anger, Tobazim strode up the steps. He arrived at the harbour-master's door to find Hersegel was an early riser. The four clerks froze. Their eyes widened as Tobazim strode across and dumped the body of the harbour-master's strongarm on his desk. All the Mieren drew back, and he realised they could sense his gift. He didn't care.

'What's this?' the harbour-master blustered. 'You've murdered my man?'

'Your man tried to slit our throats while we slept. Is that how the Mieren honour their king's truce?'

'Not on my orders, they didn't.'

'Then who ordered it?' Tobazim gestured to the injured Mieren. 'Ask him.'

The harbour-master looked relieved. 'I've never seen him before in my life.'

Tobazim signalled Haromyr. 'Bring him here.'

Tobazim caught the back of the injured Mieren's neck, bringing him forward and turning him to face Hersegel.

'Fifteen silver coins were not enough for this greedy brigand and his companions. As I see it, they convinced your strongarms to join them and rob us–'

'He lies!' The injured Mieren ducked from under Tobazim's hand, flung himself around the desk where he fell to his knees, clutching the harbour-master's hand. 'They tried to break out. We were only defending ourselves–'

Tobazim gave a bark of laughter. 'If so, why were you at the barricade when you weren't one of Hersegel's men? And why would we break out when every Mieren in port hates us? Don't you understand we want to leave this forsaken land?'

And he realised he meant it.

Boots thundered on the stairs as five burly Mieren spilled into the office, their weapons drawn.

Tobazim drew his long-knives, even though he knew fighting his way out and back to Ardonyx was impossible. Haromyr took up position at his back.

Levering himself out of the chair, the harbour-master came to his feet. He kicked the injured Mieren aside and beckoned his guards. 'Get rid of this fool.'

They hesitated, casting worried glances to Tobazim and his companions.

'The Wyrds have been wronged,' the harbour-master announced. 'I want another dozen strongarms–'

'No.' Tobazim returned his knives to their sheaths. 'No more hired thugs. I want the king's men on the barricade. We are under *his* protection.'

Hersegel lifted his hands. 'You'll have to speak to the king's agent about that.'

'I will. And...' Tobazim faced the harbour-master. 'If they are any more attacks on our wharf, I'll hold you personally responsible.'

The man grew pale.

Satisfied for now, Tobazim marched out. He suspected the harbour-master had planned to get his cut after his strongarms had murdered the Wyrds, dumped their bodies in the bay and looted their provisions. If anyone asked, he could say they'd never made it to port.

Tobazim went down the stairs to find anxious Mieren watching from across the road. It struck him that bringing the bodies here had not been the best of moves. Before rumour could take root, he jumped onto the cart seat, and summoned his somewhat rusty Chalcedonian. 'These Mieren were paid to protect us, yet they tried to slit our throats as we slept. This is what happens to those who raise a hand against us.' He gestured to Haromyr and Ionnyn. 'Unload the bodies. They're our gift to the harbour-master.'

No one spoke as Haromyr and Ionnyn lined the Mieren up on the harbour-master's doorstep.

The two initiates climbed onto the cart and Tobazim took the reins, heading back to the wharf. By the time he got there it was raining again.

Ardonyx's people were scrubbing the ships. Driven by his restless gift, Tobazim set out to rebuild and make the wharf secure. He ordered the worst of the ramshackle buildings pulled down and the wood used to repair the warehouse and reinforce the barricade.

He was kneeling by Ardonyx's side, trying to work out if he was running a fever, when Athlyn came with the news that the king's agent had finally arrived.

Tobazim had a bone to pick with him.

PART THREE

Chapter Thirty-Two

JARAILE HAD NEVER loved the king, never even liked him. She'd been fifteen when he browbeat her father, demanding that she marry him. All Charald had ever wanted from her was an heir. Their wedding night...

She shuddered.

Now, he lay exhausted after raving for the better part of five days. Only the soothing powders from Khitan had given him any peace. According to the manservant, his urine was back to normal this morning. The king had been rational, but he was too tired to lift his head off the bed. She wanted to sink her nails into the soft flesh of his arms to make him bleed, to make him suffer as he had made her suffer.

Yet everyone thought her sweet.

Once, she'd believed herself sweet. That was before she'd had to live under the king's thumb. He'd stopped coming to her bed around the middle of last year, but that didn't stop him bullying her. His hands...

She picked up the hand that lay on top of the covers. It was twice the size of hers, but thin and wasted. Only recently he'd left bruises on her with that hand.

She wanted to punish him. Since spring cusp, she'd lain awake every night thinking of her little boy, frightened and alone, all because Charald had to be rid of the Wyrds.

He didn't love Cedon. He saw their son only as a means to an end.

He didn't deserve her precious boy.

Why, if she picked up the pillow and held it over the king's face right now, he would not have the strength to fight her off. The thought filled her with righteous excitement. King Charald didn't deserve to live. Not content with bullying everyone in Chalcedonia, he'd taken his army and attacked the peaceful kingdoms of the Secluded Sea.

She didn't want him to get better. She wanted him to die before he could do any more damage to her, to her son or to the kingdom.

But she was no fool. Although she might not be as smart as the half-blood, she was clever in other ways. It made her laugh inside to see how all the others danced to Sorne's tune, while believing themselves superior to him.

Sorne understood the king. He understood the barons and he understood the Wyrds. Listening to him explain it all to Nitzane, she'd grasped the situation. Everyone feared King Charald the Great. As long as the king lived, the other kingdoms would not attack Chalcedonia, and as long as the southern barons did not realise how frail he had grown, they would not rise up against him. That was why Eskarnor was a danger. He'd lived in the palace and seen the king's growing fraility. But according to Sorne, Eskarnor could not move against the king while Charald had Nitzane's support.

It frustrated her, but she and her son needed the king. Even if they got the decree signed, the high priest, Barons Nitzane and Kerminzto, and Commander Halargon did not have the reputation to bluff their enemies. How was she going to keep her boy safe?

'There you are,' Nitzane said.

When he smiled on her, she thought the Jaraile she had been might still live somewhere inside her.

'How is he?' Nitzane whispered.

'He ate and spoke sensibly. Now he sleeps.' She tucked the king's hand under the covers.

'You are so good to him,' Nitzane said.

If only he knew.

'Have you eaten?'

'Not yet.'

'Come with me. You have to keep up your strength.'

At the door they met up with Sorne. 'How is the king?' he asked. 'Does he seem malleable?'

Nitzane didn't understand.

'I think he's had a fright,' she said. 'It would be a good time to approach him with the decree about Prince Cedon's advisors. Would you like me to do it?'

Sorne considered. She expected him to refuse, but he surprised her by nodding.

Just then a messenger arrived. The king's agent was needed on the Wyrd wharf. Sorne made his apologies and left.

Jaraile let Nitzane lead her down to the terrace, where they took breakfast. She waited until he was eating, then asked the question that had been troubling her since the day the king went mad.

'What did the king mean when he told Sorne to mind his tongue because he was speaking to his mother?'

Nitzane flushed and appeared uncomfortable.

'The Warrior's-voice is Queen Sorna's son, isn't he? The king's first son wasn't stillborn. He was born a half-blood.' She didn't know why the men tried to hide things from her. She always figured it out eventually. 'What I don't understand is why he's so good to the king.'

'Sorne's a good man,' Nitzane said. 'A better man than many True-men.'

This was high praise indeed. While Nitzane might not be as smart or as ruthless as some of the men she'd seen fawning over Charald, he was a good man. And when the king died, she was going to marry him, because he was weaker than her and she was tired of being bullied.

'Still no sign of the king?' Eskarnor joined them. A servant hurried over with a tray of food. 'Is he still feverish? You have to be careful of fevers. They can turn nasty, especially in a man his age.'

'Oh, I think he'll be up today,' Jaraile said, pretending not to understand the hidden threat. Her heart raced and she felt a little sick with fear, but she also felt more confident than she had in years. One thing had become very clear to her the day Prince Cedon was taken: she would stop at nothing to protect her son.

Once she had been a good little girl, but look where it got her – married to a king old enough to be her grandfather who raped her on their wedding night.

She was never going to be that girl again.

SORNE DISMOUNTED AND led his horse through the barricade. There was no sign of the harbour-master's strongarms, but there was plenty of activity. Despite the rain, the Wyrds were rebuilding the warehouse. Why were they going to all this trouble, when all they had to do was board their ships, load their supplies and anchor in the bay?

A lad came running over to hold Sorne's horse.

'Toresel,' Sorne greeted the cabin boy. 'Back in the brotherhood, serving Captain Ardonyx again?'

'I am. Only it'll be a while before he's on his feet.'

'Why–'

'Where have you been?' Tobazim demanded.

He'd stopped at arm's length, but Sorne could feel his power. It made Sorne's heart race, and he had to concentrate to speak. 'I came as soon as I got word.' Half a dozen big T'En men drew in behind Sorne. He could sense their aggressive gift. 'Why? What's the problem?'

'The problem was thirty Mieren trying to cut our throats while we slept. You're the king's agent. Is this how he honours his word?

Sorne took a step back and collided with a broad chest. A glance over his shoulder revealed a T'En warrior a head taller than him. Huge hands grabbed his arms. Despite this male's size, Sorne knew the real danger lay in front of him. 'The harbour-master put this wharf aside for you. What about his men—'

'Half the cut-throats were the harbour-master's men. Don't worry,' Tobazim smiled grimly, 'I delivered the dead to his doorstep.'

'If you frighten the people of the port, they'll turn on you,' Sorne warned. 'No one can stop a mob.'

'I want the king's own guard in uniform on the barricade.'

'I can organise that.' He hoped. The king's palace guard would consider the duty beneath them. They were the elite of the men-at-arms. But if the harbour-master's strongarms could not be trusted...

What was the harbour-master thinking? There'd been no trouble since the run-in over Captain Ardonyx's ships. Surely, Hersegel realised his actions had jeopardised the return of Charald's son?

If anything happened to the prince, Nitzane's son would be heir. Despite this, Sorne was certain Nitzane wasn't behind the attack; the baron didn't have that kind of cunning. But there was someone who did. If evidence could be fabricated to implicate Nitzane in Prince Cedon's death, it would drive a wedge between Charald and Nitzane. Without Nitzane and the backing of the Chalcedonian barons, the king was vulnerable.

Sorne went cold. Was Eskarnor working with the harbour-master? Events the night Toresel had been delivered to the palace came back to him. He cursed softly under his breath.

'What is it?' Tobazim asked. Sorne glanced to the hands restraining him.

Tobazim gestured. 'Let him go.'

Sorne drew Tobazim away from the others. 'You're in charge here?'

'I am now.' Tobazim's eyes narrowed. 'What is it?'

'I need to confirm something.' Sorne beckoned the cabin boy, who trotted over leading the horse. 'Toresel, think back to the night Captain Ardonyx's ships were confiscated. Who attacked you?'

'The Mieren.'

'Yes, but which Mieren?'

'How should I know?' He shrugged then added. 'The one who gave the orders spoke with a Dacian accent.'

Sorne rubbed his jaw. Just because the leader of the thugs came from Dace, it did not follow he was in Baron Eskarnor's employ. But Eskarnor had turned up at the palace with the boy that same night, claiming he'd rescued him from a mob. 'How did you come to be captured by the baron?'

'I don't know. When the ship was attacked I was knocked out. Next thing I knew I was hanging over the baron's horse.'

It didn't add up. Why did the brigands spare the cabin boy's life when they killed everyone else? Because Eskarnor needed the boy to manipulate the king into banishing Sorne. If the southern baron wanted to take the throne, Eskarnor had to divide the king from his allies. But Sorne hadn't taken offence and abandoned the king.

All this time, he had thought Eskarnor meant to move against Charald after the Wyrds left, but by then, Charald would have his healthy heir. It made more sense for Eskarnor to disrupt the handover of the prince and blame it on Nitzane. Charald had always been paranoid about betrayal. If the king turned on Nitzane, the baron would have to protect himself.

This would split the loyalty of the Chalcedonian barons because some would side with Nitzane and some with Charald, dividing the kingdom into three factions: Nitzane and his heir, Charald and his queen, and Eskarnor and the southern barons.

Sorne turned to Tobazim. 'You have to move the day of exile forward.'

'Why? The causare made a bargain with the king.'

'The bargain is no good if there's a new king.'

'What?'

'I believe the king's rival was behind the attack last night. Otherwise, why would the harbour-master endanger the exchange? Only one person benefits if the prince isn't returned, and that's Baron Eskarnor. He's ambitious and ruthless, and he's been searching for a way to separate the king from his allies. If the exchange doesn't go ahead, there will be civil war with three factions fighting for the throne.'

'Why should we care who rules Chalcedonia?'

'Because only King Charald has a vested interest in ensuring the Wyrds sail safely.'

'The T'Enatuath,' Tobazim corrected. He rubbed his mouth and looked around the wharf. 'Why should I trust your judgement?'

'Because I've been watching the king and his power plays since I was seventeen. I'm the reason your people have the prince and a chance to escape alive. And you know I'm the causare's spy.'

Tobazim conceded this with a single nod. 'Move the exile forward? Do you realise what that involves? There's all the brotherhoods and sisterhoods in the city and then there's the estates—'

'Don't trust the harbour-master. I believe he's backing Baron Eskarnor to seize the throne.' Sorne reached for his horse's reins, with a nod of thanks to the lad. 'From their point of view, there's no profit in letting you sail into exile. If they kill the lot of you on the wharf, they can divide all the riches you were going to take to fund your exile.'

Tobazim swore softly. 'If that's their plan, why jeopardise it with last night's attack?'

'The harbour-master's been skimming off everyone for years. It's second nature to him. I think he underestimated you, or his men got greedy and acted independently.' Sorne's mind raced on. 'Send a message to Imoshen. Tell her Baron Eskarnor is staying at the palace with the king, while his supporters maintain the siege. If Eskarnor learns you're leaving early, he'll tell his barons to strike while your people are camped on the road to port and plant evidence to implicate Nitzane. She must prevent news of your early departure reaching Eskarnor.' Sorne mounted up.

'Where will you be?'

Once before, Sorne had put the fate of the Wyrds ahead of his sister's safety; for all he knew, she'd died the night of the riots, but he wasn't giving up hope. There was one more place he could try... 'I'm going to ride across Chalcedonia to save my half-blood sister.'

When Sorne returned to the palace, he found Nitzane with the queen. He closed the door to the solarium and explained the situation. Jaraile grasped the implications immediately.

'Should we send Captain Halargon to escort the Wyrds to port?'

Sorne shook his head. 'If the southern barons surrounded the Wyrds, Halargon and his men would be outnumbered. They'd have to stand aside or die to a man.'

She wrung her hands. 'Cedon–'

'Is safest if the Wyrds reach port before Eskarnor realises what's happening.' He held their eyes. 'The fewer people who know, the better. Have you had a chance to speak with the king?'

'He's still sleeping,' Jaraile said. 'I'll bring up the decree when he wakes. But the agreement is only good if we can back it up.'

Sorne nodded. He was beginning to think they had all underestimated Jaraile. She had been fifteen when she was forced to marry the king. In the last four years she'd been browbeaten, given birth to a crippled son, then a stillborn boy and then lost her father. That would make or break someone.

'Eskarnor will try to discredit Nitzane. The king...' The king needed to be seen about the port, or else people would think he was fading; but he needed to be sheltered from Eskarnor. Were these two up to the challenge? 'Make sure Charald's manservant doesn't treat him. Bidern claims arsenic is medicinal, but I don't see how it can be both a poison and a medicine.' Sorne handed Jaraile his pouch of soothing powders. 'Use these if the king gets overwrought. Go to High Priest Faryx for political advice and Commander Halargon for military advice.'

'Why? Where will you be?' Nitzane asked.

'I'm searching for my sister.' It was an eleven-day journey by wagon to Restoration Retreat. He was going by fast horse, but he worried he would not make it back before the Wyrds left port. 'I have to go.'

Before he left the palace, Sorne visited the captain of the king's guard, filled him in on his suspicions and asked him to send a contingent of guards to man the barricade at the Wyrd wharf.

Then he packed lightly. He didn't have much. There was his mother's torc. The only other thing of value was the Wyrd reports, and Igotzon had the originals, so he burned his copies. Lastly, he strapped on his sword.

RONNYN SLUNG THE canvas bag of preserved food over his shoulders and adjusted the straps; then waited for Aravelle. Through the half-open front door, he could see their parents sitting close together, watching the little ones build forts in the sand. Light sparkled on the bay, and Itania's laughter rang like a bell. Tamaron was four years old today and there would be treats for dinner tonight.

What with their workload, they hadn't restocked the hide for ages. Originally a simple overhang, their father had used a winch and pulley to move large rocks to form a wall, packed the gaps, moved soil onto the top, then planted bushes until you could not tell that it was there, tucked into the hillside behind a thick screen of bushes.

His mother's voice echoed in his head. *If the Mieren come. Run. Hide. Don't come out, no matter what, until it's safe.*

'Ready?' Ronnyn asked.

Aravelle nodded and they headed out the back door, past the chicken pen, past the goats.

They walked fast until they were out of sight of the cottage, then they slowed. They saw stink-badger tracks, then found a place where the ground was churned up.

'Wild dog tracks.' Ronnyn pointed. 'Looks like the dog pack cornered some stink-badgers. Wish I could have seen it.'

'I'm glad I didn't.' Aravelle shuddered. She'd been very quiet.

That was all they said until they came to the creek bed. Usually there were several crossings, but the rains had made the water rise and they had to search for a safe place to ford the creek.

He could remember when the creek crossing had been a big obstacle, when the jump from rock to rock had been a challenge. Now he managed it easily.

Reaching the far side, he landed on the shore, feet sinking into the cool, damp sand, and turned to help Aravelle. Independent as always, she brushed his hands aside and jumped. But the river stone that had been secure under his foot shifted under hers, and she lost her balance.

He caught her, pulling her to him.

She brushed off his helping hands as though it was his fault the river stone had shifted. He wished. He was a noet, and not a good one.

'Why are you always grumpy with me, Vella?'

She looked up at him and shoved him. Hard.

Ronnyn wasn't expecting it and he went down, falling on one hip in the wet sand.

With a laugh, Aravelle took off up the creek bank. He watched her feet flashing, the curve of her calf muscles tensing with the effort, the length of her long legs disappearing under her smock.

Challenge fired him. Scrambling to his feet, he ran after her, all his concentration focused on catching her and making her pay. Before he'd gone a stone's throw, he realised he could catch her without trouble.

To make it more fun, he almost grabbed her twice, letting her get away. She was fast and slippery, but she was no match for him. Her hair came undone, flying behind her. He drove her, letting her keep one step ahead of him, all the way up the hill, until they reached the hide.

She tried to slam the hidden door on him, but he thrust it open, charging in after her, driving her up against the far wall, pressing her to the stone.

And there in the semi-dark everything changed.

Maybe it was the wild excitement of the run, maybe it was just the right time, but he felt his gift slam into him, felt it ride him then roll over her, washing around her like waves on the rocks.

It was enough for him to sense her excitement, her restlessness and that part of her which was eager for his gift. It would be so easy to...

She slipped out from under his arm, darting towards the door that stood ajar. Before she'd gone two steps, he caught her arm.

She resisted, shutting his gift out completely.

He felt the moment it happened and it infuriated him. Wordlessly, he pressed against her defences.

She held firm. More than that, she pushed back.

When she tried to pull free of his hand, he anticipated and shifted his grip. This caused the muscles in his bad arm to bite and jerk, pain shot down into his hand but he held on. He held on because he wanted her to acknowledge...

'Ronnyn?' Her voice held fear.

Fear?

It shocked him. He'd never hurt her. Never.

Taking advantage of his surprise, she slipped free. Silently, she backed up, rubbing her wrist as if to erase his touch.

He watched, fighting the urge to go after her.

His stillness seemed to reassure her; after a moment, she became all businesslike. She wedged the door open. With the sunlight streaming in, she knelt and took off her bag, then went through the food chest, restocking the hide.

A crockery container of pickles had cracked open, probably when he slammed her up against the wall. Shame made his face burn.

It was a while before he trusted himself to join her, and she didn't ask him why he wasn't helping. When he did kneel beside her, they were both careful not to touch and neither spoke.

So, they weren't going to talk about it. That suited him.

He put his share of the preserves in place and removed the old ones. Some would still be good to eat. Some would be fed to the goats.

Once that was done, he was suddenly very tired.

She closed the chest and barred it, so that even if dogs or stink-badgers broke into the hide, they wouldn't get into the food. Then she stood, hands on her hips. 'There's still the water barrel.'

She was right. They had to bring up fresh water from the creek, but he was utterly exhausted. 'We'll take turns with the bucket. You go first.'

'Fine. But you'll have to help me empty the stale water.'

He struggled to his feet. Together they rolled the water barrel until it was positioned near the crevice at the back of the hide, and then she opened the spigot. He could hear the water trickling away. The sound echoed oddly in his head.

When he turned around, she was heading out the door with the bucket.

He went over to the bedding and undid one of the bedrolls. It was almost too much effort to unroll it. A mist of exhaustion settled on his mind. He'd be all right if he could just close his eyes for a moment. As he lay down, the air went out of him in a long sigh and he let his awareness go with it.

Something nudged his back.

'Wake up. It's time to go.'

He sat up. Where...

It all came back to him. By the angle of the sun, it was late.

Aravelle slung her pack over her shoulders. She must have filled the water barrel on her own.

'You should have woken me.'

'Oh, believe me, I tried.'

He came to his knees and rolled up the bedding, tying it closed. 'You should have tried harder.'

'You think I wanted to bring all those buckets of water up here on my own?'

'I'm sorry–'

'Let's go. I'm tired and hungry, and Ma will be wondering what took us so long.'

When he straightened up, he discovered his muscles were strangely achy. After collecting his pack, he turned around, only to find she'd already left.

He closed the door to the hide and slid the bolt home, then let the bushes settle into place. When he stepped back to check, it was impossible to see the entrance.

No sign of Aravelle.

'Hey, wait up,' he called. Going a few steps along the path, he glimpsed her between the pines. She was already halfway down the hillside. 'Wait for me.'

She didn't answer or, if she did, he didn't hear. He hurried after her.

'Slow down, Vella. Don't be mad. I'm sorry I fell asleep.'

She stopped and turned back to him. Her hair was restrained in a no-nonsense plait. 'I'm not mad at you because you fell asleep.'

He swallowed.

She turned and walked off.

He should apologise, but what if she asked him to promise never to use his gift on her again? What if she threatened to tell their parents?

He ran after her. 'You can't tell Ma and Da.'

She spun around to face him so suddenly he nearly ran into her. 'You must tell them, or I will.'

The thought of tearing their family apart shattered him. 'I'll leave.'

Her chin trembled but, after a moment, she nodded.

He was devastated. Her quiet agreement was worse than if she'd berated him. 'I'll go in the spring, when the winter storms are over and it's easier to travel. We can have this one last winter together.'

She nodded quickly again, tears in her eyes.

TOBAZIM WALKED IONNYN and Haromyr to the barricade. They each carried a copy of the same message, signed by himself and Ardonyx, then sealed with the print of their sixth fingers.

As he wished them both a fast and safe journey, the rain eased off and the sun came out, reflecting in the puddles. If he was superstitious he would have seen it as a good omen. Above him a seagull cawed.

The adepts passed a wagon coming towards the wharf as they rode off.

'More of our people?' Athlyn asked. 'Wait, isn't that the uniform of the king's guard?'

The wagon stopped outside the barricade and six men climbed down. They wore the uniform and they were armed, but they could hardly walk.

Their leader, a grizzled veteran, limped up to Tobazim and introduced himself as Captain Vetus of the king's palace guard.

Tobazim looked him up and down. 'What happened to you?'

'We failed to prevent the kidnapping of Prince Cedon. We've been in the king's dungeon since spring.'

'And now you've been sent to protect us?'

He nodded. 'As punishment.'

Tobazim shook his head. He beckoned a Malaunje. 'See that these Mieren are given a decent meal.'

'We can't eat filthy Wyrd food,' one of them muttered.

'Shut up, Yano,' Captain Vetus snapped. 'If we don't eat, we'll be too weak to fight. All of you, go wait over there.'

The others shuffled off, sinking to sit with their backs against the warehouse as if that was all that was keeping them upright. The disgraced captain of the king's guard hesitated, then he inclined his head in a shallow bow. It was the closest thing Tobazim had seen to civility from one of the Mieren.

Eryx called him away, and when Tobazim next checked on the king's guard they were busy cleaning up plates of beans and lamb with flat bread.

Vetus seemed to have some sense of honour. Tobazim was hopeful that the king's guard would do their job. He had thought it would be enough for the port Mieren to see the king's colours on the barricade.

But if what Sorne said was true, the king's colours would not protect them from Charald's enemies.

Chapter Thirty-Three

'What's next?' Saffazi asked.

To keep her choice-daughter out of mischief, Egrayne had suggested she become Imoshen's assistant as they prepared for exile. Imoshen didn't mind; Saffazi was quick to learn, if a little impatient.

'Vittoryxe is setting her birds free. And here comes Frayvia with Uma.' Imoshen waved. 'It'll be a pretty sight, seeing the birds fly off.'

As they met at the door to the scriptorium, Umaleni reached out for Imoshen.

'Come to your mama, dearheart.' Imoshen swept her daughter into her embrace, delighting in the warmth of her soft skin.

'Do we have to do this?' Frayvia whispered.

'It would have been rude to refuse. They are Vittoryxe's prize birds. I spent years helping her breed them, so she wants me there when she releases them.'

'They were reared in captivity,' Saffazi said. 'They'll die out in the wild.'

Imoshen nodded. 'But they'll experience freedom before they die. It's symbolic.'

With Umaleni in her arms, Imoshen led the others through the empty chamber. It had been hard to choose only the most useful texts to take. The rest would be hidden in the crypts.

As Imoshen passed the alcove where Saffazi had nearly gotten herself and Iraayel killed, her step slowed.

'It wasn't their fault,' Saffazi said. 'I talked them into it.'

'I don't need to be a raedan to know that,' Imoshen told her.

Saffazi laughed, not at all abashed, and little Umaleni laughed because she liked it when people were happy. They stepped out into the aviary, carried on a crest of joy.

The gift-tutor sniffed disapprovingly. Her devotee mirrored her expression.

'Vittoryxe, I see you are ready.' Imoshen assumed a suitably solemn expression. The balcony overlooked the city, facing west into the setting sun.

Behind the gift-tutor, the birds called and flew about their perches, each a work of art. They had been bred for their glorious crests, brilliant colours and lilting songs, and they were Vittoryxe's passion, so it was only right that she make a ceremony of releasing them.

Two Malaunje musicians consulted with the gift-tutor, then began to play the tune she'd chosen. It was a dirge, hardly appropriate for giving the birds their freedom. Still, Imoshen had to acknowledge the depth of the gift-tutor's emotion, as tears coursed down her cheeks. Vittoryxe had been breeding birds since she was a child.

'Which ones have you chosen to take with you?' Imoshen asked to divert her thoughts.

'None.' She walked around the aviary.

'You can take your favourite pair,' Imoshen reminded her. 'I've made provision for their feed and housing.'

As if she didn't have enough to organise.

'Better for them to die free.'

It was on the tip of Imoshen's tongue to say the birds might feel otherwise, but she restrained herself.

Vittoryxe reached the end of the aviary where Malaunje servants had loosened the west wall of the cage. With a vicious push, the gift-tutor sent it crashing onto the courtyard tiles.

Umaleni jumped in Imoshen's arms, her little hands clutching in fright. Imoshen hugged her tight.

The birds chirruped, flapped and circled but did not leave. Weeping, Vittoryxe ran into the aviary to thrust them off their perches. The birds fluttered and wheeled. Squawking and shrilling, some made their way out into the world, but many did not. Vittoryxe redoubled her efforts to drive them off, weeping and cursing.

Imoshen knew that later, when the gift-tutor calmed down, she would regret her loss of control.

Right now, Vittoryxe was beyond thought. Between her cries and the birds' cries it was a cacophony.

Imoshen felt her daughter stiffen and tremble. She tried to reassure Umaleni, but it was all too much. The infant's bottom lip turned down and she wailed in sympathy. The Malaunje musicians struggled valiantly on, but their subtle pipes and strings were drowned out.

Imoshen could not console her daughter. Tears streamed down the infant's face.

What was meant to be a solemn, grand send-off became a shambles. Desperate to distract Umaleni, Imoshen went to the edge of the balcony, pointing west to where the first of the birds headed off, silhouetted against the setting sun.

'Look, there they go. Pretty birds, Uma.'

Umaleni gulped and her cries eased.

'You!' Vittoryxe's angry whisper made Imoshen turn. 'You should never have been taken into this sisterhood. Look what you have brought us to!' She gestured to the empty cage. 'Our heritage has been squandered. Our ancestors must be moaning in their crypts!'

Frightened by Vittoryxe's anger, Umaleni wailed anew. Imoshen turned her shoulder to the enraged gift-tutor and caught her devotee's eye. Frayvia took Umaleni and left the balcony.

With her distraught infant safe, Imoshen turned back to deal with Vittoryxe, but the gift-tutor had gone.

Imoshen fought to control the surging of her gift. It wasn't her fault the Mieren king wanted them gone. They were lucky to have turned genocide into exile.

One part of her was angry, the other sympathised with the gift-tutor. Since spring cusp, Vittoryxe had lost her choice-son and her prized birds, and soon she would lose her home.

The musicians came to the end of their piece, bowed and left. Doubtless, they'd talk of the gift-tutor's outburst in the Malaunje dining hall.

Silence fell, save for the call of wild birds heading home to roost. How long would Vittoryxe's birds survive in the wild?

Were their people a product of the Celestial City's hot-house? Imoshen frowned. Would they suffer the same fate? She shivered as the last of the sun's rays left the marble columns and glass doors along the balcony and, except for the highest dome and tower, the Celestial City was swallowed by twilight.

Imoshen's heart ached for their ancestors, who had striven to create beauty and harmony, never dreaming their descendants would be forced to leave the city. Her heart ached for her generation, who set off into the unknown, and for their children, who would only ever know of the Celestial City through stories and memory-sharing.

'Well, that was a disaster,' Saffazi remarked, coming over to join her. The young initiate wrinkled her nose. 'I almost felt sorry for Gift-tutor Vittoryxe.'

'You should,' Imoshen told her. 'Vittoryxe will find it hard to adjust to exile.'

'That's silly,' Saffazi said. 'It's exciting!'

Imoshen laughed. 'You're right.' She linked arms with Saffazi. 'That is how we must see exile, as a great adventure.'

RONNYN CHECKED THE hen-house was secure, then made sure the goats were safe in their pen. Finally, he walked around to the front of the cottage and stood on the beach for a moment, watching the wisp of smoke drift from the chimney.

The cries of the birds as they went to their roosts faded. The first of the night hunters took to the evening sky.

Meanwhile, their cottage rested safe and secure. The wood heap was stacked high against one wall, and the pantry was stocked with preserved food.

Satisfaction welled up in him. In the spring before he left, he would do everything he could to set up his family before leaving. Tears stung his eyes.

He could not imagine life without them, but he had to go, for their sakes. Even as he thought this, his gift rose, demanding that he use it. He forced it down.

Aravelle opened the front door. Silhouetted against the light, she beckoned him. 'Come in, the water's hot.'

Tonight was their bath. Crossing the sand, he entered the cottage and closed the door after him. Itania and Tamaron sat with their father by the hearth, where Asher combed the tangles from their hair.

Vittor knelt in the knee-deep tub, head down, as Aravelle rinsed his hair. His pale skin gleamed like the moon on a clear night. He came to his feet, innocently naked, while Aravelle wrapped a cloth around his hair, squeezing it dry. Vittor had the curls, like Itania and Tamaron, but his hair fell in long rippling waves to his thighs.

Privately, Ronnyn thought hair this length was a nuisance, but it was a matter of pride for their mother. The T'Enatuath wore their long hair in elaborate styles, so she made special scented soap, and ensured her family's hair was properly dressed, even if only in plaits.

'There's fresh hot water,' Aravelle told Ronnyn.

'You go first.' He knew she liked to freshen the bath water before using it.

'I'll be quick.' She smiled and pegged the blanket across the corner of the cottage, stepping behind it while he sat on the far side near the fire.

Ronnyn tried to build a cottage in his head, planning the frame, the timber he would need, how he would make the joints, brace the walls...

The scent of verbena-scented soap was so sharp it almost stung his nostrils. Around him, the little ones laughed and sang, but he felt isolated by the impatience that rode his body. At the same time, he felt focused by the concentration it took to rein his gift in. He could have been sitting there forever, waiting for her.

He couldn't stand it a moment longer. His heart beat like a great drum, pounding through his body. He felt his gift rise. This time he could not keep it shut away. He had to get out.

He sprang from his seat. 'I'm going to check on the animals.'

Without waiting for an answer, he went out into the cold moonlit night.

As he paced the familiar paths, his mind raced. He couldn't go on like this. He didn't want to restrain his gift. He felt she owed him the chance to test his limits. He knew she wanted it as much as he did, and didn't see why she refused.

He should make her admit it. He would...

He could not trust himself.

Surprised by this self-knowledge, he dropped to his knees in the sandy soil behind the chicken coop. Heat and power radiated from his skin, making the chill moonlit air feel luxurious.

A sound made him turn.

Aravelle stood there in her night shirt, wet hair down to her knees. She finished weaving it into a braid and flicked it over her shoulder. 'Your gift was troubling you?'

Ronnyn lifted his hands. 'It gets into my head. It changes the way I think and feel. I tell myself I won't let it, but it does.'

'You'll learn to control it.'

He didn't want to control it. He wanted to use it. 'Go away.'

'You've got to come inside.' She took a step closer. 'Dinner's ready. They're waiting for–'

He sprang to his feet, caught her arm and swung her up against the chicken coop wall; felt his gift surge.

Her breath caught in her throat. 'Don't do this. You'll be sorry tomorrow.'

He was dimly aware she was right, but...

Something slammed into the back of his knee. His leg crumpled and he fell.

'Back to the house, Vella.' Asher's voice was hard.

She ran off, but only a body length.

Ronnyn rose from a crouch, turning at the same time.

Asher stepped back, cane raised. 'Do you want to break your mother's heart?'

And the madness left him as his gift dissipated into the night.

With a groan, he sank to his knees in the cold sandy soil. Tears of shame burned his eyes, and silent sobs shook his shoulders.

'The greater the gift, the harder it is to control,' Asher said softly. 'That's why the T'En females separate the boys when they get to your age. The power surges. It clouds the mind–'

'I hate it!' Ronnyn said and, at that moment, he meant it. He rubbed his face, trying to catch his breath. 'I'm sorry. I planned to leave in the spring.'

'He did.' Aravelle backed him up.

'Too late. We'll pack up and go...'

'Ma can't travel with the baby due.' Ronnyn pulled himself to his feet, had to lean against the chicken shed. He felt tired and flat. 'I should go alone.'

'Alone?' Aravelle echoed.

'We'll talk about it tomorrow.' Asher reached out. Ronnyn felt a firm warm hand on his shoulder. 'I know you can do this, son.'

'I have to, don't I?' He sucked in a shaky breath, then looked to his father. 'I'm all right now. Please don't tell Ma.'

'We'll just tell her it's time to go home.'

So he went inside, ate his dinner and, when it was time for bed, Aravelle made herself a nest in front of the fireplace, despite his offer to sleep on the floor.

As he lay down in the loft with the two little boys, who were already asleep, he thought he'd never drift off. At the same time, he was so tired, he couldn't think clearly.

Ronnyn woke to a muffled noise. Had a possum climbed in and raided the larder again? His father would have to chase it around the cottage. No, Asher couldn't run anymore. He would have to go down the ladder, catch the silly thing and...

His mother gave a ragged cry, alarming in its intensity.

'Baby coming?' he whispered, looking for Aravelle.

But she wasn't there. The events of last night returned to him. He felt shame, but also relief now that their father knew.

Vittor sat up, rubbing his face, and Tamaron grumbled as he rolled over.

Ronnyn was going to tell them to go back to sleep, but an unknown male voice cut him off. Another unknown male voice answered.

Strangers in their cottage?

Had the brotherhood found them?

An angry curse made Vittor gasp and Tamaron sit bolt upright. Both little boys looked to Ronnyn, who lifted a finger to his lips. Vittor and Tamaron nodded.

He felt the weight of their trust.

Signalling for silence, he crept to the edge of the loft to peer down into the room below. No silver hair, or even copper.

They were Mieren.

Five men. He recognised Trader Kolbik, but none of the others.

So that was how they had been found... betrayed and hunted down by the trader. Ronnyn's stomach clenched; one of them had Aravelle by her plait.

Another, a brute with huge shoulders and a barrel chest, held their father on his knees, with his arms pinned behind his back. The fourth, a youth with crooked front teeth, held a lantern high.

The last one was a mean-looking man with a thin, ferrety face. He advanced on their mother and tried to pull Ronnyn's little sister away from her. Itania squealed as the stranger's fingers pressed cruelly into her chubby arms.

'Don't hurt her,' Sasoria cried in T'En, then switched to Chalcedonian. 'Please, don't–'

The ferret-faced stranger cuffed Ronnyn's mother. She released Itania, staggering until she hit the wall. And there she stayed with one hand under her heavy belly to support the weight.

'Sasoria!' Asher roared, struggling against his captor. The brute forced him down, crushing his face into the reed mat, muffling his cries.

The others laughed, their strange, shallow eyes gleaming.

'Bring me the Wyrd brat.' Kolbik gestured. 'Bring the lantern closer.'

Ferret-face presented Itania to the trader. Ronnyn's little sister froze; she must have been terrified. As Kolbik turned her plump little hands over to count the fingers, righteous indignation filled Ronnyn and he burned to protect her.

'She's got the six fingers and the mulberry eyes, but,' Kolbik dropped Itania's hands disgustedly, 'her hair's copper. Only a half-blood, like the parents and the girl.'

Ferret-face thrust Itania into Sasoria's arms and turned to confront the trader. 'You said there was a full-blood. So where is he? We get five silver coins for a silverhead, and only one for a copperhead!'

'What does he mean?' Vittor whispered.

Ronnyn covered his brother's mouth.

Too late. Kolbik's eyes went straight to them.

'There!' Kolbik pointed. 'There's all the silverheads you could ask for!'

The Mieren looked up.

The brute grunted in surprise. 'But their hair's white.'

'Be thankful it is,' Kolbik said. 'If it was silver, it would mean they'd come into their gifts. The children have no power.'

'Then we don't have to worry about looking into their eyes,' ferret-face said.

'Run, Ronnyn!' Sasoria cried in T'En.

Ronnyn scrambled away from the ladder with Tamaron clinging to him. Vittor joined him at the far end of the loft. The only way to go was out the tiny window. He could push the others onto the roof, then crawl out after them, jump to the ground and run, but his little brothers would never reach the hide.

Besides, Ronnyn couldn't leave his parents and sisters to the Mieren.

Ferret-face came up the ladder. He grabbed Tamaron's ankle and pulled. 'Got you!'

The four-year-old shrieked and clutched Ronnyn's legs, his nails scraping.

'Don't hurt him!' Vittor sprang towards the ladder, striking the Mieren's head and shoulders.

Ronnyn grabbed Vittor and pulled him away. But ferret-face caught Vittor's nightshirt and dragged him towards the ladder like a puppy. Vittor locked his arms around Ronnyn, holding on for dear life. Now that he was free, Tamaron launched himself at the Mieren, hitting his back and shoulders with tiny, furious fists. Ronnyn was so proud of him.

And so afraid for him; for all his family.

Ferret-face caught Tamaron. 'Catch the cub, Kolbik.'

There were muffled noises from below as Tamaron was dropped into waiting arms, then ferret-face turned to deal with Ronnyn and Vittor.

'It's all right.' Ronnyn squeezed Vittor's arms. He glanced over to ferret-face and spoke Chalcedonian. 'We're coming down.'

'Sure you are.' The man climbed up into the loft, hunching double beneath the roof.

'Go on, Vittor.' Ronnyn sent him ahead down the ladder.

Then he went next. When his chest was level with the bed, the ferret-face spoke. 'Eh, silverhead?'

Ronnyn looked up and ferret-face's fist slammed into his face.

Chapter Thirty-Four

ARAVELLE GASPED AS the Mieren punched Ronnyn. Her brother flew back off the ladder. The Mieren scattered. Ronnyn's head and shoulders hit the kitchen table with a horrible dull thud. Her mother cried out in protest. The table creaked, then collapsed.

In the ensuing silence, Kolbik swore. 'He's worth five silver coins!'

'He's not worth anything if we can't control him,' the thin-faced one said as he came down the ladder, then stepped over Ronnyn's legs. 'Now he'll think twice before he gives us trouble.'

Aravelle did not dare move, but she searched Ronnyn's face. Blood poured from his nose. Was his chest moving? Yes. Relief made her dizzy and slightly nauseous.

Someone had put a bounty on their heads.

The ferrety Mieren stepped around the collapsed table and went over to where the brute held her father down. He grabbed Asher by the hair and jerked him up to his knees. 'Where are they? Where's the precious stones Kolbik told us about?'

'Give them the torc,' her mother said in Chalcedonian. 'Vella, show them where it is.'

'Show them, Vella,' her father urged.

She understood why she should cooperate, but her heart was ripe with rebellion as she knelt in front of the hearth to remove the stone. First she pulled out the leather satchel with the brotherhood cards.

The trader exclaimed over these. 'Very fine. But I saw gems, yellow gems. Where are they?'

Carefully, she removed the mat and the box.

The trader tucked the card satchel under one arm and snatched the box from her, shook it, then tried to pry it open. He thrust it at her disgustedly. 'Open it.'

She wanted to defy him, but didn't dare. Hating herself, she obeyed, springing the catch to reveal her mother's torc.

At the sight of it all, the Mieren fell silent. One of them whistled.

Kolbik took the box from her and removed the torc. It hung from his fingers, a thing of palaces and princes, completely out of place in their driftwood cottage.

'Now you have it, take it and go,' her father said. 'Leave us alone. We've never done you any harm.'

'How much is that worth, Kolbik?' the ferret-faced Mieren asked, eyes aglow with avarice.

'As much as I can get for it. Half goes to me. That's our agreement.'

'Come on.' He hauled Aravelle to her feet. 'What else is in there?'

'Nothing.' Aravelle's voice cracked.

The leader gestured to Kolbik, who dropped to his knees to search the space under the stone. 'Nothing.'

'There's this.' Ferret-face held up the tusk their father had carved. 'That's got to be worth something. And this.' He lifted the cane.

'I'll take that.' Kolbik claimed the cane.

'Take it. Take it all and go,' Asher urged. 'Just leave us alone.'

'Not likely.' Ferret-face cuffed Aravelle. 'Collect everything of value.'

On Kolbik's orders, she dragged the quilt off her parent's bed and piled everything onto it, the pots and pans, the crockery, her father's poems, the zither, the inks and the spiced-wine herb chest. All the while she was aware of Ronnyn lying unmoving in an ever-increasing circle of blood on the collapsed table.

Meanwhile, the others drove the rest of her family outside. When she heard the hens cackling indignantly and the nanny-goat bleating, she realised the Mieren meant to take everything. How would her family survive?

Then it hit her. They weren't staying. They'd been taken captive to exchange for a bounty of silver coins. They should have gone back to their people while they still could.

Ferret-face carried the quilt filled with all their possessions outside.

'Now bring him,' the trader told Aravelle, nodding towards Ronnyn, who had not moved.

She ran around the collapsed table and knelt next to her brother. Where he wasn't covered in blood, he was pale. His nose was swollen and he breathed through his mouth.

'Ronnyn?' she whispered, hoping he was playing possum.

He did not stir. Her heart shrivelled with fear.

Kolbik laughed wildly and she looked up in time to see her parents' bed catch fire. The base, stuffed with dried dune grass, burned fiercely. As she watched, the trader tossed a burning brand into the loft above.

Smoke quickly filled the cottage, making Aravelle's eyes burn. But it was tears of rage that nearly blinded her as she slid her arms under Ronnyn's broad shoulders and dragged him off the table, out the door and down onto the sand.

The brute had her father restrained on his knees and, further along, her mother crouched in the sand with the three little ones. One of the Mieren strode down the beach swinging squawking chickens by their legs. He tossed the birds into the boat. With their wings clipped, they couldn't escape. She felt as helpless.

Aravelle dragged Ronnyn over to her mother, then knelt, holding his head so sand wouldn't get into the wound. Her mother inspected his injuries, first his nose, then the back of his head.

'Will he be alright, Ma?' Vittor asked. He had to raise his voice to be heard over the roar of the flames.

'Of course he will. Now sit still and be quiet.'

And he was satisfied, but Aravelle held her mother's eyes. This was bad. This was...

'I've seen men walk away with worse,' Sasoria whispered.

'What did he mean, five silver coins for a silverhead?'

Sasoria shook her head.

A particularly sharp crack made them both turn.

The cottage roof had caved in.

Itania clutched Aravelle's arm. Flames painted her little sister's sweet face in shades of orange, and the tear tracks glistened on her cheeks.

It was amazing how quickly the cottage burned.

Heat beat on Aravelle's face, making her skin feel tight. The blazing building lit up the night, bright as the double full-moons. But unlike that lovely silvery light, this light was filled with crazy, leaping shadows. Everything had a reddish glow, as if stained with blood.

The Mieren backed off as the flames roared, reaching into the sky. Leaping and crackling, the fire spat and growled like a pack of caged beasts, the noise so loud it drowned out all other sounds.

Beside Aravelle, little Tamaron clung to Vittor. The four year-old's shoulders shook with silent sobs, while the six-year-old stared at their burning home, the fire reflected in the depths of his furious mulberry eyes.

She had to look away. She couldn't bear to see their home burn.

Glancing over her shoulder, down the beach, Aravelle noticed the Mieren's fishing ketch. It was larger than her father's and floated in the shallows of their sheltered cove.

'Kolbik?' her father yelled. '*Trader Kolbik?*'

The trader crossed the sand to Asher, who knelt at the brute's feet. Due to the roaring fire, Aravelle couldn't hear what her father was saying, but she could tell by the way he jerked his head towards the boat that he was telling them to take their booty and go.

Kolbik laughed and turned his back on Asher, approaching the rest of her family. He caught Aravelle's arm, hauling her to her feet so quickly Ronnyn's head slid off her lap onto the sand.

Sasoria sprang to her feet and tried to step between them, and Kolbik raised his hand to her mother. Miraculously, her father pulled the trader off them. But the brute caught her father by the shoulders and swung him around. His bad leg collapsed under him and he fell, sprawling.

When Sasoria tried to help him up, the brute shoved her aside so that she fell in the sand next to Asher, who clutched his thigh, grimacing in pain.

Vittor tried to go to their aid, but Aravelle grabbed him. Tamaron and Itania sobbed inconsolably.

'Stay, Vittor.' She spoke into his ear so he could hear her over the roar of the fire. 'Look after Tam and Tani. Stay with Ronnyn.'

He nodded. The ferret-faced Mieren had hauled her mother upright. Now he swung Sasoria around by the neckline of her gown. The material tore as she staggered, falling in the soft sand.

Vittor tugged on Aravelle's arm, pointing to Ronnyn, who stirred.

She dropped to her knees and leant over him, asking if he was all right. He pushed away from her and sat up blinking, much to Aravelle's relief.

Blood drenched the shoulders, back and chest of his night shirt. He blinked as if having trouble focusing.

'My head,' he mouthed, then lurched to his knees to bring up his dinner.

She rubbed his back as he wiped his mouth. The fire's roar was dying down now. 'Are you all right?'

He nodded, then winced. 'But the fire...' He slurred his words. 'The brotherhood'll find us.'

Had he lost his wits?

'Too late. The Mieren already found us.'

He looked confused.

'The trader betrayed us. Don't you remember?' She moved out of his way and gestured to the Mieren, who were silhouetted against their burning cottage.

Ronnyn swayed on his haunches and blinked, as though the world did not make sense to him.

The ferret-faced Mieren hauled their mother to her knees. Her long copper braid had unravelled and her hair fell forward, covering breasts exposed by the ruined nightdress.

'Don't look,' the brute warned. 'They say Wyrd women can ensnare the unwary!'

'Only if you let them,' Kolbik said. 'I recommend cutting out their tongues!'

Asher tore loose from the brute. Charging the trader from behind, he pulled Kolbik's knife from his belt and stabbed him in the back before anyone could move. Even before the trader's body hit the sand, Asher launched himself at ferret-face, knocking the youth flying as he passed. The lantern went spinning.

Hope made Aravelle leap to her feet.

But the brute caught Asher before he could take ferret-face down. Aravelle saw the brute's blade flash as it sank into her father's abdomen, up high under his ribs. Asher fell to his knees.

Her father blinked once, then pitched forward onto the sand.

Aravelle's stomach turned over. She stumbled two steps, dropped to her knees and retched until she had nothing left to bring up.

When she lifted her head, she saw Vittor had shoved Tamaron and Itania aside, and sprung to his feet.

'Stop him, Ronnyn,' Aravelle hissed.

But all he did was blink slowly and stare at their father's body.

She lurched to her feet, catching Vittor around the waist. 'There's nothing we can do. *Nothing.*'

Vittor shook with emotion, and the same outrage filled Aravelle. She wanted every last one of the Mieren dead. If only Ronnyn's gift had reached its full potential. If only he had been trained by the brotherhood.

If only she had let him practise on her.

But she hadn't. She'd been too weak to trust herself.

And now they were all powerless, and she hated it. She felt like sobbing until her heart shattered, but she couldn't, not when her little brothers and sister needed her, and not when Ronnyn seemed to have lost his wits. Hatred for her own impotence seared Aravelle, erasing all thought but survival.

Dragging in a ragged breath, she searched Vittor's face. When she was sure her brother would not do something rash and get himself killed, she released him. He shuddered and sagged against her. She sat abruptly, her legs giving way. Little arms and bodies wrapped themselves around her. She would do anything to protect them, but all she could do was reassure them.

'Don't worry, it's going to be all right,' she told them. It satisfied the two little ones, and Vittor seemed resigned for now.

Meanwhile, Sasoria had crawled over to their father and rolled him onto his back.

Their father's death seemed to have sobered the four remaining Mieren. They stared at the knife hilt protruding from Asher's stomach. Aravelle could see her mother's lips moving as she whispered her father's name, searching frantically for signs of life. When she found none, she gave a keening wail of despair. It rose on the night air, carrying above the sound of the fire.

'Now you've gone and done it. We coulda got a silver coin for that copperhead!' ferret-face shouted. 'They're paying nothing for bodies.'

'It's not so bad.' The one who'd been silent so far grinned. 'Now we don't have to give the trader his share!'

Their cruel laughter infuriated Aravelle.

'You're right,' ferret-face conceded as he picked up her father's cane and tucked it under his arm. 'It'll take days to deliver the Wyrds, and he'd have fought us all the way.'

Deliver them where? Aravelle glanced to her mother, but Sasoria was lost in grief and Ronnyn was... lost, for now. At least, she hoped it was only temporary.

Businesslike, the brute pulled the knife from Asher's stomach and cleaned it. Then, grabbing Sasoria by the hair, he pressed the blade to her throat. 'Any trouble and you'll get the same.'

Ronnyn made a strangled sound of protest in his throat, tried to stand, then pitched sideways and threw up again.

'That's not the way.' Ferret-face snatched Itania from Aravelle.

She watched helpless, as ferret-face strode across the sand, carrying Itania by the back of her nightgown like a kitten. He held her in front of their mother. 'Take a good look, copperhead.' His knobbly hand closed around Itania's throat. 'One twist and no more little girlie!'

'What's wrong with you? She's just a baby.'

'She's just a copperhead,' ferret-face snapped. 'Only worth one silver coin, so don't you be giving us trouble.'

Anger and disgust coursed through Aravelle.

Sasoria held out her arms. Wordlessly, the Mieren dropped Itania onto her lap.

'After tonight, we're all rich men,' ferret-face said, gesturing with the cane. 'Into the boat with them. We should take their fishing boat as well.'

'Who's going to sail it, uncle?' the youth asked.

The man went to Ronnyn, who was still on his hands and knees, head hanging forward. The man caught a handful of his hair, jerking his head up. 'I'd get this one to help me, but it looks like we've scrambled his brains.'

The brute grinned. 'Just as well, he coulda been trouble.'

'He's only a boy, only twelve,' Sasoria protested. 'He won't make trouble.'

'Only twelve? And him bigger than most of us.' Ferret-face laughed and shoved Ronnyn so hard her brother sprawled in the sand. He curled up, holding his head.

If the Mieren knew Ronnyn's gift was already manifesting, Aravelle suspected they would have killed him.

Ferret-face pointed to Vittor with the cane. 'You. Bet you helped your father with the fishing.'

Vittor glanced to her. She was a better sailor than him. But the man didn't seem to think of her; he turned back to the others, saying, 'I've got my crew.'

Vittor's jaw worked as he ground his teeth.

Ferret-face noticed and caught Tamaron by the back of his nightshirt, lifting him off the ground in front of Vittor. 'Remember what I told your mother, silverhead. Play up when we're at sea, and he'll go overboard.'

'But he's worth five silver coins,' Aravelle said.

'Brazen bitch!' He released Tamaron to bring her father's cane down across her shoulders. The blow sent her sprawling on the sand. She'd bitten her lip, and she tasted blood in her mouth as the man stood over her. 'I can't stand girls who don't know their place.'

Too stunned to move, she lay there, her eyes watering. With a murmur of protest, Sasoria crawled to Aravelle and helped her sit up. Tamaron and Itania ran to them and held on tight.

'Look at his face.' The Mieren pointed to Vittor, who stood there, hands clenched. 'He'd kill me if he could. Try it, silverhead. Come on.'

'Don't, Vittor,' Aravelle said, quickly. 'They're just looking for a reason to hurt us.'

Ferret-face looked around. 'Wind and tide are in our favour. Get a move on, silverhead.' He shoved Vittor in Ronnyn's direction. 'Help your brother.'

When Vittor helped him up, Ronnyn stood there swaying and blinking.

The Mieren grabbed Tamaron. 'Come along.'

Sasoria thrust Itania into Aravelle's arms and struggled to her feet, holding her gown together. She went over to hug Ronnyn, searching his face, then leaned down to hug Vittor and Tamaron, before whispering something to Vittor.

'Here, what're you telling them?' ferret-face demanded.

Their mother turned. 'To do what you say.'

The man grinned. 'Listen to your mother, boys, and I won't have to throw the little one overboard.'

Then before Aravelle could say goodbye, she was being herded down the beach towards the Mieren's boat, with Itania clinging to her, too frightened to cry.

'Hurry up.' The brute shoved Sasoria between the shoulder blades.

She staggered. Aravelle slid her free arm around her mother's shoulder. 'What did you really tell Vittor?'

'To keep his mouth shut,' Sasoria whispered, fierce as ever. 'And not to give them a reason to hurt us.'

'Where are they taking us? Who's paying for our people? The king? What will he do with us? I don't–'

'I don't know. All I know is, whatever you do, don't give them a reason to lay a hand on you.'

Aravelle nodded. Survival. That's what it was all about. She focused on the sand in front of her feet, then the shallows as they waded through the icy water to the boat.

Rough hands reached down, plucked Itania from her arms and lifted her onto the deck. The same hands hauled Aravelle over the side, then her mother.

Aravelle gathered Itania in her arms and searched the beach. She was in time to see ferret-face push her father's boat into the shallows and swing his weight over the side.

As the main sail rose above her, one part of Aravelle noted that the Mieren's vessel was much like their own, only larger, with two more sails.

She glanced back to the family's boat, looking for Ronnyn. He must have been lying down. She only hoped he would be all right. At the same time, she worried what would happen when he regained his wits and his gift surfaced. Maybe they'd be where they were going by then? Days, the Mieren had said.

In the meantime, Vittor could look out for Ronnyn and watch over little Tamaron. But it was a lot to ask of a small boy.

Now that they were leaving the bay, her gaze was drawn to beach where her father's body lay on the sand, not far from the trader's corpse.

It didn't feel right, leaving their father for the island's scavengers, not that laughing, gentle man. A shudder ran through Aravelle, and her stomach revolted. She lurched to her feet and hung over the side, retching, but she had nothing more to bring up.

'Seasick already?' The brute laughed.

Aravelle did not reply, but kept her mutinous eyes lowered.

There was little wind tonight. She stole another look as they sailed out of the cove under a moonlit sky. Her home had burnt to the ground. Only the stone hearth and chimney remained, in a sea of winking coals.

Her childhood was over.

Chapter Thirty-Five

JARAILE WATCHED THE king closely. It seemed she'd spent all her married life watching the king, trying to gauge his moods. In the past it had been so that she could avoid his temper. Now...

The king settled himself in the chair in front of the fire and his manservant returned to the bedchamber, humming under his breath as he cleaned up. Today the king had managed to bathe and get dressed. She suspected he would need to go back to bed later, but right now Charald was alert and grateful to her.

It was a new experience.

For three days now, the king had been rational; in fact, he seemed to grow more alert by the day. A servant arrived with the king's breakfast tray. She'd made sure it was just the way he liked it. She knew every one of his likes and dislikes, learned from painful experience.

Charald grimaced as he nibbled the cold meat, careful of his teeth, careful of his stomach. She knew he hated admitting to frailty, but she needed to remind him before he forgot.

'It is good to see you sitting up and eating, sire.'

'Growing old is a terrible thing,' he complained. 'Better for a man to die a warrior's death than to waste away in bed, clucked over by women and servants.'

'Soon our son will be returned to us. With the way your health has been, I was worried what would become of him, but you have set my mind at rest.'

Charald's hands slowed as he tore at the chicken carcass. 'Oh?'

She recognised the signs. He did not remember, and was trying to cover his lapse. Excited yet fearful, she clasped her hands in her lap and picked her words with care. 'When you took me aside and explained how, if anything happened to you, you'd chosen four trusted men to guide our son, I was so grateful. Sorne has drawn up the decree just as you ordered. Now that you are well again, we could–'

'Where is this decree?' Charald asked, mopping up gravy with bread.

'I'll get it.' She sprang to her feet. 'Would you like me to bring your chosen advisors as well?'

'Just the document will do.'

She darted out of his bedchamber, meeting Nitzane about to go in. She caught his hand. 'The king is going to sign the decree. I'll go and get it. You keep him company.'

'Clever girl,' he told her fondly, slipping into the room.

She went straight to her chambers, collected the leather folder with the decree and headed back. Her mind raced. If she sent for everyone, they could sign it before lunch, before the king fell asleep and forgot their talk.

'And how is the king today?' Eskarnor asked, stepping out of a doorway. He must have been lying in wait for her. 'Back on his feet?'

Fighting the instinct to hide the decree, she lifted her chin. 'He's–'

'Ah, what have we here?' Eskarnor snatched the leather folder from her, flipped it open and read the first couple of lines. His eyes narrowed.

She looked over her shoulder for the closest servant.

Before she knew what was happening, the baron had lifted her off her feet and stepped into a deserted bedchamber. He thrust the door closed. Holding her around the waist with one arm against his body, he carried her across to the bed, tossed the document folder onto it, flipped it open and read the decree.

She tried to wriggle free, felt him harden.

'Don't stop. I like it when you fight back.' He flipped the folder shut and straightened up, holding her against his body. 'My, you have been busy. But then, I suspected as much.' He grimaced. 'For a people who pay no heed to other countries' laws, you place a great deal of reliance on your own laws. Don't you realise this decree is only a piece of paper with scribbles on it?' He chuckled to himself as if it was a private joke.

She glared over her shoulder at him. She hated bullies.

He laughed, gesturing to the folder. 'Sign your bit of paper. It means nothing in the long run.'

She wanted to tell him they'd anticipated his plan. He wouldn't disrupt the handover. Her son would be returned, the decree would be signed and, with the might of the church, the king and half the barons behind him, Prince Cedon would sit on the throne of Chalcedonia.

His free hand began to tug at the drawstring of her pleated pants.

'What are you doing?' She tried to stop him.

'Giving the king a reason to believe you and Nitzane are lovers. Be hard to explain away a brat.'

'The king—'

'Hasn't been near you since we got back.'

She jerked and twisted with all her strength, but it only excited him. He held her, face down on the bed, while he freed himself and settled himself in place. Then he hauled her up against his body.

She was so angry she shook with rage. 'I'll tell—'

'Nitzane? You think that puppy can stand against me?' Eskarnor whispered. 'You think those old Chalcedonian barons won't bend over for me? They swore fealty to King Matxin. They'll swear fealty to me. You think the church will do more than wring their hands and pray?'

She tried to reach behind her to claw his face, but he caught her hand and laughed with excitement, his breath growing ragged. 'Now that Charald the Great is in his dotage, there's only one man who could stand against me, but you're blind to him. You're exiling him.'

Then he was silent as he concentrated on his finish.

She endured.

When he was done, he pushed her down onto the bed while he laced up, then pulled her upright, turned her around and adjusted her breeches. 'There, if that doesn't do the trick. I can–'

Her hand swung up.

He caught it and pinned both her hands behind her back. Laughter lit his eyes. 'They have no idea about you, do they?'

'I'll tell them you raped me.'

'Who, Nitzane? He'll challenge me to a duel. Out in the plaza where everyone can see, I'll kill him in a fair fight.' He saw her stricken expression. 'No, you'll keep quiet and hope I haven't planted a babe.'

He picked up the folder and handed it to her. 'There you go. Get your bit of paper signed, but know this. Power is the only real law. I'm going to be sitting in the king's chair, sleeping in his bed and fucking his queen by spring.'

Blind with fury, she walked out.

She wanted to break something. She wanted to slide a knife between his ribs. She...

She walked into the king's chamber to find Charald and Nitzane playing cards.

'Cards?' Jaraile muttered.

'Cards.' Nitzane looked pleased with himself.

'Cards,' Charald agreed. 'I swear, it feels like a grey fog has lifted from my mind.' He noticed the folder and gestured to the sideboard. 'Just put it over there.'

'Are you all right?' Nitzane asked her. 'You look a little feverish.'

'I think...' She pressed her hands to her hot cheeks as Eskarnor's words echoed in her mind – *Charald the Great is in his dotage*. 'I think it would be a good idea if the king took a ride around the plaza this afternoon.'

'A ride?' Charald looked up. 'I'd like that. I'm sick of being shut up inside.'

Nitzane seemed uncertain.

'The king is up to it,' Jaraile assured him. He had to be. 'A rest after lunch, then a ride around the plaza. The people need to see their king astride his horse.'

Eskarnor needed to believe Charald was recovering. As much as she hated him, she needed King Charald the Great.

IMOSHEN WRAPPED A cloak around her shoulders as she ran out of the palace and down to the sisterhood gate. It was dusk, and the gate guard was just lighting the lanterns. By their glow, she didn't recognise either of the T'En men. But she did recognise Kyredeon striding up the causeway road with his two seconds.

'We have a message from Adept Tobazim,' the smaller of the two said.

'And Captain Ardonyx,' the big one added. 'They gave us two copies in case one of us...'

Imoshen nodded and took the message from the smaller man. As it started to rain again, she stepped under the gate arch to read. The two lanterns illuminated the archway above her and made the pouring rain to each side gleam like a shimmering curtain. Kiane shifted uneasily as Imoshen tilted the message to the light. One glance told her the news was dire indeed.

'What are my brotherhood warriors doing, reporting to the sisterhood?' Kyredeon demanded, as he strode into the confined space under the arch.

'These T'Enatuath warriors are reporting to the causare,' Imoshen said. She wanted to back off and put more distance between them, but the all-father would see that as a weakness. She met his eyes. 'We have to leave the city within the next couple of days, or we'll never reach port.'

'What?' Kyredeon baulked.

'Give him the other message,' Imoshen told the big T'En male.

Kyredeon read it with both his seconds looking over his shoulder. He lifted his head. 'I know you claim he's your spy, but can we trust the Warrior's-voice?'

'Can we afford to doubt him?' Imoshen countered. 'He gains nothing by warning us. He's been exiled, too.' She folded up the message. 'I'm going to the all-mothers with this. You take that copy to the all-fathers. We'll start packing tonight.'

Her mind raced. They'd be safest in one large group. Normally it took six days by cart to port, but after the rain the road would be ankle deep in mud, and who knew how long it would take.

Once the besieging barons saw them leave, they'd turn their men loose on the city. This would occupy them for a couple of days. But Tobazim had warned that Baron Eskarnor's people would try to send a message to him at the palace. Those messengers must not get through.

If her people could reach the Wyrd wharf before Eskarnor learned of it, then all they had to do was board the ships. But only four of their ships had arrived in port. They'd been hoping for a ship for each brotherhood and sisterhood. Which reminded her... the people out on the estates thought they had until winter cusp to reach port.

'Kyredeon, each brotherhood will need to send messengers to their estates, telling them to make all haste to port.' There had been around forty estates, but she knew for certain eleven no longer existed. 'Thirty messengers riding out tomorrow will arouse suspicion, so they need to make their way under cover of darkness tonight. No word of our early exodus must reach port. When we leave, the brotherhoods will need to position warriors as outriders. If they spot a Mieren messenger making for the city, they must stop him.'

'We can organise our own people,' he told her shortly, but she could tell he was pleased to be going before the all-father council with orders. He gave her a curt nod and headed out into the rain.

The two warriors went to follow him.

'No,' Imoshen said. 'I need you to ride out tonight on fresh horses. Unless we can purchase more ships, or more of our ships arrive in the meantime, half our people will be stranded in port.'

Chapter Thirty-Six

RONNYN HUDDLED DOWN low in the prow, shielding his two little brothers from wind. He shivered as the sun set on the fifth day since their father had been murdered.

'Get up. Look lively, now.' Their ferret-faced captor kicked his thigh. 'Lower the sail, cripple.'

Ronnyn came to his feet, holding his left arm against his chest. Most of the time he managed, but the cold made the muscles spasm without warning. While they'd been sailing north, weaving through the islands, he'd been playing up the problem. Anything to make the Mieren underestimate him.

Ronnyn moved slowly, stiff with cold, sore from blows, and hollow with hunger. He beckoned Vittor. Luckily, his little brother was a quick learner. He'd always wanted to go fishing with Da.

Mustn't think about Da lying dead on the beach.

Mustn't think about flames burning his home. The only home he'd ever known.

Ronnyn felt his gift try to rise as it sought to defend him, but the innate power, usually so hard to contain, was feeble, drained by days of hardship and the blow to his head.

'Like this.' Ronnyn showed Vittor how to secure the ropes.

As they approached the mainland, riding in on waves bronzed by the setting sun, the grey clouds lifted. Now that they were close, he could see a shadowy cleft in the rock face.

The larger vessel went first, between the spraying foam and tall pillars of rock. Their family's boat went next with ferret-face steering, hand on the tiller and his eyes on the sea, responding to the waves and the wind. Ronnyn admired his seamanship even as he hated him.

Inside the narrow bay it was already dusk, and the wind dropped away immediately. Ronnyn's ears buzzed in the sudden silence. The sea's surface still rolled, but there were no white caps. A single pier ran into the dark water. Three fishing ketches were moored there.

Someone shouted.

Ronnyn looked up the valley's steep slope to see people and dwellings clustered in a hollow halfway up. Chimney smoke ran straight up in spirals, above the tall pines, until the smoke left the protection of the valley and was caught by the wind and whipped away.

'They're back safe,' a lookout cried.

A youth came running down the slope from the village, carrying a lantern. An old man followed at a more sedate pace with another lantern. Dogs barked and ran back and forth. Ronnyn lost sight of the lights behind the half-lowered sails of the larger boat as it berthed.

'Don't just stand there. Get moving, cripple.' Ferret-face clipped him over the head, making the swelling on the back of the skull throb.

It had taken him three days to see straight. And he only knew this because Vittor had kept track.

Momentum carried the boat towards the pier.

'Get a move on.' Another blow. His ear stung. 'Help your brothers.'

Ronnyn secured the boat, then swung his legs over and landed on the weathered boards of the pier. For a moment, his head reeled, as he regained his land-legs.

Their captors called greetings to the fisher-folk, who watched from various vantage points on the path up to the village. They were delighted with the return of their men, delighted with the success of the raid, but underneath was an undercurrent of...

Fear.

They feared him. How strange. And how ironic, when he could do nothing to protect his family.

As he turned to help his brothers, he heard his mother's voice and little Itania's soft whimpering. No sound came from Aravelle. He knew she wouldn't cry, wouldn't complain, wouldn't give in. Ever.

And that thought warmed him.

Vittor climbed onto the boat's side and jumped down onto the boards. He staggered a little before finding his feet. As soon as Vittor disappeared over the side, Tamaron wailed, fearing he'd be left behind.

Ronnyn leaned down, caught his little brother under the arms and hauled him up and over. His bad arm chose this moment to jerk in a painful spasm and he almost dropped the four-year-old. Vittor came to Tamaron's rescue.

Mieren surrounded them, all taking excitedly as ferret-face showed off Ronnyn's family boat. If the addition of a fifth boat to the village's fishing fleet was cause for celebration, just wait until they saw his mother's torc.

The fisher folk spoke so fast, Ronnyn had trouble following them. He'd only learnt enough Chalcedonian for trading.

'Ma,' Tamaron cried in delight. Leaving Ronnyn's side, he darted between the grown men, running towards their mother.

Even heavily pregnant, Sasoria carried two-year-old Itania on one hip, but she couldn't pick Tamaron up as well. The four-year-old wrapped his arms around her, clamouring to be picked up. Aravelle hugged him.

Ronnyn headed for his family. Vittor flung his arms around their mother, who leant down to plant a kiss on his salt-stiffened white hair.

Then she looked up to Ronnyn and winced. 'Your nose... Turn around. Let me see the back of your head.' She made a disgusted noise. 'It's matted with blood.'

'It's cleaner than it was. I washed it in sea water, like you taught us. But without a comb–'

'Ronnyn?' Sasoria turned him around and searched his face, her eyes keen with worry. 'Do you remember what happened?'

'I don't remember much, apart from the headache and throwing up.' A flash of his home burning. His father's body left on the beach for the scavengers. Tears stung his eyes. He battled on. 'Couldn't see properly for a few days, but I'm fine now.'

His mother nodded. 'For all that you're not thirteen until spring, you're as big as a full-grown Mieren. That's why they hit you so hard, to teach you a lesson.'

'Then it's just as well his gift hasn't manifested,' Aravelle said, intense wine-dark eyes filled with warning.

Only she and his father knew that his gift had come on early. And Da...

He gave a little nod of understanding.

'I'm hungry, Ma.' Vittor's teeth chattered with cold.

'We're all hungry,' Aravelle told him as Tamaron and Itania chimed in.

'Be brave,' Sasoria said. 'They'll feed us soon.'

But would they?

Ronnyn looked around. The fisher-folk gave them a wide berth as they hustled about, unloading his family's goats and chickens. Two people went past with his parents' quilt, holding the corners up. He saw a flash of pots and pans, the minutiae of their life, stolen. It angered and saddened him.

'Right you lot, get a move on.' Ferret-face shoved them with their father's cane as he herded them up steep steps hacked from the rocks and into a narrow valley.

At least ten cottages were built into the sod, their thatched roofs no higher than Ronnyn's head. His family's hens and goats complained as they were delivered to the village's pens.

The fisher-folk kept pace with Ronnyn and his family from a safe distance. Dogs ran alongside them, barking

and yipping. They were shoved past cottages redolent with
the homely scent of fish stew.

Aravelle leant close to him. 'There's so many Mieren.'

Having grown up isolated on their island, Ronnyn
had never seen more than his family and their captors in
one place at one time. In the fishing village, there were
too many people to count. Ten houses with six to eight
people per house, at a guess.

Small children with runny noses clung to the adults,
who watched and murmured. And there were twice as
many youngsters as adults. Boys of eight or nine ran
about, darting in to poke his family with sticks, then
running off crowing about their bravery. Elders cuffed
the boys, telling them to keep back, while casting
worried looks at his family, at him. Just as well he had
the crippled arm. Just as well his white hair hadn't
darkened to the silver that marked him as a gifted adult
T'En.

Ferret-face and the brute drove Ronnyn and his family
onto a patch of grass in the centre of the village, where
an odd-looking cart stood. There was a hood jutting
out over the cart's seat and the back was box shaped.
The hooded seat, roof and sides were covered by what
looked like a ship's sail.

It took him a moment to understand it was a cart with
a cage built on the back. A cage for his family.

'Get in.' Ferret-face gestured to the cart with the cane.
The fisher-folk prodded them with shovels and hoes.

Aravelle went first, helping the little ones. Their
mother struggled to climb up; Ronnyn helped her. She
was exhausted and lay slumped against the cart's seat.

When Ronnyn climbed in, they all huddled together.
Ferret-face secured the padlock and went off to speak
with the others.

'I'm hungry,' Tamaron whispered.

'I think there are more dogs than people in this village,'
Aravelle said. 'Let's count them.'

While she kept the little ones distracted, Ronnyn inspected their prison. The cage had been stoutly made by boat-builders. The roof was not high enough to allow him to stand. A hinged gate was padlocked shut across the rear. The padlock was large and solid and not the sort of thing a poor fishing village would have lying around. All this was evidence of careful planning and preparation.

Given time and something to use as a lever, he could probably force the wooden slats, but he had nothing, only his nightshirt. None of them had more than what they'd been wearing when they were torn from their beds.

The weather was bitterly cold. The sail covered the roof and both sides, but left the front and back open. It kept the rain off, but did not stop the wind from blowing through. His brothers and sisters huddled around their mother, shivering and frightened.

At about a body length from the cart, their Mieren captors argued in fierce whispers. Ronnyn only caught the occasional word, but from what he gathered someone had to take his family to port to collect the bounty.

'Bounty?' he whispered to Aravelle.

'Someone's paying for our kind,' she said. 'I'm guessing it's the king.'

'Why?'

'I don't know. Ma said not to talk to the Mieren.'

Just then it began to rain. Ronnyn's teeth chattered. If he was cold, the little ones must be freezing. Much as the words would choke him, he had to ask for blankets.

'Please,' Ronnyn called. 'We need some blankets. The little ones—'

'You're a silverhead, make your own fire!' the crooked-toothed youth jeered.

Ferret-face clipped the youth over the ear. 'I told you, they don't have gifts yet. Go fetch some blankets and food.'

'Yes, Uncle.' The youth scurried off and soon returned with a blanket. His uncle unlocked the cage door, and the youth tossed the bundle in. Ronnyn unwrapped a single blanket to find stale bread and a waterskin. He passed them to Aravelle, who solemnly broke the bread, sharing it out. It was not much, but it was better than nothing, and at least they were together.

The Mieren went back to discussing what to do. He gathered the trader had been going to lead the party to take his family and collect the bounty. Ferret-face and his nephew finally volunteered to do it.

As the fisher-folk went to their cottages, the little ones settled under the blanket next to their mother. Aravelle cuddled up to Tamaron. Ronnyn lay down next to Vittor, thinking he would never sleep. The blanket wasn't big enough to cover them all, so he made sure the others had enough. Vittor's little back felt warm against this chest.

As they settled down to sleep in the cart, caged like beasts, Ronnyn's throat grew tight and tears of anger stung his eyes.

TOBAZIM WAITED WHILE the Malaunje sailor delivered their evening meal. In this quiet moment, he caught himself listening to the sounds of the ship and judging the sea by the lift and fall of the deck on the bay's gentle swells. It was amazing how quickly he had come to know the ship, but then he'd had Ardonyx as his guide. Once they were aboard, Ardonyx seemed more settled and Tobazim suspected he was healing faster than he would have on land. The cabin boy, Toresel, poured wine for them both.

'Ionnyn and Haromyr would have reached the city three days ago,' Tobazim said. 'What's the soonest we can expect our people?'

'Depends how quickly the causare can organise them. Depends on the roads.' Ardonyx shrugged and winced. It had only been six days, and he tried not to laugh or cough. 'I wish I'd been thinking more clearly when we sent the message.'

'Why?'

'The ships. One of Paragian's seven-masted vessels has arrived but we're...' He broke off as they heard welcoming shouts and laughter. There was an edge to the laughter that Tobazim couldn't place. He glanced to Ardonyx.

Toresel came running in, eyes wide. 'Ionnyn and Haromyr are back. And there's three sisterhood warriors with them.'

That explained the eager edge to the males' laughter.

Tobazim stood as they entered. He was sure there was an obeisance for welcoming a sisterhood representative aboard a brotherhood ship, but he didn't know what it was. He settled for an obeisance recognising their rank.

'Hand-of-force Kiane, of Imoshen's sisterhood,' the first introduced herself. 'We bring a message from the causare, and gold.' She dropped the heavy saddle bags on the desk. Her two companions followed suit, as did Ionnyn and Haromyr.

When Kiane offered Tobazim the message, he gestured to Ardonyx. 'This is the ship's captain.'

Ardonyx accepted the message with a smile. 'Let me guess,' he said as he broke the seal. 'The causare has anticipated the problem and... Yes, she's sent gold to purchase ships to replace those that have been stolen or confiscated.'

'Exactly,' Kiane said. 'She expects they'll leave the city today or tomorrow, and hopes to be in port in seven to eight days.'

After the sisterhood warriors left to go to their ship, Tobazim sent Toresel for more food and two more chairs for Ionnyn and Haromyr.

'Can we purchase more ships and stock them in that time?' Tobazim asked.

'We have to.'

They'd just sat down to eat when someone knocked at the cabin door.

Tobazim glanced to the door, then looked a question to Ardonyx.

'I'm guessing one of All-father Tamaron's people.' Ardonyx put down his knife and raised his voice. 'Come in.'

Lysarna entered, with Imokara. The young Malaunje woman's black eye had healed, and she radiated determination.

The old woman made a deep obeisance, as did Imokara. They remained on their knees.

Tobazim caught Ardonyx's eye. What now? They both came to their feet.

'Speak, I will listen.' As Ardonyx gave the formal response, Tobazim noted that he rested his hips on the desk, to help support himself.

Lysarna looked up, gaze fixed politely on Ardonyx's chest. 'Our all-father is far away and his brothers with him. Imokara is with child because of those Mieren. She doesn't want to birth a Mieren baby, so she asks you bestow a gift-benediction on her.'

Tobazim glanced to Ardonyx. He had read of gift-benedictions. It was an old custom that had gone out of favour, due to the risk of accidentally imprinting the mother. It was believed gift-infusing the infant when it was in the early stages increased the likelihood of the child being born T'En. He hadn't heard of it being done to increase the chance of the child being born Malaunje.

'Me?' Ardonyx asked.

Lysarna nodded. But Imokara's gaze went to Tobazim and she did not look down. Her desperate eyes were insistent.

'Why didn't she take the women's herb to prevent conception?' Tobazim blurted, his face hot.

'We were cut off, we ran out,' Imokara said. 'Do you think I wanted this?'

Lysarna raised an admonishing hand.

Imokara blushed. 'Forgiveness, Adept Tobazim.'

'She's desperate,' Lysarna told Ardonyx. 'Even if the babe is born Malaunje, it will carry the essence of all the Mieren who raped her. This babe needs a gift-benediction to purify it. This is why we have come to you, even though you are not of our brotherhood.'

'I'm not fit and won't be for a while yet,' Ardonyx said. 'By then it may be too late.'

'True,' Lysarna agreed. Tobazim realised she had known this all along, but she had to approach Ardonyx first, as the higher-ranked. 'The sooner Imokara lies with an adept and he performs the gift-benediction, the better chance the babe will be one of us and untainted.'

They both looked to Tobazim.

He backed up a step, aware of Ionnyn and Haromyr watching all this, clearly fascinated. 'I've never–'

'Would you condemn the child she carries?' Lysarna asked.

He swallowed. 'I... I'd have to walk a very fine line to imbue the babe with gift-essence while leaving Imokara untouched. If I failed...' She would be his devotee, and All-father Tamaron would be within his rights to demand Tobazim's execution for claiming one of his brotherhood's Malaunje. If this happened, Tobazim was certain Kyredeon would not protect him.

At the same time, he felt his gift clamouring to express itself. He'd been keeping it reined in since they left the city. The small amount of repair work he'd done on the warehouse had roused his gift, rather than satisfied it.

He shook his head. Although his gift needed an outlet and this would be an exquisite use for it, the very urgency of its build up made him wary. 'To be honest, I don't know if I have the skill–'

'I'll advise you,' Ardonyx offered.

'Gift-benediction doesn't always work.'

'I didn't ask for this, but now that the baby's quickened, I won't give it up,' Imokara whispered fiercely. 'It must work!'

Tobazim knew determination when he saw it. He cast a look of appeal to Ardonyx, and caught a lurking amusement in the captain's eyes.

'If you don't like women, just say so,' Ardonyx said. 'There are other T'En who–'

'I don't want another,' Imokara protested. 'Adept Tobazim has the greatest power and stature.' She lifted her face to him. 'Even if you don't like women, it is your duty–'

'I like women. It's just...'

Ardonyx beckoned him and he stepped closer, close enough to feel Ardonyx's breath on his cheek, close enough for Ardonyx to sense the trouble he had controlling his gift.

The ship's captain closed one hand over Tobazim's forearm and siphoned off a little of his power, easing the pressure. Tobazim did not resent this familiarity. Ardonyx's own reserves were still low.

'You can do this,' Ardonyx whispered. 'When the time comes, open your gift so we can establish a temporary link. Then I'll share your body and guide your gift, ready to rein it in if it slips your control.'

A rush of desire made Tobazim's heart race. This was gift-working at a shield-brother level. The intimacy required great trust, and he was honoured by the offer.

Tobazim glanced to the two Malaunje women, one old, one young, both intimidating in their determination. In good conscience he could not refuse.

In truth he did not want to. Not at all.

Tobazim bowed his head to hide the urgency of desire, fed by his gift and his hunger for this intimacy with Ardonyx.

'Are you up to this?' Tobazim whispered.

'I have to be, just as you have to be,' Ardonyx said, then raised his voice to address the Malaunje. 'Tobazim agrees. Is tonight too soon?'

'No,' Imokara said. 'Tonight is good.'

'Then go prepare yourself, while we purify ourselves.'

Tobazim waited until they left, then prowled across the cabin.

'It will not be so bad,' Ardonyx told him, his voice rich with dry humour.

'Is there anything we can do to help?' Haromyr asked.

Ardonyx shook his head, then gestured to his meal, barely begun. 'You can finish that off. I'm too nervous to eat.'

'You're nervous?' Tobazim gave a bark of laughter.

Ardonyx grinned, then sobered. 'We must cleanse our bodies and purify our minds. Run a bath, Toresel.'

The cabin boy ran off.

As Tobazim helped Ardonyx into the bathing chamber, Ardonyx said, 'This will impress our brothers.'

'I thought you weren't eager for stature for its own sake.'

'No, but I am eager for anything that will protect us from Kyredeon, and that means the respect of our fellow brothers.'

Chapter Thirty-Seven

IMOSHEN HAD HARDLY slept. She'd hoped to be ready to leave yesterday morning, but it had taken four full days to pack and load the wagons. Originally, they'd intended to make the journey to port in stages, returning with the empty wagons and carts to reload each time. Now that they were leaving all together, there weren't enough wagons and carts. People had to leave behind things they'd intended to bring, among them priceless paintings and sculptures.

There'd been tears and drama. Unable to see the irony, Vittoryxe had berated her for placing people ahead of T'Enatuath heritage.

To appease her and others like her, Imoshen had wasted precious time and resources, allocating Malaunje to move objects into the crypts. Some of these entrances had since been sealed over. Others had always been secreted behind hidden catches. Down in those dry, dusty crypts, the heavy books and great artworks should be well-preserved.

For what?

It didn't seem to matter to people like Vittoryxe, as long as the Mieren didn't despoil their heritage.

Since before dawn, the T'Enatuath had been trudging out the gate, along the causeway and up the road that eventually led to port. Several of the brotherhoods had gone first, with the intention of forming a barrier around the sisterhoods.

Reoden's sisterhood, with Prince Cedon hidden amongst the T'En children, was directly ahead of Imoshen's and now it was their sisterhood's turn to leave. Egrayne had taken the lead. Frayvia rode in the wagon with the T'En children, to watch over Umaleni.

Meanwhile, Iraayel and Saffazi kept Imoshen company as, one by one, the last few sisterhood carts prepared to leave.

A Malaunje servant waited with their horses.

'Time to go?' Saffazi said. She had been up since before dawn, but her eyes sparkled.

Imoshen smiled. 'Time to go.'

But a Malaunje cart driver jumped down and ran over to her.

'Gift-tutor Vittoryxe hasn't come down yet,' he reported. 'I have all her treatises and scrolls packed.'

'I'll get her,' Imoshen told him.

With a surge of annoyance, she strode into the palace, through the open doors – no point locking up – and across the grand foyer. Her boots echoed hollowly on the marble. Furniture and fittings stood waiting to be used, but the sisterhood's palace was empty of people, and the mix of emotions of those departing left a dissonance on the air that her gift picked up.

At a run, Imoshen powered up the central stair, and along corridors that held almost thirteen years of memories for her. When she reached the sisterhood wing, she tapped on Vittoryxe's door. No answer.

'Gift-tutor?'

She opened the door. There was no sign of the two women or their travelling kits. Imoshen felt her gift surge as every chance encounter and confrontation with the gift-tutor played through her mind.

Vittoryxe wasn't leaving. But Imoshen had to be sure, so she headed for the crypts.

As she went down the corridor towards the palace entrance, she heard singing, a male and female voice raised in solemn lament. The song broke off, ending in laughter, then silence. Curious, she crept to the top of the stairs to see Iraayel and Saffazi locked in a kiss of such intensity, the inner circle would have banished him from the sisterhood quarter.

But Imoshen took hope. Exile would force change upon her people. Some, like Vittoryxe, would not be able to face it. Others...

'Iraayel,' she called down, her voice echoing.

They broke apart, adjusting their clothing, tamping their gifts.

'What if the gift-tutor had been with me?' Imoshen admonished.

Iraayel and Saffazi exchanged a look. Somehow, they'd guessed.

Imoshen glided down the grand stair. 'Light a lamp and come with me.'

Imoshen led them down into the passages below the palace. She passed arch after arch, searching for one in particular.

By light of the lamp, she tripped a hidden catch and the wall slid back to reveal a dark opening. Immediately, Imoshen smelt the faint, but distinctive scent of bitter almond candles, associated with death rituals. She knew what she would find. And, even though Vittoryxe had been a thorn in her side since she came to the sisterhood, Imoshen felt her loss as she descended the stairs.

Iraayel and Saffazi hesitated on the top step.

'You should see this,' she told them.

The crypts on the first level were broad and deep, with small ante-chambers, decorative carvings and elaborate stone sarcophagi. Stacked neatly along the walls were the art treasures of her people.

There were several levels of crypts with many connecting tunnels, but Imoshen knew Vittoryxe; she went to the mosaic chamber that depicted the history of their sisterhood. Sure enough, that was where she found the gift-tutor, and her devotee, under a glorified representation of the past.

They lay amidst almond-scented candles that had burned down to puddles of wax. They lay in each other's arms, the devotees' head on Vittoryxe's shoulder, united in death as they had been in life.

Imoshen heard a ragged intake of breath from behind her. 'Yes, Vittoryxe chose death over exile.'

'There's not a mark on their bodies,' Saffazi whispered.

'She was a gift-tutor,' Imoshen said. 'She chose to die by the gift, taking herself and her devotee to the higher plane. Making the passage like that means they stood a better chance of reaching death's realm.'

'Poor thing,' Iraayel whispered.

'It was their choice,' Saffazi said, an edge of contempt to her voice.

Iraayel gestured to the devotee. 'What choice did she have?'

'There's always choice,' Imoshen insisted. 'As long as there's life, there's hope.'

'Exactly,' Saffazi supported her. 'They were weak.'

Imoshen was inclined to agree, but... 'They could not bear the thought of exile. I wonder how many times this has been enacted in other crypts, and been quietly sealed over.'

'We'll know by the missing faces,' Iraayel said.

'And now we'll have a new gift-tutor.' Saffazi was pleased. 'One who doesn't make learning a chore.'

Imoshen swore, startling them. They looked to her in surprise.

'Our sisterhood has no other gift-tutor.' Imoshen gestured to Vittoryxe. 'At sixty-seven, she was in the prime of life; she hadn't begun training someone to replace her.'

'Then it was selfish of her to kill herself,' Iraayel said in his calm, measured voice.

Imoshen sighed. 'Come on. The others will be wondering where we are.'

Leaving almond-scented death and defeat behind, Imoshen stepped out into crisp, autumn sunshine.

She told the Malaunje with the cartload of gift treatises to head off. Then she mounted up, turning away from the sisterhood's palace, and away from minds too rigidly bound by custom to accept a new life. 'Come on.'

All-mother Ceriane's sisterhood was headed down the causeway road. Imoshen guided her horse beside the slowly moving carts and wagons, aiming to catch up with the tail end of her sisterhood.

It was hard to tell, but she thought the last of her people would be out of the city by the early afternoon. When they left, the gates would remain standing open. It felt wrong to leave the city vulnerable to the Mieren.

They passed under the causeway gate, moving from the shadow of the tunnel into sunshine. The horses' hooves clopped on the stone causeway and the wagon wheels rattled.

The first seventeen years of her life had been spent on Lighthouse Isle, a prisoner of All-father Rohaayel's brotherhood. For nearly thirteen years now, she'd lived in the Celestial City, a prisoner of the sisterhoods' expectations and the brotherhoods' resentment.

Imoshen sat a little straighter in the saddle. Ahead of her, at the end of the causeway, the barons and their men watched them pass. The townsfolk watched from windows and balconies.

In a way, Vittoryxe was right. Exile would force change on her people, and Imoshen would be the architect of that change. She was going to oversee the end of the T'Enatuath, at least the T'Enatuath as the old ones knew it.

Imoshen felt as if she'd been set free.

SORNE FELT AS if he'd come home. He'd had no trouble finding his way back to Restoration Retreat, and when he saw the wisp of smoke drifting from the chimney of the main building, he knew he'd guessed correctly. Zabier had re-opened the retreat without telling anyone. Valendia had to be here.

As he rode up the steep switch-back road, leading the second horse, he was prepared to bluff his way past

Zabier's assistant, past the penitents to Valendia herself. After all, he wore Oskane's ring.

He half expected someone to call out to him when he approached the gate, but no one did. Above the wall, he could see the autumn leaves of the maple tree, and he could imagine the courtyard, filled with dappled sunlight and fallen leaves.

The problem was Utzen. Zabier's assistant had never liked him, and might not believe anything Sorne said. In that case, Sorne was prepared to incapacitate the old man and spirit Valendia away before the penitents realised what was happening.

He swung down from the saddle and knocked on the gate. The last time he had been here, the gate had stood open, the retreat had been deserted and he had laid the she-Wyrd's bones to rest. He had not been able to save her, but he would save his sister.

A bird cried overhead.

He waited.

When nothing happened, he rapped on the wood again. 'Open in the name of the king and the high priest of Chalcedonia.'

The eye-slot slid back. He couldn't see the person who studied him from the shadows, but after a moment, he heard the bolts being drawn and the gate swung open.

Before he could enter, Valendia threw her arms around him. 'Sorne, it is you!'

He was a little startled, as he'd expected a penitent to open the gate, but this was even better. He hugged her, pressing his lips to her forehead, whispering, 'I'm here to set you free. Play along with me.'

She pulled back with a laugh. 'I am free, silly. There's just us here. Come in.'

After bolting the gate, she led him out of the shadow into the light of the courtyard, where he tried to assimilate the long-legged, gangly twelve-year-old he remembered with this statuesque young woman, who was only half a head shorter than him.

He dropped the horse's reins and turned to her. 'Let me look at you. I've been searching for you since autumn. When no one knew where you were, I thought you'd died the night of the riots.' He finally registered what she'd said. 'What do you mean, you're free?'

She looked behind him to the three-storey building that had belonged to the True-men when he lived here.

Sorne turned to see a dead man standing in the doorway. 'Grae?' The world spun, and he found himself on his knees in the courtyard.

Next thing he knew, they'd were both helping him to his feet, laughing and chiding each other. Valendia drew him over to the table under the maple tree, while Graelen sat opposite. He'd never seen the T'En adept light-hearted, and he had trouble reconciling this Graelen with the hard-eyed assassin from Kyredeon's brotherhood.

Valendia sat next to Sorne. She was so happy she seemed to glow. 'When you told us to open in the name of the king and the high priest, we thought they'd found us. Grae was ready to deal with any threat, but then I saw it was you and... It's so good to see you!' She hugged him. 'What are you doing here?'

'I'll explain in a moment. First...' He met Graelen's eyes across the table. A leaf fluttered down, landing in a patch of sunlight between them. 'Last time I saw you...' He didn't want Valendia learning that Zabier had sacrificed their kind. 'You segued to the higher plane, taking your physical body. I thought you were dead for certain.'

Valendia laughed. 'He came and freed me.'

Sorne met Graelen's eyes. 'How is that possible?'

The adept reached across the table, but he wasn't reaching for Sorne. He clasped Valendia's hand as he spoke to Sorne. 'When I left you, I believed I was going to die and I thought of Dia, of what a waste it was to have found her only to lose her. My gift took over and our bond took me to her side. She's my devotee, Sorne.'

'Devotee?' Sorne repeated. First Frayvia, now Valendia. Was every person he loved destined to be stolen from him? 'But... when did this happen?'

'In the crypts, when I was being held prisoner before the sacrifice,' Graelen said, and Sorne remembered the powerful gift-working he'd sensed.

'I found Grae,' Valendia explained. 'When Zabier caught us together, he was very angry. He hit me.' She touched her cheek, saddened by the memory.

Graelen took up the story. 'Before they dragged us apart, I imprinted my gift on Valendia. She–'

'She had no defences.'

'Don't be angry, Sorne,' Valendia pleaded.

'It was pure instinct.' Graelen lifted his hands. 'The devotee link is the ultimate expression of the bond between T'En and Malaunje. It makes us both stronger, and it saved my life.'

'He saved me from Utzen and the penitents,' Valendia said.

Sorne frowned. 'You're bound to him for life. Did he tell you that?'

She laughed. 'I love him. I'm bound to him for life anyway. I don't need saving from Grae, Sorne.' She hugged him, pressing a kiss to his cheek. 'Be happy for me, brother.'

Graelen's features hardened. 'If you can't be happy for us, then ride away and leave us alone.'

'I can't.' Sorne wondered where to start. 'Have you heard anything of the war on the Wyrds?'

'We've seen no one since winter cusp last year.' Graelen tensed and sat forward. 'Are you saying you didn't–'

'...warn the city in time. No, Zabier drugged me. But it wouldn't have made a difference in the long run. The T'Enatuath have been exiled. The king gave them until winter cusp. After that, anyone who remains behind will be hunted down and executed. I'm here to take you back to your people.'

But Graelen was already shaking his head. 'I can't go back. I broke my vow. I swore to serve my brotherhood until the day I die, but I was weak. I chose to stay here with

Dia, even though I knew the Mieren king had declared war on my people. I am without honour.'

'Nonsense,' Valendia told him. 'What difference could one T'En warrior make?'

Graelen caught Sorne's eye. 'I bet Sorne is hungry. Do you have any of that pie left over?'

'Not the pie our mother used to make?' Sorne asked.

Valendia beamed. 'You wait here. I'll bring lunch.'

As she left them, crossing to the main building, Sorne noticed his horses were feeding on some weeds.

Graelen leant close, dropping his voice. Now he looked like his old self: intense, worried and determined. 'If I go back, All-father Kyredeon will execute me.'

'The city was under siege from winter cusp to spring cusp. After that, there was limited access, but you weren't to know that. Any reasonable–'

'Kyredeon is not reasonable.'

'You can't stay here. You'll run out of supplies, and when you go looking to trade, the Mieren will string you up.'

'If I go back, Kyredeon will do the same.'

'Then change brotherhoods.'

'Your brotherhood is for life, Sorne. Occasionally one brotherhood is taken over by another, but...' He shrugged. 'No other all-father would want me. I have a reputation.'

'I'll speak to the causare.'

'We have a causare? Let me guess, to negotiate with King Charald?' His eyes narrowed. 'Who is the causare?'

'Imoshen.'

'Ah...' He nodded. 'She's a woman, Sorne. She has no say in brotherhood business.'

'Swear loyalty to her.'

'A man can't serve an all-mother.'

'A man can serve the causare. I do.'

'You're Malaunje.'

'So I don't matter?' Anger sharpened Sorne's voice.

Graelen lifted a hand in apology. 'To someone like Kyredeon, no.'

'Here it is.' Valendia came out of the building with a laden tray and a jug. They took the tray and jug from her, and she went back inside for more.

'You can't stay here, Grae,' Sorne said softly.

'I know, but... these have been the best days of my life.'

Valendia returned with a zither. 'You eat. I'll play.'

'Aren't you hungry?'

She laughed, not bothering to answer. While they ate, she plucked a tune that started out sad and grew happier.

'Another of your songs that tell stories?' Sorne asked, when she came to the end.

'Yes. It tells our story.' Instead of putting the zither down, she ran her fingers over the strings, absently plucking lilting phrases from them.

Sorne caught the look she sent Grae, and the way she made him smile. He was happy for them, but they were safest with the brotherhood. 'As far as Kyredeon knows, you could have been kept prisoner in the crypts, Grae. By the time we get back to port, he'll be there. Tell him you've just escaped with Valendia. How is he to know otherwise?'

Graelen put his wine down. 'That could work.'

Valendia covered the strings with her palm and the sound died. 'We have to go back, don't we?'

Graelen met Sorne's eyes.

'Yes, back to the T'Enatuath,' Sorne said. 'But not back to life as it was, Grae. Exile will change things.'

'At least we have until winter cusp,' Valendia said.

'No. We have to leave tomorrow. The truce is with King Charald, and he's failing. We have to reach port before the rest of your people sail.'

At that moment, the sun went behind clouds and rain drops fell. Valendia and Graelen grabbed the food and ran inside. Sorne led the horses into the stable, where he found a covered cart and two ponies. He was happy for Valendia. And to think he used to be worried about her future. Zabier had kept her locked up from the age of four until...

He turned to find Graelen behind him, grabbed him and shoved him up against the wall. 'She was only fifteen.'

'I didn't know. It was life and death. I didn't think to ask her age and she looks like a woman. By the time I knew...' He lifted his hands, palm up. 'I'd die for her, Sorne.'

There was no doubting his sincerity. Sorne let him go.

That night, they repaired the covered cart and packed up. There wasn't much to pack: Valendia's musical instruments, some supplies and the chickens. They left the next morning. Sorne and Graelen rode, while Valendia drove the cart. It rained all day.

THREE DAYS LATER, it was still raining and Sorne found the ford he had crossed on the way to the retreat was impassable. The stream had turned into a river, running deep and fast. Impatience ate at him. He had no idea how long it would take Imoshen to pack up her people and reach port, but he knew time was running out.

'There's a bridge, one day's travel to the east,' he told Valendia and Graelen. They wore cloaks and hoods, but the rain had worked its way through after the first day. He was cold and wet, but at least he wasn't hungry.

As they went east along the river bank, they came across other travellers going west. There were three of them on horseback. Sorne couldn't tell what business they had travelling the foothills, and they carried themselves like men-at-arms, which made him wary.

'If you're heading for the bridge, it's been washed away,' the first Mieren called through the driving rain. 'We're making for the ford.'

'The ford's impassable, at least for our cart,' Sorne said. The hood covered most of his face, but he noted them looking over his whole party with calculating eyes.

'We'll try the ford,' the first one said, and the two groups parted.

Sorne edged his horse closer to Graelen. 'I don't like the look of them.'

'I don't like the way they were looking at Dia,' Graelen said.

Sorne agreed. 'We need to put some distance between us.'

'How will we cross the river? They said the bridge is out.'

'There's the new Wyrd bridge, two days ride to the east. It's sturdy, built of stone.' Sorne remembered Nitzane mentioning it.

The road that followed the river was thick with mud, slowing the cart. They pushed on. By evening, two days later they, still hadn't reached the Wyrd bridge, but it looked like Sorne's concerns had been unjustified; there'd been no sign of the other travellers.

They pulled off the road and made camp, a miserable affair of cold food and wet blankets. By now rain had worked its way under the cart's cover and everything was damp, if not sopping wet. They hadn't posted a watch while in the mountains, but since they met the other travellers near the washed-out bridge they had. Sorne took first watch.

The evening was swiftly turning dark. With the cloud cover there was no moonlight and the constant rain meant Sorne could hear nothing but its drumming. He felt like he was both blind and deaf.

He didn't like it.

He kept making larger and larger circles around their camp. When he reached the road, he discovered that even though they had pulled off the road and the lantern was turned down low, the covered cart glowed through the trees.

On instinct, he went back the way they'd come, keeping to the road verge.

He'd only gone around two corners when he spotted a dull glow. Edging closer, he found a camp fire, under an overhang. At first he thought it was another group of Mieren altogether because there were five of them. Then he recognised the one who'd spoken to him.

Sorne turned and ran. It was almost completely dark. He spotted the cart from the road, darted through the trunks and pulled back the flap. 'We need to get out of here.'

'The travellers?' Graelen came to a crouch, reaching for his knives.

Sorne nodded. 'There's five of them, and they've camped within an easy walk.'

'I'll hitch up the pony,' Valendia said.

'No.' Graelen and Sorne both spoke at the same time.

Their eyes met. They'd have to leave the cart.

'I'll get the horses,' Sorne said, leaving Graelen to convince Valendia to part with her instruments. The horses were not happy. They were cold and tired and were developing saddle sores under the wet blankets.

Working in the dark, Sorne found the bridles and fastened them. The feisty gelding showed its displeasure by trying to nip him. He sympathised with the beast. The last thing Sorne wanted to do was head off into the cold rain. But he persisted and prepared the two horses, then put a halter on one of the cart ponies.

He was debating whether he had time to saddle the horses, when he heard a shout and saw figures silhouetted against the glow of the covered cart. Graelen struggled with someone who was trying to drag Valendia away. She jerked and twisted, her cloak tearing from her shoulders. She fell. An attacker jumped on Graelen's back. The big adept threw the man to the ground.

Sorne ran towards the cart, dragging the horses with him. By the time he reached the cart, Graelen was helping Valendia to her feet. More Mieren arrived.

Graelen caught Valendia around the waist and threw her onto one of the horses, and they took off through the dark, brushing up against tree trunks and barrelling through bushes. Sorne glanced back and saw Mieren swarming over their covered cart, then his shoulder collided with a trunk and he kept his eyes forward.

When they reached the road, which appeared only as a slightly paler strip in the consuming dark, Graelen switched Valendia over to the pony and leapt astride his horse. Sorne had never ridden bare-back. He pressed his knees into the horse's flanks. Frightened by the altercation, the horses took off at a gallop, but they were sensible animals and soon slowed to a trot, then a walk. The night was just too dark and the rain too heavy to risk anything more.

Sorne had to hope their abandoned cart kept the Mieren occupied. He knew the bridge was coming up soon, and was worried they might miss it.

He only realised they were on the bridge when the horses' hooves echoed on the stone and he heard the rush of the river under the arches.

On the far side of the bridge, Graelen asked Valendia if she was all right.

'Of course I am,' she told him. Her voice sounded firm, and it was impossible to see her face.

'We need to get off the road,' Sorne said. He looked for the white stone marker that indicated the turn off to Nitzane's estate and Riverbend Stronghold.

A little later he found it and led them off the main road. At least now the Mieren wouldn't find them.

His next goal was to find the stronghold. They needed dry clothes and warm food. Going on a memory almost five years old, and his horse's instincts to find a warm dry barn, Sorne led them through the night.

Luckily, the rain eased off and the moons broke through the clouds. It seemed they'd been riding the better part of the night when he spotted the towers and battlements of Nitzane's stronghold, silhouetted against a cloudy sky.

'Not far now, Dia,' he said.

She didn't answer. He glanced back to see that Graelen rode at her side, his horse towering over the pony.

The last time Sorne had been here, the village had been dilapidated; now a sturdy gate sealed the village wall. Sorne hammered on the gate. 'Open in the name of the king.'

It took a while, but the gate-keeper arrived with a lantern. He opened up, then looked Sorne over and appeared to be having second thoughts.

'I'm on a mission for the king, with a message from Baron Nitzane for Captain Ballendin.'

The familiar names convinced the man, who stepped aside and let them through. He bolted the gate and led them up the rise. A light rain began to fall, forming a halo of drops in the circle of the lamplight.

Captain Ballendin was already at the stronghold gate, alerted by his night-watch. Sorne slid off his horse, staggering on legs numb with cold.

'What happened to you?' Ballendin asked. He was one of the few Mieren Sorne counted as a friend. 'Is Nitzane all right?'

'He was when I left the port,' Sorne said. 'We need shelter.'

'Come in.' Ballendin said

As Sorne turned to the others, Valendia pitched sideways off the horse. Graelen caught her and his wet hood fell back, revealing he was T'En.

Ballendin's eyes widened. 'What have you brought us, Sorne?'

'Friends in trouble,' he said. 'My sister's been riding all day and night.'

'And she's with child,' Graelen said.

Sorne watched, stunned, as Graelen carried her inside.

Ballendin sent the night-watch out of the guard house, providing blankets and a warm bed, then left Graelen to see to Valendia and drew Sorne over to the doorway. 'Why have you brought a silverhead into the stronghold?'

Sorne filled him in on the situation in the palace and the port. '...and Nitzane's fallen in love with the queen,' he finished.

Ballendin cursed. 'He can't resist a woman in trouble.'

Sorne nodded. 'He needs the advice of a cool head. I've been trying to think of a reason to send for you, to bring fifty good men. Now I have it.' He gestured to Graelen and his sister. 'We need an escort to port.'

Chapter Thirty-Eight

AT FIRST, ARAVELLE had watched their Mieren captors for a chance to escape. But they never let all of her family out of the cage at the same time. If she even so much as looked sideways at ferret-face, he cuffed her. For seven days now they'd followed the coast road north, delayed by rising flood waters and roads that were axle-deep in mud. Despite the sail covering the cart, the wind blew the rain in. They were wet, cold and miserable.

Each morning, they were given the near-empty porridge pot and each morning, in their hunger, they burned their fingers as they scooped up the remains. ·

Itania whimpered, waving reddened finger tips. Their mother blew on the little pink tips to cool them.

'Come here, girlie.' Ferret-face opened the cage door and beckoned Aravelle. 'Time to earn your keep.'

His nephew, crooked-tooth, guided her down to the icy cold creek. There were only two bowls and the pot, but having to clean for the Mieren at all infuriated her.

Crooked-tooth smirked as she worked. 'Does my heart good to see you scrubbin'. You need takin' down a peg or two, you do.'

She bit her tongue and gave him a wide berth as she gathered the clean pot and bowls and hurried back to the camp. The pot was heavy and she was sure if she brought it down hard enough on the back of his head, she could knock him out, but she had to choose the right moment.

Crooked-tooth stalked along behind her. By the time she reached the clearing, her teeth were chattering. She dumped the pots on top of the Mieren's travelling kit and tucked her hands under her arm pits, running over to the cage. Her mother looked relieved.

The youth unlocked the gate and Aravelle climbed in. 'That stream was freezing.'

'Here.' Their mother took her hands, enclosing them in hers and breathing on them to warm her chilled fingers.

Ronnyn rubbed her back, putting his body between her and the wind. There was a flat patch in the middle of his nose, where the bone had been crushed. It changed his appearance, so that he did not look like the brother she had grown up with.

The cart gave a lurch as crooked-tooth climbed up next to his uncle. Ferret-face flicked the reins and they started off again, rattling over the ruts. As they came out of the trees, the wind picked up, driving the rain in on them. The little ones whimpered.

Their mother tried to spread the thin blanket to cover them all, but by the time the little ones were snuggled in, there was no room for her and Ronnyn.

Aravelle didn't understand how their mother could be so calm. Whenever she thought of what the Mieren had done to Father, tears of rage threatened to blind her. She forced them down, afraid if she gave in now she would not be able to stop crying, and she refused to reveal weakness in front of their captors. She shut the rage and grief deep inside of her.

Crooked-tooth said something Aravelle didn't catch. Ferret-face laughed, his gaze flicking to her. Aravelle didn't like the tone of their laughter. Her mother sent her a worried look.

JARAILE MADE SURE she was never alone. Eskarnor let her know he was awaiting his next opportunity. When no one was looking, he would cup himself suggestively. She took to carrying a sharp paring knife, tucked in her waist band.

Although she suspected she would not get a chance to use it, it gave her some comfort.

Every afternoon, Charald, Nitzane and Eskarnor rode around the plaza. Since the king's first ride, Eskarnor had been at pains to charm, playing the bluff war baron and complimenting the king on his improvement.

Because Charald, curse him, *was* getting better, and Jaraile had the bruises to prove it. She put it down to Sorne's insistence the manservant stop treating him with arsenic. The king still had the tremor, but only when he was over tired. At first she thought he'd recovered completely – he appeared quite rational – then she realised he remained forgetful. He remembered every battle he'd ever fought, but not what he'd had for lunch.

Since he wasn't aware of what he'd forgotten, he thought he was back to normal. He refused to discuss appointing advisors to watch over Prince Cedon in the event of his death or illness, and he'd taken to treating her with casual contempt while seeking out the company of the two barons.

They walked Charald up to his bedchamber. Today the king had ridden further than ever and, for all his talk, Jaraile thought he looked tired. She suspected he would sleep now until the evening meal.

As the king sat before the fire, his manservant removed his boots. Nitzane leaned forward to say something to Charald, and Eskarnor took the opportunity to step back and adjust himself so she would notice his state of arousal.

Infuriated, Jaraile looked away. She was always regular and should have bled this morning, but she hadn't, and she was feeling nauseous. Frustration welled up in her. She had heard the Wyrd women used a herb to prevent conception, but as far as the True-men of Chalcedonia were concerned, it was a woman's lot to bear children; any attempt to prevent conception, or to get rid of a baby, was punishable with death.

She'd been pregnant twice before. She knew the signs. There was only one thing to do. She would have to seduce her husband. If the king thought the child was his, he would protect her.

She waited until the men left, then told Bidern to take the afternoon off. As she helped the king into bed, she let her hands linger, but he didn't seem to notice. Determined, she pulled the tie from her hair and felt the long plait unravel. She knelt on the bed beside him and took his hand in hers. 'I'm so glad to see you well, sire.'

Eyes closed, he patted her hand and, taking this as an invitation, she stretched out next to him with her head on his shoulder. Her hand slipped under the covers, wandering across his belly. Before she could reach her destination, the king began to snore.

She sat up. The next snore was louder and deeper. She should have known. Charald hadn't been capable for over a year now. And to think, he used to be so brutal. For all that he appeared to have rallied, his days were numbered.

She could not bear to be at the mercy of Eskarnor. Desperation drove her to check the hall. After the ride, Nitzane would retire to his rooms, strip and bathe to dress for dinner. When she was certain no one was about, she slipped into the baron's chambers.

Wearing only his breeches, he turned, startled. 'Jaraile, what is it?'

She was supposed to be seducing him, but she couldn't bring herself to lie. Instead she shook her head and ran to him. A storm of tears surprised her. She hadn't known her emotions were so close to the surface. Angry sobs shook her as he folded her against his chest.

For a moment, he just held her. When she felt him draw breath to ask for an explanation, she lifted her face to his. 'I've been so frightened.'

His breath caught in his throat, but he led her to the chair by the hearth and sat her down.

'You shouldn't be here alone. Let me get you a cup of wine, and then I'll take you back to your chambers.'

Why did he have to be such a good man? Frustration made her moan. She was supposed to be seducing him, but she couldn't stop shaking.

'Don't cry.' He knelt beside the chair. 'Tell me what's wrong.'

Eskarnor raped me. I'm pregnant and I want you to think you're the father so you'll protect me, Prince Cedon and this child. But if Nitzane tried it, Eskarnor would kill him. Good men could not stand against bullies who didn't care who they hurt to get what they wanted. Her father had been a good man, but he hadn't been able to protect her. It was a mistake coming here.

'Jaraile?'

She sprang to her feet and her vision dimmed. She felt herself collapse in his arms.

'There. What did I tell you?' Eskarnor demanded. 'Your wife is unfaithful.'

She blinked as her sight returned, and saw Eskarnor with the king in the doorway. Charald staggered back a step, hand on his heart.

Eskarnor caught her eye and gave the slightest shrug, as if to say *how could I pass up the opportunity?*

Nitzane set her on her feet. 'Sire, I swear—'

'Save your lies!' Charald turned and bellowed down the passage. 'Fetch Commander Halargon.'

Eskarnor smiled with hateful satisfaction.

It was too much for Jaraile. She ran to the king, throwing herself at him, weeping. 'He raped me!'

'Nitzane raped you?' Charald laughed, holding her at arm's length. 'Why should he, when you'd bend over for him?'

'Not Nitzane. Eskarnor.' She did not have to pretend to shake with anger. 'I ran to Nitzane and tried to tell him, but I passed out. He was helping me up.'

'Is that what you call it?' Eskarnor sneered.

'I wondered why you were so upset,' Nitzane said then bristled as he strode over to confront Eskarnor. 'You're without honour. You force yourself on the queen, and when she comes sobbing to me, you accuse me of the very crime you committed.' Nitzane could hardly speak, he was so furious. 'I swear, I'll–'

'King Charald, you sent for me?' Commander Halargon strode towards them. 'What's going on here?'

They all turned to him in the hallway. Everyone spoke at once. Jaraile wanted Eskarnor locked up. Nitzane wanted to challenge Eskarnor and defend the queen's honour. Charald wanted to believe her and Nitzane's version of events, she could tell.

Jaraile could feel the king trembling and feared his heart would give out. She tried to make them understand that the king needed to sit down, but Charald would have none of it.

A dozen servants clustered around, watching, wide-eyed.

Several of Baron Eskarnor's honour guard came running from the other direction. They thrust through the servants and lined up behind Eskarnor.

Halargon reached for his weapon. Nitzane joined Halargon, even though he was unarmed.

Meanwhile, Jaraile tried to support the king, who kept pushing her away. She gestured over her shoulder to the servants. 'Fetch Halargon's men.'

But they just stood there, gawking stupidly.

'Commander Halargon, the Wyrds are coming,' a youth in the uniform of the king's guard ran up the hall towards them. 'The Wyrds are coming!'

Charald turned. 'What is it, lad? Speak sense.'

The youth dropped to one knee. 'A merchant rode in through from the west gate, sire. He says the Wyrds are coming to port.'

'Of course the Wyrds are coming,' Charald snapped. 'They're preparing for exile.'

'No, they're *all* coming. There's thousands of them, filling the road to port. He said the first of them will start arriving tomorrow.'

'Why?' Charald muttered. 'Why leave early?'

Jaraile glanced to Nitzane, who looked to Halargon.

'I don't know, sire,' the commander said. 'But I'll make sure they get through the port to the Wyrd wharf.'

'Where's Sorne?' The king sounded plaintive. 'Where is he? He should be here.'

'I think he rode off on Wyrd business,' Nitzane said.

That reminded Jaraile of how Eskarnor had claimed Sorne was the only man who could stop him. She glanced over her shoulder in time to see Eskarnor and his men disappear down the end of the passage. 'The baron's getting away.'

'Arrest Eskarnor. He...' The king suddenly went stiff in Jaraile's arms. His eyes rolled back in his head. He dropped to the floor, his body shaking.

Horrified, Jaraile could only stare.

'He's having a fit!' Nitzane said. 'Stand back.'

By the time he'd knelt next to Charald, the king was no longer shaking, but neither was he conscious. Between the baron and Halargon, they got Charald back to his chamber. Jaraile sent for the manservant.

While she did this, she overheard Nitzane tell Halargon that Eskarnor had raped her, but she was concerned for her son.

She drew Nitzane and Halargon away from the bed. 'Commander, nothing must go wrong with the handover of Prince Cedon. You must ensure the Wyrds reach the wharf safely. That's the most important thing.'

Halargon nodded. 'I've had my people watching for men-at-arms slipping into port, and I swear Eskarnor only has his honour guard. I'll send some men to arrest him. By tomorrow, he'll be under lock and key and I can concentrate on the Wyrds.'

He headed off. Now that her son would soon be restored to her, she felt impatient with any delay.

'I'm sorry, Jaraile,' Nitzane said softly.

'Sorry?'

'I'm sorry I wasn't there to protect you.'

For a moment, she didn't know what he was talking about. Then she realised. Nitzane couldn't have protected her from Eskarnor. She was glad there would not be a duel. But she was still pregnant. She needed to think. 'I'm going to sit with the king.'

Charald lay on his bed, mouth agape, deeply asleep. Jaraile pulled up a chair and watched Charald the Great snore.

If she was going to protect her son and safeguard the kingdom for him, she needed to gather men around her who were resolute, capable and loyal. She didn't need a feeble-minded king. Charald either had to get better or he had to... The thought shocked her.

The manservant arrived, wringing his hands. 'They're saying the king had a fit. What happened?'

If the servants down in the kitchen had heard, soon the whole port would hear.

'King Charald threw a fit, and he hasn't woken up yet,' Jaraile whispered. She knew Bidern had resented Sorne's interference with his treatment of the king. 'What should we do?'

He glanced to the bed, his devotion clear. 'My brother the apothecary has been consulting the books. The shakes, the aches, the fears, the raving are common for a lot of ailments, but the red-coloured urine is typical only of one. We can give him purges and let blood to help ease his symptoms, but the best treatment is based on arsenic.'

'Then we must treat him,' Jaraile said.

'He's never had a fit before.' Bidern hesitated, then confided, 'I think I should double his dosage.'

'If you think you should do it, then do it,' she said, and she did not feel a moment's compunction.

Chapter Thirty-Nine

IMOSHEN HAD KNOWN it would be a challenge travelling with this many people. Seven days on the road and they should have already been at the wharf. Instead, they would not arrive until tomorrow. Each evening, the last of their party would catch up long after dark. The roads were knee-deep in mud. Each day they passed abandoned wagons and carts, stripped bare.

When the axle broke on one of her sisterhood wagons, they had to drag it to the side of the road, unhitch the horses and take what they could carry. Even as they walked away, Mieren came out of the fields to strip what was left. She was sure, when the roads were in better condition, they'd return with horses and take the wagon, too.

It was unnerving knowing the Mieren stalked them, but these were poor farm folk, not men-at-arms. They had been lucky. So far, there had been no attack by the barons' men. The brotherhoods had intercepted all messages Eskarnor's supporters had sent to port.

That night, as they made camp, there was no singing or laughter, only endurance. Imoshen had erected her sisterhood tent next to the healer's, and they shared the meagre warmth of a brazier, trying to heat food for the children.

The constant rain meant fires would not light. Most nights they ate cold meals, and went to bed wet and cold. Daily they were growing short-tempered and more on edge.

And they had not even sailed into exile yet.

But there was good news. Imoshen knelt next to the healer as she worked on little Prince Cedon's foot. Reoden offered her hands. 'Now rise onto your toes.'

He did this, using her hands to help him balance.

'Very good. Did you see, Imoshen?'

'Clever boy,' Imoshen told him. He'd turned three back in the spring and was fast leaving the toddler behind, growing into a little boy. He was a sweet child, and she'd grown fond of him. She hoped that by returning him to King Charald they were not putting his life in danger, but she suspected they were.

'I can jump, too,' he told her. 'Watch and thee.'

'See,' Imoshen corrected. Ree had been working on that too.

'See,' he repeated and jumped with so much vigour he nearly overbalanced.

Reoden laughed, catching him. 'My clever boy!'

'My Ree-ma!' He threw his arms around her neck.

A sharp male voice cut through the soft female chatter.

Imoshen tensed. The thought of Umaleni sleeping, vulnerable, in the wagon with the other children made her heart race and her gift rise. But surely if they were under attack, there would be screams and shouts, and the sound of fighting would have started over on the edge where the brotherhoods camped, not here in the centre where the sisterhoods were.

'I said, no further,' Reoden's hand-of-force warned.

The sisters scrambled to their feet, looking to Imoshen and the healer. Several of the warriors quietly collected their weapons and went outside. The little prince reached for Reoden.

She took his hand and beckoned her scryer. 'Watch over him, Lysi.'

'If it's Mieren, hide him,' Imoshen said, speaking T'En so the prince would not understand. 'If it's Baron Eskarnor, he'll kill the boy outright.'

'You need to come out here, Imoshen.' Egrayne sounded wary.

In the lantern-lit, rainy night Imoshen found Hand-of-force Cerafeoni and three of her warriors confronting a dozen T'En males. Cerafeoni had lost an eye the day Reoden's daughter was killed, and had never forgiven herself for failing to protect the child. She radiated distrust, her gift on alert.

The brotherhood warriors tensed, hands on the hilts of their long-knives, gifts roused in response to the threat of so many powerful T'En women. They were led by...

'Reyne?' Imoshen recognised All-father Hueryx's hand-of-force. She tried to read him, but all her gift gleaned was tension.

'Causare.' Reyne acknowledged her, then signalled the warriors who stood behind him.

They parted to reveal a frightened Mieren woman – no, a girl; she was no more than fifteen or sixteen – huddled under a travel-stained cloak. Her feet were bare.

'We caught her trying to sneak into camp,' Reyne said.

'Why?' Imoshen asked.

'She would not say.'

Unable to understand their language, the girl watched their faces. To Imoshen's gift, she radiated equal amounts of terror and determination.

Most T'En had had little to do with Mieren before King Charald marched on their city, and even less to do with them since. Knowing she had to negotiate with the Mieren king, Imoshen had read everything she could find about them. Women were only ever mentioned in relation to men, as a man's mother, sister, daughter or wife. Imoshen knew only that girls were considered old enough to marry at thirteen or fourteen, and women owned nothing, not even their children. In fact, women were considered the property of the nearest male relative.

Imoshen took a step closer.

'Watch out, causare, she could have a weapon under that cloak,' Reoden's hand-of-force warned. 'Reyne would not let us near her.'

'Did you search her?' Imoshen asked Reyne.

His lips curled in a half-smile.

Imoshen could see why the warriors were not afraid of the Mieren girl. She only came up to mid-chest on them.

Imoshen held the girl's eyes and spoke in Chalcedonian. 'What do you want?'

'I'm looking for the queen of the Wyrds.'

'She means you,' Reyne told Imoshen.

'Thank you, Reyne.' Imoshen could not keep the sarcasm from her voice. What would drive this girl to come here, demanding to see the enemy's leader? 'I am the causare. It is an elected position, unlike your queen or king. What do you–'

An infant's cry cut her off. From the sound of the cry it was a newborn, no more than a few days old. One little hand reached out, six fingers splayed.

'Half-blood,' Imoshen breathed, then raised her voice. 'She brings a Malaunje babe to us.'

Everyone relaxed, and Imoshen felt the gift tension subside.

'I have silver,' Egrayne said. She opened the drawstring purse and removed a coin. 'There you are.'

But the girl pulled back. As if sensing her anxiety, the baby whimpered and uttered a mewling cry.

'I don't want silver for her. She's all I've got.' The girl tried to soothe the baby. 'My husband threw me out. He said he didn't want a wife who birthed a Wyrd brat. I've nowhere to go.'

No one spoke.

'We can't take a Mieren with us into exile. It wouldn't be right,' Egrayne said in T'En. 'She can go to her sisters.'

'They won't take her in. Their husbands will refuse to give her shelter.' Imoshen saw the T'En women didn't understand. 'She's not one of us. She has no sisterhood to protect her. She's utterly alone.' Imoshen addressed the girl. 'Where will you go?'

'Every door is closed to me. I'll have to go to the port and sell my body to buy bread. I'd rather throw myself in the bay.'

The T'En women muttered in shock.

'But she's Mieren. She doesn't belong with us,' Egrayne said. 'Even amongst the Malaunje, she won't be welcome.'

'If we turn her away, we are no better than the Mieren who threw her out,' Imoshen said. 'I won't send her away to die. My sisterhood will take her in.' This reminded her. 'Reyne, tell the brotherhoods to call me if any Mieren want to sell their Malaunje kin.'

Then, despite Egrayne's disapproval, Imoshen sent for the leader of her sisterhood's Malaunje and the girl was taken away.

'No good will come of this,' Egrayne said. 'It's not our way to take in girls like her.'

'Exile will change our ways.'

THAT NIGHT, RONNYN tried to distract his little brothers while he waited for his mother and sisters to come back from the creek. He was weak with hunger and his gift had not stirred for days. There was never enough food, and tonight there had been less than usual. The Mieren complained that the trip was taking longer than they'd expected.

To his relief Aravelle returned to the camp with the cleaned cooking pots. Itania trailed along behind her, grizzling softly; she was tired and hungry. Aravelle dropped the pots by the fire then picked up Itania, trying to jolly her along.

'Come on,' crooked-tooth said. There was something in his voice that made Ronnyn uneasy.

The Mieren unlocked the cage. Aravelle passed Itania up to Ronnyn.

'Where's Ma? I want Ma,' Tamaron whimpered.

'She's coming,' Aravelle said and went to climb up. But the youth grabbed her by the arm, then swung the door shut, clicking the padlock closed with his free hand.

Ronnyn thrust Itania aside and sprang to the cage door. 'What're you doing? Let her go.'

'Make me,' crooked-tooth leered.

The instant the youth was distracted, Aravelle ducked under his arm and ran into the undergrowth. He took off after her.

Ronnyn shook the cage door so hard it made the cart rock. Pain spiked in his bad arm. 'Run, Vella!'

He strained to hear. There was a thump and the sound of undergrowth collapsing, then muffled grunts and thuds of flesh striking flesh.

She'd been caught. She was fast like a cat, and she might be as tall as the Mieren who chased her, but once crooked-tooth caught her, she didn't stand a chance.

Fury poured through Ronnyn. He shook the cage. His power stirred, called by the depth of his emotion.

Why hadn't he jumped out of the cage when he had the opportunity? A howl of pure rage tore from his throat.

His gift surged and skittered across his skin like stinging ants, burning him. Then it was gone, dissipating into the night, leaving him empty and exhausted.

Patches of grey came and went in his vision. His mind felt dull and flat.

He was useless – an untrained mind-manipulator, who couldn't create illusions. Tears burned his eyes as sobs of impotent fury shook his shoulders. He wept and wept. Wept until he'd worn away all outrage and only despair remained.

And then there was nothing but the catch in his throat as he tried to recover his breath.

In the silence that followed, a whimper made him turn. The little ones shrank away from him.

Ronnyn lifted his hands only to discover they were bleeding. And he recalled gripping the bars of their cage.

'Vittor, Tam...' His voice rasped, raw in his throat. 'Tani.'

The little ones hung back, frightened of him.

'I'm sorry. So sorry.' Shamed, Ronnyn crawled up to their end of the cart. 'I'm better now. Come to me.'

This time, when he opened his arms, they went to him, sobbing their hearts out. Not that they understood what was happening, but he'd frightened them and that mortified him.

Gathering them close, he hugged the little ones as their small frames shook with the force of their emotion. And all the while, he hated himself.

'Why did they take Ma and Vella away?' Vittor whispered. 'Did they kill them?'

Ronnyn shook his head.

'They killed Da.'

He shook his head again, unable to speak. He'd failed his father, and now he'd failed his mother and sister.

'Wants Ma,' Tamaron cried.

Itania hiccupped as dry sobs shook her, making Ronnyn's heart swell.

'Come here, Tani.' He lifted her onto his lap. Then he sang the song his mother always sang to put them to sleep. His voice was deep and raw, barely more than a whisper, but it was enough. Tamaron snuggled in next to Vittor.

Soon Ronnyn heard their regular breathing and marvelled that they could sleep. He certainly couldn't.

When he was sure Itania was asleep, he tucked her in between Tamaron and Vittor.

And then he waited.

When his mother returned, he helped her climb into the cart then stopped, not sure what to do.

His mother took in the little ones, huddled together, and her gaze flew to Ronnyn's face. 'Where's Vella?'

'Crooked-tooth took her.'

Sasoria swung around to clutch the frame. 'You promised me. You promised!'

Ferret-face finished bolting the padlock, shrugged with a satisfied smirk and moved off towards the fire.

Ronnyn bristled. He couldn't sit still. Not when Aravelle was still out there.

A sob escaped his mother.

He hugged her. She smelled like ferret-face. It made his stomach turn, but kept his arms around her. 'Did he hurt you, Ma?'

'He promised not to touch Vella,' Sasoria whispered. She went very still, then thrust his arms away, lurching to the side of the cart where she vomited through the bars. It didn't take long. There was not much in her stomach. Ronnyn rubbed her back, his own stomach heaving in sympathy.

When she was through, he offered the waterskin. 'Here.'

Sasoria rinsed out her mouth and washed her face. Ronnyn didn't like the way her hands shook.

'I'm all right,' she whispered. 'I'm just so angry...'

The cart door swung open. Aravelle stood there, her mouth and nose bleeding, her nightgown held in place with both hands.

'Vella,' Sasoria moaned.

Ronnyn crept forward to help his sister in, but she thrust his hands away. He could only sit back and watch as she crawled to the far end of the cart, near the little ones. And there she huddled, shivering occasionally, knees drawn up under her chin.

Crooked-tooth locked the cage and swaggered back to the fire.

Ronnyn looked to their mother.

She grimaced, hugging her belly, as she drew her breath in through clenched teeth.

'The baby's coming?' Ronnyn could not believe their bad luck. 'Now?'

She nodded, unable to speak, and her free hand reached out for him. He caught it in his good hand, marvelling at her strength as she panted through the contraction. When it had passed, she fixed on him, fiercely determined as always. 'The baby's had the full year, so it is not too early. Don't worry. I'll be all right.'

He nodded. They sat in silence while the Mieren settled down for the night.

After a while, his mother's gaze became unfocused again and her breathing changed as she rode the pain of another contraction.

Ronnyn had never delivered a baby. When Itania was born, he and Vella had been sent outside to keep Vittor and Tamaron busy. Back then, he hadn't been afraid. Their father had been with them and it seemed they lived a charmed life. Now...

'Vella, I need you.' Ronnyn called softly over his shoulder. No answer.

'Vella?'

'Leave her.' Sasoria squeezed his arm, recovered for the moment. Her lips twitched. 'I'll be fine. I have done this before, you know.'

He had to smile. 'I know, it's just...' He gestured to the cage.

'Babies come when they are ready,' Aravelle said, suddenly at his side.

Relieved, Ronnyn reached for her.

'Don't touch me.' Anger contorted her face as she brushed his hand aside. 'Don't...'

She shuddered and he lifted his hands and backed off, but he couldn't go far. He watched as his mother and sister put their heads together.

'What needs to be done?' Aravelle asked, sounding practical and firm, as if she hadn't nearly fallen apart when he touched her.

'Not much,' their mother said. 'I'll ride the contractions. Right at the end you'll need to ease the baby's shoulders out. But what about you? Did he hurt you?'

'He can't hurt me.' Aravelle lifted her head to glare through the cage at the Mieren. 'Nothing he could do could ever hurt me.'

In that moment, Ronnyn loved her more than he had ever loved anyone.

'Oh, Vella,' their mother whispered, but before she could say more another contraction took her.

All that long night, while the little ones slept, Ronnyn remained where he was, unable to help. Aravelle wouldn't let him near her or their mother. He wished there was something he could do to ease his mother's pain. Sasoria bit on a wadded cloth and held onto his sister's hand each time the contractions took her.

Each time he almost succumbed to sleep, he'd jerk awake, heart racing, nausea coiling in his belly. He would not sleep, not while his mother suffered. If he stayed alert, ready to help, then Aravelle would see and soften. She would forgive him.

Looking back, he remembered Itania's birth as being quick. It had all happened in one afternoon, and his mother had been showing them the new baby by supper time. But not this birth; it went on all night.

Meanwhile, Aravelle watched over their mother. She didn't seem to sleep. She didn't speak to him. She didn't look at him. Half of him wanted to shake her and tell her it wasn't his fault.

The other half of him wanted to weep with her.

If only she'd weep.

THAT NIGHT, JARAILE and Nitzane took supper in the king's private dining chamber, where Commander Halargon found them.

'Where's the king?' he asked.

'Sleeping,' Jaraile said. Charald had been confused when he woke and complained of pain. They'd treated him with the Khitite soothing powders and Bidern had started him on the arsenic medication. 'What is it?'

'Eskarnor got away with his honour guard. They'd disappeared when I took a contingent of my men to his chambers. I've told all the gate keepers to watch out for him.'

'He could take passage on any ship leaving port,' Jaraile said. 'We should declare him outside the law and his lands forfeit.'

'Do that and the southern barons will unite behind him,' Halargon warned. 'The king must make that kind of decision.'

'I wish I could have challenged Eskarnor,' Nitzane muttered. 'That would have settled it.'

Jaraile wished Sorne was here. 'The more time we give Eskarnor, the more trouble he can cause.'

'His honour guard consists of twelve men,' Halargon said. 'The king's palace guard counts sixty, maybe seventy if I call in a few favours.'

'What if he goes to the harbour-master?' Jaraile asked. 'Sorne said he was in league with Master Hersegel.'

'If the harbour-master went through every tavern in the wharf district, he could muster maybe thirty or forty strongarms, and half of them would be drunken sots. We've time.' Halargon shook his head. 'Tomorrow, when the king is feeling more himself, he can decide what to do about Eskarnor.'

And Jaraile had to be content with that.

Chapter Forty

FEAR CONSUMED ARAVELLE. Her mother had been in labour since last night, and it was now mid-morning. Aravelle had given her sips of water, rubbed her aching back and tried to ease the jolting of the cart. Ronnyn had kept Vittor and the little ones occupied, returning every so often to Aravelle's side to check on their mother.

When the three little ones had fallen asleep, Ronnyn crawled over to join Aravelle, just as another pain took their mother. She curled on her side, panting.

He whispered under the cover of the rattling cart. 'The other births did not take this long.'

'Nor tax her so hard,' Aravelle agreed. There was almost no point in whispering. When the contractions struck, their mother was lost to the pain, but she did not make a sound.

'I hate feeling useless.' Ronnyn flexed his hands, his poor, cut, swollen hands. Aravelle felt for him. She knew he blamed himself and feared his gift would rise, but she couldn't sense the slightest hint of power.

The cart's creaking stopped as it came to a halt on the crest of a rise. Ferret-face pointed. 'There it is. Port Mirror-on-sea.'

'Go look,' their mother urged. The contraction had passed. It was amazing how she could be completely swamped by pain one moment, then alert the next.

Aravelle came to her knees. In a half-crouch, she peered through the slats past the Mieren's shoulders, across the valley. A long line of people, carts and wagons stretched along the main road, all heading for the port. From this distance, it was hard to make out much detail.

Port Mirror-on-Sea. She couldn't see the sea, only the port's defensive wall, and behind that, the buildings. The rain had stopped. It was one of those clear, windless, cold, sunny days. Smoke drifted up from myriad chimneys, collecting over the city.

'So many Mieren,' Aravelle whispered.

'Who would have thought?' Ronnyn looked grim.

First the fisher-folk, then the villages they'd skirted, now this... the size of Port Mirror-on-Sea stunned her.

'Which do you think is the king's palace?' Ronnyn whispered.

She had no idea. There were many spires and domes. Would the exchange take place at the palace? How many other T'En and Malaunje had been captured? Why was the king paying a bounty for her people?

Ferret-face twisted in the seat to inspect her family. What he saw seemed to confirm something, because he nodded to himself, then he flicked the pony's reins. But the cart didn't go down the track toward the port; they turned off the path.

'What?' crooked-tooth muttered.

'No baby yet. I won't be cheated out of my fair share,' ferret-face said. 'We'll wait for the baby to come. But we need to do it out of sight of the road. Don't want anyone grabbing our prizes.' He turned the pony towards a copse of trees nestled in a hollow.

Their mother moaned as the cart lurched over a rock. Ronnyn moved to support her.

While the Mieren made camp and prepared food, the little ones stirred. They wanted something to eat. They wanted Ma to tell them stories. They wanted to climb into her lap. They wanted her.

But she was focused inward each time the pain took her.

Every so often ferret-face would come over to check on them, then go back to the fire. Here in the hollow the cold was deep and damp, and went right into the bones.

The three little ones slept under the blanket. They seemed to be sleeping a lot. Aravelle suspected it was because they were cold and hungry, and huddling together was the only way to keep warm.

She sent Ronnyn to watch over them, while she did what she could for their mother, who panted as if she was running a race and the hill just kept getting steeper. Her moan was low and soft, and desperate. It was a terrible sound.

Ronnyn came back. The pair of them crouched over their mother, worried eyes meeting. Something was wrong.

Aravelle touched her mother's shoulder when the moaning stopped. 'Ma? Ma, do you need a midwife?'

She knew her mother heard her, for she went very still.

There was a long pause; so long that another contraction came. Ronnyn rubbed their mother's back. Aravelle felt her stomach go hard as a drum.

Surfacing from the contraction, Sasoria caught her breath. 'Yes, get a midwife.'

Ronnyn went to the end of the cage, calling to the Mieren by the fire. 'Our mother needs help. You need to send for a midwife.'

Ferret-face came over to study their mother through the bars. He poked her with the cane.

Sasoria opened her eyes. 'Please.'

Ferret-face turned back towards the fire.

'Should we send for a midwife?' crooked-tooth asked.

'She's still making sense. She'll be all right.'

'But–'

'If we go to the locals for a midwife, they'll find out about the silverheads. They'll take them from us.' They went back to the fire.

Aravelle grabbed the bars of the cage. 'If you don't get a midwife, you could lose our mother and the baby.'

'The three silverheads are worth more.'

Anger ignited Aravelle, but she kept her voice even. 'The baby's going to be a silverhead.'

Crooked-tooth looked to ferret-face.

'Nah,' ferret-face answered his unspoken question. 'Even if we fetched a midwife, the mother and baby might still die, and we could lose the three silverheads. A bird in the hand is worth two in the bush.'

'How can he risk Ma and the baby for a few silver coins?' Ronnyn muttered. 'I don't believe it.'

Aravelle had no trouble believing it.

TOBAZIM AND ARDONYX met the captain of the king's guard at the barricade.

'I've just had word from Commander Halargon,' Vetus reported. 'He says your people will be arriving soon. His men are going to escort them across the port.'

'Then we'd better make room for them.' Tobazim set off across the wharf, then slowed his step to allow for Ardonyx's injury. Over the last few days, people from their estates had trickled in and been ferried across to the ships. The problem was lack of ships. They'd purchased five vessels, but only two had been delivered. 'Seven ships in all. Brotherhoods will be forced to share, I fear the all-fathers will–'

'They should be grateful we've manage to segregate the brotherhoods from the sisterhoods.'

Tobazim shrugged. 'I had been hoping to have a ship for each brotherhood and sisterhood, but–'

'The other three vessels may be delivered by evening, but we still won't have enough. Nine brotherhoods and six sisterhoods between ten ships...' Ardonyx glanced up to the sky, his sailor's eyes judging the time from the sun's position. 'Almost midday.'

Athlyn spotted them and came over at a jog. 'The first of our people are here. All-father Kyredeon led them.'

By the time they reached the barrier, wagons, carts and people were piling up inside the wharf.

'It's going to be chaos,' Tobazim muttered.

'We'll start loading the ships and work through the night. I'll take Kyredeon on board and oversee the loading while you coordinate the wharf.'

Tobazim took over, directing the wagons and carts. They had two berths, where they could load ships, and two sets of stairs leading down to floating jetties. Meanwhile, their people kept arriving, a constant, steady stream of refugees.

With the T'Enatuath pouring through the port gate, Baron Eskarnor would know he had to make his move before they sailed.

IMOSHEN RODE THROUGH the unnaturally quiet streets of the port, watched by sullen-eyed Mieren. She rode beside the wagon where Umaleni travelled with the other T'En children. They were part of a long train of people stretching behind and in front of her.

Kyredeon's brotherhood would have reached the wharf by now. All-father Paragian had volunteered to bring in the rear, and his brotherhood would reach port by dusk.

She sat tall in her saddle, trying to contain her impatience. Meanwhile, her gift buzzed under the surface of her skin like a hive of bees, waiting to be released. She'd done the exercises to take the edge off her gift readiness, but nothing could prevent her instinctive reaction to being surrounded by ten thousand Mieren.

It wasn't just the innate threat their kind presented to hers. It was also the weight of their presence. For every Mieren who had natural defences, there were two who didn't. The port contained a miasma of emotion, layered deep by time. She couldn't prevent her gift from reading that one there, hanging over the flour merchant's balcony. The woman positively glowed with satisfaction as she fed on the T'Enatuath's shameful exile. Below her, a merchant burned with greed as he counted heads and calculated how much gold he could make out of supplying her people. Meanwhile, that boy with the eyes full of wonder felt a sense of loss and confusion keen as a knife, and would remember this day for the rest of his life.

Imoshen reined in her gift and focused on organising their departure. With a ship for each brotherhood and sisterhood, but only two berths it would be a challenge to load all the stores and people. She didn't know how long it would take to load each individual ship, but suspected they didn't have that much time.

If Sorne was correct and Eskarnor sought to disrupt the handover of the prince, he would do it here, in port in the next few days. Where was Sorne?

As she rode through the barricade gate, her heart sank. The Wyrd wharf was no larger than a city block. Already it was packed with people, carts, horses and belongings. She could see two ships at the berths. People clambered all over them, carrying supplies aboard, but it wasn't happening fast enough.

'Causare?' Ardonyx's voice reached her through the din. He was walking with the aid of a cane. Her heart rose to see him.

She swung her leg over the horse and dropped to the ground. Someone took the horse's reins. What were they going to do with all these horses and wagons?

The crush of people entering the wharf drove her forward, into Ardonyx, who steadied her. She wanted to throw her arms around him, and her gift tried to rise. For his sake, she forced it down and kept her distance.

'Up here,' a voice called from behind them and she turned to see Tobazim on the barricade by the gate.

Ardonyx forged through the crowd, drawing her with him. She climbed up next to Tobazim, who offered Ardonyx his hand, hauling him up. Up here, people's heads were about level with her knees, and she could see the extent of the crowding on the wharf.

Imoshen shaded her eyes. At least it wasn't raining. 'We'll never fit everyone in.'

'I've tried to divide the wharf into sisterhood and brotherhood,' Tobazim reported. 'But you're right, we're not going to fit. I've already started ferrying people and stores out to the ships.'

'Can we use the land beyond the barricade?' Imoshen indicated the open space between them and the slums. Ardonyx and Tobazim looked doubtful. 'Just for tonight? Make a barricade of the wagons?'

'We could. But I don't trust the Mieren,' Ardonyx said. 'I'd rather get everyone onto the ships, stack all our belongings and supplies inside the barricade and keep loading through the night.'

'How long will it take to load all the ships?'

Ardonyx and Tobazim exchanged looks.

Imoshen's heart sank. 'You haven't been able to get more ships?'

'We've signed the bill of sale and paid a deposit on five ships, but only two have been delivered,' Ardonyx said.

'Gold—'

'Won't help us this time. Sorne suspects the harbour-master is working with Baron Eskarnor, and he has all the ship owners in his pocket.'

'How many ships do we have?' Imoshen asked.

'Seven.'

'Is that enough?'

'It will have to be. We can't wait for the other three ships. While we're sitting here on the wharf, we're vulnerable. Brotherhoods and sisterhoods will have to share vessels.'

'Any sign of Parazime and Tamaron?' The all-mother and all-father were missing.

'Not yet.'

They were running out of time and she hadn't heard back from the Sagoras. Where would her people go?

First, they had to escape the port. The seemingly endless parade of wagons, carts and people dismayed Imoshen.

'A little less than a year ago, the port Mieren turned on us, burned our warehouses and strung up anyone who tried to escape,' Imoshen said. 'There are king's guards directing our people, but there are ten thousand Mieren and fewer than two thousand of us. While we're spread out through the port from here to the gate, we're vulnerable. There's no time to call an all-council and decide which brotherhoods will share ships. The all-fathers won't like it, but you'll have to allocate ships and start loading up, Ardonyx.'

'And blame the causare, if anyone complains?'

She laughed. 'Exactly.' How she loved his wry smile. 'Which is my ship? I'll share with Reoden.'

JARAILE COULDN'T SEE the Wyrd wharf from the palace balcony, but she could see one of the main thoroughfares down to the port. It had been choked with carts, wagons and Wyrds since midday. Somewhere in amongst those thousands was her son. She wanted to stride in there, find him and reclaim him. Impatience tore at her control.

'There's been no reports of Eskarnor leaving via the port gates,' Nitzane said. 'He could have taken passage on a ship already.'

'To do what?'

'Unite the southern barons behind him.'

'He's better off disrupting the handover of my son and fabricating evidence to blame it on you. Then, after you and the king battle, he can march in and mop up what's left.'

Nitzane laughed. 'You sound like Sorne.'

'Where is Sorne? He should be back by now.'

Nitzane covered her hand. 'Don't worry, Commander Halargon will ensure the Wyrds reach the wharf safely. All they have to do is load up and set sail. We'll meet them at the headlands and they'll hand over the prince. My ship is ready to sail at a moment's notice.'

'I wish they'd just hand him over now. I hate to think of him down there, so close, but out of reach.'

'You're a good mother.'

But she wasn't. She'd stepped out of the nursery for a moment, and in that time he'd been stolen. Until she held him in her arms again, she would not be whole.

And when she did, she would stop at nothing to protect him.

'VELLA, IT'S TIME.'

Aravelle helped her mother sit up. Ronnyn supported her back.

It seemed like days ago that her mother had warned about all the things that could go wrong during a birth. Sometimes babies came with their feet first, and sometimes with the cord around their necks. More often than not, T'En babies were stillborn, or they were born deformed and died within days. What would she do if...

There was no time to think. This part of the birth was as quick and violent as the beginning had been long and exhausting. Three pushes and she saw the baby's head. She eased the shoulders out, just as she'd been told. The baby was shockingly hot and slippery.

As the rest of the infant boy slithered onto the bare boards, a rush of blood followed him. Too much blood.

Aravelle's mouth went dry with fear.

The baby mewled, as if too exhausted to cry. But he was breathing and, as far as she could tell, there was nothing wrong with him.

Her mother managed a tired smile. 'Keep him warm.'

With tears of joy on her cheeks, Aravelle gathered him in her arms. The cord still pulsed with life. She had to wrap him or the cold would kill him, but all she had was that dirty blanket.

Ronnyn eased their mother down until she lay on her side. Then he hauled off his nightshirt, tearing a small strip to make himself a loin cloth. The rest he handed to Aravelle, who wrapped it around the baby.

Then she placed the baby next to their mother. 'He's perfect, Ma.'

Her mother tried to focus on him, but she seemed too tired.

Aravelle could remember Tamaron and Itania as babies. Tamaron had been completely hairless, while Itania had been born with a crown of red hair. This baby was bald and so pale that, when she'd wiped the birthing blood off his skin, she could see the fine veins mottling his flesh like marble.

He was pure T'En. She felt an unworthy stab of jealousy. By a twist of fate, this baby would belong to the elite, while she and Itania would be servants.

At that moment, if Aravelle could have cast aside her gender along with her Malaunje nature, she would have. Both were failings, both made her a victim.

It was only worthwhile being female if you were T'En.

The babe gave another mewling cry.

'Baby's born,' crooked-tooth announced.

Ferret-face came over to peer into the cage. 'Just in time. We'll reach port before they close the gates.'

When Aravelle looked into his shallow blue eyes, she read only calculation, no pity or compassion. Bitterness sat in her chest like an undigested meal. She closed her eyes, channelling her anger.

Ferret-face climbed onto the cart seat and turned the pony towards port.

The jolting woke their mother. She pulled herself up on one elbow and smiled down on the baby. 'We'll name him after your father.'

Aravelle could hear the unshed tears, thick in her mother's throat. Now the same tears stung her eyes and filled her chest, until she felt it would burst. But she pushed them down, refusing to give in to emotion.

'Baby, Asher,' Ronnyn whispered, stroking the tiny curled fingers.

'No, Ashmyr,' their mother corrected. 'That's the T'En form of the name.'

The baby gave a stronger cry, which woke the little ones.

'Baby's here?' Vittor was excited.

'Wanna hold him.' Tamaron clambered over. 'Lemme see.'

Little Itania was also fascinated. They did not understand the significance of their mother's grey skin, and Aravelle and Ronnyn shielded them from the blood.

'You can hold him soon.' Sasoria pressed the baby against her body as she caught Aravelle's arm, pulling her closer. 'You'll need to cut the cord and tie it off. The afterbirth will come soon...' A groan cut her off.

Their mother seemed too tired to put any effort into expelling the afterbirth.

They needed a knife to cut the cord. Only the Mieren had knives.

'Ronnyn.' She nudged him. 'We need to cut the cord.'

He came to his knees and called to the Mieren as they drove the cart. 'Can I borrow a knife to cut the cord?'

'Chew through it,' ferret-face muttered. 'That's what dogs do.'

Shock robbed Aravelle of coherent thought.

'But–' Ronnyn began.

She shoved him aside, snatched up the cord and tore through it with her teeth, backhanding her mouth with a shudder. 'There. Now tie it off.'

He stared at her.

She tore a scrap from her tattered nightgown to seal the baby's cord, then passed the baby across to Vittor. 'Take him down to the far end and show the little ones. Keep him warm.'

The next contraction drove out the afterbirth, followed by another great rush of blood. Aravelle tried to stop it with their one thin blanket, but it was soon drenched.

Ronnyn's terrified eyes met hers. 'Ma needs a T'En healer.'

'We'll be there soon. Hopefully...'

'You hear that, Ma?' He lifted their mother's head in his arms. Her eyelids flickered, but did not open. She was so pale her lips were blue. 'We're going to a T'En healer.' He smoothed matted hair from her forehead as brooding grey clouds gathered overhead. 'Just hold on.'

But there was too much blood and they had no way of knowing if there would be a T'En healer in port.

Chapter Forty-One

SORNE RODE INTO port with Captain Ballendin and fifty of his men. They'd only gone a short way beyond the gate when the wagons in front of them stopped moving. In the gathering twilight, it was hard to tell what the holdup was.

'What is it?' Captain Ballendin directed his question to a woman standing in the doorway of her shop.

'The Wyrds. Must be thousands of them. Started arriving around midday today. It's been so bad decent folks haven't been able to get around.'

Sorne stood in his stirrups. The wagons were moving, but too slowly. 'Come this way.'

He led the others through the back streets. It was amazing how people got out of the way for fifty armed, mounted men. They reached the royal plaza without trouble.

Sorne turned his mount to face Ballendin. One part of him wanted to go to the palace to ensure that Nitzane and Jaraile were coping, but he belonged with his people. 'Find Nitzane. Tell him the king has to make sure the Wyrds get onto their ships, or he won't get his son. I'll be down at the Wyrd wharf.'

As Captain Ballendin rode off with his men-at-arms, the prayer bells rang out and Sorne was reminded of Scholar Igotzon. He turned his horse towards...

'The Father's church?' Valendia protested. 'I spent eleven years locked up in there.'

'There's one more thing I have to do.'

'What?' Graelen baulked. 'Tell me why I should take Valendia into that place again.'

'We have to find and destroy the reports that led King Charald to realise he could conquer the Wyrds.'

'Why?' Graelen countered. 'The Mieren have called our bluff.'

'Very few people know the true limitations of Wyrd gifts,' Sorne said. 'I've seen what one little old Wyrd woman can do to a room full of war barons. King Charald has banished the Wyrds, but more half-bloods will be born and they'll eventually produce T'En. In the future, our kind will need the mystery of the gifts to protect them. If I destroy these notes, they'll stand a chance.'

He took them down one of the narrow streets that ran alongside the church, found the old gate and handed his reins to Graelen. Standing on the saddle, he climbed over the wall, dropped to the courtyard beyond and let them in.

'Only a few dedicated scholars come to these old halls,' he told them. At this time of the evening, Igotzon should really be at prayer, but Sorne suspected the scholar would work through the evening prayers. 'Leave the horses and come with me.'

This was the old section. It was dim and near-silent. From far away, he could hear the chanting of prayers. Sorne recognised the door and opened it to find the desk empty, but a lamp still burned.

'Scholar Igotzon could be back any moment.' Sorne pointed to the chest. 'Open that, Grae. Oskane's journals should be in there. Valendia, come with me.'

He went down the length of the wall until he found the right row of niches. 'Hold out your arms.'

He piled up Wyrd scrolls, but what he really needed was Igotzon's reports and he didn't know where they were.

Back at the desk, he found Graelen kneeling by the open chest. The adept showed him a journal. 'These?'

'Yes. Tip the scrolls into the chest, Dia.'

Footsteps came from the hall. He gestured for them to step to one side of the door and stood near the desk, just as the scholar entered.

'Sorne.' Igotzon was genuinely pleased to see him. The scholar walked in, unaware of Graelen and Valendia in the shadows. 'Where have you been? I have that list of questions for you. I put them...' He searched his desk.

'Igotzon, how many copies of the Wyrd reports did you make?' Sorne asked.

'Just the two. One for me and one for the high priest. No one else cared.'

'And where are these copies?'

'You said the high priest's set was destroyed. My copies are... Here's the questions.' He offered Sorne a sheet of cramped writing. 'If you answer these, I can start on the history of King Charald's reign. They're saying his mind is going, and he won't last much longer.'

Sorne went cold. 'Who's saying?'

'Everyone.'

'Where are your Wyrd reports?' Sorne pressed.

'Why? Do you want to check their accuracy? I must admit, I would like to get someone who knows to look them over. You... What's wrong?'

'Is it true?' Sorne had just recalled something the scholar said the first time they'd met. 'You once said you remember everything you've ever written.'

'I do. I've trained my mind to hold an image of this church. Every corridor contains doors, and behind every door is related information. I just have to find the right door,' Igotzon said, then frowned. 'Why?'

Graelen stepped up behind him, waiting for Sorne's signal – a knife through the ribs, a twist of his neck, or, failing that, the adept could wipe the scholar's mind and leave him a gibbering wreck.

Igotzon glanced over his shoulder, spotted Graelen and Valendia and gave a jump of fright. 'Sorne?'

Graelen caught the scholar's arms before he could run.

'What's going on, Sorne?' Igotzon asked.

'The information you collated in your reports led King Charald to believe he could attack the Wyrds and defeat them.'

'All I did was seek the truth.' Igotzon swallowed audibly. 'Knowledge–'

'...is power,' Graelen said. 'We can't let him live. Step outside, Valendia.'

Sorne had killed in self-defence. He had stood back and watched others die because he could not prevent it. He had watched Graelen die, or thought he had, and it had killed something in him.

'Grae?' Valendia whispered.

'Sometimes it's necessary to kill. I don't want you to see me do this, Dia.'

'I thought you valued knowledge, Sorne,' Igotzon whispered, stricken. 'I thought I'd found a friend.'

Graelen put his hands on the scholar's head.

'Please, no.' Igotzon closed his eyes. 'There's so much I don't know.'

'Wait.' Sorne swallowed. 'Would you like to write the history of the Wyrd exile?'

Igotzon's eyes widened. 'How can you ask?'

'It would mean leaving your home, sailing–'

He was already nodding.

'We can't take a Mieren,' Graelen protested. 'He's not one of us.'

'My Wyrd reports are in the chest.' Igotzon gestured to the chest, then realised it was open. 'Oh, I see you already found them.'

'Do you need to pack?' Sorne asked.

Igotzon nodded.

'Make it quick.'

He collected ink, pen and paper, and added this to the chest. 'Ready.'

Sorne had to smile. 'Good. By now the road to the wharf should be clear.'

TOBAZIM CROSSED THE wharf. Clouds obscured the sun, bringing an early twilight. He could not believe the number of people and the amount of supplies they had ferried out to the ships, but looking around him there was so much more to load. He rounded the warehouse to find Ardonyx with Hand-of-force Reyne.

They'd put Hueryx's brotherhood on the same ship as Kyredeon, simply because his brotherhood had arrived next. All-father Hueryx was not happy, but at least he could load his supplies. The rest of the brotherhoods and the sisterhoods had to to ferry people and the lighter stores from the two floating jetties.

Ardonyx sent Reyne off and turned to Tobazim. 'I wish we knew how much time we had. If we don't load the holds properly, the ships will be unstable in high seas, but we might be better off loading everything onto the ships' decks and sorting the holds while we're at anchor in the bay. I wish I knew where Sorne was.'

Before Tobazim could comment, they were hailed by Captain Vetus.

The veteran Mieren escorted two rough-looking brigands and a child of about five or six, who was wrapped in a stained travelling cloak. Stolid, wine-dark eyes looked up from under the hood and the child hugged a bundle under his cloak as if it was the most precious thing in the world. Tobazim noticed small, bare feet, blue with cold.

It started to rain and they stepped into the warehouse, where several Malaunje were preparing a meal for those who would not make it onto the ships in time for the evening meal. The smell of the spicy beans made Tobazim's mouth water, and the child looked hopeful.

Vetus indicated the unsavoury-looking Mieren, who gripped his sword hilt aggressively. 'They've come to claim the reward.'

Ardonyx pulled open his pouch. It was very light now. 'That's one silver coin.'

The two Mieren exchanged looks.

'Five silvers,' the older of the two corrected and he pulled off the child's hood to reveal white hair. When the child turned his head, Tobazim saw that a copper streak grew above one ear.

'Five silver coins for *each* of them.' The Mieren flipped back the boy's cloak to reveal the child held a baby with the wine-dark eyes and downy white hair.

Tobazim glanced to Ardonyx. This was the first time anyone had delivered a T'En child, let alone two. The boy and the baby had to be the only survivors of a sisterhood estate. Tobazim bristled. What had happened to everyone else?

'So that's ten silver coins you owe us,' the older one said.

'Which sisterhood did you come from? Where's your choice-mother?' Tobazim asked the child in T'En. Stony mulberry eyes stared up at him. Was the boy dimwitted?

'Where's our reward?' the brigand asked.

Ardonyx beckoned the cabin boy, Toresel. 'Go tell the causare two T'En children have been delivered. We don't know which sisterhood they belong to.'

The lad ran off.

'What's he saying?' the brigand demanded of the king's guard. 'What's going on?'

'I don't have ten silver coins.' Ardonyx jingled the pouch to show it was nearly empty. 'So–'

'Don't you try to cheat us,' the younger one warned and gestured to Tobazim's arm-torcs. 'What about them? They've got to be worth ten silvers each.'

Tobazim glanced to the silver arm-torcs. Embossed with the symbol of his brotherhood, they weren't his to give away, and they symbolised much more than their worth in silver. 'They're not–'

'Don't try to cheat us!' They younger one snatched the boy, and both brigands began to back off towards the door, knives drawn.

'Here.' Tobazim pulled the torc from around his right bicep. 'Take this. It's worth twenty silver coins.'

He tossed it to the older brigand, who caught it, inspected the workmanship and nodded to his companion, who shoved the boy aside, sheathing his knife. Tobazim darted forward, catching the child before he could trip and drop the baby.

During all this, the boy had not made a sound but, now that Tobazim held him, he could feel the child trembling. What had he seen and endured?

'You're safe now,' he told the boy, kneeling to look into his eyes. 'What's your name?'

But again the child only stared at Tobazim.

Meanwhile, Ardonyx had stepped between him and the brigands. 'Get them out of here, Vetus. And make sure they leave the wharf.'

As soon as the others left, Ardonyx came over to Tobazim. 'Is he all right?'

'Yes.' Tobazim stood. 'But he might be deaf.'

Ardonyx snapped his fingers. The boy's eyes went straight to his hand. Ardonyx grinned. 'I don't think so.'

The boy smiled tentatively.

'What's this about T'En children?' Imoshen asked, as she entered the warehouse with her voice-of-reason, and Healer Reoden. Tobazim came to his feet, but he kept a hand on the boy's shoulder.

Imoshen glanced to the boy. 'You said there were two children. Where's the other one?'

Tobazim parted the boy's cloak to reveal the baby.

'Oh...' As Imoshen dropped to her knees in front of the child to inspect the baby, her mouth parted in a delighted smile.

'I should check the baby for injuries,' Reoden said.

'Give me the babe.' Imoshen went to take the infant from the boy, but he stepped back, hugging the baby to his chest. This put him in contact with Tobazim and Ardonyx, and he seemed to take comfort from their support, because he remained there with his shoulders pressed against their thighs. As Tobazim rested his hand on the boy's slender neck, he felt the child relax into his touch and experienced a protective surge that surprised him with its intensity.

'Don't worry.' Imoshen spoke to the boy as if trying to calm a wild creature. 'I won't hurt you or your brother. Just give the babe to me.'

Even knowing how powerful she was, Tobazim was drawn to her, but the boy resisted.

'Where did you come from, little man?' Imoshen asked. 'Who was your choice-mother?'

The boy stared at her, but did not lower his guard.

'He can hear, but I don't think he understands,' Tobazim said.

Imoshen reached out to cup the boy's cheek in her left hand. Tobazim felt her gift stir as a tendril of power curled through the boy and into Tobazim. It happened so fast there was no time to raise his defences and, by the time he realised what was happening, he didn't want to relinquish contact. Instead, he revelled in her exotic feminine power as he lost track of everything but the intensity of the moment.

Imoshen let her hand drop.

Heart racing raggedly, Tobazim had to consciously repress his gift and rebuild his defences. It had been a long time since he'd come so close to betraying himself, not since he was a lad struggling for gift control. Embarrassed, he glanced to Ardonyx, but the ship's captain had eyes only for Imoshen.

The causare stared at the child.

'Well, Imoshen, what did you learn?' the healer prodded after a moment.

'He thinks we look odd. He has never seen adult T'En before. I caught a glimpse of his home and his parents. They were Malaunje,' Imoshen said. 'I'm guessing his parents were born of Mieren parents, who never gave them up to the T'Enatuath. I got the impression there were others like his parents living nearby. No wonder he doesn't understand our language.'

'So the stories of the free Malaunje village are true?' Egrayne whispered.

'Maybe. There were mountains and no Mieren in the glimpse I had,' Imoshen said. She switched to Chalcedonian. 'What is your name, child?'

'Light-of-my-Life,' he answered in the same language, and love enriched his voice.

'I'm sure you were,' Imoshen said. 'And where are your mother and father?'

'Da didn't come back from fur trading. Then bad people came and Ma told me to hide in the cave, but she didn't come back for me. I've been looking for her ever since. Do you know where she is?'

'Oh, you poor boy,' Imoshen whispered, tears glistening in her eyes. She summoned a smile. 'Don't worry, you and your brother will be safe with—'

'The baby's not my brother,' the boy said. 'I found her hidden in the neighbour's chicken coop.'

'A T'En girl!' Imoshen's voice rose with excitement. She glanced over her shoulder to Reoden and Egrayne. 'A baby girl!'

T'En girl babies were rare. Tobazim expected to see avarice in the causare's mulberry eyes when she returned her attention to the boy, but he saw only joy.

'A dear little girl,' Imoshen marvelled. 'Imagine that, free Malaunje producing two T'En children? Why, it's just like the legend of how the T'Enatuath originated!' She sprang to her feet, addressing Ardonyx. 'The Mieren who delivered them, did they say where they found the children?'

'I didn't think to ask them. They demanded payment and, when I said I had no coins, they drew a knife.' He gestured to Tobazim. 'We gave them one of my brother's arm-torcs.'

'Egrayne, see that Kyredeon is recompensed,' Imoshen said. Her happy gaze returned to the boy and the baby girl. 'We'll have to call an all-council to assign the children choice-mothers. And the boy will need a brotherhood when he grows up.' She turned back to Ardonyx. 'Should we hold the all-council on one of the ships?'

'No time for an all-council. We'll be loading and manoeuvring ships all night,' Ardonyx said. 'If we left our stores unattended, the poor from the rats-nest would strip the wharf bare by morning.'

Athlyn thrust the door open to report, 'The first of All-father Paragian's brotherhood has just arrived.'

'Good. He's the last one. The sooner we are all here, the sooner the ships are loaded and we can leave,' Imoshen said. The baby started to cry.

'She's hungry,' the boy said. 'But I've run out of—'

'Give her to me.' Imoshen sat on a crate and began to undo her bodice. 'I'll feed her.'

The boy hesitated only for a moment.

'The commander of the king's guard wants to speak with you,' Athlyn told Tobazim.

He climbed the platform by the gate, where Captain Vetus introduced him. 'This is Commander Halargon.'

'You're Baron Tobazim?' the grey-haired Mieren asked.

'I'm not a baron. I'm a scholar,' Tobazim corrected. 'Thank you for escorting our people through port.'

'The king sent me. When do you want to hand over the prince?'

Tobazim had no idea. 'I'll send a message up to the palace when we're ready to sail.'

The commander nodded and rode off.

SORNE HAD THOUGHT all the carts would be at the wharf by now, but they came up behind another one as they neared the rats-nest. When it passed under a shop lantern, three little children stared out at him, two T'En and a Malaunje, and he felt a jolt of surprise. It had been over four years ago, but he recognised them; these were the Wyrds of his vision – the children he'd seen loaded into a cart by Mieren.

What was the use of his visions, if he couldn't prevent them from happening?

Feeling as if he already knew them, he led his horse closer to the children. Igotzon walked on the other side of the horse, and the chest was tied across the saddle. Graelen and Valendia rode behind.

'Are you all right in there?' Sorne asked the children in T'En, then repeated it in Chalcedonian for good measure.

'No,' a voice called in T'En. A moment later a near-naked boy of about twelve peered through the slats. 'My mother's just had a baby. She needs a healer. Can you help us?'

'Hold on. We're nearly there,' Sorne said.

They'd entered the rats-nest now. The Mieren seemed restless tonight. He caught them watching from dark doorways, heard shouts and swearing, a scream that was abruptly cut off. Then they were through to the far side. The open area before the wharf was packed with empty carts and wagons.

The cart stopped ahead of them, at the barricade gate.

'We've come for the bounty,' one of the cart drivers announced. The gates swung open and they entered. The wharf was packed with supplies, stacked higher than Sorne was tall in some places. Between the supplies on his left he saw a seven-masted ship being loaded by lantern light. Everywhere he looked, people moved with purpose.

'What do we have here?' Tobazim asked as he jumped down from the platform by the barricade gate.

'We've come for the bounty,' the cart driver repeated.

Sorne went to meet Tobazim. 'We have several cold, hungry children and a woman with a newborn, in need of a healer.'

'That's lucky. The healer's in the warehouse.' He directed the cart to follow and fell into step with Sorne. 'Did you find your sister?'

'She was in the crypts beneath the church all this time.' Sorne gestured to where Graelen was helping Valendia dismount. 'Along with a brotherhood warrior. Where's All-father Kyredeon?'

'Over there.' Tobazim pointed to the seven-masted ship. 'And the causare?'

'In the warehouse, with–' Tobazim broke off as he caught sight of Scholar Igotzon. 'What's the Mieren doing here?'

'He's going to write the history of the Wyrd exile.'

Tobazim rubbed his jaw, then shrugged as if nothing would surprise him now. He signalled the cart driver. 'That's far enough. The causare will deal with you.'

When Tobazim moved off, Graelen caught up with Sorne. 'I'll take Valendia and report to the all-father. We'll see you on Kyredeon's ship.'

'No, I'll be with Imoshen's sisterhood.' As soon as he said it, he realised there was never any doubt.

'You're leaving us, Sorne?' Valendia whispered.

'You have Grae. I have someone in Imoshen's sisterhood. Be happy for me, sister.' He hugged her, kissed her forehead, then clasped Graelen's forearm. 'I am happy for you.'

'And I for you. Although I don't know how a wild Malaunje will take to living with the T'Enatuath.'

Sorne grinned and handed Igotzon the horse's reins.

When he opened the warehouse door, he spotted the causare with Egrayne and Reoden. They were speaking to a little boy while several Malaunje prepared a meal. The smell of cooking made his stomach rumble.

'Sorne!' Imoshen hurried over. As she approached, he realised an infant slept in a sling across her body. 'Did you find your sister?'

'Yes.' He was touched she'd remembered.

'I'm glad. Is the king–'

'I've no idea. I came straight here, but I sent a message to the palace. Imoshen, the children from my vision are outside in a cart. Their mother's just given birth and she needs a healer. I–'

'Where do I put this?' Igotzon asked, as he arrived with his chest.

Imoshen turned to Sorne for an explanation.

'This is Scholar Igotzon. He wants to write a history of the Wyrd exile.'

Imoshen blinked, then laughed. 'Why not?'

Sorne felt relieved. He'd been afraid they would execute the Mieren scholar on the spot.

'Do you have time to deliver him to my devotee?' Imoshen asked. 'She's on the flagship.'

Sorne's heart rose. 'Where's your ship?'

Imoshen smiled and pointed between Kyredeon's ship and the end of the barricade. 'Take the stairs down to a floating jetty, get in line and ask for the causare's flagship. Do you know how long we have to load?'

'No idea. The sooner the better.'

'That's what I feared.' She beckoned the healer. 'Reoden, we need you.'

He took one side of the chest and Igotzon took the other. But he stopped at the cart. Three little ones looked up at him, and he saw two older children down the back with a woman. 'The healer's coming. Don't worry. You're safe now.'

'Thank you,' the eldest boy said, coming to the bars. His hands were swollen, his voice rasped and his nose had been broken recently. 'Thank you so much.'

Since he was seventeen, Sorne had stolen power and used visions for his own advancement, causing death and disorder on the way. He did not deserve the lad's gratitude. 'I did nothing. Save your thanks for the causare and the healer.'

He turned back to Igotzon and, between them, they carried the chest towards the steps, dodging people, supplies and carts on the way. As they passed Kyredeon's ship, Sorne saw Graelen and Valendia being escorted up the steps to the rear deck and into the cabins.

'Look at the queue,' Igotzon said.

When they reached the top of the stairs, they found a line of refugees leading down to the crowded floating jetty.

Rowboats ferried people and their possessions out to the ships. It looked like they'd be waiting a while.

'There's another set of steps over near the cliff end of the wharf, but it's probably just as busy,' Sorne said.

He put the chest down and Igotzon promptly sat on it. The scholar seemed stunned, but happy.

Sorne looked along the length of the wharf. From here he could see the gang plank to Kyredeon's ship. A steady stream of porters carried supplies aboard, while winches swung laden nets onto the decks. The same thing would be happening on the other arm of the wharf, but even if they worked all night and the ships took turns, they wouldn't be finished loading for several days.

As soon as he settled Igotzon and saw Frayvia, he needed to get back to the palace and find out what Eskarnor was up to.

RONNYN TOOK HIS mother's cold hand. 'Did you hear that, Ma? The T'En healer's coming.'

But his mother didn't respond. Her skin was pale, her lips bloodless. When the newborn whimpered, she didn't respond.

'Open this cart,' a woman ordered.

Ronnyn looked up to see the silhouettes of two T'En women. One was only half a head taller than ferret-face, who fumbled with the padlock. The other was a full head taller than him.

'Bring the lantern closer,' the smaller woman told a Malaunje servant, as ferret-face swung the gate open.

Ronnyn blinked in the light. He'd never seen adult T'En before, and they appeared strange to him.

The smaller woman frowned. 'Just look at the state of these poor children. Dressed in tatters, their hair all matted and filthy, caged like beasts.'

She glared at ferret-face, who backed off.

Aravelle caught Ronnyn's eye. 'Tell her.'

He raised his voice. 'We asked them to fetch a midwife, but they wouldn't. The baby was born all right, but...' He trailed off because he didn't want to worry the little ones. There was so much blood, he feared the worst.

The two T'En women exchanged looks.

'This is Healer Reoden and I'm Causare Imoshen,' the smaller one said. 'You're safe now. Come out, children, so the healer can get to your mother and the baby.'

The three little ones looked to him and Aravelle.

'You take them,' he said. 'I'll stay with Ma.'

She scrambled out with Itania in her arms, then helped Tamaron down. Vittor climbed out on his own.

'Ronnyn?' his mother whispered.

He leant close and she grasped his arm, with surprising strength, fixing determined eyes on him. 'Promise me you'll never forget your Malaunje kin. Swear it.'

'I'll never forget, Ma.' His throat felt so tight he could hardly speak. 'But the healer will save you. She'll—'

The cart rocked on its axles as Healer Reoden climbed in and shuffled towards them on her knees, oblivious to the blood.

His mother released his arm and lay back, exhausted. Ronnyn edged away, so the healer could crawl closer to his mother.

'The baby came, but the bleeding wouldn't stop,' he whispered. 'We didn't know what to do. You can fix her, can't you?'

The healer looked grim as she took in the circle of blood. Then she rubbed her hands together and met his eyes. 'I promise I will do everything within my power.'

He felt a rush of awareness, of sharpened senses, and realised he'd sensed her gift.

Just then, his baby brother whimpered. He went to pick up Ashmyr, but the healer stopped him.

'Leave the newborn with me.'

Ronnyn hesitated.

'Out you go.'

He glanced to his mother. She gave him a single nod.

It felt strange leaving her, as he scrambled to the end of the cart and climbed down next to the causare. When he did this, he realised two things: she carried an infant in a sling across her body, and she was the same height as him, which meant he was no taller than a small T'En woman. And to think, he'd believed himself a man.

Aravelle and the others stood at the entrance to the warehouse. As Ronnyn watched, one of the Malaunje servants draped his robe over Aravelle's shoulders. But when Vittor and Tamaron tried to stand next to her, the Malaunje separated them. Ronnyn's heart sank. This was why his parents had run away. He shivered.

'You poor lad, you're half-frozen.' The causare rubbed his arms, and he felt a pulse of warmth that did not come from touch alone.

The way they summoned power, and guided it with ease, impressed him. But... 'We thought we were being taken to the king for the bounty.'

'I'm paying the bounty. That reminds me.' She moved over to pay ferret-face.

The causare was the reason his father had been killed?

As she returned she saw his confusion. 'The bounty ensures the Mieren deliver our people alive. Some of our estates have been attacked and everyone massacred.'

He shivered again. She took off her robe, settling it around his shoulders. It carried the warmth of her skin, a subtle, sweet scent and a hint of her gift, which was both exotic and rich.

'Wait with the others. As soon as we return to the ship, we'll find you some hot food and warm clothes.'

She went into the warehouse, and Ronnyn noticed ferret-face had left his father's cane leaning against the cart wheel. He grabbed it in memory of Asher, hiding it under the robe.

Chapter Forty-Two

TOBAZIM RETURNED TO the platform beside the barricade.

'Glad you're here,' Vetus said. 'We've got company.'

Tobazim looked where he pointed, into the dip towards the rats-nest. Moonlight gleamed between scudding clouds, and he could just make out figures gathering under the tenements.

'It's just a pack of desperate slum dwellers. We should be able to fight them off,' Tobazim said.

'They have the numbers,' Vetus warned. 'And, with the abandoned carts and wagons, they have cover. If they make a concerted effort and storm the barricade, they'll overrun it.'

He was right. Tobazim had been so focused on getting people and supplies aboard their ships, he'd lost track of the wharf's defences. He'd never be a hand-of-force.

Spotting Athlyn, he jumped to the ground. 'Go along the length of the barricade to the sea. Tell them to be on alert. The rats are gathering.'

The youth nodded and ran off.

Tobazim looked in the other direction and spotted another T'En youth. 'You, come here.'

When the youth turned, he realised it was Imoshen's choice-son, Iraayel. Tobazim had been going to tell him to run down the barricade towards the cliff, but he sent him to warn the causare instead.

Just then Ardonyx caught up with Tobazim. 'You'll never believe who came back from the dead. Kyredeon's assassin. We'll have to... What's wrong?'

'The rats are gathering. They might be half-starved skinny brats armed with knives and homemade cudgels, but there's hundreds of them. I have to warn the defenders on the barricade. Wait here.'

But Ardonyx paced alongside Tobazim as he strode towards the cliffs, warning the barricade defenders. He didn't like it. They were too strung out. They should draw back and form a smaller defensive perimeter, but he didn't want the rats looting their supplies. He would have to bring in more defenders from the ships.

When they reached the end of the barricade, Ardonyx drew him aside. 'We need to reinforce the–'

The ragged screams of attacking Mieren cut him off. It sounded like they were concentrating their assault on the gate. Tobazim went to go help, but Ardonyx caught his arm, pointing to the cliff. At least two dozen dark figures slid down on ropes, with more coming.

'Those are not half-starved skinny brats armed with knives and homemade cudgels,' Ardonyx whispered. 'They're strongarms, and they're coming in behind our defences. We have to retreat to the ships.'

AT THE SOUND of the screams, Sorne spun around to see dozens of thin, desperate Mieren storming the barricade gate. Valendia was safe on the ship, but the children...

He grabbed Igotzon's shoulders. 'When you get to the causare's ship, ask for Frayvia.' Then he ran through the stacked supplies towards the cart, where he found the five children huddled together outside the warehouse.

'Quickly, come with me.'

'We can't leave our mother–' the eldest girl protested.

The boy pointed to the cart. 'Our baby brother's still in there.'

As Sorne thrust his head into the cart, he sensed the healer's power, but she was closing the mother's eyes. 'Mieren are attacking. Come quick.'

'I'll get Imoshen.' She picked up the newborn, tucking him inside her vest. 'You take the children to the ship.'

Sorne nodded.

He darted back to the children. 'Come with me.'

They hesitated.

He scooped up the four-year-old boy and headed for the stairs. The girl took the six-year-old's hand and the eldest boy picked up the toddler.

Sorne led them through the maze of stores and supplies. The shouting and clash of metal told him the barricade was holding, for now.

When they reached the stairs, Sorne found piles of abandoned possessions littering the steps. About a dozen people still waited on the floating jetty, and several dangerously overloaded rowboats were heading towards the ships. Trusting that the rowboats would return, Sorne led the children down the steps. When he reached the jetty, he couldn't spot Igotzon. He hoped the scholar was in one of those boats.

'We should have waited for Ma and the baby.' The oldest boy looked up the stairs, as if he was thinking of going back for them.

'Wants Ma,' the small boy in Sorne's arms whimpered.

Sorne felt for him, for all the children. Now was not the time to tell them their mother was dead. He almost asked after their father, but suspected the worst.

Just then a rowboat returned, and everyone piled in.

'To the causare's ship,' Sorne told the oarsmen.

As soon as Imoshen slipped into the warehouse, the little boy spotted her and ran to her side. She hushed him and beckoned Egrayne. 'There are more children outside, desperately in need of a bath, warm clothes and food. I think they must be the children of loners like these two. We need to go back to the ship. We can–'

'Everyone out,' Iraayel said, even as he thrust the warehouse door open. 'The Mieren are massing to attack.'

The Malaunje started to pack up, but before they could finish, the roar of attacking Mieren came through the open door.

'Leave everything,' Egrayne ordered. 'Go.'

The boy whimpered. As Imoshen cupped his cheek, she felt a shiver of fear run through him and her gift surged. She caught a glimpse of his thoughts... no, it was a memory. She saw two bodies amidst the wreckage of a one-room cottage, heard a baby crying and found the poor little thing, hidden in the chicken coop.

She dropped to a crouch, taking the boy's shoulders in her hands. 'You're safe. You're both safe.'

He didn't believe her.

'Iraayel, come here.'

She took the boy's chin in her hand, held his eyes and let him feel the force of her gift. 'This is my choice-son, Iraayel. He's very brave. He'll protect you.'

The boy's gaze dipped to the sleeping baby tucked against Imoshen's chest.

'And I'll protect her. Come.' Imoshen sprang to her feet.

They were the last out the warehouse door and they found the healer climbing out of the cart. She carried a newborn tucked inside her vest. Imoshen's gift surged. Reoden would protect the infant with her life.

'The mother?' Imoshen asked.

'Dead.'

'Where are the children?'

'Sorne took them to the ship.'

The roar of the fighting was so loud she could hardly hear herself think.

Two skinny Mieren youths ran towards them, swinging cudgels. The youths paused to look them over, but Egrayne advanced towards them. She had been a gift-warrior, and it showed in the way she moved. The two youths took off, in search of easier prey.

'Come quick.' Egrayne led them towards the steps.

They dodged supplies and running Malaunje, some of whom were making for Kyredeon's ship, while others ran for the steps and the floating jetty.

But when they reached the steps, the jetty was empty but for discarded possessions, and an overloaded rowboat was already halfway back to the vessels.

'To the brotherhood ship,' Imoshen cried. They ran around piles of supplies. She glanced towards the warehouse and saw Ardonyx and Tobazim, with a dozen defenders, coming her way.

TOBAZIM RAN ALONG the barricade, driving the defenders back to the ships as the brigands came down the cliffs behind them. Ardonyx ran at his side, bent double over his stomach wound. Tobazim heard a shout and glanced behind them.

Slum rats spilled over the deserted barricade. But instead of coming after the defenders, the rats made for the supplies, focused on looting.

A band of about thirty brigands had gathered at the base of the cliff. One of them pointed at Tobazim's group, and they gave chase, weapons drawn.

Tobazim swung his arm under Ardonyx's shoulder and ran. Ahead of them, the two Mieren who had delivered the latest cartload of children were trying to turn their cart and pony to escape.

As Tobazim and the defenders darted around the cart, he saw Imoshen and the others with the little boy.

'You can't fight. You can barely run,' Tobazim told Ardonyx. 'Take the causare to the ship. I'll buy you time.'

Without waiting for a reply, Tobazim turned back to deal with the brigands. He hauled the crooked-toothed youth off the cart seat and put his shoulder to the cart, tipping it over. The older Mieren who'd been leading the pony objected and the pony panicked. Tobazim cut it free from its traces then slapped its rump, driving it towards the brigands. To his right, he saw several defenders piling up supplies to form a barrier.

They were level with the barricade gate and all the defenders were concentrated in this one area, protecting Ardonyx's ship and the stairs to the nearest floating jetty. He didn't know how the rest of his people were coping on the other arm of the wharf. He had to trust they would escape from the floating jetty, and the ship would be able to cast off.

When the brigands reached the makeshift barricade, they came around each end, funnelled towards the waiting defenders. As a burly Mieren attacked him, Tobazim fought the temptation to reach for his gift. He blocked, brought his second knife around and gutted the man.

One of his people fell; his killer stripped him of his valuables before returning to the fray.

A brigand with three sets of torcs down his arm lunged for Tobazim, who ducked, kicked the man's knee and stabbed him before he could regain his balance. There was no time to retrieve the arm-torcs.

Step by step, Tobazim and his people fell back. He saw Captain Vetus and three of the barricade defenders running in their direction. The king's guard stumbled as he was struck over the head. A horde of slum rats poured over him, cheering and whooping as they scattered to loot the supplies.

The three Malaunje warriors joined Tobazim. He was down to half a dozen able-bodied defenders. At least Ardonyx had escaped.

He wondered if they could make it to the floating jetty and glanced behind him, only to see Ardonyx guiding the causare and the others along the edge of the wharf towards the steps.

With a curse, he ran to meet them at the top of the stairs. 'What happened? I thought you were taking them to your ship.'

'I was, but Kyredeon cast off before we could get there.' Ardonyx was furious.

A dozen cheering slum rats ran past. Others loaded crates onto already-overloaded carts but the brigands kept coming. This was no random attack. Tobazim saw them pointing to the boy Iraayel was trying to protect.

Imoshen gestured to the floating jetty, which was covered in abandoned possessions. 'We'll have to trust they send back the rowboats.'

'Go.' Tobazim shoved Ardonyx.

While the others went down to the jetty, Tobazim returned to the last of the defenders.

They fought a rearguard action to the stop the stairs, then backed down, holding off the brigands, who now had the advantage of the high ground.

The last woman warrior plunged off the steps, taking one of the brigands with her. A Malaunje warrior moved into her place, but almost immediately a lucky sword thrust skipped over his defence and took him in the throat. His attacker thrust him aside.

As the Malaunje warrior toppled into the dark bay, Tobazim glanced over his shoulder to see the T'En women on the floating jetty shielding the boy, while Ardonyx signalled the nearest ship.

Still no sign of a rowboat, and they were only four steps from the jetty. Iraayel drew his long-knives. Egrayne had found a sword.

He looked up the steps, seeing at least fifteen brigands jostling to attack them. They had to put to sea.

Tobazim was reminded of the night they'd escaped the winery on a floating jetty. He turned to the last two defenders on the stairs. 'Hold them.'

Then he hacked at the rope that tied the jetty to the stair bollard. The rope was as thick as his wrist and tough. A brigand jumped onto the jetty behind him, and another followed. Iraayel tackled the second, as the first tried to run Tobazim through. Sidestepping the blow,

Tobazim kicked his attacker into the water and freed one end of the jetty.

Then he darted around the fighting figures. The second rope's thick fibres seemed to take forever to cut through. Finally, he shoved the jetty away from the steps.

Four or five of the brigands were still with them. One tried to make the jump, and Tobazim kicked him into the sea. Egrayne was only using one arm, but the last Malaunje warrior caught her attacker from behind and held him, while she dispatched him. Reoden and Imoshen shielded the little boy with their bodies. Iraayel struggled with a brigand who tried to throw him into the sea. Ardonyx was on his knees wrestling, blood soaking his belly and thighs.

Tobazim went to help him, but a brigand came out of nowhere, swinging a cudgel at his head. He tried to duck. Too slow. The cugel struck him above one eye. Stunned, he fell to his knees, head swimming. The brigand raised the cudgel to brain him, and there wasn't a thing he could do about it. His body refused to obey him.

The causare appeared behind the brigand. She touched the man's neck and he dropped like a sack of grain. She didn't even lose consciousness as she ripped the Mieren's life force from his body and sent it to the higher plane. Tobazim shuddered at this casual display of power.

She did the same to the brigand who had Ardonyx by the throat, then went to help Iraayel, but he had already thrown his attacker into the sea.

And with that, there were no more brigands on their makeshift raft.

As they floated across the bay, Reoden went around checking each person for injury. She felt Egrayne's shoulder and adjusted it, then reached for Tobazim.

He refused her touch, indicating Ardonyx who sprawled beside him, his belly and thighs covered in blood.

Her hands moved over Ardonyx and Tobazim saw his frown ease. A long sigh of relief left the sea captain.

When Reoden was done she moved towards Tobazim, but he gestured to the injured Malaunje warrior.

'I'm fine.' His vision was blurry and he felt nauseous. 'Heal him next.'

He was glad he'd insisted when she rolled the Malaunje warrior over and he saw it was Maric, from the winery. As the healer worked on him, the causare knelt between Tobazim and Ardonyx. She had such a sweet face, like spring after a cold winter...

Her hand clasped his, fingers entwined. The skin of her forearm was softer than silk, warm and tingled with power. He saw she'd taken Ardonyx's hand, too. 'You saved our lives, thank you.'

It was all the warning he had as she gift-infused them both. Her power, so rich and exotic, rolled through him, like waves of sunshine sending warmth into every limb. All pain banished, his mind rose beyond the everyday to a point of such acuity, he lost himself in the pattern of the brocade trim on her vest.

Lost himself entirely...

JARAILE READ THE king to sleep, then bid his manservant good night and went out to the balcony. She'd been standing on one balcony or another all day. Now she heard shouting and the clash of weapons from the Wyrd's wharf.

No!

She ran to the dining room doors and threw them open, startling Ballendin, Halargon and Nitzane, who had lingered to drink and talk. 'They're attacking the Wyrd wharf. Come see!'

The three men crowded around her. In the distance, they could hear the roar of fighting.

'But Eskarnor doesn't have any men other than his honour guard,' Halargon protested.

'He found some somewhere, and Cedon is down there.' Jaraile was so angry she shook. 'I want you down there right now. I want that wharf protected. Nothing must interfere with the handover. Nothing!'

They didn't argue. In no time at all, they'd strapped on weapons and assembled the king's guard in the stable yard. All around her, they mounted up.

When she tried to climb up on the horse behind Nitzane, he dismounted. 'Be sensible, Jaraile. It'll be dangerous.'

'But what if he's frightened? What if he needs me?'

Nitzane laughed and hugged her. 'Trust us to look after him.'

But she didn't. No one loved Cedon as much as she did.

'We can't be worrying about you,' Nitzane told her. 'Stay here.'

She nodded. 'But–'

'But nothing.'

And they rode off, all the kingsguard, all of Captain Ballendin's men. Surely they could keep her little boy safe.

Chapter Forty-Three

SORNE HELPED THE children out of the net that had hoisted them onto the deck. They thanked him, then ran to the side of the ship, where Malaunje and T'En, adults and children crowded to watch the fighting on the wharf.

'I lost the chest, Sorne,' Igotzon said. He was dripping wet.

'What?'

'The people on the stairs panicked. I was knocked into the sea. I'm sorry.'

'Sorne.' Frayvia threw her arms around him. She kissed him and he forgot everything.

RONNYN DREW HIS brothers and sisters close as all around them people pointed to the wharf overrun with Mieren. He should never have left his mother behind. How was she going to get to the ship now?

'Is that the healer?' Aravelle asked, pointing to a knot of defenders fighting a rearguard action down the steps to the floating jetty.

'Where's Ma? Where's our baby brother?' Vittor asked, his voice rising in panic.

'See the way the healer's holding her arm across her chest,' Aravelle said. 'I bet baby Ashmyr's inside her vest.'

But there was no sign of their mother, as the causare and the healer urged a small boy onto the jetty. Only a few T'En and Malaunje warriors survived, and they battled at the base of the steps, trying to hold back the attackers.

'I think they've cut the jetty free,' Aravelle whispered. Sure enough, the floating jetty left the base of the stairs, and the last of the attackers were beaten back and thrown into the water.

The whole ship cheered.

'And now there's a rowboat going back for them,' Aravelle said.

'But where's Ma?' Vittor repeated.

They all looked to Ronnyn. He was the last one out of the cart. He knew the healer had done everything she could, but...

A storm of tears shook Vittor's small frame. Aravelle hugged him. Sobbing loudly, Itania threw herself into Aravelle's arms. Ronnyn went to console Tamaron, but his little brother was no longer by his side. Where had...

Ronnyn turned around and looked across the deck to see a Mieren warrior holding a knife to Tamaron's throat. A dozen armed men surrounded the warrior.

'Bring out Prince Cedon,' the man yelled.

'No,' Ronnyn protested.

SORNE FROZE.

'Bring out Prince Cedon or the boy dies.'

'Eskarnor?' Sorne looked over Frayvia's head to see the baron surrounded by his fiercely loyal honour guard. Eskarnor held a knife to Tamaron's throat.

'Come on,' Eskarnor said. 'Why should Wyrds care who takes Prince Cedon?'

'Where is the prince?' Sorne whispered to Frayvia.

'In the far cabin, with the healer's T'En children. They'd have half a dozen gift-warriors, but...'

He assumed her hesitation meant Eskarnor had a point. Why risk one of their own for the hated king's son?

'Bring him out here or the boy dies.' Eskarnor shook Tamaron, who whimpered.

Sorne saw Ronnyn come to his feet, raising the cane like he meant to use it. The lad would get himself killed.

'Take me instead.' Sorne stepped forward, unbuckling his sword belt and tossing it aside. 'Take me hostage.'

'You?' Eskarnor's eyes gleamed. The baron would gladly gut him, just because he could.

'We have him,' a one-eyed sisterhood gift-warrior announced. She left the cabin with four other warriors, who fanned out. Sorne could see by the way they watched Eskarnor, they were judging the right moment to attack.

'This is the prince.' The one-eyed gift-warrior led a small boy. He had fine white-blond hair and pale blue eyes, and did not walk with a limp. In his face, Sorne saw Jaraile's sweet features. Sorne was not handing Prince Cedon over to die at Eskarnor's hands.

'Looks like I don't need you, half-blood,' Eskarnor said.

The one-eyed gift-warrior gestured to attract Eskarnor's attention. 'Let the T'En child go and you can have Prince Cedon.'

'Oh, no. You send the prince to me.'

Slowly, she walked Jaraile's son forward. Meanwhile, her warriors tried to flank Eskarnor's party. Sorne feared they'd panic Eskarnor's men and Tamaron would be killed in the confusion.

'So you planned to kill the prince and implicate Nitzane all along?' Sorne asked and deliberately began to edge closer to distract Eskarnor.

'Nitzane's a fool, but I'm not. No closer, half-blood.'

'How did you stage the attack on the wharf?' Sorne asked. 'I've had people watching the port. Your men-at-arms haven't filtered in.'

'Why should I sacrifice my men when there's a slum full of hungry vermin ready to die for a chance to loot your wharf?'

'And the harbour-master?'

'His strongarms have orders to bring me every small boy-child they find. But they were only a diversion while I boarded the causare's ship and got my hands on the prince.'

'Cedon, no!' Reoden cried.

Sorne turned to find Imoshen's party had climbed aboard. As Ronnyn and Aravelle pleaded with them to save their brother, Reoden handed them the newborn.

Sorne saw the healer take in how Eskarnor held the little boy. She opened her arms. 'Come to Ree-ma, Cedon.'

The prince ducked away from the gift-warrior and ran towards her. The instant he started moving, the gift-warriors attacked Eskarnor and his men.

Sorne was already running.

Too slow. He saw the baron cut Tamaron's throat, cast him away and run for the side. Sorne dropped to his knees beside the boy, and clamped his hands over the wound. Too much blood.

'Out of the way.' The healer thrust him aside. 'Get back!'

He felt her power like the heat of a naked flame and knew it could consume him. Tamaron's brothers and sisters were too close. Sorne picked up Cedon. 'Back! Everyone back!'

He drove them away until they were a safe distance from the healer.

'Can she save him?' Ronnyn asked Sorne.

'She couldn't save Ma,' Aravelle said.

'She deliberately provoked Eskarnor. She must have thought she could save your brother.' Sorne only hoped the healer was right.

The gift-warriors dispatched two of Eskarnor's honour guard who were too slow going over the side of the ship. Then they cleaned their weapons and formed a circle around her and Tamaron.

'KEEP THE CHILDREN back, this is powerful gift-working,' Imoshen told Sorne. She was so angry she shook as she stepped over the two dead Mieren. 'Throw their bodies overboard. No honour in death, for those who have no honour in life.'

While several Malaunje moved to obey her, she approached Reoden's hand-of-force.

'Stand back, Cerafeoni. I only want to help,' Imoshen said. 'Ree's already exhausted. She tried to heal the children's mother, then she healed all of us who were injured in the scramble to escape the wharf.'

'Imoshen's right, Cera,' Reoden's voice-of-reason said.

Seeing Nerazime, Cerafeoni's shoulders sagged. 'We couldn't save both boys. We–'

A soft thump made the circle of gift-warriors step aside. The hand-of-force sank to her knees and rolled Reoden over. 'All-mother?'

Nerazime joined her, touched the healer's face and closed her eyes. 'She's drained her gift.'

'Is our brother all right?' the children cried. 'Is Tamaron all right?'

Imoshen knelt beside the small, bloodied boy. He was cold and pale and so very still. But under all that blood, there was a neat silver scar across his throat.

A wave of relief made Imoshen dizzy. 'I can't be certain.' He'd lost a lot of blood. She hoped Reoden had been able to heal him before his mind began to shut down. Usually the healer urged the flesh to knit, and that was enough to speed the body's natural healing process. Due to the nature of Tamaron's wound, she'd had to heal him completely. 'We'll know tomorrow.'

'Can we see?' the children pleaded.

'Let them come over, Sorne.'

The children crowded close, peering over her shoulder or crouching beside their brother.

'Why isn't he moving?' the eldest boy asked.

'He needs to rest,' Imoshen said.

The littlest girl began to wail. Imoshen came to her feet and caught Nerazime's eye. 'See to the children, Nera.'

The voice-of-reason beckoned a Malaunje servant, who led them away. Meanwhile, the gift-warriors carried Tamaron and the healer into the cabins under the foredeck.

'Ree-ma?' Prince Cedon tried to get down out of Sorne's arms. 'Wants my Ree-ma.'

'She needs to rest,' Imoshen told him.

'I should take Cedon back to his mother,' Sorne said.

'No.' Imoshen held out her arms and the prince went to her. She tucked his head into the curve of her neck and stroked his hair. 'This is what's going to happen. You go back and tell King Charald we have his son. We could sail out of the headlands with him right now and he would never see the boy again. But we will return the prince, if our conditions are met.'

JARAILE PACED UP and down the balcony. She wished she could tell what was happening. Her stomach churned, and she felt sick with worry. She'd given up praying to the Mother. Now she prayed to the Warrior. Just let little Cedon be safe.

Heavy footsteps on the dining room floor. She spun around. 'Is he–'

It was Eskarnor.

'How did you get in here?'

Eskarnor laughed and gestured to his honour guards' bloody weapons.

'What are you doing here?' Jaraile backed up.

Eskarnor kept coming, through the doors, along the balcony.

She realised he meant to take her and ran for the balustrade.

'Oh, no, you don't. I need you to legitimise my claim to the throne.' He caught her around the waist, threw her over his shoulder and strode inside. 'Once Charald and the brat are dead, you're the closest thing to royalty this kingdom has.'

She drew her paring knife and stabbed him in back, once, twice.

'You little bitch!' He swung her off his shoulder. She flew through the air and landed on the dining room table. He plucked the knife from her hands, tossing it aside.

She sprang up, trying to slip past him.

He cursed and his fist slammed into her head. She felt her body fly sideways, then nothing.

SORNE CAUGHT UP with Nitzane and the two military men on the wharf. By the time it was secure and the Wyrds could load what remained of their stores, it was after midnight. Nitzane left Captain Ballendin in charge of the wharf, while Commander Halargon searched the port for Eskarnor and the harbour-master.

Meanwhile, Nitzane and Sorne returned to the palace. As they walked the corridors, he filled the baron in.

'...so I doubt the Wyrds will hand over the boy until their terms are met,' Sorne said. 'Jaraile is going to be disappointed.'

Nitzane tapped on the queen's bedroom door. 'Jaraile?'

The old woman who served as her maid opened the door. 'The queen is waiting up for you in the dining room.'

But Sorne found the dining room empty. He took in the overturned chairs and the words carved into the mahogany table. *I have her, E.*

'Eskarnor.' Nitzane cursed. 'I swear, if he hurts her, I'll...'

Sorne didn't hear him for the rushing in his head. 'He won't hurt her. He needs Jaraile to legitimise his claim on the throne.'

'I love her, Sorne. I can't bear to think of her in his hands.' Nitzane sank onto a chair, devastated. 'What am I going to do? You've got to help me save her.'

'The king—'

'The king had a seizure two nights ago.'

'Did he sign the decree appointing the five advisors to guide Prince Cedon until he comes of age?'

Nitzane shook his head. 'He refused to discuss it. And when he learned Eskarnor had raped Jaraile, he had a fit.'

'Is he rational?'

'His wits come and go.'

Sorne's mind raced. The king was not in his right mind. Nitzane wanted to save the queen, but Eskarnor wouldn't hurt Jaraile. Sorne still had to ensure Prince Cedon was returned.

'Poor Jaraile.' Nitzane moaned then looked up at Sorne. 'I'll do anything to save her, anything. Just tell me what to do.'

To all intents and purposes, the kingdom was Sorne's.

Epilogue

WHEN HE WAS seventeen, Sorne had seen a vision of King Charald hugging a small boy on the deck of a ship. Now it unfolded before his eyes.

The rest of the Wyrd fleet had already sailed through the headlands. Only the causare's flagship remained, its sails painted by the dawn sun. The prince was lowered onto the deck of Baron Nitzane's smaller ship in a net. He climbed out and stood there looking uncertain.

King Charald directed him to jump, then walk. Seeing his club foot was cured, the king knelt on the deck, swept Prince Cedon into his arms and declared him fit to be his heir.

Sorne knew Jaraile would have hugged him first, then marvelled over his recovery.

ISBN: 978-1-78108-011-5 • US $7.99 / CAN $9.99

ROWENA CORY DANIELLS

BESIEGED

BOOK ONE OF THE OUTCAST CHRONICLES

"Page-turning, plot-twisting, breakneck adventure."

Sorne, the estranged son of a King on the verge of madness, is being raised as a weapon to wield against the mystical Wyrds. Half a continent away, his father is planning to lay siege to the Celestial City, the home of the T'En, whose wyrd blood the mundane population have come to despise. Within the City, Imoshen, the only mystic to be raised by men, is desperately trying to hold her people together. A generations long feud between the men of the Brotherhoods and the women of the sacred Sisterhoods is about to come to a head.

With war without and war within, can an entire race survive the hatred of a nation?

Rowena Cory Daniells, the creator of the bestselling *Chronicles of King Rolen's Kin*, brings you a stunning new fantasy epic, steeped in magic and forged in war.

 WWW.SOLARISBOOKS.COM

Follow us on Twitter! www.twitter.com/solarisbooks